BALLAD
OF THE
BLACKSMITH'S
SON

To a Friend
of Annette –
May you Find and Follow
the White Stone God has for
You!

Rick Taylor

Sept 2023

D1707196

RICK TAYLOR

outskirts
press

PART 1

THE BALLAD OF THE BLACKSMITH'S SON

WHEN ERIK RULED THE HOARY LAND
    FROM NOVGOROD TO ARCTIC STRAND,
THE MESSAGE CAME THAT EASTERN MEN
    WITH FOREIGN GODS WERE THREAT TO THEM.

BUT, LO, THE WOLVES HAD THREATENED LONGER
AND DROOLED, AS FIEND, FROM CLOSE TO YONDER
AND GAVE THE WISE MEN PAUSE TO PONDER:
"WHICH IS WORSE, AND WHICH IS STRONGER?"

From *The Ballad of the Blacksmith's Son*

FATE

Keri Ellison shook off his leather gloves so his fingers could better grip the stiff deer hide thongs looped around a pile of birch logs. Having spent more than half his sixteen years swinging a blacksmith's hammer and a woodcutter's axe, his thick callouses protected him from the cold while he worked in the snow.

He turned his head to the sound of a crunch. Twenty feet away a golden yellow she-wolf stepped out of the brush and paused, questioning him with eyes that reflected the blue sky. Keri leapt to his feet and snatched a hand axe from his belt. She raised her head and tilted it to one side, looking. Keri edged toward his larger tree axe. He wiped a snowflake from his eye and shivered. The wolf sat down, watching like a village dog hoping for a bite from the master's table. Her soft eyes followed him, then narrowed.

He tensed.

Her ears went up, alert, as her eyes darted behind him.

Keri swirled to find a massive black wolf crouched for an attack ten feet away. Throwing the hand axe, the lad jumped over his birch logs to grab the larger axe. The black wolf dodged, then fled as the hand axe thunked into a tree. Keri swung back to the yellow wolf, who still sat watching. He stomped his boot at her. She dropped her head, sighed, and trotted away.

Shaking, the blacksmith's son searched the snow-glazed forest for either creature but saw nothing. He pulled his hand axe from the tree where it struck and found a rune carved into the trunk. Nine lines interwoven. Keri hesitated, then touched it. "The Web of Wyrd," he whispered. "Everything past, present, future touches every other thing." *Brother Hamar says everything happens for a reason. Even these wolves? Is God telling me I'm still vulnerable as a calf?*

"Hmph," he snorted. *Some Viking I would have been. Almost eaten by a wolf. No one would find my bones until spring. Who cares anyway? When the Norns cut the thread of my life, will they notice? Who am I that the old gods or Brother Hamar's Jesus might notice me? Father might miss me. He needs the help.*

One of the many snow-covered pines that sparkled in the sun above bent to drop a basketful of snow. The resulting whoosh sounded like a distant whisper and dashed the air with sparkling powder. Keri's shoulders relaxed. *Soft as a kiss*, he thought. *Bah, what do I know of kisses? Even the forest mocks me.*

Keri sighed, checked for the wolves, and gathered his tools. Sunrays glowed like golden bars through the treetops and ridge lines above. He knew this time of year the sun would not rise enough to chase the shadows from where he stood under a white-blue sky.

Grabbing his gloves, he stomped a foot, and flipped the logs onto his back. *Mother won't miss me. She says having the biggest kid in the village means she has to cook more. More bread…warm bread. Bread would be nice.* His stomach grumbled.

He shouldered past the drooping white firs to the snow-packed trail. It was a fair walk east and down through the dense white forest to Keri's first destination and that much up again to the village of Rentvatten farther north. With less than two hours of daylight left, he hurried. Breathing deep he left great clouds of condensation coiled in the frozen air. He shook the shaggy yellow hair out of his eyes and pressed his thin lips together.

A flying chunk of snow crust the size of a shield exploded off his load, covering him with fine cold crystals. He dropped the wood and whirled around just in time to catch a second white blast in the chest. His dark blue eyes blurred, and he couldn't see what knocked him into the snowy undergrowth.

His attacker stood laughing on the trail with squirrel fur gloves on slim hips. "By the ancient saints, Sakarias Ellisson, you are slow-witted today. If I'd been a wolf, you'd have been dinner." Not as tall as Keri, nor as thick, the teen had gray eyes and black hair more characteristic of the southern people than Keri's Nordic looks. The boy's smile showed bright teeth under the wispy beginnings of a mustache.

Keri cleared his eyes. "Eli Gregerson, you skinny otter, I hope you have not eaten today because you are about to devour enough snow to freeze your liver!"

Keri lunged up, but Eli dodged and tripped him into a snowdrift. The hunter jumped right back up, but the prey was too quick. They laughed as Eli bounced away but when he landed on the woodpile, a log slipped, he yelped in pain, and staggered. Keri bear-hugged him from behind, lifting Eli off the ground. He stalked to a large mound of snow.

"Not there. That snow covers a huge boulder."

"Really? Well, how about this tree?" With a grunt, Keri threw Eli into the lower branches of a white-draped evergreen. The flailing boy dislodged snow from thirty feet of branches down on his head. He rolled to his back with the tree's avalanche sending icy messages down his fur collar. Buried to his neck, he looked like a reclining black-haired polar bear.

They laughed as Eli reached out a hand. Keri clasped his arm and launched him to his feet.

Eli winced, lifting one foot. "Ouch! 's wounds! I think I twisted my ankle." He tried to walk but ended up hopping and grabbed for his friend's shoulder.

"Well, so much for the fastest runner in all Rentvatten. But that's what you get for calling me 'Sakarias.'"

"It's your name."

"It's my mother's only mistake. It's too formal for a mere black-smith. Otherwise she made me perfect." Keri knelt. "Let's see that foot."

"Oh, no. If the foot is going to swell, it will never get back in the boot for the walk home. Leave it be."

"In faith, I'd leave you here, but two wolves stalked me a while ago and your arrows barely stop the squirrels."

"Wolves? This high up? They're early, or late."

"Aye, but I have to get going. Cnute makes charcoal tonight and wants this load." Keri picked his hand axe out of the snow and flipped it before securing it in his belt. He shook his head. "I'd like to know if I'll ever be able to use a real battle-axe and fight in a war like Sigvard."

"Your chance to find out rode into the village at noon. That's why we have to get back before evening prayers."

"Why? You just go to prayers to watch the girls."

"At least I go." Eli smiled. "But tonight, you want to go. The king's messenger arrived on a huge warhorse and will speak to the village before church. We should go now if we want to hear him. That's why I came to find you."

"A real horse? Not one of those ponies or mules like Asaph the trader uses?"

"Yep. He's almost as big as you."

"The messenger?"

"No, the horse!"

"That I want to see. Is it war?"

"I don't know. He hasn't said."

Keri laughed. "Who'd want to come up here to fight? We're not a rich town like Novgorod or something."

"I don't know. Asaph says Turks are harassing Vladimir's Rus down south."

"A Christian-Arab war? A crusade? Will we march to Byzantium?"

Eli threw up his hands. "What war? For all I know the announcement is about a royal wedding! I don't know! But I thought you'd like to see the horse and weapons before he leaves. We need to go."

"Cnute's wood first. Can you walk?"

"Maybe." Eli stepped with his injured foot. "'s wounds!" He hopped around slapping the snow off his leg with his leather hat.

"Where's all this 'His wounds' come from? Doesn't sound like you. You been working around Sami?"

"All the men say it."

"No, they don't. I don't say it and it sounds wrong on you, like you're faking it. And Brother Hamar says it's a sin."

"As long as I don't say 'God' in front of it I'm all right. Besides, what should I say when I'm frustrated: 'raging weasels'?" Eli hopped over to pick up his ever-present bow and quiver.

Keri shrugged. "You always were a baby about pain, but don't let Brother Hamar hear you. Or the messenger. The king's edict about being Christian includes no swearing…I think."

"No matter what I say, I can't walk fast."

Keri rubbed his hairless chin. "Humm…turn around." Rewrapping the pile of wood in its leather thongs, he placed it on Eli's back. Then he turned his back, stooped, and picked up lad and load together. "Hang onto my neck like the child you are." With a grunt, he started down the trail.

Eli bounced at each step. "If I had known…I had a ride… down the mountain, I'd have gotten… a load of wood… for my mother… too!"

Halfway down a second ridge they heard an angry voice. Entering a clearing by a frozen pond they found a smudged, disheveled man swearing as he shoveled dirt on a waist-high stand of vertical birch logs. He stopped to drain a large wooden cup and threw the empty vessel at a nearby shack where it clattered off the log walls. "B' God's wounds yer a small cup w' sech weak ale!"

Eli sniggered. "See, everybody says 'by 's wounds.'"

"Hush." Keri lowered him to the ground and approached with the wood. "Cnute!"

The reeling man turned to glare at the boys. His potbelly distorted an otherwise skinny frame. Soot covered both his badly shaved head and round face marred by discolored scruff and frozen spittle around the mouth. Keri couldn't tell the original color of his torn, mud-caked wool clothes. Dominating Cnute's features, an empty red eye hole glared at the world.

"Wha'?" His voice a guttural growl, "Yer t' late can't ye see. I've a'ready started th' oven. Who d' ye think ye are, boy, t' come s' late." He scratched his stomach.

Keri straightened up and towered over him. "The agreement was one more load before dark. The days are getting shorter, but there's daylight enough for this wood."

"Take yer beardless face away from yer elders, ye insolent milk-suckin' child. I'll say when yer on time 'r not." Cnute leaned on his battered wooden shovel to remain standing. He slapped his leg, then scratched.

"Where's th' ale that's due me, curse ye?" Cnute looked up.

"It's waiting at Father's anvil for you when you deliver the charcoal."

Cnute dropped to his knees. His tone changed and he fell, piteous, sobbing with his bare hands in the snow. "How's a man t' do all 'is work with n' ale?"

Eli stepped up. "You could get more at the village."

"I don't want t' go t' th' village," Cnute snarled and struggled to his feet.

Eli flipped a thumb behind him. "You might today. There's a messenger from the king."

The charcoal maker sneered. "I hates th' king. I spit on 'is messengers. What ha' they done f' me? Where's m' blessing for bein' a good villager? Did he answer m' prayers? Did he save m' Liisa? Did h' help m' revenge on th' black wolf? Forget th' king an' 'is blasted demands an' 'is vague promises. His plans mean nothin' t' me. He's as powerless as any man 'gainst wolves or th' Tunturri, or fate."

Keri stepped between them. "Well, there will be news tonight, maybe war, and we are going to go hear it. Here is the load I promised you. May God bless you to turn it into charcoal without the help of ale." Dumping the wood, he lifted Eli on his back, and tromped through the snow toward the village. Cnute shouted insults at them but stopped mid-sentence.

"Look," whispered Eli.

Glancing back, Keri saw Cnute squinting at a louse he pulled from his tunic. He squeezed until the louse snapped and then popped it in his mouth. He scrunched up his nose, flared his eye, and savagely attacked Keri's load of wood with his shovel.

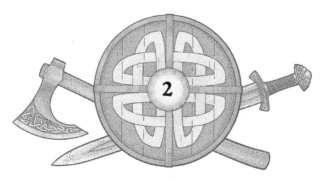

MESSENGER

Approaching the village gate Keri saw a crowd gathered outside the long stone and log building that served as council room, feast hall, market, and church. A raised platform adjacent to one side faced an open space and a slight hill with the community well. The thick beams of the building and its steep thatched roof rose over the pointed log palisade surrounding the village. Two sentinel towers at opposite sides loomed in the fading light.

Keri dropped Eli at the gate and stretched back up to his full height. "Try to look like a man as we walk in, will you?"

Keri kissed his fingertips and hopped to touch the village crest above the gate. Eli tried to jump but barely left the ground. He hobbled on his good foot, grumbling.

Keri stood behind him. "Go again. Three generations of Rentvatten boys have kept that brass shiny. Besides, you need the luck." Eli jumped. Keri caught his belt to thrust him higher.

"Made it. Thanks, but remember I touched the crest a full six weeks before you could reach the lintel post."

Keri laughed. "Four weeks, but I bagged my first caribou before you."

"And a tiny one it was, too."

"Your little sister carried yours home."

"At least I didn't puke when I gutted mine."

Keri shoved Eli harder than he meant to and had to pick him up. "Sorry."

Split logs turned flat side up in the snow formed an uneven main street. Dozens of branch and wattle houses spider webbed out in rough rows forming lanes. Each was separated from its neighbor by a low crude fence of woven sticks or hedges with a large open space to the back. Goats, pigs, and an occasional shaggy cow shivered in the yards. Some houses were thatched with steep piles of straw while others had roughhewn board roofs. There were some stone chimneys, but most featured only a smudged smoke hole in the thatch.

Eli limped in holding Keri's shoulder. Keri turned in to the second trampled snow street to drop his tools at his father's blacksmith shop. He swallowed a dipper of iron-tasting water from beside the warm forge and hurried back to where Eli waited, leaning against a low fence. They moved into the square and found a festive atmosphere with people chatting and laughing. Small children ran among their elders with shrieks of joy.

Away from the crowd, but watching with a sideways stare, Keri saw Fum. Fum's skin was young and smooth but his parched eyes examined them from a body that bent as if carrying the world's woes on one shoulder. Keri shivered and wondered again how old Fum really was. Fum's pale wool shirt was too big, a gift from a widow, and he wore no socks in his woven straw boots. The only villager who owned no leather or fur, he clutched a rude straw cape over a rough wool blanket. His pure white hair fell over nearly pink eyes and his complexion was the whitest in the village both winter and summer. He stood motionless except to finger the lamb's bone whistle on which he played the same nameless tune as always.

Eli released Keri; they nodded at Fum, and moved into the throng. Eli pointed. "The king's emissary."

A man in a scarlet and gold tunic trimmed in wolf fur stood near the platform, conferring with the elders. He shined like a jewel against the muted browns and grays of most of the townsmen. Even the blues, greens, and rusty reds of the women were dull by comparison.

Another stranger, more commonly dressed, stood to one side. A finely trimmed black beard mocked his bushy eyebrows on a long, thin face. He wore a black fur-lined travelling cape that draped nearly to the ground.

A tall, well-muscled warhorse stood stomping a hoof in the shelter of the overhanging roof. He twitched among a gaggle of wide-eyed children and young boys squealing at this rarest of beasts. Behind it a small shaggy packhorse dozed completely ignored. Keri and Eli approached and listened to the chatter. "How fast are they?" "How much can it carry?" "How much does it eat?" "Do they bite?"

Jesspersson, a tall, thin teen, announced he saw them in Novgorod once before his father died. "They can outrun an eagle. They step on wolves, eat lingonberries, and only bite evil men." At that moment the horse reached out and bit white-clad Brother Hamar, the town's cleric. When the monk jumped away, the horse began nibbling straw from the thatched roof. The boys laughed. Jesspersson looked at the ground. "It *could* step on a wolf," he mumbled.

"Not the one I saw today," said Keri.

As the kids turned to Keri, Fum sidled up and, without looking directly at the horse, reached out his hand to touch the well-groomed mane. The horse turned toward him and stopped quivering. He nuzzled his big head into Fum, who hugged him. The boys all gasped. With a final touch Fum walked away playing his tune. The horse nodded as if asleep.

Eli smoothed his hint of a mustache. He glanced at Jesspersson. "Does anyone know what the messenger has to say, or is he just here for lingonberries?"

"I heard him, and he talks funny," said Keri's young brother, Soren.

Bue, Eli's cousin, spoke up. "Father says that's the high language of the court. He thinks he might be a tax collector."

Eli shrugged. "I know that man wearing black next to him. He's Firth Black Collar from up north in Drakestad. Father tangled with him over some sheep last year. He's a crafty dealer, cousin."

Keri followed his gaze. "What do you suppose he wants?"

"I don't know, but if anything involves Firth, you'd better put an extra watch on the gate. He might try to slip the feast hall into his cape," said Eli.

Bue laughed and gave his cousin a friendly push.

Keri noticed Jesspersson glance around then slip a dried apple from the messenger's pack into his tunic. He ducked around the corner, eating it. Keri started to speak but Eli nudged him. "Seven brothers and sisters...no father... They have a short table. An apple is a treasure. Let him be."

Keri shrugged and they moved to the platform where the council counted the crowd.

Chubby Tharn nodded to the others, his face barely showing behind his furry side whiskers. "The Proverbs say, 'In a multitude of people is the glory of a king.'"

Brun Two Beards rolled his eyes. "Don't you have any words of your own?"

"You should learn to read the Scriptures," said Tharn. "Ha! You should learn to read."

"I read the signs of deer and bear."

"Fie! I bagged my first deer before you did."

Brun scoffed. "And a tiny one it was, too!"

Tharn pushed Brun. "Your little sister carried yours home."

Brun laughed. He swung a tiny girl pulling on his leg up into his huge arms and kissed her cheek. He handed her to his wife, who helped release the child's grip from the two braided forks of his fiery auburn beard. He had the chest of a bear mounted on the legs of a satyr and moved with a grace that Keri envied. He leapt up onto the raised wooden porch in front of the hall and gazed over the east wall at an eternity of sky. Smiling, he sucked in a chest full of the cold, clear air.

Old Valdemar the tanner, head of the council, climbed up and waved his tannin-stained hands for quiet. His tangled spotty white beard kicked as he spoke. When no one listened, Brun scooped a large crust of snow off the low roof and threw it into the crowd. The people protested, but Brun, with finger to lips, pointed to Valdemar. Fum lowered his whistle and studied Brun.

"Friends," said Valdemar, his voice squeaking. "King Erik sent us a messenger. Three months he trekked from village to village around the edges of that great snow desert, the Tunturri." Valdemar's skinny arms spread out from his cloak. "Up the tributaries of the Archangelsk River south and west, he braved the early snow while moving toward the Dnieper, where the great ships wait for the summer thaw. Higher and higher he climbed up to Lake Ladoga and the graves of our valiant Viking grandfathers. He traversed the borderlands of the northwest, defying the wolves from town to town until last night he stopped in Drakestad. Tonight he will sleep here under the northern lights." Valdemar took a long breath and raised his head. "His noble steed has trodden the rocky shores, the flinty cliffs, and dodged the jagged snow slides. Our good king has…"

Brun put a hand on his shoulder and stepped in front of him. "Enough, old friend. You have all winter to tell us how big the country is, how deep the snow gets, and how huge the wolves who rule the Tunturri. Let the messenger speak." The crowd laughed.

Valdemar sighed. "Bah, you have no respect for ceremony, or the ancients." He waved. "Turn your ears, people of Rentvatten, to hear Johann, emissary of the king!" The crowd cheered as Johann stepped forward. His broadsword hung from the wide strap across his chest. The clasp bore the king's crest with gleaming brass and shiny steel like the sparkle of his sword hilt. Cropped yellow hair, matching his short beard, cushioned the steel helmet. Keri and the other boys nudged each other with wonder at the spectacle of red, brass, and silver. Eli pointed to several girls staring dreamily at the tall man.

Keri tossed his head in their direction. "Humph, silly girls excited by a fancy hem." He turned back to stare at the messenger's sword.

"Hear ye, fellow countrymen," said Johann in an accent more Slavic than Nordic. "I thank God and King Erik for this chance to see so many fine villages like Rentvatten that make up the kingdom. The king himself sends ye greetings and says he remembers his passage through these lands with his father. He wishes me to bring him some of your famous smoked salmon."

The village cheered. Valdemar looked down his hatchet-like nose at Tharn and whispered, "Who gets the honor of providing salmon for the king?"

Tharn shrugged.

Johann raised his hands. "But that is not why I am here. There is threat of war from the east: Turks, yellow horsemen, heathens. We must be prepared. The king requires each village to send him one crew of thirty men this spring. They will train a season with the king's army. Then, if we must, we are ready to fight for our God, our freedom, and our lands."

The villagers broke into excited talk, and the old men nodded. The boys stood wide-eyed with the prospect of armies and great battles. Several older women cried out "No!" and pressed their children close.

Johann spoke louder. "Friends! There is no danger yet, thanks be to God. And if we show ourselves strong and able, the spies of the enemy may advise him to leave us be. Will ye send men across the Tunturri to answer the king's call?"

The boys cheered. The wives and girls looked uncertain. Many men stayed quiet. Grandmothers shook their heads and grit their teeth. Keri heard one say, "How much the cost of freedom this time? Twelve dead at the battle of Lake Ladoga."

"Aye," said another, "but each man came home with five silver pieces and the widows received ten! And spoils! That's how they built the mill and the great hall."

"I'd rather have the father of my children than a hundred silvers."

"Aye, and what will it cost to supply the men who must go? Our winter stores will disappear."

A man next to Keri asked, "Can we get the crops in with thirty men gone?"

His friend replied, "Or the sheep. They start dropping lambs in two months."

"And Rainar saw a wolf today."

"Already?"

"Yep, a shiny silver."

Fum dropped his head as Brun shouted, "Rentvatten, lift your heads. Would you be free under King Erik, whose yoke is light, or serve a heathen master who wants your fields, your women, and your soul? I will serve the Christian king and bring him thirty of the best men in all the land!"

The crowd cheered feebly. Brun jumped down and hugged his wife and kids. Eli and Keri turned to each other smiling. Keri lifted him off the ground. "We'll make our fortunes if I have to carry you to Hilhelm myself."

"You'll have to catch me first," said Eli.

Over Eli's shoulder Keri saw the dark stranger, Firth, in the shadow of the eaves, examining the crowd. He nodded and smiled behind his black beard. Fum stared hard at his face.

A WEE TEMPTATION

E li's eyes darted around the great hall as he waited for the evening prayer service to start. Tables lined the walls and benches served as pews. The stone fireplace in the middle provided light and a semblance of warmth. Johann in his red and gold made the room sparkle from his seat of honor up front. Fum knelt in the rear corner. The room buzzed and Brother Hamar, a green cloth draped over his rough white cowl, struggled to settle the unusually large congregation.

A golden-haired young lass walked right between Johann and Hamar, swirling her blue shift as she turned up the aisle. She splashed into the lap of Pekka, the miller's pimply son. He jumped and fled to the back. She frowned, glanced around, and saw Keri. Eli saw a smile creep on to her face. She stood but two girls her age pulled her toward them, and she sat down. They giggled.

Eli whispered to Keri, "I guess we can start now. Stjärna has arrived."

Keri was studying the rivets on Johann's helmet. "Huh?"

The candles were lit as the older devouts sang loud to suppress the whispers of the young people. "O Bright Morning Star gladsome of the holy glory of the Immortal Father, the Heavenly, the Holy, the Blessed,

O Jesus Christ…" The young girls calmed down long enough to recite the Psalm of praise Hamar taught them: "Thou hast been magnified exceedingly…" But after the Litany of Peace with its frequent congregational responses, the whispers picked up again. Eli rolled his eyes at the girls and elbowed Keri, who craned in his seat to see Johann's scabbard. The room murmured.

Brother Hamar stomped his round, powerful body down from his makeshift dais, stood in the aisle, and stared the offenders into silence. His brown eyes flared reminding them he was not a Norseman by heritage or mother tongue. Eli looked down at the monk's hairy fingers. Hamar raised one totally wild and untamed eyebrow and glared sideways at the young girls. They hushed. "Ironic it is that we prevail on oer heavenly Lord wid a Litany o' Peace only moments after we are prevailed upon by oer earthly lord t' participate in a war." He shifted his eyes to the boys. Eli nudged Keri, who peered at Johann's chain mail.

"But sure, God's ways are nae men's ways and the two events are nae doubt juxtaposed for His good reasons. An' sure, is it not good that before we pick men t' go for the king, we ask God t' pick for us?" His eyes swept the congregation.

"This is nae great adventure for honor and glory. Surely this is a sober moment when we shall be sorely tested by enemies both earthly and heavenly. Some o' you young men may be tempted, even forced, t' do things in battle you would ne'er be doin' otherwise. Those of you stayin' behind will have new problems because 'tis not just in battle we are tempted. Who do you think you are that you alone can withstand the sins t' which so many others hae fallen?"

His eyebrow went up and aimed at Eli, Keri, and the other young men. Keri looked up caught, surprised.

"Call on God now t' be with you not only t' acquit yourself well as a warrior, but t' acquit yourself as God-fearing men…and women." Hamar's head jerked toward the girls then back to the boys. "For sure, you may hae the strength t' hold your place in the king's shield wall, but can you even find your place in God's army?"

Eli restrained a smile as Keri squinted to listen. Hamar's accent always puzzled him.

Hamar smoothed the long green stole with a white embroidered square cross; the only vestment he owned. "Don't ye know, 'tis no accident that we chant Psalms asking God t' 'Deliver me, Oh Lord, from the evil man: gathered together for war.' And then we ask God t' 'incline not m' heart t' any evil thing.'

"As we oppose the wicked," Hamar said, "let us remember that both those who go and those who abide here are one wee temptation away from bein'…" he narrowed his eyes, "the wicked." Eli and Keri dropped their eyes.

The service was completed in appropriate solemnity.

CHOOSING

Fum sat on the council house roof playing his whistle. He watched both the crowd below and the gate. Rentvatten gathered below for the selection of the thirty. Fum eyed Firth, the black-cloaked stranger from Drakestad, standing to one side of the platform. The king's messenger, Johann, had gone well before first light carrying enough smoked salmon to satisfy King Erik and the egos of seven village women.

Fum craned as he played to see beyond the gate. He frowned and then turned to watch old Valdemar and Brun Two Beards mount the platform with an iron pot.

"Friends," said Valdemar. "Our high king calls on us daily to be good subjects, but he seldom calls on us to undertake great things in his name. Today he calls. The Scriptures and our traditions recount the lottery as the best way to fill the king's draft. The council has determined that any man between fifteen and forty-five deemed physically capable is eligible. Per Scriptures we will not accept any man married less than a year. Further, we will not consider any man whose wife is with child, or who has read the banns already to announce his marriage. In addition, no household may be left without a capable man or to send more than one."

Murmurs ran through the crowd. Wives took their husbands' hands and more than one mother hugged her young son in quiet relief or anxiety. The embarrassed or disappointed sons struggled to be free. Keri and Eli smiled and pushed each other. Fum pursed his lips and glanced back toward the gate.

"Therefore," said Valdemar, "we have filled this caldron with one hundred and twenty-seven stones representing the one hundred and twenty-seven men we deem eligible. Thirty of the stones are white, the rest dark. Those who draw the white shall pull the great sledge with its load of life-giving firewood across the snow-drifted, treeless Tunturri. They will brave the last storms of winter on the open land."

Brun rolled his hazel eyes and put his massive fists on his hips.

Valdemar ignored him. "They will cross the frozen river before the thaw sets in and hurl night fire into the faces of the wolves who stalk them. They will hearken to the king and..."

"By the beard of St. Peter," said Brun, snatching the pot. "Get on with it!"

"Wait," said Tharn, clumping onto the platform. "The sage says, 'Haste is only good when the house is on fire.' Before we begin, let us ask God to guide our hands. Brother Hamar?"

Fum stopped playing his whistle and listened.

Brother Hamar stepped up and bowed his head. "Lord," prayed Hamar, "the Psalmist says, 'Through you we push back our enemies.' So it is that we surely ask your will t' be done t'day. Show us each oer role. In Jesus' name, amen." Most of the crowd murmured "amen" and crossed themselves.

"Delightfully brief and to the point, Brother Hamar," said Brun under his breath.

"An' sure, the Good Book says not t' babble," said Hamar.

21

Fum smiled, glanced toward the gate, and resumed playing over the crowd.

Brun looked sternly at the assembled men. Then a fierce white grin split his autumn-colored beards. "Ha! Har!" he roared, holding out the pot. "Let us see who the Lord has chosen!"

The men and older boys pressed forward to the caldron. Hands pulled out stones to roars of approval, disappointment, and jest. The women stood off wishing their men to stay but most reflected courage in face of a white stone.

As if tapped on the shoulder, Fum looked around to the gate, where he spotted one-eyed Cnute creeping toward the commotion below. Fum raised his eyes to the sky then back to watch the drawing.

Sturl, a hunter, father of seven, was chosen. Viktor, a trapper, found white. Keri chewed his lip until his father drew black. "I can draw!" he shouted. Stocky Mantas pushed two men aside and drew white. "'s wounds! I'm goin'!" Two farmers and the carpenter each pulled a white stone. The council declared the chronically ill rope maker ineligible to draw. Eli's cousin, Bue, and Godwin danced in a circle at their selection.

Arn the cheesemaker drew but concealed what he had. Fum's eyes followed him. Arn saw Jesspersson draw black and took him to one side. Arn talked and Jesspersson fingered three silver coins as he walked in a daze with a white stone to where Brother Hamar wrote names on a piece of bark. "I'm in after all," he said.

Brother Hamar raised an eyebrow at Arn, who walked swiftly away. Then he saw the three pieces of silver and sighed. "You've made a good and brave sacrifice for your family."

At the caldron they turned away Rainar because his son, Pekka, already drew white. Pekka's mother flailed at her husband and clutched her squirming son.

Jon's wife of thirteen months wept openly when he drew white.

Sami, the only man carrying a sword, drew a black stone and cursed furiously showing the stone to anyone who would look. Brother Hamar tried to quiet his rude words. Sami pushed the monk off, unleashed another oath, and threw the stone over the great hall, almost hitting Fum. He stalked away behind a nearby house and leaned against the wall where sweat soaked his shaking body. He composed himself, wiped his eyes, and forced a thin smile. He glanced up at the hall, saw Fum looking at him, sneered and walked away. Fum shook his head.

At the platform Keri and Eli pushed forward to take their stones. "Not so fast, Eli," said Valdemar above the crowd noise. "The council declared you physically unfit because of your injured ankle."

Eli's face fell. "No! It is just a sprain. You know I am fastest in the village. It will pass."

Valdemar kept his hand up. "No stone for you, Eli. The council has spoken."

"This cannot be, sir. We will not leave for three months. Surely I will be whole." Eli turned from Keri to Brun to Tharn. "Sirs, how can a temporary injury have so much weight? You create a coward's way out if you allow a sprain to eliminate a man from the selection. And you deny an eager fellow like me a chance to win his fortune."

"He's right," said Tharn to Brun. "Any man in the village who limps tomorrow could escape from the sled and stay home in the arms of his wife."

Valdemar folded his arms. "It's too late. The number of stones was set, and the cauldron is nearly empty. It cannot be changed now."

Those close enough to hear the exchange murmured. Eli with his accurate bow and his speed would be a good representative of the village. His exclusion seemed an untimely fluke.

Brun shrugged and held the black pot above his head. He reached in and felt around. "Two stones. The one is mine, the other yours, Keri. Will you choose now or last?"

Eli whispered in Keri's ear. Keri's eyes went wide.

"I choose now," said Keri. He reached high into the pot and brought out his clenched hand. The crowd looked at Brun to see what the last stone would be.

Brun reached into the kettle and roared, "Who are you, Keri Ellisson? You've taken both stones, you imp!"

All eyes turned to Keri, who stood smiling with Eli. Each held a white stone in their palm. "Keri and I both claim the right of selection as we each hold a white stone," said Eli.

The crowd rippled in cheers, jeers, and astonishment. Brun bellowed and then laughed. "What shall I do with such impudent children?"

"Spank them!" shouted someone laughing. "If you can."

"Let him go!" said several in the crowd.

"But what about my chance to go?" said Brun.

"Brun!" shouted some. Men argued. Keri and Eli held fast to their stones and looked for a champion. Valdemar waved the council to the platform and they talked. Brun spoke loudest, but everyone spoke.

Finally, Valdemar looked at each member in turn and they nodded. Brun threw up his hands and laughed his loon-like laugh. Valdemar climbed the platform. "Friends, by rights one of the two white stones belongs to Brun. By possession, however, Eli holds a white stone. We have agreed that Eli shall go, if…in four weeks he is able to beat Brun in a foot race around the palisade. If the Lord heals him to run, he will be among the chosen. If not, then it is Brun: it is up to the Lord."

The villagers cheered. Keri slapped Eli on the back and Brun smiled a clean, fierce grin while the twin forks of his red beard fairly twitched with joy.

Fum sighed and climbed down from the roof.

Stjärna Dirksdottir wiggled her lips as she stared across the crowd at Keri and Eli. She straightened her slim posture and lifted her chin. She tossed her thick blonde braid, but neither boy seemed to notice.

Glancing around to insure she had space, she twirled her blue shift and walked straight toward Keri.

He looked up.

She changed course.

With her head turned away, she scrunched her nose and caused a tear to form in her deep blue eyes. Then she bit her lip and gazed back at Keri until she was sure their eyes were locked. Striding away she wiped the tear and flipped her blue cloak as she swung around the corner of the nearest house and ran hard into Sami.

"Well met," said Sami pulling her close with one arm and wiping his nose with the other. Grease spotted his tunic.

She pushed away with an anxious glance at the corner.

He appraised her and licked his lips. "It looks like we will be spending some time together with everyone else gone. The sauna will not be so crowded. I could make it hot for you." He had ale and pork on his breath.

She laughed derisively. "I'll keep the dirt, if you are keeping the sauna."

He leaned in close and whispered, "My brothers and I are building our own sauna. It may have some surprises for you. You should come see."

"The surprise will be if I come. Where will you put it in that pigsty you call home," she snapped as she glanced again at the corner.

"Father left us pigs. It was enough for Mother. When did you stop eating pork?"

"When it reminded me of you. Go. Leave me alone."

"Waiting for something?" He nodded toward the corner.

"Yes. I'm waiting for you to leave."

"Well, so far I find my pigs more entertaining than you. But the day will come when you need some company. Maybe even some protection." He slapped the sword. "And all those fools will be gone. I think you will be in a better mood then, to play sow to my boar."

She jolted and pulled her cloak tight.

He laughed and sauntered away.

Stjärna watched until he was gone, pursed her lips, and peeked back at the crowd. Keri and Eli were shoving each other and laughing. Her shoulders fell. She leaned against the house and felt a shiver. Then she saw Fum watching her. She hung her head and walked home.

CHOICES

As Keri and Eli left with the crowd another voice crackled above their heads. The stranger Firth Black Collar bowed on the platform in his black cloak. "People of Rentvatten, you go too quickly to your beds. There is one more challenge to be made here."

He threw his cloak over one shoulder, winked at a pretty girl, and then slowly gazed around the whole group with a questioning smile peeking out of his trim black beard. Firth stood tall and wiry with long, thin arms that made grand gestures. His eyes sunk dark as dungeon cells under bushy eyebrows, but they glittered as they simultaneously seduced and warned. After he made a circuit of the crowd, the village fell silent, almost frozen. Keri quivered.

"Many of you know I am Firth, of your neighbors at Drakestad village, just a short day's journey north. We see so little of you, yet you are ever on our minds. Had I known the king loved your smoked salmon I would have come more often, for it is marvelous to be in the smoked fish center of the kingdom." He licked his lips and rubbed his stomach in exaggerated appreciation. Some in the crowd laughed, several frowned.

"But I come today not as a food taster but as a representative of our council. Drakestad, too, has been asked to send thirty men to the king's army. We already conducted our lottery and designed a great sled to pull across the Tunturri. We plan to move by St. Ioakim Day three months hence. Will your men and sled be ready then? Will you have dealt with this new wolf in the neighborhood? Will you have enough smoked fish?" Firth pretended to pop tidbits into his mouth. Children laughed but the men growled.

"What is it you want, Firth?" called Tharn. "You've stalked through our streets for a day now and I'm beginning to worry about my geese."

Firth looked concerned. "It is a wise man who worries about his eggs, Tharn. Especially…" He gestured like a wizard, and a small leather bag appeared in his hand. "Especially when I come to you with a bag of silver from Drakestad and a proposition to make it yours."

Tharn stepped up on the platform and poked at Firth's thin belly. "Are your stomachs so empty at Drakestad that you must buy our smoked salmon for your sled?"

"Ah ha," said Firth, hand to forehead. "We are all famished, but not from lack of fish." He poked Tharn's belly, laughing. "It is lack of sport! We offer you this silver as a wager. We propose a race: your sled and ours to Hilhelm. Let the winners take a bag of silver from the other."

Keri nudged Eli and smiled.

Tharn's voice rose an octave. "A race? Across the Tunturri? But these aren't hand-picked crews; these are winners of the lottery. How do we know you haven't packed your sled with your best men?"

"Look at me," cooed Firth, spreading his cloak. "All dried leather and hollow bones am I. And yet I am on the sled to Hilhelm." He wrapped himself tightly again. "Surely, I am no match for even one of your boys." He gestured at Keri and Eli, who involuntarily stepped back.

Valdemar climbed up and swatted at Firth with his fur hat. "Away with you. We'll have none of your sly deals here. Our council's money has too many needs to be chanced against some scheme of yours. We will not be tempted by the sin of pride."

The crowd of villagers murmured. Fum, walking back from the gate, lowered his head and began to play his whistle.

"Aye," said Tharn. "The sage says, 'Happiness within is better than wealth.'"

"Ah," Firth sighed to the heavens. "I *thought* money would not tempt your honest village. I told them as much." He upended the bag into the snow. Out poured scrap metal and stones. The crowd stepped back. Eli laughed. Fum stopped playing and looked at Brun.

Firth bowed. "Perhaps something more symbolic would be an acceptable wager?"

Keri bit his lip, but Eli spoke up. "Like what?"

"Well…the winning village gets the crest of the losing village for a year."

Keri's eyes grew bright. "Aye."

Brun stepped forward. "Perfect! Let the council meet now to accept this challenge."

Brother Hamar spoke up. "Ach! It's pride you're showin'."

"Oh, fie!" said Brun. "Would you have us wager Ellendottir's goat?"

The crowd laughed, but Valdemar frowned, determined. "Why must we wager at all? And how do we know they will not cheat and leave early?"

"Oh, my most worthy Valdemar." Firth put an arm on the old man's shoulders. "Do you think your neighbors so dishonorable? Do we not worship the same king's God? Or do you think that a meager village like ours violates the command against stealing when we invite a prosperous village like yours to a little race?"

A snowball smacked into the wall beside Firth. The crowd turned to see pure white Fum staring at the ground.

Keri heard a widow whisper to the women around her, "Fum knows evil."

"Aye," came a chorus of replies.

Tharn said, "Drunken men and children tell the truth."

Brun scoffed. "Don't be silly. Fum's no child and this is not a truth issue; this is sport." He turned to the crowd. "We will race for the honor of Rentvatten!"

Eli pounded Keri's back in joy as the village men cheered.

Fum gazed at Brun and sighed.

Valdemar stammered, "Even Saint Peter fell to temptation. How can we keep each other on the straight and narrow? Pride can lead to sinful cheating."

"Well, old friend," said Firth, smiling. "How about we exchange one of our chosen men for one of yours two days before the start, so we can keep an eye on each other?"

Brun clapped him on the back. "Done. I will beat young Eli in four weeks and you in eight more!"

Fum hung his head. Firth smiled and headed for the gate.

Tharn and Brother Hamar stood to one side as the crowd broke. They gestured for the other council members to come.

Brun clasped Tharn's arm. "A white stone for you! We will test some of your proverbs in the Tunturri."

Brother Hamar tapped the list of those chosen. "'Tis an interesting problem we have. Cnute Pieterson, the charcoal maker…a white stone he drew."

"What?" said Sigvard, an aged veteran of the last sled. "We counted him as eligible even with only one eye, but no one expected him to come in for the drawing. We can't let him go; he'll disgrace the whole expedition."

"'Twas not us chose him," said the monk. "God did." He crossed himself. Fum smiled behind him.

Sigvard's hands shook and his beard flared. "That may be, but we owe it to our king and our kin on the sled to see he is not among them.

I doubt he can even walk the distance much less pull the sled. He's a drunk with the temperament of a wasp."

"Aye, that he has been," said Brother Hamar. "But his face...you should hae seen, when he pulled the stone."

Tharn enacted the scene. "When Sami was blustering, Cnute scuttled in from behind the hall. He glared at Fum up above and put his hand in the pot. Fum, he just nods, and Cnute... when he saw he had a white stone, his face softened. It was as if he had found a pearl."

"Or a devil," said the cleric. "All around he looks, to see who noticed, and then up agin where Fum he finds, looking at him, a smilin'."

"Fum? Fum never looks at anybody," said Brun.

"He does sometimes, and you can feel it," said Sigvard.

Tharn jumped back in. "Fum looked at Cnute Pieterson, who then walked his scraggly shaved head over here meek as a rain-soaked lamb to make sure we had his name. It was like he'd seen the ghost of his wife."

Sigvard folded his arms. "He's probably scared as a rabbit dangling from an eagle. He's so flabby and dirty no one will want to be in the traces with him."

"Dirty, yes," said Brun, fingering his beards in thought, "but I'd not say flabby. His clothes are absently patched, but he does a man's work out there in the dark. Ever tried to chunk dirt from the frozen ground in winter?"

Brother Hamar sighed. "An' remember...he chose to pick a stone an' God His own self chose to give him the white. 'Tis his right to be on the sled against something happening t' knock him off."

Sigvard shrugged. "Like falling down drunk in the snow and freezing to death?"

"The sage says, 'The lame man runs if he has to,'" said Tharn.

Valdemar looked sideways at Brun. "Maybe...but then maybe he is the solution to the problem between Brun and Eli." He raised an eyebrow.

"Perhaps..."

FUEL

Supper at the Ellishouse table was subdued that night as it was in twenty-nine other homes. Keri and his "almost eleven"-year-old brother, Soren, tried to remember all those chosen for the sled. Marta, their mother, was unusually quiet as she fed their little sister, Galina. Keri looked up from his stew. "Father, Cnute Pieterson is among the chosen. If he goes, who will make charcoal for the forge?"

Ellis stopped mid-bite and considered his wooden spoon. "Pieterson? Hmmm...I don't know. He has no apprentice. Nobody wants to put their son with *him*. His temper...and his speech...you know. I am just about his only customer."

Soren frowned. "Pekka says Cnute is cursed and creates the devil's own fire."

"He has had his share of bad luck." The blacksmith scraped his bowl. "But curses are for witches and spirits. He did not seek out his troubles."

"Really?" Marta flipped hair from her eyes. "The dumbest man in the village would not have done what he did."

Ellis nodded and poked at his empty bowl. "You're right about that, Marta. He was tempted or bewitched as you say, and it cost him nearly everything."

"And he has done little to fix it."

"How do you fix the dead, wife?"

"Well, what about his eye?" Marta mumbled as she shoved another bite at Galina.

Keri turned his head back and forth with the conversation. He opened his mouth but nothing came out.

Soren broke the silence. "Is Cnute able to make the trip? If they excuse Eli, they should excuse him."

"Well, he drags his sled of charcoal up the mountain to my anvil in all weather, but I don't know his real strength. He's often full of ale and staggering when he gets here."

Keri bobbed his wooden spoon in agreement. He glanced at the empty kettle, then at the empty bread board.

Ellis sucked his mustache. "He has no use for anyone. He's a hermit out there with his smoldering night fires. He has no family now. Few will miss him except us."

Marta mumbled, "The wolves might miss him, but I won't."

"Can he make enough charcoal to last you through the next year, Father?"

"No, Soren, I fear not. He's having trouble making enough now. It will grow worse as the sled's chosen call for new helmets or swords. It takes several days just to make a week's worth of charcoal the way he does it. I suspect he will be even slower when people distract him seeking pine tar to seal their traveling clothes."

"Perhaps..." Keri's chin sat in his hand, "I could help him make charcoal until I leave."

"I could help too," said Soren.

Marta glared across the table at Soren. "What? Work with that madman? He's wrestled with Satan and lost. His hut is almost down among the wolves. I don't want either of you out there any longer than it takes to drop off a load of wood."

Ellis looked at Keri. "Well, it would help if you could drop off more wood than usual. Bigger charcoal mounds don't take much longer than small ones." He scratched his beard and then waved a hand at Soren. "Maybe you could make Cnute's deliveries and Keri could keep him working at the stacks instead of walking into the village. He loses three days to fresh ale when he comes in."

Marta rolled her eyes. "It would help if you didn't pay him in ale."

"I pay him in ale at his request. Therkel pays him in copper, which he spends on ale. But it might help if you sent some bread when Soren takes back the empty sled."

Marta shook her head. She unconsciously lifted one of Galina's hands out of her bowl and pointed a finger at Keri. "You be there whenever Soren is there and don't leave until he leaves, mark me!"

BLUE

Old Jodis Jurgensdottir, from her home by the gate, saw all the village activity. She saw which girls left with which flocks and when. She knew who had a fresh deer. She saw Eli work his ankle each day and put some spring back in his stride. Brun ran well in his teen years, and a decade of spear hunting added genuine strength to his quickness. It would be a good race, she thought. Keri prepared too. He piled bigger loads on his back and trotted in the gate instead of merely walking. Keri brushed it off when his father praised him, but Jodis saw him smile when Ellis turned away.

Another set of eyes noticed too. Eyes that knew when Keri came and went. Eyes that gauged the loads of wood and wondered at the strength. Eyes so blue to make a Viking think of a distant sea. Eyes so wide as to be pools. Eyes so soft they caressed when she smiled.

Eyes that watched Keri's eyes and knew that he was not harboring feelings such as she felt. Eyes that saw Annika gazing at Keri in church.

Eyes that narrowed with the realization that if she didn't act soon, she might never know the status of being on Keri's arm.

At that realization, Stjärna Dirksdottir ceased to be a young girl smitten with the idea of a beau. She determined to be noticed by this boy. She had to get closer. She had to do it soon. She had to be subtle. Or did she? Hook or crook, she would get him to see her. Pursue her. Fie on Annika! Stjärna knew she must capture Keri's heart before he took it to war so she could display it after he was gone.

"Marta," said Ellis, coming in from the anvil. "You were right. I think it is beginning."

"Sweet Annika or skinny Dirksdottir?" Marta looked up from her cutting board.

"The blue one, Stjärna Dirksdottir. She has been lingering about the square, peeking at the house. Every time I get more charcoal or greet a customer she ducks behind the hall."

"Ach! She would ambush the boy. She may be named for a bright star, but she has a dark heart." Marta plopped chunks of onion into the pot. Her strong hands shifted the black kettle to the hook over the fire.

"Shall I invite her in when Keri gets home?"

"No," she snipped. "It will be harder for her in the cold." Her hands slapped her wide hips, but her voice turned soft. "They do not have much time before he must leave. Make them go slowly."

"Bah!" barked Ellis through his drooping yellow mustache. "You act like they will be married soon. Does she even know who he is? And he doesn't even know she exists."

"He may know tonight," said Marta. Her shoulders relaxed. She smiled remembering. "If the Lord wills it, he will know tonight."

36

Eli met Keri at the village gate. They jumped to touch the crest and walked in.

"I could see the top of your load five minutes before I could see you, Keri. You're a mule for carrying wood."

Keri's opened his sweat-soaked tunic and cloak to the cold air. "If a hunter sees my tracks he'll think a Rime Giant walked by. A goose could disappear into my footprints in the snow."

"Well, maybe you can carry the sled straight to Hilhelm and save them pushing it."

Keri laughed. "As long as I don't have to carry you, I don't care. Your constant chatter would drive me mad. Besides, you still have a hint of a limp."

"Don't worry about me. The limp is to attract sympathy from the girls. I ran to North Pond and back today without much pain. When the sled leaves, I will be out in front finding the best routes. You will be like a great ox plodding in the traces."

"I may be an ox, but you'll be wolf food if you wander too far in front alone."

"Not me. I am as fast as a deer, bright as an owl, and can outmaneuver any wolf."

"Deer may be fast, Eli, but if they are so quick, what is it that makes the wolf's coat so shiny and his shoulders so powerful?"

"Slow lemmings?"

They laughed.

Eli jogged toward home. Keri dumped his load before the wood-shed and began to stack it. He bit a splinter from his hand. His nose twitched as he smelled fresh bread and clean air-dried clothes. He turned and almost bumped into Stjärna Dirksdottir.

She stood a forearm shorter than he, but her erect carriage made her appear tall. As usual Stjärna was dressed in shades of blue with the buff apron common to her village. A thick pale-yellow braid started high on her head and went heavily down her back. Bangs framed her wide eyes.

"I'm sorry." He backed up, stumbled on the wood, and fell flat on his rear. "I thought you were my mother," he stammered.

"Your mother?" She tilted her head to the side.

"Well, the sweet sniff of bread and clean just reminded me of my mother." Wood tumbled from the pile as he tried to stand.

Stjärna looked at herself. "I don't think I look like a mother yet."

"No, no, you, uh, certainly don't look like a mother."

"Do you mean no one would have me to be a wife and mother to their children? Are my breasts too small?" She gestured at her apron and his eyes went wide.

"No, no, anyone would love to have you for a mother."

"So, I do remind you of a mother." She half turned away.

"No!" he wailed. "A wife, a wife! Anyone would love to have you for a wife."

She turned back, leaned down, and drowned him in her eyes. "Even you?"

"Yes, of course. Even me." He froze.

"Well, I may not be available." She sniffed, turned on her heel, and walked chin up off the field of battle.

Keri watched her go and for the first time noticed how well her straight frame moved. He marveled at the golden hair woven down her back. He saw the rise of her breasts and the color of her round cheekbones as she turned the corner and disappeared. He remembered the sweet scent of her and how her eyes drifted through seven different depths of blue. He felt as if he had never seen her before and had to see her again soon. But the image she planted that rose highest in his newborn mind came to his lips in a single question: "Breasts?"

Keri sat on the wood, stunned.

"Oh, she's a live one," whispered Marta to Ellis behind the kitchen shutters. "She's slapped her paw on his tail and is thinking up new games."

BOYS

Rainar bellowed at a special meeting of the council in his best embroidered cape and tunic. His wife, cowering behind him, clutched at his pimply-faced son, Pekka.

One hand on his silver-handled knife hilt, Rainar concluded his point. "So even though my son drew white and I was denied a chance to draw, as head of my house I request, no, I *demand* the right to exchange myself for Pekka on the sled."

The council sat open mouthed. Brother Hamar cleared his throat. "'Tis the Lord chose Pekka. That's wha' we prayed for. Are ye askin' us to deny God's will?"

"He's too young. He's too weak, and…and…I am the head of my family. It is my *right* to determine who does the work required of my house."

"Do you think you could go?" Brun asked Pekka.

Pekka's eyes widened. He nodded vigorously. His mother wailed.

Rainar leaned on the council's table. "He is not a sufficient candidate! I am sufficient. I should be the one going on this quest for glory."

Brother Hamar fingered his simple wooden cross. "The Lord does na choose sufficiency as men do. Faith! His miracles show more power, don't ye know, because the men He bids to do 'em are so weak."

"Immortal gods! He is not man at all!" said Rainar. "He takes more pride in cooking than hunting, darning socks than butchering sheep, weaving than chopping wood. He hasn't shown interest in girls *and* he favors his left hand! He will disgrace us all. I will bring us honor!"

Pekka's shoulders slumped.

"Are men defined by hunting, butchering, chopping?" Tharn stroked his side whiskers.

"No, they are defined by what they do," said Rainar through his teeth, "and this child does nothing."

Brun sat up tall. "Yet many a time I have seen him in the woods chopping and hauling. In the spring I have seen him breaking the soil, clearing, and planting. What makes him less than his fellows?"

Rainar stomped his foot. "He is worthless. He is not mature. He needs to stay here with his mother and learn to be a man. I must go in his stead."

"Thank you," said Valdemar, rising. "Go about your work at the mill. We will tell you our decision before evening."

Rainar flared. "I *will* go on this sled." He turned, almost stumbling over Fum, grabbed Pekka's arm, and berated him out the door. Rainar's wife glared at the council, broke into tears, and fled.

Gotthard snorted. "You would think one of the richest men in the village would want to stay behind and tend his money. Arn did."

Brother Hamar cleared his throat. "Per's widow and her children will eat this winter because Jesspersson accepted Arn's stone. If the Lord blesses him, they might even have more silver when he returns."

Brun poked the fire. "Do you think Rainar really wants to go or is he just placating his wife? She uses tears to steer the ox."

"Pekka is their only child," said old Sigvard. "She fears the wolves."

Brun sighed. "Rainar ran pretty wild until she put a halter on him. I miss the old Rainar, but I guess the mill needs him."

"It's not his money or his mill," said Valdemar. "Grandfather Leksa still makes all the decisions."

Sigvard warmed his wrinkled hands. "Old Leksa may be keeping things from Rainar… and Pekka. Leksa missed the sled in my generation, you know. His mill is his soul and he won't give it up."

Gotthard laughed. "Maybe Rainar just wants to get away and show up the old man."

Tharn nodded. "The prophet says, 'The parents eat sour grapes and the children's teeth are set on edge.'"

Brother Hamar folded his hands in his cowl. "'Tis pride scraping agin pride."

Sigvard nodded. "Doesn't help when Leksa calls his own son 'birdie legs.'"

Brun popped his fist into his hand. "They are turning Pekka into an empty shell."

Gotthard gestured at the fire. "Send the kid with the sled and we'll fix him. Nothing like a bunch of guys talkin' around a campfire to teach a lad how to be a man."

Brother Hamar slapped the table. "What? And will ye be gettin' him a painted woman when ye get to Hilhelm? From the smoke into the fire he'll go."

"Nah," said Gotthard, laughing. "Didn't Rainar say he doesn't like girls?"

"Ah," Brun scoffed. "Remember Snorii Stagkiller? He didn't hunt anything but deer until he found Brida Ragnardottir gutting a deer of her own. He had twelve children by her. God awakes each man when it's time."

There was laughter.

Brother Hamar stood, hands on hips. "Half jokin' you are, but yer sayin' things that give young boys a false idea o' what 'tis to be a man. Ye be far from the image of God."

Gotthard snorted. "What? Would you have him be like your Jesus, all meek and mild? Jesus wouldn't last a season up here."

Hamar turned on him. "Be sure, fellow sinner, Lord Jesus was displayin' humility in ways ye certainly do not, but 'twas Jesus also whipped the moneychangers. 'Twas He drove out the legion of demons. It's God makes ye powerful but for the benefit of others. It's strong ye are in His image so's ye can do the hard things for those too weak to do it for themselves. And each of ye," he pointed at Gotthard, "are an answer to someone's needs, someone's prayer. Do ye ken that?"

No one spoke.

Hamar sat again, hands to the fire. "Half right ye are, Gotthard. Ye older men need to be talkin' on the way to be showin' true God-like manliness t' the younger ones. No woman can do that. But be sure, taking a woman does na make you a man any more than eating grapes makes ye a wine barrel. Saints be praised, manhood starts with your earthly father an' ends with the peace of Father-God over your deeds." He sighed. "Now, I'll be dealing with Rainar. Ye men find ways to teach Pekka, Keri, and t'other boys on this trek so they be comin' back men, not idiotic pride-filled braggarts."

Fum played quietly in the corner as the men left.

THE EYE

Keri and his brother, Soren, pulled an empty sled through the part of the mountain forest where birch prevailed. They walked in a twilight of overcast skies and soft drifting snow.

Conscious he would soon pass this job to his brother, Keri was teaching. "Cnute likes pine best for tar and birch for charcoal. I learned that one day when he threw a stack of oak at me." Keri picked out a slim birch tree and began to chop at the base.

"Cnute yelled at you? What did he say?"

"Who knows? You can't understand him half the time."

"Pekka says that Cnute is really a conjurer who turns wood to solid smoke. He says birch is the Devil's spotted tree like Jacob's spotted lambs and not acceptable for sacrifice. He says Cnute howls at the moon when it's full and…"

"Stop." Keri put down his axe. "When Cnute's wife died, Father and I made charcoal until he went back to work. Are we Satan's servants?"

"Well, no, but I've heard him howl at the moon."

"He does howl sometimes but usually it is because he's been

drinking and is weeping for his wife, Liisa. Losing a wife so young is sad for a long time."

"Do tears come out of his good eye and his...eye hole?"

Keri grimaced. "I don't know."

"Well, if he's howling how can he make charcoal?"

"Charcoal is just slowly baked wood. You don't have to think much once you start. Cnute piles the wood just so and buries it. That makes an oven. Then he starts it burning very slowly, putting dirt on places where the smoke comes out too fast. After about three days, the wood turns to charcoal."

"That doesn't sound so hard."

"It's a lot like baking bread. There is a certain knack to it, and you have to stay awake for a couple nights." Keri sighed. "It's a lonely job and Cnute fills the hours with ale. That makes him mourn his wife, and that makes him cry, and *that* makes Pekka think Cnute howls at the moon." Keri tentatively chopped at the tree.

"So how did his wife die? No one tells the same story."

"She was killed by a wolf."

"What happened?"

"Ah, that's the part that makes Cnute crazy." Keri looked up as if the slate sky would remind him of the tale. "They used to live near here. Their old cabin had a clearing for his fires and a stone hearth for making pine tar. He was very proud of it. One night not long after he married Liisa, Cnute started his charcoal oven."

"Did he still have two eyes then?"

"Yes, he was an ordinary fellow."

"What happened?"

"With a cup of ale and a torch he was making his nighttime rounds when he heard whimpering. There, crouching by the door, sat a small black wolf cub looking weak and harmless. He thrust the torch at the pup, and it backed into the shadows, growling. All wolves fear the light. Cnute took pity, however, and didn't harm it." Keri whacked the tree.

"Mindful wolves might be around, the next nights he went out armed. The black cub kept returning, however, and they figured it was orphaned. So Cnute went out with a bone for the cub and ale for himself. Soon the wolf cub let him touch it. When the thing followed him on his rounds, Cnute decided to make it a pet." Keri sighed.

Soren jumped up. "Is that when the wolf ate his wife?"

Keri tapped the tree with the back of the axe. "Well, Liisa was worried. The wolf would disappear during the day. She was afraid and wanted no part of it. Cnute laughed and said the wolf was like a flagon of ale; a good companion on the dark nights.

"At first no one in the village ever saw the wolf, but one evening Cnute appeared where the path breaks out of the woods and looks down on the gate. The wolf was with him."

"Did you see him, Keri?"

"No. Father did. He said the wolf was black as night. Head to tail. Unusual for a wolf. And bigger than any wolf he'd seen. Cnute called it his poor whimpering cub but it was big. People worried about that wolf out there with their children tending goats and gathering wood, but no one wanted to offend Cnute, so they didn't say anything. Especially since they never saw the wolf. They only heard it." Keri drew a long breath. "I remember hearing it: howled like a horn from hell."

"But Father saw it?"

"That time at the gate, Father said, this is strange…Father said the wolf stopped on the path overlooking the village. It snarled and bristled, ignoring Cnute's commands. Sigvard started to shut the gate and called for some men to get their spears. People scurried in, scared, but Fum stepped out and started up the hill. The wolf doubled his snarling and ignored Cnute's commands to settle down. Fum walked right up to it and spoke. The wolf fell to its knees and rolled on its back, whimpering. Fum pointed and the wolf jumped up and fled, never to be seen by villagers again."

Soren stood straight. "Fum spoke?"

"Yep. Only time I've ever heard of. No one could understand the words, but they say it sounded insistent. The wolf couldn't stand it. Like the noise hurt its ears."

Keri studied the snow at his feet. "That night…it was the winter Jesspersson's father died…that night Cnute came reeling into the village screaming his wife had been attacked by the wolf. The men ran out and found her dead with her heart ripped open. They followed a blood trail down the slope but found nothing except Cnute's ale cup. They set traps and poisons but never even saw a track. The black wolf disappeared." Keri pressed his temples. "I wonder if it is the one I saw awhile back?"

Soren glanced into the woods.

Keri's eyes were distant as he continued, "Cnute went mad. He disappeared below the tree line into the Tunturri with his spear. People heard him shouting among the rocks and snowfields, but they couldn't find him. He disappeared."

Keri went back to chopping.

Soren waited a moment but couldn't hold it. "And then?"

"That's when Father and I started making charcoal. The village whispered God punished Cnute for harboring an evil thing in his house. A few pointed to his drinking. People regretted never saying anything to help or warn Cnute. Some blamed Fum for allowing the wolf to run free. He had power over that thing."

Keri stopped cutting. He looked straight at Soren. "One evening when he'd been gone forty days, Cnute returned. His spear was gone, and he was nearly frozen. He limped into the village square, weeping and raging. He had shaved his head and face and was bleeding from a dozen cuts. He raved that he prayed for God to let the wolves kill him. Since they didn't, he said he had to make some kind of a sacrifice to be forgiven." Keri shivered.

"In the torchlight Cnute pulled out his knife and backed off the crowd. Then he shouted about how Christ said it was better to pluck out your eye than to be cast into hell. Brother Hamar ran up and said that God didn't want sacrifice, but your heart. 'Remember, Jesus died so you don't have to sacrifice like the pagans.'"

"But Cnute just glared at him. 'How can a man take and take from God and never pay? You say God offers me life today and forgiveness tomorrow. Therefore, I owe Him. I have to pay!' Then he plunged his knife into his eye and…" Keri paused, feeling a little green.

Soren put a hand to his mouth.

Keri talked faster. "The village went crazy. Women dragging their children away, men pulling their knives, Brother Hamar praying and rushing to stop the blood gushing all over. Cnute thrashed about, like he was possessed, and bit his tongue something fierce. That's why he talks funny now.

"Brun grabbed the knife and Sigvard knocked Cnute on the head… They dragged him off… Sometimes I still see the black blood in the snow and his eye lying there stuck on the knife."

Keri swallowed and shook his head. He looked up at the tree and gave it a tentative push. He turned back to Soren. "Cnute stayed with Brother Hamar, tied up and babbling for a while. Fum sat by his side for days playing that song but in a sad, solemn way. When Cnute stopped raging, Father brought him to our home. You were less than two. After a week he left, moved to that hunting cabin down at the pond where he lives now. He said he was invading the wolves' territory. Challenging them to come for him. He started making charcoal again, but he also began drinking his wages."

"What happened to the eye?"

"I don't know."

"Is that the same knife Cnute carries now?"

"No, maybe… How should I know?" Keri scowled. He whacked the tree three times hard.

"What a waste." Soren gestured to the trail. "He has to walk farther with his charcoal, and we have to walk farther to find him."

Keri wiped chips off his axe. "You shouldn't judge him too harshly. He's only about fifteen years older than me and he doesn't have anyone to help him. His family was long dead, and her family disowned him."

"What about you and Father?"

"I was younger than you, so I didn't know what to say. Cnute pushed off Father and everyone else, even Brother Hamar. He kept saying that if God wanted him, God knew where to find him."

"He lives a dangerous, charmed life. He runs from pitifully meek to instantly angry. He never carries protection against wolves when he tends his fires and has no fears of walking across the snow long after the gates are shut against the night creatures. He never even carries a torch."

Soren looked into the woods. "Maybe he is the Devil's servant if he can walk the night."

"Maybe. He won't go to church."

One last swing and the tree came down with a whoosh. Soren whacked off the branches while Keri cut it into lengths. By early afternoon they had two small trees down and loaded but the sun was low, so they hurried the sled toward Cnute's lakeside cabin.

Keri paused at a turn in the trail. "Let me do the talking with Cnute. If he's drunk, he can be dangerous."

Pekka crossed their path with a sled of firewood.

Soren waved. "Where are you going?"

"Mill. Home." Pekka looked at his feet.

Soren pointed his thumb at Keri. "We're delivering wood to Cnute."

"I wouldn't go near that place." Pekka eyed the trail to the pond. "Mother says he is crazy, and he ate his eye."

Keri laughed. "Hardly, but he can be cantankerous."

Pekka brushed the hair off his face and looked up at Keri. "You're not afraid because you're big, but I walk an extra half league to stay away from him. At the mill we can hear him wailing to the wolf spirits at night. It scares Mother so that she sleeps with me. You're lucky you live inside the walls of the village."

Keri shrugged. "Your stone walls at the mill are pretty high. You need a ladder to reach the threshing floor. You *could* sleep in your other house in the village."

"No wall is tall enough to keep out Cnute's evil spirits. I'll see you tomorrow when the sun is up, and he has lost his night powers." Pekka trudged away.

Keri and Soren crested the low ridge above the charcoal maker's cabin. They saw Cnute with leather helmet and shield fighting the air with his spear. He grunted and spun and knocked himself off-balance. When he saw Keri and Soren starting down the slope, he quickly retreated behind his snow-drifted cabin.

Keri cupped his hands and shouted, "Cnute Pieterson! We bring you wood." He dropped his voice and spoke to Soren. "Stay behind me. If he has been drinking, he might just throw that spear."

They trudged down to the cabin where Cnute, unarmed, came around the corner with a crooked smile. "Keri."

Soren peeked around his brother. "And Soren."

"An' Soren." Cnute touched the sled. "More wood 'an I spected."

"Yes, more wood than you expected." Keri studied him. Cnute's clothes were still ragged but he had washed his face and wore a bright red woolen stocking cap that sloped to cover his missing eye. There was no ale cup in sight.

Keri watched for a weapon. "Did you win your battle?"

"Huh? Oh. No. M' battle lies ahead."

"Father is worried about his supply of charcoal after you go to Hilhelm."

"Yer father—always wis' t' plan ahead." Cnute stood straight, then sagged.

"Father said perhaps you could make bigger piles and more charcoal before you leave."

"Ha!" Cnute tilted his head and looked sideways up at Keri. "Can't make 'nough t' last 'im a year, d' ye think?"

"Well, you could call a truce in your battles. Father thought I could bring more wood, you could make bigger piles, and Soren here could haul the charcoal to the anvil for you."

"Help? Have t' pay f' help." Cnute's voice sharpened. Then he lowered his eyebrow and looked hard at Soren. He rubbed his scarred, shaved head and then knelt to equal Soren's height. Peeling off a torn glove he reached out his scarred and calloused hand. It shook in the cold air. "Young Soren, f' yer father's sake I'll fin' ta way t' give ye part of m' earnings." His voice was all gravel but even.

Soren looked at Keri and then Cnute. Keri nodded though his eyes narrowed, and he tightened his grip on his hand axe. Soren took Cnute's outstretched hand.

"Thank you for your offer, sir, but I understand my father pays you mostly in ale and I have quite enough."

"Ha!" Cnute stood suddenly, pulling his hand away. He shivered and fidgeted with his face. "Got t' change that. Tell yer father I needs only a little ale, an' a lot o' bread…an' perhaps some meat. I also needs some work on m' father's helmet. But you, Soren, got t' have some payment f' yer work or I'm not t'agree t' this arrangement."

"Thank you, sir."

Cnute turned back to Keri. He sighed. "Keri, we be on th' sled t'gether. You an' yer father ha' tried t' help me in th' past. I may needs yer help agin." He reached out his hand.

Keri hesitated; then they clasped arms. "Sir, you are not yourself today."

"Indeed, I've not been m'self since I drew th' white stone fer th' king." Cnute clapped his hands together. "I'm called agin t' th' wilderness. It's either God or tha' hell-wolf." He looked vacantly down the mountain and shook. His fists clenched and he ground his teeth. "Put th' wood there an' go." He walked stiff-legged into his cabin.

Keri and Soren dumped the wood and walked in silence up the hill.

Soren looked back as they left but saw no Cnute. "He didn't seem so scary up close."

Keri noticed there was no smoke from the chimney. "No, not to-day. But be wary: you saw how he changes like the moon from light to dark."

PLANS

Sigvard and the other two aged veterans of the last trek across the Tunturri came out the gate to talk to Eldman, the carpenter. They found him and Tharn looking at a drawing in the snow.

"The old sled was too fat to get through some of the gaps," said Sigvard. "We had to re-figure our route probably twice a day in the mountains."

His comrades nodded. "Yep."

"Yep."

Eldman stroked his gray beard. "So you said."

"And it has to be high enough underneath to not suddenly catch on snow-covered rocks. We about jerked out our teeth." Sigvard poked at a gap in his yellow teeth.

"Yep."

"Yep."

"But it can't be too high. You heard how the last one fell over." He put out his arms and tilted back and forth.

"Yep."

"Yep." The veterans sipped their ale.

"Thank you." Eldman closed his eyes and took a slow, deep breath.

"And we need to make the width of the skis wide enough to hold the weight and not sink in the snow."

"Yep," said Sigvard.

"We are thinking one long ski on each side instead of a separate one at each corner."

"Yep."

"Yep."

"And don't forget the river," said Sigvard. "If it is too heavy it will break the ice and sink like a devil laden with sin."

"Yep."

"Yep."

Eldman nodded. "Yep."

Everyone gazed at the pattern drawn in the snow.

The three elders folded their arms in unison. "Well, call us if you need anything else." Sigvard looked at his friends. "More ale?"

"Yep."

"Yep."

They trudged back in the gate.

Tharn shook his head. "We've been doing this for days now. I'm getting snow blind looking at it."

The carpenter nodded. "Don't your books have any answers?"

Tharn laughed. "I only have one and all it talks about is chariots."

"Hamar's book?"

"Nope, book about dead Romans, no sleds."

Eldman grimaced, chin in hand. "Well, it won't be so top heavy after the first week as the load gets lighter. Maybe we could chance a capsize for that long."

"If it tips over, we lose a day getting it unloaded and upright again. Besides, the first two weeks are the most uneven through the passes and creek beds. The sage says, 'Better a mule that bears me than a stallion that throws me.'"

"Yep."

Eli and Pekka appeared up the hill from the gate, each pulling a sled piled with wood. Eli's was short and wide while Pekka's was taller with more freeboard. The boys trudged down and began to unload their wood at the growing pile of logs for the trek.

Eldman glanced at the two and slapped Tharn on the back. "Two sleds! We make two sleds: one big, one small, both narrow enough to slip through the hills and not so tall as to topple. And the second sled becomes firewood when it's empty!"

"Brilliant!" shouted Tharn. "And because they are lighter, they ought to move easier."

Tharn erased the latest snow drawings with his boot and they started anew.

After a few days, the sleds' outlines began to rise from the snow and shavings by Eldman's shop. He built the biggest five paces wide: enough for two lines of men to pull in front side by side. Nine paces long, it would hold about forty nights of firewood stacked taller than a man. Once on the Tunturri Eldman knew there was only frozen marsh grass and scrub brush barely good for kindling. Wood provided not only warmth but created light that held the wolves at bay. His second, smaller sled featured a shelf for the lighter items while the ale kegs and food boxes found space below.

Meanwhile the village collected food in the meetinghouse. The building smelled of strong rye crackers, smoked hams, salted deer, game birds, and cheese. Bags of hazelnuts and dried crab apples came along in quantity with turnips, onions, leeks, and pickled cabbage. Disappointed earlier, several women provided enough smoked salmon for the men and the king.

At the woodpile Soren and Pekka stacked logs. Dirk, Stjärna's father, stood gazing at the sleds, watching without joining in.

Sigvard kicked a split log. "You can never have too much wood. Once the wolves find you, they get bolder each night. On my trek, Ole Sigson fell asleep on guard duty, letting the fire go down. He awakened us all screaming as a wolf dragged him into the night."

"Mother says wolves hate the light like a devil hates the Word," said Pekka. "We keep our hearth fire big to ward off Cnute and the wolves."

"Why do the wolves avoid the village?" asked Soren, plopping on his sled.

Tharn heaved a sigh. "Wolves don't fear man, but they fear the gifts God gives men. Like fire that burns them and illuminates their schemes. Wolves prefer darkness or solitary places like the wilderness to hide their work."

"Aye, only the foolish farmer sets his cabin close to the wild," said Sigvard. "Dirk, you remember Lindstrom. He built a hut two days down the mountain. Built a nice barn and had a great summer with good grass for his sheep, but wolves took nearly his whole flock one evening. We went to see what we could do and the wolves chased us into his hut all night. There must have been thirty wolves outside howling and snuffling until dawn."

Dirk shook out of his silence. "I remember. We stabbed through the door at them but never seemed to hit one. It was tense." He sighed. "I think that may be my life's only adventure. I dearly wanted to be on this sled."

"Tsk," said Sigvard. "No stone for you. My daughter, your wife, is pregnant again. Praise God!"

Dirk snorted. "Praise God? Probably another worthless daughter. Isn't three enough?" He turned and stalked into the village.

Sigvard shook his head.

Only Pekka saw the flash of blue and blonde that ducked behind the gate. He also heard the choked-back sobbing.

GREEN

The days until the race between Eli and Brun crept past. Brun assured everyone he would win and began organizing the crew. Eli declared himself healed and ready, but Keri knew both men spent time running the back hills.

The same time passed too quickly for Stjärna Dirksdottir. She thought of Keri's departure with the same sickening sensation she felt when looking down from a tall cliff. Her attempts to catch his eyes hadn't worked and she wanted that arm in hers. A blacksmith's woman commanded respect.

Keri, on the other hand, lost track of time as he worked to build his own endurance and gather extra wood. He also lost track of the number of occasions he caught himself seeing Stjärna Dirksdottir as if for the first time.

Surely, he thought walking to the woods, *she has always been at the well each morning these past years. Surely, she has always been Sundays at church. Surely, she has passed my house every day before now in pursuit of her chores. Why am I now aware of her laughing voice across the square, how good she looks in blue, how her blonde bangs frame her eyes, the shape of her body? I must not let her catch me staring but how can I help it? How can I even talk to her when my mouth dries up every time she walks by? Who am I to think she even wants to talk to an oaf like me?*

Surely, I sound like a cow bellowing at the well, thought Stjärna, walking across the square. *Surely, Brother Hamar thinks I am deaf for having moved up front in church. Surely, Mother must think I am a lost deer going past Keri's house on every errand no matter where she sends me. Maybe Keri doesn't like blue. Maybe I should grow out my bangs. Am I too skinny? Why won't he talk to me?*

I need to be bold, thought Keri one morning. *I need to place myself at the well and speak to her. She is just a girl, not a wolf. I am a man on his way to war. Surely, I can talk to a girl!*

I need to be bold, thought Stjärna one morning. *I need to place myself by the gate where everyone will see me talk to him before he leaves to cut wood. He is just a boy, not a wolf. I am a woman well able to run a household. Surely I can talk to a boy.*

"Mother," said Keri that morning, "I will draw your water before I go to the woods today."

"Mother," said Stjärna that morning, "I will be slightly delayed bringing in the water today. Jurgensdottir asked me to stop by the gate."

Keri sniffed his wool shirt, wrinkled his nose, and slipped on his Sunday tunic. Running a hand over his wool vest, he flipped out some bits of twig and pine needles. He used his fingers to push the hair back over his ears and peered into his mother's brass mirror, wishing for a hint of beard. No luck. He considered a leather hat but left it behind. He didn't want to appear to be doing anything special. He did, however, take an extra moment to scrub at his sap- and charcoal-stained hands. Keri grabbed a bucket and was out the door into the morning darkness.

Stjärna sniffed her bluest frock and whitest collar. She pressed and smoothed the wool until they were the image of order and purity. Under protest, her younger sister braided her hair three times. A pinch on her cheeks to add color and she was at last through with the brass mirror. Grabbing up an empty basket, Stjärna was out the door and into the morning darkness.

Stepping outside with the water bucket Keri dawdled by the corner to see if Stjärna was at the well yet. A variety of village girls came in twos and threes, but not Stjärna. He went back and chopped some kindling to pass the time but worked slowly so he wouldn't sweat. The sky changed to a rose color over the palisade wall but still no Stjärna.

Stjärna went directly to the village gate, which meant bypassing the well. As she arrived, she slowed her pace to see who was approaching. An accidental meeting would take some finesse. She sauntered by, exchanging greetings with old Jodis Jurgensdottir, who stood shaking out a tunic by her front door. She walked past the gate and around a corner to where she could see the opening and waited, trying not to be obvious. She doubled back twice to keep moving in the cold, but Keri didn't come.

"Sakarias," called his mother out her door, "I'm going to need that water soon."

Keri looked anxiously at the well. Jodis Jurgensdottir tottered up the short hill with her bucket behind some girls, but not Stjärna. "Yes, Mother," he replied.

"Yes, Mother," echoed Eli coming down the lane. "Oh, Sakarias," he said in a high, squeaky voice, "has the woodcutting been too difficult so you must now only carry water?"

"Hush, you skinny raven," said Keri. "I'm just helping Mother."

"Then is Soren out doing the real work with the axe?"

"Drawing water is real work. Mother gets tired. It fits a son to help," hissed Keri.

"Perhaps, but drawing water is woman's work in a house where the labor is divided properly. Will you do laundry and bake bread next, Sakarias?"

"Not unless I end up a bachelor like you will because no girl will tolerate your bad manners and running mouth," barked Keri. "Besides, the forge requires water too and no one will say smithing is woman's work. Here, take this other bucket and we will go show those girls we can draw for the forge like men."

"Ah, ha! Now you are closer to truth. You should have told me this involved a girl. Perhaps one with a name from the heavens?" Eli winked.

"Why…uh, no, I'm…it's just…my mother…"

"Keri," said Eli, interrupting, "I am your friend. I know you are distracted these days and so am I. As it happens, I am also looking for an excuse to go to the well at the right moment, and you have provided it. And I am interested in a name from the forest, Laurel Larsdottir.

There she goes now. Come with me, let us draw water as Isaac's servant did and see if it leads to romance."

Keri hesitated. "Who's Isaac?"

"Bible guy. Pay attention in church. Come on."

Laurel Larsdottir had a bucket and crunched through the snow up to the well. Both her dark green frock and cream-colored apron were embroidered with evergreen trees. Her deep brown hair was tamed by a green head scarf into a long smooth river that went straight down her back. A fresh evergreen twig was tucked above her ear. She measured just shorter than Eli with a delicate almond-shaped face and sharp hazel eyes. Her closed-lip smile welcomed the boys.

Eli's voice bounced. "I see that your father has no need to go for wood today, Laurel."

"And why would that be?" she answered, still walking.

"Why, you carry the forest to him on your clothes."

"Are you saying I should throw my frock in the fire?" She looked down at it. "Is my friend Gudrun's embroidery so bad?"

"No," said Eli, looking into her eyes. "But I am surprised it hasn't caught fire from the warmth you carry within it."

"If my uncles hear you talk so they will thrash you like summer wheat. What could you know of my warmth, Master Gregerson?" She raised an eyebrow.

"Certainly nothing from personal experience." He bowed. "But the fire in your eyes burns in my heart and surely it must come from a wonderfully warm soul."

Keri rolled his eyes.

Laurel laughed. "You had best speak to my father before you speak to me again that way."

"With your permission, I will do that today."

She paused, then smiled just for him. "I would be pleased if you would."

"I will go this very moment. When you get home, I will be camped

61

at your door." They both laughed as he sprinted away with only a hint of the limp.

Keri stood with two buckets and a puzzle on his face.

Laurel turned to him. "If you would like to carry a token from a girl of this village when you cross the Tunturri, I think I know a blonde who would be willing to give it," she said.

He quivered. "How can you talk so openly, so easily about things in your heart? I can hardly bring myself to be in the same street with the girl who has caught my eye for fear I may say something stupid."

"It is simple. You have good parents, good will, and a good heart. Even Brother Hamar smiles when he hushes you in church." She took his hand and looked into his eyes. "Just be who you are."

"But what if she doesn't like me?"

"Everyone likes you, Keri. The real question is how much she likes you. Take time. Talk to her. Find out if God suited you for each other."

"That's easy to say. Eli is good at talking, I am good at…chopping wood."

Laurel smiled and shook her head. "The Lord has given you all you need. Look at how easily you are talking to me. I suspect Stjärna will be even easier."

He scratched his hair. "Yes, I *am* talking to you. *Surely* I can talk to Stjärna." Keri's eyes lit up as he took her other hand in his. "Thank you. Thank you. I *will* speak to her."

He dropped her hands and grabbed her bucket. "Let me fill this for you and then we can walk to your house and see how Eli proceeded with your father."

Jodis Jurgensdottir came by Stjärna with a pail of water from the well. "If you're looking for Keri Ellisson," she said, "he's headin' for the well. He's not been out the gate today."

Stjärna stammered, "Why…uh, no, I'm…it's just…my mother…"

"Sure, sure," said gray-haired Jodis. "I've seen lots of other girls lurking around these gates with an empty basket and a wandering eye. Yesterday it was Gudrun trying to catch Jesspersson and before that it was Annika. I spent a little time here myself before Ole noticed me." She sighed. "That was a long time ago. Now, go. You are wasting daylight. Try again tomorrow. Keri's detained today." She went inside chuckling.

Other girls? thought Stjärna. The idea hit her like an arrow. She marched to the square and looked up at the well. Keri was holding Laurel Larsdottir's hands and gazing deep into her eyes. They smiled, and he filled three buckets and carried them as they walked off toward Laurel's house *in front of the whole village!* The world blurred as Stjärna's eyes filled with tears. She fled out the gate to the woods. A stone throw behind, Fum followed, shaking his head.

A wolf howled somewhere down the valley.

In the next days Keri looked for an opportunity to talk to Stjärna, but she made sure there were none. She traded chores with her sisters and seldom left the house unless one of them saw Keri leaving to cut wood. She even feigned illness to skip church. "I am not going to let people see him make a fool of me like that ancient Jodis Jurgensdottir. Who does she think I am?" For over a week Stjärna disappeared from Keri's sight.

He began to think God was saying, "Look elsewhere."

ANOTHER AXE

K eri trotted over the snow with a bundle of wood piled high on his back. He was surprised to see his father, Ellis, waving him to a small clearing where the sun sparkled bright on the new fallen snow.

"Put down your load, son."

Keri frowned but obeyed.

"Sit while I talk," said Ellis, gesturing with an odd-shaped leather and fur bundle.

Keri settled on his stack of firewood.

Ellis's drooping mustache had ceased to hold a civil shape and sparkled with silver strands. His body bent at the waist from too many years over a forge. He looked disheveled, foolish to a stranger, but his heavily veined and muscled hands could crush the jaws of a bear. Keri thought those hands seemed gentle as they stroked the long fur wrapping.

Ellis took a deep breath. "My son...when my father turned forty-five years old, he brought me up to these woods and told me again the stories of the family. He told me of the pagan Konrad, how Lorn converted to the faith at the battle of the Ladoga Lake and earned a sparkling red stone from the king. He told his own tales of trading

64

BALLAD OF THE BLACKSMITH'S SON

among the Arabs where the rivers don't freeze and a man's skin turns dark. Finally, he remembered his own part in the War of the East with Sigvard.

"I think you know these stories already," said Ellis.

Keri nodded and glanced at the fur parcel.

"You also know that I have the sword of Lorn with the jewel embedded deep in the hand guard. It is rightfully my sword for several more years, but I was not chosen to wield it during my lifetime. I was too young to draw with Sigvard and drew black in this season. The Lord apparently has other plans for me." His smile held no enthusiasm.

Keri's eyes lit up and he looked again at the bundle in his father's lap.

"By rights that sword should go to you, my oldest son," said Ellis. "I hope someday to give it to Soren instead."

Keri stood, then sat. "Father, have I offended or sinned in your eyes? Of course, the sword is too valuable to send to Hilhelm with me. Who do I think I am?"

Ellis smiled. "No, you have been all a father could ask. What you have done is grown too big."

Ellis began to unwrap the bundle, exposing a thick oak handle with a leather loop. "Few men reach your height and fewer still achieve your strength. Not many of our ancestors were so big. Neither were their foes. What would be a perfect weapon for them would be too small for you."

Ellis paused. "Keri, you have heard that you resemble your mother's great uncle, Ubbe. He was big like you and the strongest man in the village in his lifetime. I'm sorry you never got to see him. He used to lift my father's anvil and balance it over his head with one hand. He also was too big for a sword."

Keri eyes widened and he looked again at the bundle.

"Your mother and I went to her uncle Vigge and asked for a boon.

65

Here it is: the battle-axe of your great-uncle Ubbe. The axe they call the Wild Boar."

Ellis unfolded the last length of fur and revealed a double-headed axe-hammer. The handle, reinforced with a banded iron sleeve, came up to Keri's waist. The large axe head was fluted and curved. Its opposite side featured a long hammerhead almost two fingers thick. Two hand grips, one near the center and another at the bottom, were double wrapped in oiled leather strips. A lanyard helped keep the weapon close. On the top gleamed a mean spike as long as a knife.

Both axe head and hammerhead showed use, but the blade radiated a certain arrogance. Even in Ellis' huge hands the weapon looked heavy. He handed it to Keri.

"Is this the one he used on the river?" Keri touched the spike.

"Yes," said Ellis. "From Ladoga and Kiev. The bards say he once hit the bow of a Slavish longboat so hard the whole keel detached and she sank."

"Why did Uncle Vigge give it up?"

Ellis shrugged. "His children were all daughters. He ate well but hunted alone. Even now there is only one grandson to inherit, and he has another family sword."

"That is sad."

"Daughters are good. They are better at caring for their old parents than sons."

"I will never be like that."

"I hope so, but you have sisters," said Ellis. "Do you remember the Corinthians Bible passage Lorn used to dedicate his sword?"

Keri scrunched his face. "Wasn't it something like 'Our weapons are not man-made but made mighty through God's power'?"

Ellis laughed. "You may have it clearer than the actual words: 'The weapons of our warfare are not carnal, but mighty through God to the pulling down of strongholds.' In any case, it applies here too. It will be

God's strength, not yours, that makes Wild Boar powerful. You must always remember where your power really comes from."

Keri nodded but his eyes stayed on the weapon. He stood and tentatively swung it, feeling the weight. It pulled him off-balance.

"See how it has two grips?" said Ellis. "You will learn to use the length of it to reach over your shield wall to pull down their shield wall. And it is good for close-in fighting when you grab the middle grip. And like a sword you can slice or stab. It scares your mother that you will not have a third hand to hold a shield, but, gripped in the middle, you could use one hand for the axe and the other for your shield."

"Will you teach me how to use it?"

"I can show you a little, but you'd best talk to someone in Hilhelm who uses one. The trick seems to be to keep your feet on the ground as an anchor to the weight of the axe."

"Maybe Sigvard knows more…" said Keri.

"Slowly, my son," said Ellis. "You already know much about iron, steel, swords, and their needs. We will talk more of this weapon but first let us pray you never have to use it, and if you do, that you use it only for the right. Tharn read somewhere, 'A man's honor lies in his sword's idleness.' And all truly great adventures begin with the Lord's blessing. Remember where your power comes from."

Keri nodded absently, caressing the hammerhead, and licking his lips.

WARMTH

After church Brun called the crew of the sleds to meet him with their gear for the trek. "You, too, Eli. I might decide I don't want to go." Tiny snowflakes and low-flying clouds turned the afternoon a light gray as the thirty men stood around Brun in front of the meetinghouse. Fum huddled by the doorway studying faces. Sigvard, with his two old sled comrades and a flagon of ale, came and sat on the platform.

"All right," Brun shouted, his twin braided red beard twitching. "We start by checking to make sure you have what you will need for the journey. Let's start with boots. Everyone has two pair? One to wear, and one to stay dry until you need them? Hold up your second pair." He walked around looking at their boots.

"Timonen, that is a sorry second pair. If you kicked a wolf, he would laugh. Look at that seam. Viksten, you're good with leather. Help Timonen make these ladies' slippers stand up to the Tunturri."

"Yep." Viksten stepped over.

Brun continued around, pointing and ordering improvements.

"Keri, do you have a hat? Bring it. You too, young Bue. Get one from your cousin, Eli. He won't be going." Brun winked at Eli, who frowned.

"Socks! Let me see your socks. At least four pair. Jesspersson, that's only two."

"It's all I have." He hung his head.

"These don't fit me anymore," said Keri, tossing him a pair.

"I have some spares too," said Eli.

"You won't need any, Eli. You'll be here hunting squirrels." Brun laughed. He put a friendly hand on Jesspersson, handing him the socks, but turned to the rest of the crew. "Tunics and trousers. At least two pair. Show me. Show me!" He toured again.

"Pekka." Brun smiled. "Did your mother choose your clothes? They are beautiful." Then his voice rose word by word until he was shouting. "Quickly now, run home and get those heavy trousers I saw you cutting wood in last week. We're not going to a wedding!" Pekka fled with his bag. "And bring some decent gloves!"

Brun turned and looked at Cnute's trousers. "By the beard of St. Cynibild, those look like they were put together by a drunk and invaded by the king of fleas."

"So's yer beard," Cnute growled.

Brun looked hard into Cnute's eye. Cnute returned the gaze and raised an eyebrow over his empty eye socket. Everyone froze.

Brun also raised an eyebrow. "You need a seamstress who doesn't drink much."

"I got one who drinks little but gots n' skill."

"I have a mother-in-law who drinks less and has skill...but is cold."

"I gots charcoal would keep 'er warm."

"Her work would keep you warm long after you have left."

"Sounds better 'n drink."

"I drink to your new trousers." Brun smiled and stuck out his hand. They clasped at the wrist. Everyone breathed again.

Brun fingered his own beards. "And do I see a new beard?"

"An old beard coming home." Cnute looked down and smiled.

Brun nodded. "I pray we all bring our beards home to grow old."

"Amen," said Tharn.

"Yep," said Eldman.

Brun shouted at the group, "Sleeping furs! Let's see them."

The afternoon faded into twilight while Brun checked their gear. As darkness approached Brun brought the men together. "You've all seen the sleds Eldman is building. We're going to store our weapons, shields, and skis on the outside for easy reach. Our clothes go inside." He picked up a hinged box about the size of a cradle. "Everyone needs to build a box just like this for your stuff. Same size. They pile easy and will help us load faster. I want yours done by Sunday. Put your rune or mark on it to help keep order. If something doesn't fit in the box, it doesn't go."

The men looked at each other.

"We are going to practice pulling and skiing every morning before sunrise except Sundays. You'll have daylight to do your family work. And if you think you can't do it, look at Eldman, here. He's the oldest man on the trek. He's already spending most of his day working on our sled and most of his night doing for his family. We will rest in Hilhelm. Warm lodging, good food, and nothing to do until the horsemen show up.

"All right. Go home and fix your things. I'll see you in the morning. Pekka, I need your help for a minute." Pekka wiped the hair from his eyes and looked up.

The men gathered their gear and headed home.

"Pekka, take this box back to Eldman's shop. Then pick up the board he gives you. It has the measurements for their boxes. Take it around to everyone's house. Thanks, I'm counting on you. Go."

Sigvard came over. "Warm lodging and good food? Do you know who warms the lodging and cooks the food?"

"Aye, you've been talking about it for twenty years. But by the time we get there we will think a woodshed and a piece of horse leather are luxurious."

"Yep," said Sigvard. His comrades folded their arms and nodded.

After a week, many of the men limped or smelled of liniment. Brun's favorite change, however, was how Pekka responded to Brun's attention. The boy showed a new eagerness in his step and looked up when he spoke. Brun's biggest smile came at church when Pekka moved from his mother's side over to the far end of Annika's bench. Annika smiled even bigger.

AFOUL

The day arrived when no one left the village. Eli and Brun were to race around the palisade. The whole village turned out, plus Firth Black Collar from Drakestad who argued wagers with Mantas and Gotthard. Money changed hands and Eli saw a coin drop unnoticed. Jesspersson also saw the coin and kicked snow on it. When the others moved off, he picked it up. Fum, playing his merry tune just uphill, hit a bad note, and frowned. Eli laughed.

Eli stood in a knot with his cousin Bue, Keri, and several of his friends. Jesspersson walked up with Gudrun and started offering advice. Eli, craning to see around him, wanted him to shut up.

A group of older men surrounded Brun, talking and slapping his back. He tied his auburn mane back at his neck and captured his beard in two short braids that jumped when he laughed. Other groups stood around speculating, gesturing, and enjoying the holiday atmosphere. Annika held Pekka by the arm and talked excitedly to him. He alternately smiled at her and at his feet.

Eli felt a warm hand touch his hair. Laurel stuck a pine sprig into his leather headband and whispered, "I would prefer you stay safe here with me, but I know this sled means a lot to you. It is my competitor for your affections this day. But God will choose right, and you should know that you are very dear to me no matter who wins."

He turned to respond but she slipped away with a hand to her eyes.

Tharn blew his hunting horn and the crowd noise dropped to a stream-like mutter. Even Fum stopped playing. Brother Hamar blessed the runners and asked for God's wisdom.

Valdemar stepped forward. "The race starts here." He scraped a line out from the gate in the packed snow. "The first one around the village and back across the line wins and fills the last spot on the sled." The crowd murmurs grew. He waved his arms for quiet. "Brun, Eli, are there any questions?"

Brun stepped forward smiling. "I stand ready to run, but I want to know what I am to do if this lad bumps me and I stumble. Who will judge if there is a foul?" The crowd noise increased again.

Valdemar and Tharn looked at each other. Two other council members stepped up and they huddled, breath steaming in the cold air. Valdemar shrugged and waved for silence. "There will be no fouls," he said. "This is a no-rules race. We want our most resourceful men on the sled and that will be the one who can get around the palisade first by any means."

Brun threw his head back, "Ha, har! Perfect!"

Eli's stomach lurched. Brun weighed a barley sack more than he did and flexed forearms that could knock down an ox.

"Sir," cried Keri, "that is hardly fair. You said it would be a foot race, not a half-league-long wrestling match."

Tharn put his hand on Keri's shoulder but looked into Eli's eyes. "Cicero said, 'Laws are silent in times of war.' Son, war is not fair, and it is much more than a half-league-long wrestling match. We would rather see Eli lose here than lose somewhere else with a spear in his chest."

Eli grimaced but nodded his assent. He shrugged at Keri and

moved up to the line. His parents stepped up and spoke briefly, his mother shivering. She hugged him and whispered a prayer for safety in his ear, but he knew she wished him to lose.

Brun winked at his wife holding their latest toddler and stepped to the line. The racers grasped each other at the wrist in a rough but friendly shake. Brun smiled. "I'll try not to hurt you, lad, but I won't let you pass me and I will *not* lose this race. I've waited all my life to be chosen to cross the Tunturri."

Eli felt the grip and wondered how a man could be so strong. He forced a smile. Brun laughed and stooped to adjust his boot.

Eli glanced around for Laurel. He saw Stjärna with Pekka and Annika in the crowd before he spotted Laurel alone away from the starting line. He smiled, but she cocked her head and then rolled her eyes, signaling to look behind him. He peeked over his shoulder but saw only Fum staring away at the snow.

He turned back to her. She squinted to see if anyone was noticing and then jerked her head to gesture behind him. He looked behind him again and back at her with a puzzled frown. She rolled her eyes impatiently, arched her eyebrows at Brun, threw up one elbow, and then rolled her head to indicate behind him again.

Eli's eyes widened. He looked again over his shoulder and smiled. Fum played his whistle. The villagers strung out around the north end of the gate where they could see the first hundred paces of the race. Eli nodded at Laurel and she bowed.

Valdemar started a speech about upholding the honor of the village, but Brun interrupted. "Start the race. I have chores to do before dark."

Everyone laughed. Brun moved to Eli's right, closest to the wall.

Eli casually asked Valdemar, "The winner is the first one to cross the line after going around the village, right?"

"Of course," said Valdemar. He held up his hand.

"Ready?" They nodded. Brun cocked his arm and made a fist.

"Set?" Eli tensed as a hiss escaped from Brun, "SSSSS."

"Go!"

"Taah!" Brun's arm flashed out to catch Eli in the stomach, but the boy jumped back. He spun around and sprinted down the village wall in the other direction. Brun took a step to catch him but realized he could never make up the distance. The crowd yelled in amazement. People pointed both ways.

"Go! Go!" Jesspersson shouted. "Catch him in the middle as he comes around!"

Brun took off running in the opposite direction from Eli. The crowd parted as he charged along the wall.

The sled crew's practice had packed the snow close to the palisade and Eli found good traction. He flew around the first corner and thought ahead. *Brun. Must stay away from those arms.*

Eli reached the back wall first. He ran a quarter of the way before Brun turned the corner in front of him hoisting a large grin and a larger icicle from the corner tower. He charged toward Eli. Eli ran wide. Brun ran wider. Eli darted toward the wall. Brun swerved toward the wall. They both swerved wide again as the distance closed. *We're going to crash. Need one more fake to get by.*

Suddenly, Brun hurled his icicle at Eli's feet. Eli jumped and Brun hit Eli's legs like a tree branch, throwing him hard in the snow. With fingers like talons Brun grabbed Eli's arm and leg. "SSSSutaah!" he cried, lifting him high over his head. "Let's go see your friends! Ha har!" He lumbered down the wall; Eli flailed helplessly above him.

Eli stopped struggling and Brun folded him over his shoulder like a sack of wheat. Eli's arms bounced on Brun's back. His fingers occasionally scraped the rough logs and ice along the palisade. When Brun turned the corner, Eli grabbed the corner log and kicked forward with his legs. His kick and Brun's momentum swung Brun off-balance and slammed him into the palisade. He fell to the ground in a daze.

Loose, Eli raced away on his original course.

Brun staggered up raging but soon stumbled toward the gate. He was closer to the finish, but winded from carrying Eli and addled from his crash. He fell twice until the cold snow cleared his head and he pounded toward the last turn.

The villagers at the far corner saw the crash and yelled the news. Laurel and Keri waited at the opposite corner looking for Eli. At last he appeared, moving like a deer chased by wolves. His feet flicked the ground as he ran high on his toes. Even so Brun lumbered around his last corner and headed for the gate a full three heartbeats before Eli came into view.

The crowd jumped and screamed as the two ran toward the line and each other. Eli was eating up Brun's lead. Valdemar and Tharn backed the crowd away from the line. In the final sprint Brun's eyes lit up. "Ha har!" His legs pumped not just at the finish but at Eli.

They hit the line simultaneously, but Brun put his shoulder into Eli's stomach, tackling him backward. The two tumbled into the spectators, Brun on top, and both gasping for air. The crowd jumped like a tormented sea. Voices cheered Brun the winner. Others cheered Eli. Valdemar and Tharn both spoke at once: "Eli," said Valdemar. "Brun," said Tharn.

Brun rolled on his back laughing, his breath steaming into the air. He stood and reached down a huge arm to Eli. Eli retched trying to recapture the air knocked out of him. "Breathe deep and live, boy," said Brun. "Such a lad as you shall represent us well on the sled."

"I won?" gasped Eli.

"No, you lost," said Brun, raising his voice for over the crowd. "I claim victory because we both ended up on my side of the line. There is no proof Eli ever crossed the line."

The crowd broke into shouts, arguments, and cheers.

"Peace," Brun shouted. "I also claim a place on the sled for the lad because Rentvatten's finest midwife, my own bride Gayle, tells me that Jon's lovely wife is four months gone with child. That means she was blessed by God with a child before the choosing of the stones. That means Jon is not eligible to go, so I claim his place for young Eli here, who is nearly the fastest runner in the kingdom."

There was a pause, consternation, then cheers as everyone ran to congratulate someone. Eli's friends and family surrounded him. Jon's friends and family surrounded him and his blushing wife. Tharn broke through to Brun and slapped him on the chest. "Why didn't you just say so?"

"Have you never done something just because it was fun?" said Brun, laughing. "And it settles a question that would have haunted us forever: who really is faster?"

Eli's father, Greger, bragged to his friends with one arm around his son. Eli's mother, with tear-filled eyes, dabbled at a trickle of blood on Eli's lip. Eli's eyes darted around the crowd. He saw Jesspersson and Gudrun running over the hill, and Pekka looking curiously at Annika.

At last he spotted Laurel standing away from the mob of well-wishers, nodding her head. When their eyes met, she cocked her head and smiled a tight-lipped smile. A fir sprig twirled in her hand. Looking over the crush of people he mouthed the words, "Thank you." She raised her brows and shrugged.

Eli disengaged from his parents and pushed through the back-slapping, jabbering people. He tried to be polite but wanted to get to Laurel. When she saw him coming, she turned coyly on her heel and started walking slowly up the woodcutter's path. He broke free, brushed past Mantas and Firth arguing about a coin, and caught up to her in a couple of bounds. They walked slowly together up the trail. Him gasping still, and her hiding a tear.

Keri broke out of the group of well-wishers too. He saw Eli and Laurel walking hand in hand and turned to scan the crowd. *There!* A flash of blue. Stjärna walked alone through the gates. Keri ran to her, remembering to jump and touch the village crest for luck.

"Stjärna," he stammered, stumbling to her side, "may I speak with you?"

"Do you need something?" Her eyes narrowed.

He missed her sharp tone. "May I speak with your father about seeing you more often?"

She turned on him like a cornered snake and hissed, "Who do you think you are, shopping the whole village to see how many girls you can entice at once, you panting dog?" Her face was red but her clenched teeth showed white-hot anger between curled lips.

Keri's eyes opened wide but he plunged on. "I have asked no other man permission to see his daughter. You are the only one I have ever sought like this."

"I should have known. Laurel Larsdottir, with her bright ideas, would never seek her father's permission to do anything. But if you think a lumbering moose like you can court me and hold hands with her at the well under the same moon, you are sadly mistaken. I don't care what that green toad tells you is fashionable: I will not play by her rabbits' social rules."

Keri stood stunned. *Lumbering moose? Toad?* His cheeks colored. He clenched and unclenched his fists. *Laurel Larsdottir?* He closed his eyes and shook his head. *Lord, what is this?* Then it hit him.

His eyes popped open. Stjärna was striding away. He caught up and blurted, "'Twas Laurel who took my hands Friday last to convince me I could speak to your father as Eli had just gone to speak to hers. I have spent the time since trying to find you for a private moment."

She stopped, wheeled, and put her finger in his face. "If you think for one candle flicker I am going to believe a lie like that, then you take me for a bigger fool than you have grown to be yourself."

He backed up in face of her tiny furious finger and noticed a flash of green over her shoulder beyond the gate. "'Tis true," he cried. "Look." He pointed up the hill to the woods. Just disappearing up the woodcutter's path went Laurel's green frock with Eli's arm around her.

Stjärna's eyes went wide. Her finger wilted. She looked at the spot where Laurel disappeared, then at Keri. He smiled at her. Her eyes suddenly broke into tears. "Look what you have done. You ruined everything!" She fled down the village street, pushing through Pekka and Annika, leaving a bewildered Keri in her wake.

Jodis Jurgensdottir walked arthritically by Keri on the way to her door. "Well, you got the first part right. You didn't lose your temper. Hamar says it is written you must forgive seven times seventy. Give her a chance to think. If you demand anything from her now, you will only make it worse."

"What?" said Keri.

"You can't live by the village gate," said the old woman, smiling, "and not see a lot of couples come and go. Bible says, 'love is kind and patient.' She needs a lot of patience right now. Go chop your wood."

He scratched his head a while and then went for his axe. In the distance, Fum's whistle played up the wooded trail.

COURAGE

Several days after the race Keri crunched out of the forest to the woodcutters' path, his head down under a load of wood.

"Were I a wolf, you would make an easy dinner," said Laurel Larsdottir, leading her goats onto the same path.

He looked up startled but recovered enough to say, "Aren't you brave, so unarmed and unescorted far from the walls? Jesspersson saw a wolf just yesterday. You would make an easy prey, but I fear you are too small to be worth eating."

"When you herd goats properly, they warn you of danger." She nudged a goat along. "Besides, village gossip would tell you I was probably dishonorably escorted."

"I know naught of gossip, but I know Eli is well south gathering cedar for arrow shafts."

"Well, perhaps I have a defender left in the village after all," she replied with a quizzical smile. "It seems everyone else would rather call me a wicked girl now that Eli and I have determined to look harder at each other. Did you know that Annika is no longer allowed to draw water when I am at the well?"

"No." Keri frowned. "That hardly seems fair. You've been friends since birth."

"We are breaking ground, it seems, Eli and I. We are among the first of our birth years to think seriously beyond childhood. Some of the parents are scared. Yet we do nothing they did not once do."

"Maybe that's what scares them." Keri shifted his load.

Laurel laughed. "Perhaps it would help if some of our friends began to look more seriously at the future." She raised an eyebrow at Keri.

He shrugged his load. "Annika seems to be following Pekka. Or is it the other way around?"

"No, she's trying to wake him up. He's a doe-eyed puppy. He still watches for her when he jumps for the village crest. Maybe the sled will give him courage. No, I mean someone who has deeper thoughts, like Eli and me." She plucked a pine sprig from a snow-weighted bough and twirled it in her hands.

"What about Jesspersson and Gudrun? They always seem to disappear at the same time."

"Only their friends have noticed. If her father finds out, Jesspersson could be in for a beating." She tucked the pine sprig into her green scarf.

"Really? Do you think…?"

"I'm not sure what to think but Jess is giving Eli ideas and Eli says Sami is pressing Jesspersson to pounce. If they've gone as far as Eli fears and no one confronts them, they may start an avalanche of kids disappearing into the woods." Laurel whacked a goat.

Keri gulped. "Are you…?"

"No." Her head snapped up. "But we might as well be by the way people talk. We are accused of things Jesspersson and Gudrun might be doing. That's why I would really like you and Stjärna to be seen together to take some of the talk off me and Eli."

Keri sighed. "You of all people should know Stjärna is avoiding me."

"I didn't know. She avoids me as well." She cocked her head. "Did you say something?"

"No, well, yes, I mean 'no'…I didn't say anything, but she thinks, or thought, or something, that you and I were 'thinking seriously' because she saw you take my hands at the well. When I pointed out you and Eli after the race, she just popped like pine sap in a fire."

Laurel wrinkled her eyebrows. "So that's it… Well, that helps me a lot. Now that I know what the problem is maybe I can talk to her."

"That's wonderful but how is it that I can't talk to her? I can talk to you or Annika or any other girl but not her. Why is that?"

"Only last year we all spent a day on the ice laughing and slipping around. You talked to Stjärna all the time."

"Yeah, but I talked to everyone!"

Laurel kicked along the path. "Once we were all children, with hardly any differences in our bodies. We talked and teased and played without much thought. Then we grew up and grew towards roles God planned for us. Those new roles changed many things."

"I suppose that's true."

Laurel snapped off another sprig of fir. "You suddenly consider Stjärna to be special, more than a friend, so talking to her is different. It is like you are walking across ice. If you slip with a friend and both fall down, you laugh and go about your way. But if you slipped and hurt her, you would feel ashamed or guilty. A fall while talking might hurt someone's inner feelings and if you slip there…you may never know what you broke. You might feel rejected."

Keri studied her. "When did you get so wise?"

"While you and Eli were beating each other with wooden swords I sat by the fire and listened to the elders. They know stories of old courtships and romantic disasters. There is more to the history of our village than the battle of Ladoga Lake."

"So, you are saying that since I like her in a new way, I may never be able to talk to her?"

"No. What I am saying is that until you are sure that she likes you in that same different way, you will treat her like the silver communion cup Brother Hamar saves for weddings. *After* you two reach an understanding you will be able to talk about anything."

"Well, how can I ask her how she feels about me if she won't let me talk to her?"

"You need to show her that you have a special interest."

"I tried that. I've taken firewood to her house. I spread wood chips to absorb the mud around her door. I even found three perfect red bullfinch feathers and gave them to her mother to give to her."

Laurel sighed. "You are a man at heart. You think we women want you to fix everything and give us presents. To be sure, we like it, but what we really want is something from your heart. A declaration or a gesture that publicly reveals that we are special. Not just owl eyes like you did when those Gypsy women came through last year. You made those same silly eyes at the messenger's horse." She stopped and gazed down the trail. "We seek something that says to the world, 'this girl is special to me.'"

Keri rolled his eyes. "Do you want me to write it on the well?"

"No, that's childish, like Gudrun's carvings on the hall benches. Besides, you can't write, and Stjärna can't read." She laughed. "So, since you can't talk to her directly, you must find some other way."

"How about you tell her?"

"Nope." She shook her head. "That is almost worse than gossip. And it says you don't care enough to step up on your own."

Laurel studied the snow and then smiled. "You need to ask her father, Dirk, for permission to court her and you need to do it in a public place."

Keri stopped, stunned. His history included things a boy considers brave. He'd slept in the woods, killed a few caribou, faced down a boar, and beaten all but one man in the village at wrestling. But how could he talk to a father about his daughter. "Uh, I...uh..."

"Her father's not a bear, you know." Laurel laughed. "When you get up the courage, she may give you a chance. Until you have that courage, you remain a boy. And alone." She danced down the snow-covered path, chasing her goats. "Remember," she called over her shoulder, "you leave in six weeks and then she will be unattached in the village for at least six months…with all those men who aren't going…and are smart enough not to give red feathers to a girl who wears blue!"

Keri paused at the top of the hill overlooking the gate. He saw Dirk Thorlofson, Stjärna's father, dragging a sled piled with animal fodder over the mushy snow to the gate as the sun disappeared behind the mountains. Through the gate, Dirk stopped by the meetinghouse to speak with Timonen and Olaf. Fum huddled near them in the growing shadows.

Brun stood with Pekka by the gate, waving at Keri and a few others to come in as the shadows became night. Keri trudged to the opening, put down his wood, and jumped to touch the village crest. When Keri crossed the threshold, Brun put his shoulder to the heavy gate. Ice weighed down the base and he had to dig deep to move it. His muscles powered the breath straining through his teeth in a long hiss. "SSSSSuut-TAAhhh!" he cried, breaking the gate free. Pekka, helping push, fell in the snow. They laughed.

As Keri continued up the split log street, he noticed Dirk still talking by the meetinghouse. Keri started to turn down his lane, hesitated, then changed directions to approach the group.

As Keri settled his wood on the platform Olaf said, "Any wolves today, Keri? Or is your new friend, Cnute, wolf enough?"

The men chuckled.

"No, sir," he replied. "I have a question for Dirk, sir."

Dirk looked up.

"Sir…" Keri bit his lip. "I think I have taken an interest in your daughter, Stjärna, and would like your permission to see her."

Timonen and Olaf burst into laughter. Keri turned salmon red and felt a burning in his neck, but he stood stoutly as one about to be punished. Dirk's sympathetic smile and eyes held him in his place.

"So, Sakarias Ellisson, it really is you who will be first to break my daughter's heart and cause my wife to have sleepless nights," said Dirk. "It is hard enough to find peace in the house with three daughters but now another man comes to disturb it."

Keri had not anticipated this. Anger maybe, questions about intentions maybe, simple rejection even, but not this. "Uh, I mean no harm to your house, sir, only to see if your daughter and I are of similar minds."

"Ho, ho!" blurted Olaf. "We know what similar young minds find to do!"

Dirk turned on Olaf. "You'll not insinuate your rude thoughts on my family or honest lads like Keri here in my presence. Be still or be gone."

"You are right, Dirk," said a subdued Olaf, offering his hand, "I was rude. I merely remember the joy of my youth and wish that happiness on others. I expressed myself badly."

Dirk nodded and turned back to Keri.

"You, young Keri, are about to go on a great adventure. Do you wish to tie my precious star to a promise on such short notice while you slip away to palaces, taverns, and futures unknown?"

"No, sir." Keri squirmed. "I wish to impose on no one; only to know my own heart better and perhaps that of Stjärna. The tale is often told of men who wander far and stay too long because they had nothing but a forge or goats to bring them home. If there is a star here for me, I would know it now so it may guide me home."

"Well spoken, Keri Ellisson," said Dirk. "But you may find many temptations crouching at your heart in Hilhelm. Stjärna is the heart of my life, my firstborn. I gladly spend scads to keep her in the blues she so loves. Will you? She is of surpassing value to me. Be wise beyond your years, young smithy. Temptation is a double-edged dagger full of false pleasure and true pain." Dirk looked hard at Keri, then smiled. "You may see my daughter if you can find her, and may God reveal His will to you both."

LIONS

The next dawn the crew practiced loading and unloading the smaller sled in the early twilight. Brun grunted pleasing noises as his designated leaders worked their six-man harness crews. He'd told them to encourage rather than disparage and laugh rather than rage. So far the result was happy banter coupled with willing cooperation.

He ordered the boxes stacked against the palisade. Keri tripped over a box.

"Stargazing, Keri?" boomed Brun. "Or are ye lookin' for a star coming out of Dirkshouse?"

Keri stammered as the men laughed.

Brun slapped his shoulder as he turned to the men. "Eldman says we test the small sled tomorrow. The Lord knows we have proved we can pack and some of us can ski, so today we run and then… Follow me!"

The men trotted around the palisade. When they approached the gate the third time Brun led them into the village. The whole group almost fell as Keri and the younger men leaped to touch the village crest. They crashed down into the others.

Gotthard pushed Pekka into Eli. "Grow up!"

Thirty-year-old Mantas, near the end of the group, jumped and touched the crest. Brun laughed at him.

"You never know," said Mantas, touching the intertwined three horns of Odin he wore around his neck.

Brun shook his head and led them to the great hall. "I want each crew to set up benches inside facing the firepit. Shake the snow off your boots like your mother taught you. And each bunch take in a log for the fire. Pekka, grab that big log for us. You can handle it. Everyone else, let's go."

Pekka flipped the hair from his face and smiled. Brun leaned down and whispered, "I used to tie back my hair to keep it off'a my face."

Inside they found a fire already started and Fum helping Brother Hamar tap a small keg of ale. Everyone grabbed a cup and a seat. Brun squeezed in beside Eli, who was tying a broken bowstring around Pekka's hair. Brun winked at them.

Brother Hamar smiled at the men by the fire. "So it tis that Brun's been tellin' me he's pleased w' yer preparations. Working well together he says, an' peace in yer souls w' one another, saints be praised. Ye know me. Yer soul is one o' my major concerns an' pleased I am to have received confessions o' faith in Jesus Christ as yer soul's Savior from many o' ye." Hamar nodded at Bue and several others.

"An' the rest o' ye, God bless ye, have heard me speak on this, an' remind you 'tis never too late t' repent o' yer sins an' receive that same blessed assurance o' salvation w' Jesus. How is it ye think t' survive God's judgment wid out Christ standin' beside ye?" He shrugged.

"But today it's somethin' else I have for ye." He sipped his ale. "The Apostle Paul prays that yer whole spirit, soul, and body be kept blameless. The saint, he divides ye in ta three parts: body, soul, an' spirit ye know...three. Brun's sayin' yer bodies will be too tired t' find trouble in Hilhelm. An' remind ye, I just did, how t' be makin' yer soul blameless. So, it's the third part we'll be lookin' at: this blameless spirit part."

He poked the fire and watched the sparks drift up. "Ye know t' Bible says Satan prowls around like a hungry lion, he does, seekin' someone t' devour. Now then, have any o' ye ever seen a lion? No? Not me. They don't live up here, Saints be praised, nor back in me blessed Hibernia. But is it that ye believe they exist? Aye, me too. I know. Vicious they are as wolves, an' about half the size o' yer bear. The Bible an' the cursed Romans talk o' them. The pagan emperors used them for sport, don't ye know! T' kill Christians! So though I never seen 'em, I believe there's lions."

He raised his hands. "Never have I seen Satan either, but I know he exists. 'Tis he appears in the Bible more 'n lions. But rare it is in physical form. Ye can't touch him, ye know… sneakin' in as a spirit… ghostlike." He stirred the fire. "Oh, seen his work, I have. In the impulsive act o' a frustrated father beatin' his wee children or his wife…in anger o' a jealous man who turns on a friend account a too much ale… in t' desperation o' a disappointed woman who deserts her own begotten family. I been there after the crisis…eyeballin' the scattered broken pieces, don't ye know? Too many times people cryin' out 'I dinna know what I was thinkin'!' See Satan? They didn't, but he was there…as a spirit…a spirit…that third part Paul's a-prayin' for." Hamar shook his head. Several men dropped their eyes.

"By the saints, ye have a spiritual side an' there is it that Satan be tryin' t' devour, deceive, an' tempt ye. Book says we are not at war wi' the physical, but wi' t' spirits an' powers o' t' air. An' today that is what we will be talkin' about, save yer souls. King Erik will be leadin' ye against t' eastern horsemen, but who will lead ye against yer cruelest eternal enemy?"

Before the sleds left for the Tunturri, Brun ensured the men spent several mornings there with Hamar talking of battles of the spirit and where to find help. After the sleds departed, Brother Hamar talked with the women as well because they, too, were targets of that roaring lion. He regretted not talking to them sooner.

RISING STAR

Twilight turned the snow a light blue as Keri split wood for the sled by the gate. He kept one eye looking for Stjärna. Pekka and Eli came up dragging small sleds loaded with logs.

Pekka nodded to Keri. "Seen Annika?"

"Nope."

Pekka instinctively flipped his head even though he now held his hair with a broad thong. He shrugged and trudged off to his village house while Eli unloaded his wood.

"So, you are finally doing some man's work," said Keri.

Eli laughed and shook his dark hair. "I might as well. Dirksdottir and Laurel are friends again, so I've lost my companion in the woods to another girl."

"That may stop the village wags a bit."

"Perhaps, and that's good for Laurel. She deserves no bad repute even if she does have very warm hands." Eli smiled. "But I miss her prodding the goats while I cut wood. She sings to them and talks to me to help pass the time."

"Are you sure she is not singing to you and talking to the goats?"

"She may well be for all I remember of what she said, but it is more pleasant company than you grunting about heating iron, butchering deer, and battle-axes."

"Huh." Keri leaned on his axe. "That's what happens when you spend too much time among girls; you lose interest in the things that keep us alive."

"Maybe. But I am teaching her to shoot my bow and that helps keep me alive." He sighed. "Having her close as I guide her hands to the bow makes me think there are other things besides eating and fighting that make life interesting."

"Hush. I get enough ideas from Sami's constant bragging about his wife's …uh, details."

"He exaggerates for his pride. Ignore him."

"How? Johanna is a lovely girl and I never thought of her, uh… the way Sami talks. Now I have trouble looking at her and not seeing Sami's, you know…hands."

Eli looked down. "Me too. But Sami's just trying to make up for not going on the trek. That's why he's so talkative. It makes him feel important when he's not."

"Yeah. He's just a quivering hedgehog even with that silly sword he carries. But that whole marriage is strange to me. Two weeks from nowhere to married. What made Johanna suddenly go from sweet and quiet to putting herself out there like that?"

"I don't know." Eli stacked another log. "Laurel says Johanna was lonely and wanted attention. Her mom was pregnant and already had two little kids to chase and her father pretty much forgot her when her younger brothers turned old enough to hunt."

"Really? She doesn't seem that anxious now."

"No. Once she and Sami married, she became quiet and timid again. I guess a man in her bed wasn't the attention she thought it was." Eli emptied his sled.

Keri pushed the yellow hair from his eyes. "That's too bad. Still yet, he's talking about things I never thought of before. I have trouble getting them out of my mind."

"What Sami is telling you is old information." Eli shook his head. "The neighbors say there are a lot more tears than…joy going on in those walls. Forget it."

"Old news or not," said Keri, "the ideas stick like pine sap."

"Well, don't just sit there like a dog waiting for a scrap. Change the subject. Put those half-true images of his on some back shelf with your mom's pickled cabbage. Talk about hunting or the forge."

"Hey, even you say I'm boring when I talk about them."

"No, really!" said Eli. "Isn't that what Brother Hamar said about temptation? Flee. Pray. Talk about better things."

"Are there better things?"

"There must be because my folks at least don't…ah…do that all the time and they still talk and laugh together."

"What do you and Laurel talk about? If I ever find Stjärna before we leave, I have no idea what to talk about besides iron, deer, and learning to swing my battle-axe. I doubt she wants to hear that."

Eli brushed falling snow off his eyebrows and kicked at the sled. "If you don't know what to say, ask her questions. It works for me. Then she does all the talking. Try to focus on her answers, not her charms. Besides, her opinions will help you decide if you really like her."

"I fear her charms are what first got me into this mess. I love to look," said Keri. "And she's the one who first brought up her breasts."

"What?"

"I mean…she said…doesn't matter. Besides, she keeps avoiding me."

"Really? 's wounds."

"Jeez, you sound like that crow Sami when you talk like that."

"Sorry. Slipped out. What is the problem between you and Stjärna?"

Keri pondered. "I'm not sure. At first I thought she was angry at me. Now I think she is angry at herself. Mother thinks it's pride. And I need a chance to ask her, but I can't find her."

Darkness fell as Keri nodded to Brun and Pekka at the gate. Jodis Jurgensdottir called him to her doorway as she wrapped a loaf of warm bread. "Would you be so good as to take this to Timonen's house for me? My bones ache."

Keri's task took him past the well in the half light. It was unusual for anyone to get water so late but there was Stjärna with her back to him raising a bucket. Keri quickened his step to catch her, but he wrinkled his brow. *Laurel said to make her feel special...Eli said ask questions...Jesspersson said do things for them...*

The well axle squeaked when Stjärna cranked it, so Keri arrived unheard and unseen. As he reached around Stjärna to take the full bucket, his voice croaked, "Did you know that when you wear blue it is my favorite color, and so can I carry your water?"

Startled, Stjärna jumped back, causing him to lose his balance and pour the bucket over her apron as they both fell to the ground.

She scrambled to her feet, hissing, and turned on him with her hands on her hips. His eyes quivered and she sucked in a huge breath and pointed a finger at him. But no words came. The rising moon twinkled in her eye and the pointed finger became an open palm offering to help him up.

He took the hand and leapt to his feet.

"My, what a rough hand," she said.

"And clumsy too, I fear," he said.

"My clothes are starting to freeze. Could you possibly help me get home?" She smiled. "*With* the water?"

He whipped off his fur cloak and placed it on her shoulders. She pulled closer as he did and he felt her warm hand touch his face. "Thank you," she said. "That helps a lot." She took the bread and flipped her golden braid from under the fur.

"It's nothing." He lowered the bucket into the well.

"I hear you spoke to my father," she whispered.

"Yes."

"That was nice." She smiled.

"It was terrifying."

"I'm glad you did it."

"I'm glad you're glad because it gives me a tickle in my gut."

"Ew." She crinkled her nose.

"No! It's a nice tickle. I like it."

He refilled her bucket and stood looking at her like a puppy. She took his free hand and led him toward her home as if it were a commonplace thing for them. His heart was racing, for Keri knew it was not common.

"Why are you drawing water so late?"

"Jodis Jurgensdottir said Mother needed it. Where were you going?"

"Jodis Jurgensdottir asked me to take that bread to Timonen's house."

They stopped and glanced down toward the gate. Jodis Jurgensdottir was silhouetted in the dark by the light from her door, her shoulders shaking with laughter. "I will drop a load of wood at her door tomorrow," said Keri.

"That would be nice." Stjärna leaned into him. "Maybe we could walk home the long way past Annika's house?"

Keri nodded. She smelled of clean air and fresh bread and he liked it. He saw the evening star bright over her shoulder. Fum's whistle played gaily by the feast hall.

FEAR

Pure white Fum sat high in a bare linden tree bathed in the first rays of dawn. He raised his hands to the sun. Far below him, where shadows still ruled the deep snow, Brun formed the sled crew in five groups with torches sputtering in the quiet morning. Sigvard and friends watched.

Brun's eyes darted among the men. "All right, Eldman says the small sled is finally ready for testing, so today we finalize harness crews. Sigvard suggested long legs pull better with long legs and short legs with short legs. Six men in each crew, so we have some adjustments." He twisted his lips in thought. Pacing up and down, he pointed for individuals to move among the groups. Tharn and Eldman made some suggestions until the three of them stopped switching and counted one last time.

Keri gazed at the morning star. It reminded him of Stjärna. He sighed and glanced at his new harness mates. Brun set Sturl with his seven-tailed fur hat as their leader. A known hunter he stood almost as tall as Keri. Jesspersson, and somewhat shorter Gantson, from a dairy family, were with Keri. Eli served under Tharn, while Cnute and Pekka fell under Brun. Older Eldman led Laurel's father, Lars, and Eli's laughing cousin, Bue. Gudrun's uncle, Gotthard, headed the fifth harness team.

Hands on hips, Brun nodded. "We're going to put one crew at a time on the small sled. Four men to pull and two to push from the back. We'll put two harness crews at a time on the big sled: one to pull, the other to push, and keep the blessed thing from tipping over. The fourth group will scout for the best routes and clear the path. And the last bunch serves as flank guards while they ski along with the sleds. We will rotate the crews several times each day."

"Will we pull with skis or without?" asked Pekka.

"Without. We need to be able to stop the sled as well as move it, so the traction of feet is better than the slide of skis."

"I'm glad, because all I do so far is slide on the skis. I don't stop so well," said Pekka.

"You're still learning. You'll be fine." Brun gripped his shoulder. "Now, let's try this. Tharn, your crew to pull the traces. Two men push the back corners. Sturl, put your men into the sled and act like heavy wood."

"We need to make these harnesses longer," said Tharn. "We'll trip on each other."

"No, no, no," said old Sigvard, waving his cup of ale. "Use separate traces for each man. One man stumbles, only one man falls."

"Yep."

"Yep."

They all took another sip of ale.

"Eldman?" said Brun "Can you…"

"Yep."

They fixed the harnesses and Brun tried again. "Sturl, your crew inside. Tharn, gently at first. Go slow and then we will build up speed. Ready? Push."

They took up the slack and the sled popped forward out of the rut where it had been built. Inside Keri stumbled and grabbed for the wall but Jesspersson slammed into him and the whole group fell. The weight shift jerked the sled askew as the men pushing tried to compensate.

"Stop! Stop!" Brun grabbed a corner and pulled up to look inside. "You look like a dovecot after a fox raid. Sit down. Again!"

They struggled with the unaccustomed job. Eldman stopped everyone twice to trim the runners, but they eventually made it around the palisade.

"Now let's try it with two crews inside."

And so it went for the morning. Each day for a week the men pulled for longer distances, watching anxiously as the big sled neared completion. They finished each morning exhausted, aching for a sauna. Keri and others complained of vicious leg cramps shattering their sleep.

One foggy pre-dawn the big sled stood ready. Brun put eighteen men inside with two harness crews outside to pull and push. Fum climbed up and sat on the back ledge of the sled, playing his tune over the men. Most of the village came to watch, so the men stood tall in the early darkness.

Keri waited on the left side to pull beside his leader, Sturl. He saw a splash of blue in the crowd and smiled to think Stjärna's eyes were watching him. She called his name and waved.

"Keri!" sang Eli in a falsetto voice from inside the sled. The men laughed.

Keri blushed but waved at Stjärna. The wall between them had melted and he was glad. She talked and talked, which puzzled him, but he delighted in hearing her voice, seeing her eyes, watching her face.

"Keri! Will you be joining us? Or are you still watching your morning star?" bellowed Brun after Keri ignored him twice.

Keri shook and stammered.

Brun laughed. "Do I need to put blinders on you like a Novgorod cart horse?"

"No, I...uh..."

Brun turned away. "Everybody take up the slack. Set your feet. Remember, start with a steady pull, not a jerk. Here we go. Put your weight on the slings and...PULL."

The harnesses stretched and almost hummed as the men strained. Nothing happened. "Push, you men at the back! Lift and push!"

Men grunted at the effort. Feet slipped, Pekka fell, and the sled stood fast.

Sami and his brothers pushed through the crowd and jeered at Pekka. "You're gonna get left behind on the Tunturri and die. God's wounds! I've seen squirrels with more muscles."

"Halt!" cried Brun. He pushed Sami away and walked around the sled with Eldman. They looked at the skids with a torch. "If we can't move it with men inside, how will we move it packed solid with wood?"

Brun shrugged off his cloak and took a place at the corner of the sled next to Cnute. "Again. Ready? Wait, wait. Pekka, switch with Cnute. I want his strong shoulders at the post and your strong legs at the back with me. All right. Take up the slack...and push!"

They pushed and pulled but everything stayed frozen until rising above the grunts came Brun's unmistakable hiss, "SSSSSuut-Taah!" and the sled broke free. The men seated inside scrabbled against the lurch while the men on the outside stumbled to keep upright.

Brun slapped Pekka on the back as the two crews adjusted to keep the sled moving. "She was frozen at this corner, Eldman." Brun pointed at some yellow snow. "Perhaps a dog fondly remembered the tree."

"Or a hungry wolf," sneered Sami. "You're gonna die."

Tharn turned on him. "We might, but the good book says, 'The fear of the Lord is a fountain of life, turning a person from the snares of death.' What do you fear so much that you carry that sword everywhere?"

Sami bristled and gripped his sword. "I'm not afraid of you."

"Then it must be the wolves. It's a good thing the Lord did not choose you for this trip."

"Mark my words," snarled Sami. "There will come a day you will wish I was there beside you with my sword."

"Mark my words, 'He who draws the sword, dies by the sword.'" Tharn turned and followed the sled.

FUNNY CREATURES

Stjärna spotted Soren pulling a sled and caught him at the gate. He rolled his eyes at her voice and looked away.

"Do you know where Keri is in the woods?" she asked so passersby could hear.

"I do."

"Is it very far?"

"It is not."

"Would you take me to him?"

Soren hadn't looked at her yet. He scratched a flea on his leg and glanced at the low sun. He peered at her sideways. "Don't you have chores?"

"Oh, I won't stay long. I have to help with supper, but I have some time while the sun is still above the hills. I know Keri wants to see me."

Soren sighed. "Come on."

Stjärna chattered pleasantly at him about people, weather, Cnute, and charcoal.

They topped a rise and Soren pointed at a birch shivering in a grove below. "That's Keri."

When they arrived, the tree had fallen, and Keri stood over it with his hand axe taking off branches. When he saw them, Keri walked right by Soren, handing him the axe, and stood in front of Stjärna. "You are out late today. I thought you wouldn't be able to come before dark."

"I bribed Kirsten to start my chores."

"I'm glad you are here."

"I'm glad I'm here, but I wish we were walking in the village."

She sighed.

He sighed.

Their eyes were locked as were their hands.

"Your hands are warm," he said.

"Your hands are cold…and rough."

"The thick skin is a warm glove."

"If you don't help me with this wood," said Soren, "we're all going to be warmed by our fathers' hands for coming home after the gates close."

Stjärna glanced at Soren, startled as if a troll had appeared. Keri let loose one hand to hush his brother, but Stjärna released the other and stepped back. "I must not slow your work. Soren is right, and I can stay only a few moments."

Keri gritted his teeth at Soren but pulled his eyes away from Stjärna long enough to grab the big axe and attack the tree. Soon Soren's sled was full, and Keri helped him push it to the top of the rise. Soren disappeared toward Cnute's and Keri pounded down the hill to where Stjärna waited. Their hands touched.

"Can you walk me home?" She smiled up at him.

"I'd rather stay with you here a while."

"Why?"

"Because I like to look at you and no one harasses me when I do it here in the woods."

She looked down. "Is it too much trouble to look at me in the village?"

"I do it all the time."

"But why do you chafe so when Eli or Jesspersson teases you?" She raised her brows.

Keri paused, gazing into her eyes. "I have no idea. You know, it wasn't so long ago they cheered me for tying your pigtails to Annika's. We used to think of you girls as funny creatures like mice and cats."

"Am I a very funny creature to you?"

"No, you are a very perfect creature to me."

"I like that you say that."

"You should love Eli then," said Keri. "He has a very clever way with words."

"But he doesn't have your strength or blue eyes."

Keri's hand reached up to touch her cheek. "You are the one with blue eyes. I don't think anyone in the village has such eyes as yours. They call to me like the morning and evening stars."

"Well, they like to look at you." Her voice barely moved the air.

Keri quivered from his chest to his stomach, his hand paralyzed on her cheek. His mind tried to form words but instead formed commands that his hand, his lips, his body struggled to perform. All the years of childhood games and teasing slipped into a deep hole in his brain, replaced with new ideas he had only heard but never dared.

She leaned into his chest a little and slipped her arm inside his. They hesitated a moment and she closed her eyes.

For a heartbeat Keri felt like a spectator watching two other people. He leaned down and lightly kissed her lips. They both shuddered with a strange thrill. He closed his eyes and kissed her again.

They pulled a little closer together and she lifted her head for a third kiss. This one proved more deliberate. When it was over, like the bellows at Ellis' forge, they slowly relaxed and began to breathe again.

Stjärna opened her eyes. She smiled. "You are looking at me like the last piece of Yule cake."

"You have erased all memories of cake from my mind. One can get full of cake, sick even. I don't think I could ever get full of doing that."

They reached for each other again, but the air crackled with a voice calling, "Stjärna!"

They jumped back and looked up the hill. Soren was there. He cupped his hands and called, "Stjärna, your uncle is out looking for you!"

She glanced quickly at the hills and saw the sun was nearly gone. "Raging weasels! I am in trouble now." She laughed. "But Gudrun will be delighted."

"Huh?"

"Nothing." She looked at Keri and took his hand gently. Her voice softened. "Thank you." Then she rushed up the beaten snow path toward home. The evening star twinkled above.

Keri watched her go, his hands still out as if holding her. "Thank you?"

STUPID STUFF

Jodis Jurgensdottir moved into line behind Stjärna and Laurel to wait her turn at the well.

"He never says *any*thing," said Stjärna to Laurel.

"Don't his lips say anything?" Laurel's eyes crinkled.

"No! Kissing him makes him even quieter. He just gets dreamy eyed and sits there."

"What do you want him to say?" Laurel hung her bucket from the rope.

Stjärna opened her mouth but nothing came out. Laurel laughed.

"He is obviously talking to you, Stjärna. What is he saying that is not what you want to hear?"

"Oh, he talks about the sled and his harness team, and how much more wood he can carry, how his calf muscles test his trousers, and his battle-axe...you know: stupid things. What does Eli talk about?"

"Pretty much the same stuff only you can change the axe to a bow and replace Keri's calf muscles with Eli's chest splitting his tunic."

They both sighed.

"If you young ladies aren't actually going to draw water out of the well," snipped old Jodis, "may the rest of us get a bucket full?"

"I'm sorry, ma'am." Laurel hauled up her bucket and hooked on Stjärna's. "We lost track of what we were doing."

"Indeed, boys will do that to you. Maybe if you figure out what it is they want *you* to say, then they will say what you want *them* to say."

"You mean they are not happy either?" Stjärna cranked up her water.

"Oh, they are probably very happy to have two lovely girls like you spending so much time with them." Jodis handed the girls her bucket. "But until you say what they need to hear, they will probably keep talking about 'stupid stuff' and never figure out what you want to hear."

Stjärna knit her brows. "Keri has never asked me to say anything in particular. Do you know what he wants?"

Laurel cranked up Jodis' bucket. Jodis led them away from the well and stopped. "Most men need to know they are appreciated but they don't know how to ask. Instead they do silly things or talk about 'stupid stuff' hoping for the reaction they want."

"Like what?"

"Well, you know how the boys all jump up and touch the crest at the gate?" The girls nodded. "They want you to notice how agile they are or how high they can jump."

Laurel sneered. "So, when they jump, I should say something like 'Oh, my, Eli, look how high you can jump'?"

"Yes." Jodis put down her bucket. "But you have to make it sound sincere. Make it sound like jumping counts for something to you."

"That sounds so pretend."

The old woman touched Laurel's arm. "It certainly can, but it is ale to a thirsty man. Some girls learn to do it early and often and how to control a boy. But eventually the boy revolts." Jodis smiled. "But it sounds like Eli and Keri need to hear how you noticed their muscles are growing and how much you admire their ability to handle weapons.

Until they know you see how important that is to them, they may not have the confidence to talk to you about other things."

Laurel put her hands on her hips. "You mean they are intentionally not talking about anything besides their own muscles and skills?"

Jodis sighed. "No, they have no idea they are avoiding you. They just know they are comfortable talking about things they know better than you do. Then they can't be embarrassed by being wrong."

"Is being right so important?"

"Maybe," said Jodis. "Somehow it is part of how men and boys are made. If they are to be head of their own household, then they must be right about a lot of things. As husbands, if they don't cut enough wood, or keep the goats alive, or thatch the roof properly, they could cause their family a lot of discomfort, even death."

"But my folks always talk together about things," said Stjärna.

"Yes, and that is why yours is a happy house. But if they can't agree, who makes the final decision and then has to live with the results?"

"Father."

"Yes, Father." Laurel nodded.

"So, what those boys are looking for you to say is that you trust their ability. Once they feel you trust them or respect what they think is important, then they will venture into opinions about what you think is important; what you want to talk about."

"Oh!" said the girls together. Then they giggled and started to run down the hill.

"Wait," said Jodis, cackling in their trail. "Have you thought about what you want them to say?"

But they were laughing and chattering and didn't hear her. "That will be a later lesson." Jodis smiled and turned toward her house. She nodded to Annika, who stood with her bucket watching them. Annika smiled back and then looked over at Pekka's house.

Keri's father heated a barrel hoop at the forge. A stack of them waited for the cooper. Keri sat distracted with his tree-cutting axe in one hand and an idle whetstone in the other. Ellis smiled. "Sure, you're gonna miss your girl at the gate if you don't get going pretty soon, son."

Keri shook his head as if to wake up. "My girl? Is that how you see her?"

"Well, that's a bit premature, I suppose." Ellis pushed some wood in the fire. "But she shows you off all over the village and seems taken with you."

"But how do I know she is really taken with me? I mean, I have done nothing to impress her and I really have no achievements. Why me?"

"Well, you're on to something there. You're a fair enough looking lad, but that doesn't last over time. Pleasant features are more like bait than glue."

Ellis studied Keri. "You're kind, and slow to anger. That counts for something, but it doesn't win a heart for life. There's lots of despicable men who can fake that to get what they want."

"Like Sami?"

"Or Firth…" Ellis nodded. "And you're right. You don't have any brave deeds, or a history of being faithful. But ferocity and fidelity alone will not hold a woman. If they did, then your mother and the rest of the village women would have flooded Sigvard's house when he returned with the king's own dagger. No, women do not swoon because a brave or faithful man kills a sea dragon or a bear. Many a man has wasted his youth, strength, and hoard thinking deeds can win love. They end up bitter about women. No, what a woman wants is different, and sometimes she doesn't even know what it is."

Keri looked up. "Laurel says gifts are nice, but girls really want to know they are special. Don't gifts show her that she is special?"

"Sure they do. And if your woman puts great weight on gifts, then bring her things: flowers, trinkets, interesting stones. It shows her you think of her. But look further to see what she wants from life. It may not be so different from what you want. For instance, why were you anxious to be selected for the sled?"

"This is a great adventure where I could make my fortune."

"And do you think you are the only one who likes adventure and wealth?"

"No, all the boys wanted to go."

"What about the girls?"

"Why do they care? They don't like the open country the way men do."

"No? Most, maybe, but they want the thrill of adventure just the same. They all attended the race between Brun and Eli, and don't they all shriek when someone wears their token in a wrestling match?"

"Well, yes, but that's not the same as being the wrestler. What adventure is that?"

"It's having a stake in the match." Ellis pulled the bellows. Sparks flew. "They make a claim to a contestant, win or lose, and that gives them a reason to care. They have chosen a good horse and worked with it until they are a part of it, so to speak. Then they have bragging rights just as you have by going on the sled."

"Sounds like a horse."

Ellis smiled. "No, women don't seek a horse." He brushed a spark off his leather apron. "But some women like to go on their husband's adventures. Brun's wife often goes to the woods with him to help set traps and dress pelts. Jodis loved to help drive boars through the forest toward the men's spears. I've heard that some women follow their men to war and our grandsires fought alongside shield maidens."

Keri twisted his mouth, "I don't think I could fight a woman."

Ellis laughed. "Oh, you will." He glanced toward the kitchen. "But for most women, the great adventure includes solving problems of life with her husband. Problems like rearing children, tending fields, managing the Lord's bounty, surviving long winters. That is an unrecognized adventure. Husbands and wives face life together like it is a dragon, sharing victories and defeats. Even if women don't push the plow, they share the responsibility with one eye on the weather and another on the storage jars. They fight the battle against winter, against hunger for each season."

Keri's father tentatively tapped a hot iron hoop on his anvil. "For some men, home, crops, family, work are all the adventure God gives them. Few women get to marry a war hero or sea trader. But they want to be a part of their man's fight for life, to share in his plans, success, and even failure." Ellis stared into his fire, one hand absently reaching for his cup.

Keri realized his father's adventures seldom went beyond his forge or a hunt. He felt a quiet sadness. "Raising a family is kind of a victory, isn't it?"

Ellis straightened up and took a long draw, finishing his ale. He swirled the empty cup and tossed the last few drops hissing into the fire. "It is. Yes..." He cleared his throat. "And through it all the wife needs to know that she is special to her man, whether it be by his gifts to her or wearing her token or hearing her opinions. Special enough to fight for her against nature's harm or village scorn. She wants him to hear her thoughts, understand her views, consider her opinion before deciding. She wants to know he will come find her when she is frightened or hurting, or when *he* is frightened or hurting. And she wants to know he will stand by her, even if she is wrong."

"Wrong?" said Keri. He hadn't considered that Stjärna might be wrong about anything.

Ellis looked for another sip in the empty cup, sighed, and put it down. He studied Keri. "Some men, and women, yell when things aren't perfect in their house. Not doing it their way is wrong to them and they feel they have to say so. Your mother, and every other woman, occasionally burns the bread or rips a hem. Is she wrong or did she just make a mistake?"

Keri shrugged. "I guess it is just a mistake."

"How you react to things you don't like, such as burnt bread, will set the tone for your house. If you yell about it, frown about it, before you listen to her side, you may as well live among the bears. In the long run, burnt crusts and tattered clothes are small issues compared to life and family."

"Father, I take your point. But how do I show Stjärna I won't yell if she burns bread someday?"

"Ah! That's why you take your time to know a girl. You need to see her burn some bread and she needs to see you react so that you really know each other. And she needs to see you stumble so she can see what life with you could be like. At your age getting to know girls is really like seeing if squirrel, rabbit, or fox makes a better glove. Try several before you choose. Don't take things too seriously. Don't trust first emotions or make big promises. Look how mad Stjärna was after the race. She was holding herself and you to promises only she had made. It is all practice, like on the sled. It wouldn't hurt you to look at several girls."

"Other girls?" Keri tilted his head.

"Yes, learn about their differences. See what's out there, so you choose wisely. Marriage is a horse a wise man only buys once."

After the dawn sled drills Eli found Keri beside the palisade staring at a snow squall in the direction of the Tunturri. Fum stood ignored in the nearby woods.

"Worried about wolves?" asked Eli.

Keri shivered, glanced at Eli and then away again. "No."

"Worried about the yellow horsemen?"

"No."

"Well, you look worried about something. Did you get bad news? Has your goat died?"

"Don't pick at me. You sound like Stjärna."

"Sorry. Laurel does that sometimes too. So does Mother when she thinks I'm hiding something."

Keri looked at him. "I guess I am worried about Stjärna."

"Oh."

"Yeah." Keri made a snowball and threw it at a tree.

"Nice throw."

"Unh."

"Worried that she won't wait for you to come back from Hilhelm?"

"No, it's not that. No, it's not Stjärna, it's…" He paused and looked across the snow.

Eli started a snowball. "What did she say?"

"Nothing!" Keri stamped the snow. "It's that rabbit-brained Sami. I ran into him coming down the mountain and he started talking about the joys of married life again."

"What, hot food and a warm bed?"

"Yeah, but mostly the warm bed…him and Johanna. I didn't understand half of what he said but my, uh, body seemed to understand and suddenly I saw Stjärna in a whole new light." Keri stood stock-still as his nose dripped in the cold.

"By 's wounds, I know that feeling," said Eli. He hunched against the breeze. A snowball landed at his feet. Fum was looking at him. Eli waved. "Sorry." Fum looked away.

"Yeah, well, I know what it means, and I know it's in my future to find out more but… I feel like the future should be sooner than later." Keri looked directly at his friend.

"I can help you with a lot of stuff, Keri, but not that. My father said it is perhaps the hardest part of a man's life waiting for the marriage to be performed."

"Well," said Keri, staring at his feet, "I am able to put it out of my head while we haul the sled, and it fades if I'm tired, so maybe hard work is a good salve for the ache."

"Yeah. Hard work," said Eli. "And I think I've been feeling this way longer than you have."

They both stared at the slope.

"Crow over there."

"Yeah."

"Stjärna likes to kiss, you know," said Keri.

"So does Laurel…and a little bit more."

"I know my folks giggle a lot and touch. Even my mother. Girls must have some desires besides talking."

Keri glanced at Eli and then away. A gust whipped snow in their eyes.

Eli's words spilled out. "Well, all the teasing and gossip Laurel and I tolerated over the past month is suddenly more than just irksome. Now I struggle with not trying to make it a reality. And I'm not sure I don't want to make it a reality. And…and…" He lowered his voice to a husky whisper. "Sometimes I think Laurel struggles too." He stalled, then burst out, "And what about the idea that we could be dead in six weeks. What are we missing? Will we ever get a chance to know? What about that?"

They both stared hard at the distant slopes falling away to a dim snowy mist. Fum, quiet, forgotten, closed his eyes and bowed his head.

"I asked Brother Hamar about it," said Eli. "He said children are a gift from God and that creating them is pretty sacred stuff."

"Children!? I wasn't even thinking about children," exclaimed Keri. "I just want to hold Stjärna in more ways than I had ever considered."

"Yeah, well, you know one usually leads to the other. In any case, Hamar says that we need to ask God's special blessing before we get that far. That's marriage, and getting the blessing first not only pleases God but it purifies and sanctifies the whole, uh…you know."

"All right, but what do we do with these feelings until we get past the sled, the war…until the marriage?"

"Hamar says, 'Master your sin.'"

113

"Is it sin to dream and then remember the dream?"

"Just master it!"

"Swell, how do I do that?" Keri stomped at the snow.

"Ask God, I guess."

"Great, but I think I'll chop more wood while I ask."

"Yeah. Chop wood."

They left in opposite directions.

Fum smiled.

LURES

J odis Jurgensdottir held court by her door near the village gate. Gudrun swore she saw a she-wolf. That prompted the ladies to talking of wolves and the danger to the girls, which led to the favorite subject of village romances. Jodis took center stage with accounts of the comings and goings of various young ladies through the gate with or without their goats. The affairs of certain passersby always interested her neighbors.

The talking prompted Keri's mother, Marta, to find Stjärna's mother privately. "Lisbeth," she said, "we have blessed children, you and I."

"Yeah, though one of my daughters seems to have gone light in the head." She rolled her eyes.

"If my son could see that light, perhaps they would both come back to earth."

"Is this good, with him gone so soon?"

"That is true." Marta folded her plump arms. "Still, we should be careful nothing unwanted happens should they suddenly realize their attraction is mutual and their time is short."

"From the giggling I hear between Stjärna and Laurel, I think that realization has been partly realized. Shall I lock up my daughter or shall you lock up your son?" Lisbeth put her hands on her hips.

"Oh, no! Unripe berries can intrude on all your thoughts if you've been told you can't have them."

"True, strange how that works. But what are we to do?"

"Pray?"

"I have prayed for my children since before their birth. I was hoping for something more practical."

"Perhaps if we tell them some uh…practical truths about the berries they seek?" Marta cocked her head.

"Hmmm…" Lisbeth smiled. "Every girl prepares to be brave during child delivery but every man squirms at the very idea. Make Keri squirm?"

Marta nodded.

"And I," said Lisbeth, "will tell Stjärna the truth that once a man has had any woman, his body thinks he needs to try every woman."

"Aye." Marta grinned.

"May God be with us and our children," said Lisbeth.

"He is whether we ask it or not."

A day later Keri's father kept him from the woods to finish some helmets. Keri's mother appeared in the dusty workspace with two cups of ale.

The two smiths nodded in thanks and drank deep.

Ellis smacked his lips. "You are the best brew master in the village."

"And you are always wise not to consume too much," said Marta. "I am proud to say our son follows your example."

"Yes, such a son." Ellis smiled at Keri. "And you bless us with your conduct. We know you will be brave should you have to fight, and we trust you will remember our counsel and God's will in all your other activities."

Keri smiled. "Father, your trust in me is like silver in my palm. I pray God will not let me stray into any temptation that will bring shame to you."

"Amen." Marta wagged a finger. "And that city, Hilhelm, will bring you temptations. You will be free of us and have your first purse full of coin. Taverns, strong sweet mead, and foolish ideas will tempt you. Be gentle as a dove, but wise as a serpent. Stay out of the dark and in the light. And remember, many of those who would befriend you at Hilhelm are really after your purse."

Ellis considered his cup. "The work may be boring, and the king's food dull, but poverty is a weight like no other. Chasing pleasure for pleasure's sake is the path to poverty."

"There are wonders to see there, I'm told," said Keri. "I don't suppose the tall buildings will want my silver just to look."

Ellis rocked back and forth. "Well, wonders can be like a lure to a fish: the eyes are fooled and you get pulled in before you know it. Women who flash their wonders can conceal an especially nasty hook."

Keri looked at his parents. "I've never known a woman and wouldn't know what to do with one if she jumped in my arms."

"Well," Marta looked him hard in the eye, "you may soon find one in your arms and I hope you will know what to do."

Keri blanched.

"I think your mother means that she hopes you will know that your body is a gift of God and you must honor it. We learned on our wedding night that the body will tell you exactly what to do when the time comes. You won't need instruction."

"Aye." His mother's face softened. "It is all natural. Who teaches the elk or the rabbit?"

Keri's face turned red over pink.

"Still a woman's labor is not a thing to be caused hastily." Ellis took Marta's hand.

"Amen, again. It was very trying, delivering you." She smiled at

117

Keri but leaned towards Ellis. "Do you remember the day I gave birth to this child?"

"Day? It was at least two days: long and loud."

"Margaret said he was the biggest child she had ever pulled from a woman."

"Most of Rentvatten heard you howl like Cnute on a full moon."

"I was loud because I had such a son to be proud of, but getting him here?…exhausting!" She slumped a little.

"And the cleanup! Who knew you two could leave so much blood behind?"

Keri reeled from a sudden heat. He expected tears and spiritual warnings over his departure, but not this. He grabbed his vest and stumbled out the door mumbling about getting more wood.

Marta dropped her voice. "Did we say too much?"

"No, I think we just opened a piece of his mind that he hadn't explored yet."

"Heavens, do you think we've made him curious? Will he do something rash?"

"I don't think so." Ellis swished his cup. "If he can barely talk to us, I doubt he will be able to talk to anyone else for a while. He needs time to think."

Marta twisted her lips. "Keri will pick up a lot of talk on the sled."

"Perhaps, but Brun is a good one-woman man, and a man of faith. I think he will watch out for the younger men. Tharn too, and I am glad Keri is on Sturl's team, not that boor Gotthard's."

"Lord, grant me more faith." Marta clasped her hands heavenward. "It is going to be hard to release my son to Your hands, Lord, knowing that I won't be there to help You."

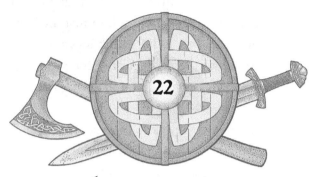

In the Fire

Keri shivered carrying a load of pine on his back in the early twilight. He glanced at the evening star and smiled. The afternoon had been dazzling. Snow sparkled as if dancing to Fum's distant whistle but now the frozen snow crunched under his feet. Keri laughed when Stjärna appeared singing below in the vale.

He waved and gestured where he was going. She waved back and cut around some trees to intercept him near the frozen stream. He was halfway there when he heard Stjärna scream. Dropping the wood, he snatched his axe and ran around the trees.

Stjärna thrashed in a pool of silver water with most of her body trapped under a shelf of ice. She apparently didn't see a snow-covered artesian well and broke through the ice. Completely drenched, the immobilizing cold and weight of her wet, heavy clothes pinned her to the stream bank. Grunting inarticulately, she sounded more angry than afraid.

Keri stepped into the exposed water, grabbed her arm, and pulled her with such force that the ice ripped her apron. Stjärna's face flushed red, but her lips pulled back in frozen agony as she clung dripping to him.

He swept up her legs and lifted her across his chest. She instinctively wrapped her arms around his neck as he began trotting toward Cnute's charcoal cabin just over the near hill. At first she fussed, but the cold penetrated from her icy hair to her numb toes and she just gasped pitifully. They jarred across the snow, Keri talking between breaths. "Be brave, you'll be warm in a few minutes. Hang on. Just be brave and hang on."

Cnute's cabin came into view but Keri saw no smoke from the stone chimney. He hollered as he ran but no one answered. Stjärna's wet clothes soaked through his open coat and it crackled as it began to freeze his tunic. Dripping water stung his legs. More burned down his neck from her limp arms. Shivering, he kicked open the door.

He placed Stjärna on the fur-covered bed built into the wall. "Get under the covers and get undressed."

She didn't respond.

He looked in her dim eyes and shouted, "Stjärna! Get out of the wet clothes while I make a fire!"

She dropped over and crumpled on the floor.

Keri tore off her frozen mittens and chafed her blue hands. No response. He fumbled with the broach that held her slushy cloak and ripped the fabric as he threw it wet and heavy into the corner. Her blue tunic was also soaked and freezing. When he ripped that away he found even her under-tunic sparkling with ice.

Keri remembered the bear hunt when Ole fell into a creek. The men stripped Ole naked and wrapped him in furs. Keri reached for Stjärna's remaining garments and stopped. He gulped. Time mattered. He squinted his eyes and ripped away the last crackling wet fabric, feeling her strange cold softness beneath his clammy, wet hands.

Her blue skin looked frail and he feared to touch her lest she rip like the wet clothes. Overcoming the last vestiges of his boyhood taboos, he lifted her naked body and gently tucked her into the furs. His eyes darted everywhere while his mind tried to see nothing.

120

Her shallow breathing gave off soft puffs of fog. Frozen strands of hair stuck out like a blonde Medusa. He shivered of his own accord but turned to the wood to make a fire. "Oh, Lord, oh, Lord…"

He snatched Cnute's flint, steel, and tinder box from the hearth. His first attempt to put a spark into the tinder caught, but drips from his sleeves fell and extinguished it. His frozen hands fumbled to get another piece of dry tinder. His toes tingled and his neck hurt from the cold. He jerked at his coat to find it frozen to his vest. He flumped it on the earth floor of the cabin and blew at a new spark in the tinder. He blew it out. His tunic felt like a leaden shroud; soaked and freezing. He struck the flint twice more and flipped a spark into the tinder. It flared. He nursed a small flame, which he put in some dry shavings. They caught. His hands shook and his clothes were stiff with ice. He tore off his wet tunic and boots. By the time the fire snapped with steady self-assurance, he wore only one sock in front of the growing warmth.

Slowly both light and heat began to spread. He felt relief as he turned around in front of the flames, warming both sides. Self-conscious, he grabbed a boot to hold in front of himself. The cabin leaked heat from years of neglect and Cnute's indifference to pain. He stepped toward Stjärna but the heat dissipated only a few feet from the flames. It would never penetrate Cnute's bed and reach Stjärna's frozen body. Did she have enough body heat to warm herself inside the furs?

"Stjärna?"

Stjärna groaned, dribbling saliva, which froze on her lip, but the furs lay stock-still. Her panting almost died out.

"Can you feel the heat? Are you getting warmer?"

He stepped across the painfully cold earth floor and put his hand inside the furs to her shoulder. Though his own hands were still numb, he felt warm compared to her. She flinched and he jerked his hand out.

How could he get heat into the furs with Stjärna? The ground lay stone-cold frozen in front of the fire. One whole side of Cnute's rope bed was part of the wall and wouldn't budge. Keri needed to bring heat to her.

He stood his full height and stared at Stjärna's wrapped form lying there before him. The final step the bear hunters used on frozen Ole was when his brother stripped down and rolled into the furs, lending him his own body heat. Ole lived today to tell the story.

Keri shivered in the cold and stared. Stjärna began to convulse under the furs. The image of her delicate body shook him. His own body felt warmer now but he shivered in the drafts as the fire steamed moisture off his skin. His clothes sat in a frozen, dripping pile. He looked at the furs. He looked at Stjärna's blue lips and shallow breath. He tried to focus on what needed to be done and not on what he was about to do.

The fire flared a little and lent heat to his back. He threw in the remaining few logs, licked his lips, and lifted the furs. He dropped the boot. "Lord, please be with me. Please be with us." He lowered himself into the bed, under the furs, and close to Stjärna.

His body instinctively tried to pull away from her cold skin but he pressed against her back and wrapped an arm over her shoulders to pull her into his chest. He shivered again and ran his legs up around hers. She was totally limp and he held tight to keep her from slipping away.

"Oh, Lord, oh, Lord…"

His mind and body jangled with sensations and visions. Stjärna's cold skin against his made him shrivel into himself yet his mind boiled. He pulled the furs over their heads and held on as she began to mold into his body. Slowly, as if hours passed, he could feel their two skins finding a common temperature. The ice in her hair dripped. She murmured deliriously with her eyes shut tight. Suddenly she rolled over and burrowed the still cold front of her body into his, holding him as tightly as he held her.

He spoke her name but she lay as in a trance or a deep dream.

After what seemed like hours, warmth spread between them and filled the furs. She relaxed and fell into a hard, deep sleep. He started to push away but she held him tight, grabbing the skin on his back to the point of pain.

Night fell and the fire dwindled to embers. He heard crunches on the snow and a snuffling sound around the door, a whine, then panting. He tried to sit up on one elbow to see, but Stjärna whimpered and pulled him back down. He called out but no one answered.

"Oh, Lord…"

More time passed and he felt the warmth of their bodies reflected in the furs. He became obsessed by the new softness of her arms, the pressure of her body, and an acute anxiety in his gut. The panting and shuffling outside the door came back and then faded away. Silence. Silence. Only the flutter of her breath. Then the empty sound of a distant wolf howling at the midnight sky. They were truly alone under warm furs in the middle of the night.

He quivered. She nuzzled. *So soft, so close, so exciting…so close.* He struggled to hold still, to forget his hands. He wanted to touch, to kiss…her neck, her shoulders. He wanted…

"I love you," he whispered into her tangled, matted hair.

And the wolf howled again across an endless night answered by another and another. A night owl screeched. Death stalked the night.

He squeezed his eyes tight, trying to squeeze his mind shut. *Lord, do not be far from me.*

And then it was quiet. In the dying fire a knot flared and sparked. Exhaustion hit Keri like a pole axe. He fell dead asleep. Delicious, dreamless sleep.

Unheard in the distance voices called, followed by hasty crunches in the snow. The door flew open. Cnute, Olaf, and Stjärna's father, Dirk, stumbled in together where their torches lit the scene: two naked young people sound asleep under the furs across from glowing coals.

MOSTLY CONFUSION

"We both apparently fell asleep," Stjärna said, grinning, "and then Cnute, Olaf, and Father burst in the door."

Gudrun giggled. She and Laurel were combing out Stjärna's hair by the Dirkshouse hearth. "What did they say?"

"Cnute said, 'Thank God,' but Olaf just laughed. Father started yelling." Stjärna imitated her father's voice. "'Villain! Who do you think you are?' He jerked Keri from the bed, started kicking him. Keri curled up in a ball, but he wouldn't fight." She sighed. "I ruined my best apron."

Laurel and Gudrun both stopped combing and sat slack-mouthed. Stjärna turned back to the fire and put her hands to the warmth. Though she still shivered periodically, she smiled. "Father kept kicking Keri until Cnute pulled him back. Even when Keri and I explained what happened and showed him our icy clothes, he was still angry. He glowered at me and yelled at Keri."

"How did you get home?" asked Laurel.

Stjärna shrugged. "Cnute gave me some of Liisa's things to wear. He threw a ratty tunic to Keri. I dressed and found my boots had mostly dried out, so I wrapped up in Father's cloak and we started home. At first Father wouldn't speak. He wouldn't even turn off to see where I fell through the ice. He just kept mumbling about Brother Hamar and the village. Then he stopped, looked at me, and...I think he was crying. Suddenly he just grabbed me and held me so tight. Then he took my hand and led me home." She sagged on her stool and smiled.

"Was Keri with you?"

"Keri stayed behind with Cnute and Fum. I guess they will be back soon."

Laurel paused her braiding. "Fum? Where did he come from?"

"I don't know but he was outside the door."

"Well, Olaf is now the most popular man in the village." Laurel shook her head. "He's been down at the great hall telling people the story all morning."

"How did it feel?" asked Gudrun.

"It was painfully cold like needles of ice." Stjärna leaned into the fire. "The water froze my clothes so quickly I felt like I was being paralyzed. Then when the air froze my hair..."

"No! Not that." Gudrun looked into Stjärna's eyes. "What did it feel like to be naked with Keri?"

Laurel stamped her foot. "By the beard of Saint Herman! The girl almost died."

"But she didn't." Gudrun stuck out her chin. "And she has had an opportunity you, uh, we have not yet had. Jesspersson was so anxious but I am afraid and...and...we may not have much time before the sled leaves. And there's no one else to talk to about it! How did it feel?"

Stjärna just sighed.

Laurel glared at Gudrun. "Drink some more broth, Stjärna. Brother Hamar will sort this out."

Stjärna's eyes went wide, smiling. "Oh, do you think there will be a fight for my honor?"

"A fight? Tradition says, 'yes'," said Gudrun, clapping.

"No! Hamar won't allow it," said Laurel.

Stjärna thought a moment. "Still, the village will talk and you two must know to tell the truth. Nothing happened. I was delirious or unconscious or asleep for almost all of it." She hesitated. "But I think I would know if something happened."

Gudrun laughed. "Oh, I would hope so!"

"Hush!" Laurel slapped her shoulder.

Stjärna smiled at the flames. "As I was sort of waking up, you know, before the door crashed in, I know I felt safe and…and…uh, comfortable."

Gudrun giggled but Laurel just glared at her.

Brother Hamar sat fidgeting by Olaf, who had been given too much ale by too many people. Olaf smiled blankly from a bench near the great hall's fire.

"Olaf, me friend, an' sure we must finish hearin' yer tellin' o' what really happened, don't ye see, before this gets out o' hand. You were tellin' us how Stjärna told everyone she was a goin' t' find Keri."

Olaf smiled and snorted a laugh.

Hamar sighed and poured him a little ale. He set the pitcher aside. "Now what was it ye were seein' when ye got to Cnute's cabin?"

Olaf leaned on the table and considered his words. "Panic…confusion…joy…terror…but mostly confusion." He smiled and leaned back.

Keri's father and Tharn hovered over Olaf. Each started to speak. Hamar's hand went up. "Now, who was it ye saw that was panicked?"

"Dirk! Her father panicked. Jurgensdottir said Stjärna went out the gate an hour before sunset. It was almost dawn and we'd been all over. We were almost out of torches. Dirk feared his daughter was killed by a wolf. What Dirk saw was worse! 'Villain! Who do you think y' are?' he kept shouting. Panic it was!" Olaf smiled and put up his finger.

"Also, young Stjärna panicked when she realized she was naked with Keri under her father's eyes!" He laughed and his eyes wandered away, following his hands, which were flitting like birds. Suddenly he focused.

"And then there was joy. When Dirk realized his daughter was alive, not dead." Olaf drooped a little and then raised up. "And Keri rejoiced to see her alive, but he quickly turned to confusion when he realized he was naked! Ho, ho!"

Olaf nearly fell off his seat. He caught himself and stiffened. He leaned forward and squinted. "And then Dirk filled with terror that the jewel of his life was smudged by the grimy hands of the blacksmith's son! And that filled Keri with terror as Dirk began kicking and cursing him. And then Cnute jumped in to stop Dirk, and Stjärna jumped up to protect Keri, and I jumped up to cover Stjärna, which was safer and far more pleasant work." He winked at Tharn. Tharn spilled his ale.

Olaf gestured to illustrate his words. "Cnute guarded Keri. Stjärna, all wrapped in a fur, grabbed her father and blurted out about falling through the ice and being carried to Cnute's cabin. But that's all she knew. Keri filled in the rest about frozen clothes, building a fire, and Ole on the bear hunt. But Dirk kept looking at their nakedness and stamping his feet." Olaf leaned back and chuckled. "God forgive me, but she is a beautiful girl to wrap a fur around!"

Ellis rolled his eyes as Hamar leaned in close to Olaf. "By the saints, is there any reason ye have to be thinkin' that young Keri be lying?"

"What are you asking?" said Tharn. "How can one tell if a woman has had a man?"

Olaf folded his arms and spoke as clearly as he could. "They were both truly embarrassed. She showed nothing but gratitude for Keri and pleaded for her father's mercy. She even invoked God and Jesus that she remembered nothing but feeling warm and safe. Keri likewise swore he did naught but try to save her life. Tears fell as he spoke, and I believe him. And Fum believed him too."

"Fum? Saints alive! Where did he come from, do ye know?" Hamar glanced around.

"He was sitting outside the cabin door like a mushroom when we arrived."

"An' why is it that you think Fum is believin' the lad's story?"

"He started playing that bone whistle while Keri talked."

"And you believed it?" said Ellis.

"Yes."

Tharn nodded. "Children and drunk men tell the truth."

"And I believe both my daughter and Keri," said Lisbeth, coming out of the great hall's doorway. Fum scooted in behind her.

"I have spoken with Stjärna, asking questions that you men may not understand. I am satisfied they are as chaste as when they woke yester morn."

Olaf smiled and nodded vigorously while snatching Ellis' untouched cup of ale.

Hamar looked at each person in turn. "I believe ye to be right. Saints be praised, Olaf's testimony kens the truth, do ye see? The young ones be more relieved than contrite. But don't ye know, the ones who matter be Dirk and your family. Is it that ye will be demandin' retribution?"

"I will not." Lizbeth moved to leave. "And Dirk knows how I feel. But Dirk has a strong, proud mind. You must talk to him."

"There will be a fight to restore honor," said Jesspersson. "That's what Hamar, Ellis, and Stjärna's mother are talking about."

Sami slashed his sword at imaginary enemies by the sled. "Sure there will and Dirk will crush Keri."

"What honor is there to fight for? I hear nothing happened," said Pekka, unloading wood.

"I hear she is with child," said eleven-year-old Leifson.

Sami swung over the boy's head. "You're an idiot. It takes more than once. I've waited a long time to see somebody crush Keri."

"Really?" said Jesspersson.

Pekka stopped working. "Keri is bigger than Dirk. How can he get crushed?"

"Dirk is infused by the gods he is so mad. He'll go berserk on him. And Keri won't want to fight his girl's father. It'll be a slaughter."

Leifson laughed. "You're still tipped that Keri beat you so easily wrestling at Jon's wedding."

Sami pointed his sword at Leifson and forced him back. "Keri is strong, but no one can beat me with a sword. I've carried a blade since I could walk, beat my brothers every time. I know more moves than a tomb has runes. Keri knows nothing except polishing that dumb axe he sleeps with."

Pekka slapped the sword aside and stepped into Sami's face. "Would you like to try pushing someone without your sword?"

Sami stepped back and raised the sword between them. He sniffed and turned away. "If Dirk doesn't fight him, I'll do it just for fun. When I'm done, Keri won't be in any shape to pull the sled. He'll have to stay here and watch Stjärna be given to another man."

"Would Dirk give her away?" asked Leifson.

Sami sheathed his sword and started to push the boy but Pekka stepped up. "He could try but I don't know if anyone will have her now. I know what happens when a man and a woman climb in bed. The man becomes a man but the woman becomes just another breed sow. You know that, Jesspersson. You made a man out of yourself with Gudrun, eh?"

"What? No...yeah, I'm as manly as you are!"

"I kind of liked that one myself. Gasps like a pig, huh?" Sami made a rude sound.

Pekka put a hand on the boy. "Shut up, Sami. Leifson is too young for your crude talk."

"Shut up yourself, kid. You'd have done it too if you had the chance. Keri's your sled mate, but now Stjärna's rancid cheese and Keri's a horny goat. The whole village knows it."

"Says who?"

"Olaf, that's who, you skinny stoat. I heard it myself at the great hall. I don't play your children's games and fetch my own water anymore. I have a woman to do that work. I stand among the adults and go when and where I please."

"Then what are you doing here with us?" said Pekka.

"Dropping crumbs to the dogs." Sami spit as he turned and marched off.

"I be believin' ye, young Keri," said Brother Hamar, nodding with his hands tucked in his woolen sleeves. They sat at the blacksmith's forge by a dying fire.

Keri dropped his eyes.

"But there's somethin' else troublin' ye, is there."

Keri hesitated. His eyes flicked up. "Nothing happened, but that doesn't mean I didn't want it to. I tried to pull back, I prayed, I tried to focus on the night sounds, I...I couldn't help but feel...her! She eventually warmed up but I couldn't get free. And I didn't want to get free. I...I...finally just...fell asleep wishing for...for..." Keri dropped his head in his hands. "What do I have to do to make up for that sin?"

"Sin?" said Hamar. "By the grace o' God ye did difficult an' brave things t' save a life. That's nae sin. Besides, ye know God doesn't forgive sin by what ye do, but by what ye believe."

Keri sighed. "Oh, I know. Jesus is the sacrificial lamb who died to pay for all my sins, but I feel like I should still do some...penance? My desire to...to...my pleasure at...I, uh, it feels like a sin. And it feels like I should pay for it."

"Well, even if yer sayin' the Lord's prayer all night, there's naught we can do that could repay God for anything. That's His grace, His mercy, don't ye know? Only Jesus, bein' perfect an' all, had anything t' be offerin' God. But do ye see? A big test ye faced, huge. An' with God's help ye won."

Keri just shook his head and stared at the ground.

Brother Hamar pulled back his white cowl. "Ye said ye prayed."

"Yes."

"An' despite huge temptation and opportunity, do ye see, you still didn't do any wrong. By the Blessed Mother, do ye see the connection?"

"I suppose. But in the end, it sure felt more like a pleasure than a test."

"Aye. A temptation it was, an' probably one that old Satan himself put there t' stop ye from being what God wants ye to be." Hamar crossed himself.

"What is it that God wants me to be?"

"Heaven's gates, I don't be knowin' what it is for ye. Righteous, certainly…obedient, but we each ha' different gifts, do ye know, an' God has different plans for each. Maybe God's plan for ye is out there on the sled, don't ye know?"

"Well, I don't know how holding Stjärna that way is supposed to help me fight for the king or please Jesus."

"True. It's puzzling. Ye beheld beauty ye may not ha' been ready to see. If Eve was t'other half of the image o' God, the half that Adam lacked, then ye was seein' the love and beauty God wants ye t' have t' complete your life, don't ye see?"

Keri shook his head.

Hamar looked heavenward and crossed himself yet again. "Ye must think o' her as more than a beautiful form. Saints alive, God intends for a woman t' be completin' a man, so we be one in the image o' God. Women, they have more o' His ability t' express love, forgiveness, an' peace. They nourish the children an' sacrifice for their families. It's a healing touch they have, don't ye know, an' a central piece o' the unity of a home: keeping the fires going, the food stored, and the noses wiped. Without them, saints be praised, man's life is more crude, more work, less honest. Did ye see Cnute after his Liisa died, God love him? When we come t'gether with a woman's soul we be findin' a peace in our souls, praise God. Like a Sabbath, ye know." Hamar stared at the embers.

"Is that what making love does?"

"Nae, nae. Anyone can take a woman's body. True pleasure, true peace is sharing your souls first so that when ye be together in body, ye be sharin' your spirits. Outside of that, don't ye know, just two animals ruttin'.

"M'lad, a glimpse ye had o' her, and she o' you. But do ye know the rest o' each other? Are ye bemused by how silly girls be, or is it that ye are entranced by how willing the lass is t' share her innermost thoughts? Is it that yer ready to be tellin' her yer soul's thoughts?"

Keri shrugged. "What should I tell her? That I have a desire to one day kill a bear? That I want my shield to hang honorably outside my door?"

"Sure, an' if those be important things t' ye, proud she will be t' have yer trophies on her walls. But don't ye know she wants a part in putting them there? She wants ye t' be comin' t' her with yer hidden fears before ye be huntin' that bear, or going to war. By the saints, she's wantin' to' know ye will be a safe place for her t' talk o' her fears to."

"What does she have to be afraid about?"

"You, lad, you, don't ye know? If ye are t' be her husband. Will ye be ridiculin' her fears? Laughin' at her desires, her dreams? Is it that ye will always be hungerin' for her the way ye do now? How will it be, she wants t' know, when she makes a mistake, or, heaven forbid, disagrees? Oh, and you will disagree. An' will ye be lovin' the things she loves? Her children?"

"Father said this too." Keri stirred the embers. "But what do I do? Just walk up to her and say, 'Hello, I will never laugh at your fears or dreams'?"

"Ah," said Hamar, leaning back. "That bein' the hardest part, ye ken. Women don't be gettin' to the point as directly as men an' ye may have t' wait like a fisherman for the right bite. 'Tis many a stream a lass can wander, don't ye know, before she be findin' the fish she wants to talk about."

"Is all this in the Bible?"

"Nae, nae. Not all of it. I guess ye could say, bein' a monk is m' second life."

Keri cocked his head.

Hamar straightened up. "Don't ye be worryin' about that. Just listen to her, young Keri, and be patient."

"Patient? It's only three weeks before we leave, and I don't even know how to talk to her. I don't even know if Dirk will let me talk to her!"

"Aye. There's that." Hamar adjusted his dingy white robe. "Saints above, the whole village be waitin' t' see what happens betwixt your families. An', don't ye see, no one wants t' know the outcome more than Stjärna."

OLDEFAR

Dirk stood at his door and watched Eli trot away in the gray morning. The boy's footfalls slapped hard and crisp on the frozen mud. He looked north as a wolf howled, causing Dirk to shiver. He turned in to his wife. "He wants to meet outside the great hall at midday." He studied his three daughters. "Very well. Best clothes on all of you. Go!"

Stjärna clapped her hands, smiling. "For me?"

"Go!" Dirk opened the chest that kept his grandfather's old helmet and took his sword and shield off the wall. He sighed, "Lord, help us."

An hour later the family passed Dirk's inspection and he strode out the door with his shield on his arm. He glanced at the smudge of sun in the overcast sky and nodded. The family followed stiffly except for the youngest, who hopped beside her mother, Lisbeth. Dirk glanced over his shoulder at Stjärna. Her eyes danced and a smile quivered at her lips when she saw the people watching them. He caught Lisbeth's eye and she shook her head. Laurel, her lips pressed tight, stepped out of a side street and walked beside Stjärna.

Dirk saw most of the village gathering by the great hall. Brother Hamar, praying, stood by Valdemar on the platform. Branches traced a wide circle in the snow before them. Brun, armed and grim, sat next to Pekka on the platform.

As Dirk arrived his brother appeared from around a corner and walked in bearing shield and spear. Annika walked out of the crowd and stood by Laurel and Stjärna. "Where's Gudrun?"

Annika shrugged, then glanced over at Pekka. They both smiled.

Dirk saw Keri coming up the main street. He wore an old helmet and a shield over the battle-axe on his back. He stumbled as he shifted his shoulders several times to even out the unfamiliar load. His father walked beside him with Soren. Ellis wore Corinthian, the family sword. Marta and the baby followed.

Eli on Keri's other flank carried his bow and a leather helmet. Various armed relatives of both families formed up behind their principals. Eli looked around, then whispered to Soren.

Soren shrugged. Dirk guessed they were looking for Jesspersson.

Both parties stopped on opposite sides of the circle. Valdemar looked from Keri to Dirk. "What are your intentions that you come here armed?"

"I am Dirk Thorlofson by his wife Marti Sigvarddottir. My family is as old as any in the village and I stand to protect my family honor and the women God entrusted to me." He felt Stjärna push up beside him, bouncing on her toes. She beamed. He looked at Keri.

Valdemar turned to Keri and raised an eyebrow.

Keri pulled again at the shield. "I am Sakarias Ellisson by Marta Alfdottir. I am guilty of holding Stjärna Dirksdottir in my arms while we slept. She was dying of cold; I was warmth. I am here to accept whatever punishment or deed Dirk thinks is appropriate to restore his honor, but first I claim the right to fight any man who claims Stjärna is guilty of any wrong."

Keri marched into the center of the circle and looked at Dirk. Dirk tilted his head and thought. Then he nodded slowly and stepped back. Stjärna clasped her hands and hugged them to her breast, smiling. Keri turned to the crowd. He pulled his shield off his shoulder and the axe dropped. Mantas laughed. Keri fumbled with the shield's straps and grabbed his axe in three different places before he was satisfied.

The wolf howled again.

Fum's tune echoed down a side street.

"Any man," Keri said again. His helmet pressed hair in his face. He brushed it away. Then his eyes slowly moved around the crowd. Several men dropped their gaze as did many women. He stopped and locked on Sami's leer.

Sami glanced left and right to see his brothers and friends looking at him. His wife sneered and raised an eyebrow. He turned back to Keri standing flat-footed in the snow.

Valdemar pointed to Sami. "Do you wish to challenge the girl's honor?"

Sami canted on one hip and studied Keri. "She gave her honor to Keri Ellisson. And if Dirk has no stomach to thrash the boy, then by the gods of our forefathers, I will remind him how it is to be done." He threw aside his cloak and revealed his helmet, shield, and sword ready at his side.

Stjärna gasped.

"Come into the circle, then, with your pagan tongue," said Keri, "and I will show you how an honest man fights for an honest woman."

Stjärna started to move but her father held her in place. "Too late," he said.

Sami threw his cloak at his wife and crossed into the circle. He made a show of putting on the helmet, then slowly drew his sword and swung it until it hummed. He drew swift patterns in the air, springing lightly on his feet. After a few passes, he stopped, raised his shield to eye level, and aimed the sword at Keri. The crowd froze.

Stjärna grabbed Dirk's arm. "Father...I never..." Her voice cracked.

"Hush, daughter. This has left your control."

Fum's whistle seemed to be coming closer.

Keri crouched with his shield and readjusted his grip on the axe. He grimaced, stood to his full height, and threw the heavy shield in the snow. Grabbing Wild Boar with both hands, he swung the huge blade horizontally, stepping unsteadily forward. The crowd murmured seeing the legendary weapon for the first time in twenty years.

Sami's eyes went wide. He instinctively stepped back.

Wild Boar gleamed along its blade as Keri fussed for a comfortable grip. Irritated, he shook his head like a wet dog and flipped off the helmet. His eyes narrowed and he glared under a forehead of blond hair.

Sami hesitated. Mantas and Gotthard jeered. "Two silvers on the ugly one!"

Sami looked at Keri's feet facing squarely at him, unbalanced. He saw the nervous grip on the axe, the discarded shield. He smiled, paused, spun in a circle, and sliced near Keri's midsection. The axe flashed down with a thud into the ground. Keri stumbled backward. He touched his tunic and pulled away a bloody hand.

The crowd sighed.

"No!" cried Stjärna, but her father held her back. Tears streamed down her face.

"Do it again, Keri!" called Gotthard. "We need to dig a new well."

Mantas belched and laughed. "Two silvers on the shiny one!"

Sami laughed and twirled the sword as Keri jerked the axe from the earth.

Fum's music grew stronger, then stopped.

"Wait!" shouted a raspy voice.

Old gray Sigvard entered the circle. His trek mates stood behind him each with a mug of ale. Fum followed. Sigvard wore the battered helmet and the travelling cloak he wore on the Tunturri so many years ago. An old chipped shield and a long, heavy spear with a bronze tip quivered in his hands. A white stone dangled from a leather thong about his neck. Brun stared, mouth open.

Sigvard spoke to the crowd. "I am Sigvard Ivarson, grandfather to Stjärna Dirksdottir. As oldest in her line, I have first right to fight any man who accuses her." He looked at Keri, then at Dirk. "I do not relinquish that right." Then he looked at Sami.

Brother Hamar bustled up to the old trekker. "Brother Sigvard, an' certain it is that ye have the right, but do nae let the foolishness o' this Viking tradition be causin' two deaths today. If God wills Keri or Sami to die, let that be enough, don't ye know. Do nae be a bloody preface t' another death."

Sigvard smiled at the monk. "You once said even though I was old, God was not through with me. Maybe it was for such a time as this that I have been saved. It was the last thing on my mind when I awoke. But as I dressed, I heard Fum outside my door and I felt a call to be a grandfather."

"David an' Goliath this isn't," said Hamar. "By the saints, God hates this fight for pride."

"Ach! Maybe I can make it a fight for truth." Sigvard smiled. "Please stand away and let God decide."

Fum tugged Hamar's white robe. Hamar hesitated, then stepped back.

Stjärna rushed by Hamar to Sigvard. "Please, sweet Oldefar, do not put yourself in harm's way. My grief at this moment is already to the bursting point. I don't even know how to pray. I never expected this. The whole family is in danger because of my stupid vanity."

Sigvard freed a hand to touch his granddaughter. "There is no stupidity in truth. Besides, it is well that the oldest should die first, not the youngest. The young will go on to their lives, the old to their rewards." He smiled. "But you assume it is I who will die. God called me here and may well have other plans for your oldefar."

He kissed her on the forehead, disengaged her hands, and turned to Keri.

"Young Keri," he said. "Your honor and your bravery are noted, but it is my right to be here. Step aside and let God and our traditions settle this."

Keri looked at Sigvard and then at Stjärna. Tears streamed down her quivering face. "You, sir, already have the love and respect of the girl I would fight for. Let me fight and win a share of her affection."

Sigvard waved his shield at him. "Bah! Winning a woman in a fight is the stuff of fireside tales and ballads. Neither valor nor fidelity will hold a woman. A quiet hour on a kitchen stool talking of her dreams and fears is worth more than dead dragons or fresh venison. Show a woman she is chosen, pursued, adored." Sigvard shook his head. "A fight does not prove your love."

Keri hesitated and turned to Stjärna. She nodded, bursting into sobs on her mother's shoulder. Keri backed off. "May God be with you, sir."

Sigvard glanced across the circle to Sami, who was leering at a girl in the crowd. Sigvard removed his cloak and called to Pekka. "Come be my shield bearer for a few minutes." He handed him the cloak and Pekka tightened his helmet. Sami exaggerated a yawn as Sigvard turned toward him.

Sigvard spit at Sami. "Ignorant puppy. You strut with a sword on your hip like some sort of Roman. Your gods and your sword are solid as smoke. Your late father should have slapped you to Danesland the first time you waved a stick at a crippled dog. Your flashy circles show you know nothing of battle or the horrors of the shield wall. Come, let me teach you."

Sami curled his lip. "Sad old man, trapped in a past so far back even the battles have been forgotten. Since your frightened family sends you, it is obvious they know their god is weak, dead on a cross. They hold honor in low esteem. I will finish the big oaf after I discard you. Your rheumy eyes will never see the blade that sends you to some dead god's Valhalla."

Sigvard shrugged. "I doubt you will see Valhalla this day or ever. But neither will you see Heaven. You are too prideful to grasp it."

Tharn leaned over to Brun. "One should listen when an old dog barks."

Brun bit his lip.

Sami sneered, clapped his sword on his shield, and marched forward. Sigvard stood fast with his shield and spear point wavering before him.

The crowd shouted and Hamar kneeled to pray. Fum's hand squeezed his shoulder. Keri and Dirk both stood quivering with rage as the fight began.

"Two silvers on the old goat!" shouted Mantas.

"Taken!" said Gotthard.

Sami whirled his blade in swift patterns about his head and charged. Stjärna screamed.

Sigvard's spear point quivered and then suddenly flashed out like a snake strike at Sami's feet. Sigvard's shield deflected the sword as the spear point skewered Sami's foot to the ground. Sami fell face first.

It was over in a moment with Sigvard pinning Sami's sword arm under his knee while holding the king's own dagger at Sami's throat. The white stone about his neck dangled in Sami's ear. "Cry 'yield' and live, Sami the lame. God may have work for you yet."

Sami winced at the dagger's edge and the agony in his foot. He dropped his sword and whimpered, "Yield."

Keri saw Sami's bloody foot and gagged. Stjärna fainted into her father's arms.

Sigvard's old friends touched their mugs together.

"Yep."

"Yep."

Sigvard stood and jerked the spear from Sami's bloody boot. Family and friends ran to him. Pekka, wide-eyed, placed the cloak around the old man's shoulders. As they left the circle, they bypassed Sami like a dead snake.

Laurel rubbed some snow on Stjärna's face and she jerked awake. Her father held her close. "It's over, my jewel. All is well." She buried her face in his shoulder, clung to him, and wept.

Sigvard looked to Stjärna and smiled. He then took Keri's arm and brought him to Dirk. Dirk held Stjärna under one arm and grasped Keri's arm with the other. The women exchanged embraces, then began to fuss with Keri's wound.

He waved them off. "It's like a branch scratch," he said.

Dirk whispered to Lisbeth, who nodded. He took Stjärna and gestured to Keri to follow. They mounted the platform and Dirk called out to the crowd. "This is done. The Lord has shown us His judgment and His grace." Dirk placed Keri and Stjärna's hands together. "No banns today, but no banes either. They have earned the right to be trusted together. And though the timing is odd, this is a courtship we would not oppose. It is up to God's direction for them, which I suspect He will tell them, not me...nor any of you." He looked pointedly at several groups of people talking excitedly. Then he walked off the platform.

As friends swamped the two families, Sami limped off with his brothers. "Sami the Lame," said one. "I think Father would have enjoyed something different." Sami snarled but then gasped at the pain in his bleeding, broken foot.

Sigvard turned to Keri to show him Sami leaving. "Learn, young lad. In the shield wall it is not the man who stands tallest who wins. It is the man who can keep his feet. That's a lesson in life as well. Keep your feet on the ground and let God worry about the glory."

One of Sigvard's old friends handed him a mug. They nodded.

"Yep."

"Yep."

"Yep."

Sigvard smiled at Keri. "We each have been given our own gifts, young Keri. One of mine is the spear; one of yours is your size. Your great-uncle Ubbe would be glad you have Wild Boar. I saw him use it a few times. Perhaps I could stop by and tell you what I remember."

Keri nodded vigorously. "Please, sir. I need some help."

Sigvard whispered to Keri, "Lesson one: if blood makes you gag, bite an ale-soaked piece of wood." Sigvard winked.

TALKING

K eri and Stjärna went to their respective homes to re-order their day. Keri's mother tended his "scratch."

Keri broke free and went to Dirkshouse just before sunset. Dirk said Stjärna would come out, but it wasn't soon. When she appeared, red-eyed and distant, Keri clasped his hands behind his back, and they walked silently between the houses and out the gate. The twilight faded into a gray haze.

Stjärna stopped. "Why don't we just talk here by the walls. I don't need to go to the forest today, do you? Besides, Mother fears that wolf." Her voice cracked.

"Huh? No, I guess this is fine."

They moved down the wall and around the corner.

Keri looked at his boots. Stjärna looked at her mittens.

He cleared his throat. "I, um…I'm sorry I got you in this mess."

"No, I'm sorry. It was my fault. You must think I'm a fool for falling in the creek."

"No, not at all. You hear of it all the time."

"Thank you for standing up for me even when that pig Sami drew his sword."

"What else would I do? He is a lout."

"But you could have been hurt. Sami said he wanted to kill you… and Oldefar."

"It was the right thing for me to do. I'm sorry your grandfather was in danger though." Keri bit at his lip.

She sobbed. "I never meant for anyone to be hurt. I…I…it was like one of Hamar's tales with Artur and I was…everybody was looking at me… I didn't think anything would happen." She grabbed him and cried into his chest. He held her gently, tentatively. When she stopped crying and straightened a little, he let her go.

She turned away. "Well, I suppose this is a good time to say good-bye then." She stiffened her face. "I mean you have to get ready and go off and pull the sled and be a warrior and see Hilhelm."

His head jerked up. He stared at her. "Are you that angry?" His voice rose. "I didn't know what else to do."

"Well, now that the village thinks you are a hero and you've saved a silly girl's life, you must have other deeds to do."

"A hero? I was too scared for a hero. What if I had lost you?"

"Then you wouldn't be a hero and I would still be a fool."

He moved to face her. "Stjärna, I did all that for you, not for me."

"And I almost got you killed!"

"But you didn't mean to."

She hung her head. "I think I did…accidently. I was mad at Father for keeping me so close to home. When he made his last trip to Lake Ladoga I was determined to be practically pledged when he returned."

"So?" Keri stood back, puzzled.

"You still don't get it. I chased you. I made you like me so you would walk me around the village. If I had let you be, I never would have fallen through the ice and you never would have had to fight Sami. You could have died just because I wanted to show Father I was ready to be a respected woman, not just a useless girl."

"Your father loves you."

"I know that now, but…" She teared up again.

He reached for her hands.

She pulled away. "You don't have to do that."

"Have to? I want to."

"Well, you didn't want to when we were walking in the village."

"I thought you didn't want to."

"You didn't ask."

"I've never asked." He was puzzled.

"Maybe it is time you did. You never ask me anything. You don't know anything about me: how mean I can be, how selfish, how thoughtless."

Keri spread out his hands and leaned down toward her. "With you I never feel any of those things."

"You just wait. You don't know me. You never ask me anything."

"Yes, I do. I'm always asking how your family fares, how you made your hair so nice. I even remember you said you liked smoked trout better than salmon."

"You never ask me anything important."

"Like what?"

"If I have to tell you, then you aren't really interested." She stiffened again and flared her eyes.

Keri sagged and rubbed his brow. He lifted his head. "Is this about…how I made you warm that night?"

She rolled her eyes and turned away. "You don't care how I feel."

"I do care."

"Then why don't you ask?"

"Ask about what?"

"How I feel?"

"Feel about what?"

"Exactly."

Keri brushed at his vest. Stjärna watched a distant cloud.

Keri took a deep breath. "Well, we're not getting anywhere, so let me say what I came to your house to say."

"Oh, is this where you tell me goodbye?"

"No! Stjärna, let me talk."

She folded her arms.

His eyes found hers and he put a calloused hand gently on her hand. "I just wanted to say that I'm sorry…I couldn't find some other way… some not so embarrassing way to keep you from freezing to death. You must think I'm like Sami, one of those fellows who just wants to leer at you. I'm sorry, it was the last thing on my mind."

"Really? Is that what you think I think? That's where you are so wrong." Her voice was rising. "That's what you need to ask me about. Don't ever try to tell me what I am thinking. Ask me what I am thinking, and I will gladly tell you."

She put a finger in his face. "I think you really are a hero. I love how you saved me, and I loved waking up in your arms." She began to cry. "What I am upset about is the whole village that looks at me like I am still as naked as the moment Father charged in the door. They laugh and nod at you like you did something fun and got away with it, but they laugh and point at me as if I was Tamar playing the harlot."

Keri stood back. "Who's Tamar?"

She rolled her eyes. Tears tracked her face. "How can I hold my head up in this place? And then you go and walk beside me through the village just now like we are sister and brother. Are you ashamed of me too?"

His mouth fell open. "No, I thought you were mad at me."

"There it is again. Ask me how I feel! Don't guess."

He pulled her hands to his chest and took a big breath. He let it out slowly and tried to breathe normally. He whispered, "I love you."

Her face rose and changed from tight to soft to softer. "That's not the first time you've said that to me, is it?"

"No. I said it in the cabin as I prayed for your life…for our life."

"Then it wasn't a dream." She was whispering too. She pulled closer. "I love you too."

His body shook. "And I will tell the whole village of my love from the platform in front of the lodge."

"No." Stjärna relaxed in his arms. "Just show them. We only have a little time left before you go. Let them see that you love me. That's all I ask. And show me too by talking about something besides hunting, heating iron, and sleds."

"That may be all I really know." Keri buried his face in her hair.

"Oh, I have a basket full of things you know that you haven't talked about." She pushed back to look up at him.

His eyebrows went up. "Like what?"

"Like, how did you feel when you woke up in Cnute's cabin holding me?"

He squinted in thought. Then his face relaxed. "Your father interrupted the most peaceful sleep I ever had. Holding you was like warmth from the finest furs in the whole world."

"Oh?"

"Oh! I'm sorry! I don't mean to say…I mean I, um…weasels!" Keri released her hands and stood back. "I'm sorry. I hope you don't think I just, um…well, you felt…I mean."

She laughed. "You liked it?"

He squirmed. "Well, yes…a lot." He smiled from his bowed head.

"Good. I didn't know what you thought and it's nice to know we both liked it."

"You did?" He pulled her close again.

"Yes, but we'd best see what else we share before we follow that path too far."

"That's pretty much what Hamar said." Keri sighed and relaxed his grip.

"Good. Then let's try to empty that bucket you call a head and see what's in it."

"What are you talking about?"

"I'm talking about talking." She disengaged herself from his hug and led him by the hand toward the forest. The evening star rose over the mountaintop. "You say you don't know anything to talk about. Well, here's just one of many things you know that I do not: What would you want to name your children?"

A heretofore unnoticed portion of Keri's brain suddenly awoke and leapt into a time after the sled. He struggled like a puppy walking, but eventually Stjärna had him talking about things he had never considered. Each was amazed at what the other said and they both laughed a lot. Keri laughed so much he forgot to jump and touch the brass crest over the gate when they came in.

A SCROLL

The next three weeks went quickly. With so much to do and talk about, the village hummed. Hamar heard Jodis Jurgensdottir took credit for having brought Keri and Stjärna together. Several pregnancies needed discussion. Sami lost two toes. Would the men have to fight when they reached Hilhelm? Wasn't Cnute cleaning up nicely in his red knit cap? And was Pekka's skin clearing up?

Then, to Hamar's joy, Asaph the Jew came singing through the woods one afternoon, leading his two well-armed sons, his massive dog, Goliath, and a string of mules full of trade goods. Fum greeted them dancing at the gate and piped him up the log street to the great hall. Out of Asaph's round girth and impossibly tangled black beard came a deep baritone voice that sang along to Fum's happy tune in some foreign tongue. His dark eyes shined down from under a black brimmed hat which crushed a bramble of curly black hair. The blunt-faced dog licked Fum's outstretched hand but growled at every other adult who approached. Even Keri backed up.

"Brun! Hamar!" boomed Asaph in his strange accent. "Long we have not seen each other." He waved vaguely behind him. "My sons!

148

Look how they have grown! One year only it has been. Joseph, hold back that dog!"

The village quickly spread the news, and curious folks soon surrounded the visitors. He paid respects to Valdemar and negotiated the usual fee for permission to spread his wares in the great hall. The children gladly helped him and his sons unload his packs and lead his shaggy beasts to the Widow Jonsdottir, where visitors normally arranged shelter and fodder.

Brother Hamar took Asaph's arm and led him toward the great hall. "Is it that ye have eaten, old friend?"

Asaph looked at him and they both laughed. "Well, later then," said Hamar. "After evening mass. Aye, a wee bit o' ale in the great hall."

"Yes, yes. After we eat. Joseph! Water! For the animals."

As they walked off Keri approached Hamar. "They never eat with you or anyone else. Do Jews not eat?"

Hamar shook his head. "'Tis under the old laws they are. Naught but their own utensils and stores, ye know. Friends, they have in the villages, but they dinna go near a pig or what might o' touched one. But fine storyteller he is. Come and listen after mass."

Hamar smiled as acquaintances and the village stayed after prayers to hear news of the outside world. Like a minor prince holding court, Asaph came in and sat by the fire with his silent sons, alternately answering questions and singing songs far into the night.

Asaph worked the western mountains, so he knew little of the potential war east at Hilhelm. "Kipchak Turks maybe?" He did have news of births and deaths among the hills and news from further west. "Your Danish kinsmen have settled affairs with the Saxons."

"But now new wars. The Pope in Rome sends white-clad knights to free Palestine from the Musselmen. He tells them, 'Sing Kyrie Eleison as you fight your way to the Jerusalem.'" He paused, looked heavenward.

"May my tongue cling to the roof of my mouth if I do not remember you, Jerusalem, my highest joy." He shrugged. "'Kyrie Eleison?' Greek, they tell me, not the Latin. It means 'Lord have mercy' I am told. These armies, they pass through Constantinople. Ah! Trade there is good."

The fire dwindled. Asaph finished his last horn of ale, and said, "We must sleep. May the Master of the Universe bless us all."

In the morning Asaph spread his goods along a wall of the hall. One table held cones of salt, small blocks of dark sugar, and slivers of tangy ginger. He put out medicinal barks and herbs in clay pots, large metal spoons, simple kitchen knives, and some decorated daggers. He displayed one chain mail shirt, some helmets, and several swords. People handled interesting bronze goblets, plus iron pots and pans. They examined heavy hooks to hang meat or pots and great padlocks with massive keys. A large box held metal heads for sickles, hoes, axes, and mattocks.

The women clustered where Asaph put bolts of Asian silk, Egyptian cotton and linen, and plain homespun wool in plaids of a far-off design favored among the Goths. They tried on felt hats and soft head scarves.

At the center table the dog stood guard over pendants of polished stone, some semi-precious gems, and finger rings. Some were plain, some woven with thin strands of steel or even silver. He displayed a basket full of ceramic beads next to another of seashells. There was even a small stack of Egyptian paper.

Fum sat playing his whistle in the rafters.

"Pelts!" said Asaph to the crowd. "Pelts, I am seeking. All kinds. Martens and stoat are wonderful, but don't forget squirrels and fox. Also, wax and honey I want. Maybe some small wood carvings, needle-work, or finished leather." His fuzzy hair bounced under his wide black hat as he shouted and walked among the people.

Asaph filled the hall, bickering and trading with each potential buyer until both were satisfied. Though well-known as honest, Asaph knew he was only a guest and worked hard to ensure neither he nor his sons offended. It was dangerous to be alone and of a different tribe, so he sometimes traded good profit for goodwill.

After two days Asaph felt he drained the village of most of its trade pelts and he began to pack his goods into manageable loads. Keri, Soren, and Eli came into the nearly empty hall and went first to the remaining weapons and then to the table of stones and rings. Soren found himself face-to-face with the dog.

Joseph, Asaph's oldest son, met them. "Goliath, sit!" The great beast went behind the table to his master. "How can I help you lads?"

Eli gestured at Keri. "We two are on the sled, sir, but would like to leave something behind for some special girls."

"Hmmm…special girls…" Joseph raised his black eyebrows and peered at what the boys carried that might be for trade. "Do I see pelts in that bag?"

"Sixteen fine squirrels," said Eli.

"Are the skins punctured by arrows?" The trader nodded to Eli's ever-present bow.

"No, sir, I used blunted arrows: broken heads, not broken skins. Sometimes I had to twist their necks."

Keri winced.

"Very wise. May I see?" Joseph examined several skins, nodding. "Not bad. Let's talk."

"How about…" Eli reached for a silver cape brooch.

The dog stood. Eli hesitated and Joseph laughed, pushing the dog back. "Nope. You can't begin to afford any of the silver but maybe we can agree to one of these bronze brooches."

Eli sniffed at them. "Actually, my heart had been set on a silver hat band for myself but then a girl came into my life." He sauntered to one side. "How about this bolt of green cloth?"

"Nope, but you could afford three of these head scarves. There is a green one."

151

"I only want one."

"A fine fellow like you has only one girl?"

"I can't afford more than one."

"Very wise again."

While Eli and Joseph sparred, Asaph came over and nodded to Keri. "What is it you wish, Sakarias Ellisson?"

Keri's face showed surprise.

"They call me Keri."

"Keri, then, but you must know that Sakarias is one of our prophets."

"One of ours too, I'm told."

Asaph studied Keri.

"I was hoping for something blue," said Keri.

"Blue beads I have, not much else. A royal color, blue. But…something unusual from a countryman up from Kiev…last spring." Asaph reached into one of his packs and pulled out a folded cloth. He unwrapped a leather thong with an oblong, opaque blue stone caught in a twist of shiny steel wire.

Asaph dangled the stone in front of Keri. "Sea glass. From an old Roman window or bottle, perhaps. Broken long ago, long ago on the Black Sea, smoothed by the sand and sea since the destruction of the temple maybe."

Keri's eyes went wide; then his face sagged. "I could never afford that. I only have three jars of honey and a box of wax."

"Perhaps not." Asaph laid down the stone and shrugged his shoulders. "But a proposition I have for you. Soon you go with the sled. Hilhelm I have not seen for many years. Once I had there relatives and friends. Today it is daughters I seek from among my own people to marry my sons. Your honey and wax I will take for this stone, if to Hilhelm you will carry a message for me, bring me the answer, and bring a scroll they will give you."

"A scroll?"

"Writing on rolled skins."

"Surely, I will do this, but who am I? You have had many men from the sled here trading with you these past two days."

"Who are you indeed? This question many men ask themselves and get the wrong answer." Asaph rolled his eyes and shrugged again. "People I have asked. 'On the sled, who is reliable?' I ask. 'Him,' they say, and 'him,' but often they say you: Sakarias, named for our prophet. You, son of Ellis, the smith. And him I owe a favor."

"What has Father done for you?"

Hands up as he shrugged yet again. "Directly? Nothing. But I know I take business from him with my Novgorod-made metal. Yet oppose me he does not when I come." Asaph smiled. "Good will is a good favor and hard it is to find ways to repay. I hoped you would come in to trade."

"But is this message really so valuable?"

"What could be more valuable than good wives for my sons and the word of God?"

"You want me to get a Bible for you? The cost would be huge."

"True." Asaph lifted a hand to his heart. "But my people have been copying books of what you call the Bible for centuries. On scrolls! Sheep skins or sometimes Egyptian paper. Bring me a scroll of the prophets." He gazed at the ceiling. "A prophet who wrote when my people were in Babylon: Daniel, Ezekiel, Zechariah, your namesake! Again, I would hear the promises of God to bring my people home."

"Wait, I could never remember all those names."

"I will write them for you."

"I can't read."

"No...you won't read." Asaph sighed. "Your people do not value reading enough to know your own history, much less the prophets."

"I can trace my family back seven generations to Daneland."

"Seven hundred years to Hispania I know my people. And two thousand more to Moses! But a scroll I have to help me."

Keri squinted his eyes. "Well, I know Brother Hamar said I knew enough to go to heaven."

Asaph took a breath, let it out, and smiled. "You know? May you be right to think you are pleasing God, but were we to debate the merits and fine points of our faiths? Ah, either of my sons would embarrass you with how little you know. You do not read, so you cannot know."

Keri stepped back. "Well, Jesus is the Messiah. And that's all I need to know."

"Really?" Asaph raised his hands palms up. "Brother Hamar reads many books I read. Messiah will be a conquering strong man, they say. A king, punishing the oppressors of my people. Jesus? Did he do that?"

"No."

"No? Then wrong you may be. Brother Hamar and I—hours we debate our prophets and your Jesus. We cannot agree. But you? How can you even understand our talk? You have not, *cannot* read the most important books in the world."

Keri leaned back and examined Asaph. "Are you a priest?"

"No. I am of Judah. Priests were Levites. But every man should seek God with all his heart, soul, and mind. Both my prophets and your Jesus said that. If you do not read, you can seek God only through others' ideas, and thoughts."

Keri was thinking when Asaph leaned over the table and put the pendant in his hand. "But we cannot solve a mystery of a thousand years, you and I. Write, I will, a message to my people in Hilhelm. They will know what I want and give it to you. They will know. Can you do that?"

Keri looked at the blue stone. "I will certainly try. But what if…uh, you know, I don't come back."

"God forbid, and my prayers will go with you, but let us enlist your friend to stand with you on this task." He glanced down the tables. "Eli. Ah! Another with a name from my people! Come. You were looking at these silver clasps. You cannot afford them but a proposition we have for you."

Asaph and Keri explained the proposal to Eli. After some questions and an exchange of squirrels, honey, and wax the boys walked out with a fir tree-shaped bronze clasp inlaid with a strip of shiny steel and a blue sea glass stone on a leather thong. Fum smiled from his overhead seat.

The next day Asaph gave Keri a tightly wrapped and wax-sealed envelope of oiled sheepskin the size of his hand. Strange writing surrounded the seal. "Show this to any of my people, Sakarias. They will know."

Keri tucked it in the bottom of the box he would carry on the sled.

CHOICES

Brother Hamar persuaded Brun to declare the day before the sleds departed as a time of worship and family. Consequently, two days before they left, the sleds sat in front of the great hall ready to go. Split logs packed the big sled so tight that a spider could not squeeze between them. Spears and shields hung from the sides with skis standing tall in a rack at the back. Wooden hooks held swords on the swing-out front door. The smaller sled carried barrels for ale, forty-two food chests, and each man's personal box. The runners sank a hand's breadth into the snow.

The great hall rocked with laughter and light. Brun looked over the room. Almost the whole village was there. Benches and tables lined the walls while ale kegs crowded one corner. Beef and pork sizzled on the open spit. Bread and dried apples sat on wooden platters. Smoke, people, talk, and laughter filled the room. Valdemar recited the battle of Ladoga Lake and several young men, notably not Sami, wrestled or sparred with wooden swords in an open space. A couple sang favorite ballads accompanied by Annika's lap harp. Mantas almost started a fight when he pinched one too many girls.

Brun bounced his youngest on one knee and his wife on the other. He noticed Fum standing quietly near the fire. Beckoning Pekka and Bue, he pointed toward two shallow hand drums hanging on the wall. They nodded, grabbed Annika and the drums.

Pekka and Bue began a moderate rhythmic beat. On the downbeat Annika struck a chord. Bubump bump thrum, bubump bump thrum. They kept at it and the crowd quieted. Brun and his wife led several couples to their feet. Timonen and his wife pushed back some benches and joined in.

Then it began, simple and soft, coaxed by the beat of the drums and Annika's harp: Fum's whistle played a few measures of his tune. He paused, found his spot, and played the beginning again in earnest. The couples, not daring to look at him lest he stop, began to dance in slow circles around the room.

Bubump bump thrum, bubump bump thrum. Young and old the dancers swished around, skirts lifting on the turns. People began to clap to the beat. The whistle came again and played a few new measures.

Keri looked at Stjärna, who smiled at him. Eli and Laurel waved to them from among the dancers and they rose as one to join them.

Fum played his entire tune twice. He began it again and a second deeper tone came in. People glanced over where Asaph and Joseph added harmonies to Fum's basic tune using deeper wooden flutes. The music swelled. The dancers bounced and spun and bumped and danced and did it again. Sigvard and his cronies slapped the tables and laughed at the collisions. The women and girls at the edges pointed and talked of the grace, the clumsiness, and the beauty. Soren grabbed his little cousin and whirled her around the floor. Other children danced in little twirls on the edges of the crowd or bounced by their parents. Jesspersson and Gudrun collided and fell amid loud giggles. A cat took the opportunity to lick the bowls at an empty table.

The musicians played on, sometimes improvising on the basic theme of Fum's tune. Slowly the drummers increased the speed of their beat until the dancers staggered, dizzy. Cold, sickness, grudges, war, the sled, the wolf's howl outside all dried up like a tear. Old people nodded, young parents cuddled, and the dancers laughed. The music cleansed the room with peace, love, and joy.

Suddenly Fum stopped. So pronounced was his halt that the others played only a few notes and then faded to nothing. Fum assumed a pensive look: hands at his side and head askance, looking at the door. After a few stumbling seconds the couples stopped, the laughing stilled, and the room grew silent save for the dancers' heavy breathing and the crackle of meat on the fire.

The hall's great door opened to Firth Black Collar. Behind him stood a large young man of about twenty years with a thin beard and his hair pulled tight back in a low mud-colored braid. He carried a short sword and a large bundle in his bulging arms. Fum stared sideways at him.

Firth, always wearing black, smiled his seductive smile. "Good day! Don't stop for us! It is good to see you in such great spirits!" He gestured for the lad to wait at the door, eased around Fum, crossed to avoid the three Jews, and went to Valdemar. Whispering, the dancers found their seats. Some pointed toward the young man. By the time Firth reached Valdemar's table, the whole room knew the moment had come.

Tharn moved over to Brun and nodded at Fum, who gazed at the tall youth at the door. "Fum knows. Look how he stares at him. A bad tree does not bear good fruit. There is something amiss here."

Valdemar gestured at Brun, who brought a small bag from the center post. Valdemar addressed the crowd. "We all know why Firth is here: to exchange our man for his. You know I oppose this race and this trade to ensure its honesty. I ask you: is this a good idea at all? Let us keep our men together, let this man pull with his village, let us think of nothing except the prize put before us: service to our king."

Firth spread his arms. "I am only here as we agreed. Wise men proposed this months ago and it merely adds trust to our little bet. You cannot lose by taking Gath, one of the biggest men in Drakestad. Surely we will be the losers in this bargain."

Valdemar shook his head. "Who loses if we merely do our duty and send thirty men to the king?"

The crowd murmured.

Firth raised an eyebrow at Brun. "Shall we not keep this agreement?"

Brun lifted his bushy red head. "I was anxious to run this race when it was merely a race. But now I have pulled in the traces with our men and I know each of them better than before. If the king were to cancel everything, I know I would have twenty-nine new brothers with whom I shared hardship and dreams. True community is made not by accident of birth, but by shared effort."

He lifted the bag. "In this bag are thirty stones. Whoever draws the lone white stone is to go with Drakestad. But I want no man to go. We are a crew. I cannot think of a single man I would be content to lose to Drakestad even to have the muscles of this small giant here. And I would die in my heart if I was drawn."

He lowered the bag. "I propose we allow Firth to take this young man back to Drakestad to pull with his friends. If Firth has been honest enough to allow such a fine specimen to be their offering, then I think he will be honest enough to run a fair race. Besides, if we were to send any man back who is less in stature than this young Thor, they would cry 'foul.' Let us run with the men we have and let God choose the winner."

Led by the men of Rentvatten's sled, the crowd cheered. Brun raised an eyebrow to Firth.

Firth smiled. He waited for the crowd noise to subside and waved at his companion. "This is Gath." Gath looked down and shuffled his feet. "We groaned when he was picked for this trade, but I told my people never to fear, you would never take him." Firth gestured.

Gath grimaced and emptied his bag onto the nearest table. Instead of his kit, out tumbled two huge smoked hams. "Gifts." His deep voice rumbled. "One to eat today, one to eat on the sled."

Valdemar led the clapping that filled the hall.

Fum walked up to Gath and held out his fist. Gath reached out his hand and the silent spirit gave him a crudely carved wooden cross strung on a leather thong. The young man held up the cross and then stared at Fum. Fum stared back. Gath shivered and Fum moved off.

Brun broke the silence. "A remembrance of our shared faith. Wear that well, young giant. Now eat with us!"

Keri jumped to slice the ham.

The room filled with happy noise again. Jesspersson and Gudrun brought Gath a wooden bowl with a steaming rib. He absently stared at the cross in his hand.

"Who was that person?" he asked.

Gudrun smiled. "Fum."

"What's wrong with him? He's so…"

"Wrong?" Jesspersson finished his cup of ale. "Nothin'. Few people are as content as him. Even fleas don't bother 'im. He's blessed by the living God."

"How did he get like that?" Gath looked around the room. "Where did he go?"

Gudrun laughed. "He likes to disappear. My mother says a man named Zach found him in a wool-lined basket in the forest. Years ago, just before Brother Hamar arrived. Since Zach and his wife had no children, they raised him, but it was clear from the start he was not a normal child."

"Were they as pure white as he is? His hair is like a snowfield and his eyes are pink as a sunrise." Gath coughed.

"Oh, no." Gudrun shook her head. "Zach and Elizabeth had brown hair and blue eyes."

Jesspersson filled his cup from a nearby flagon. "Some people thought he's one o' the pale horsemen from back east 'til Asaph the Jew declared Fum was o' his people."

"I know the Jew." Gath nodded at Asaph. "He trades in Drakestad. How did he know the child was his?"

Jesspersson wiped his mouth with his sleeve. "Not his, but a Jew. I dunno know for sure, but he said the eyes were wrong t' be a horseman an' that the horsemen are a dusky brown. One o' the women said Asaph saw baby Fum being bathed an' suddenly declared 'im a Jew." Jesspersson belched. His head nodded down, eyes closing.

"I wonder why? They are not the same color."

"Nope, that's not it." Gudrun leaned into Jesspersson. "I think Mother knows but she won't tell me."

Gath narrowed his eyes. "Did Asaph try to take him? In Drakestad, some say Jews eat Christian babies."

"No, but Fum always runs to him."

Gudrun looked up. "Isn't Asaph the one who gave him the bone whistle?"

"I think so."

Gath finished the rib and threw the bone into the fire. "How old is this Fum?"

"God knows. He's been that big and that small since I was a boy. And his sort-of parents died long since."

"How does he live?"

"People try to take him in," said Gudrun, "but he usually sleeps in the hall here or wherever he wants in the summer. And eats with Brother Hamar…only bread and honey. Except when Asaph is here. Fum is the only one who ever eats with them."

"Do they speak the same language?"

She shook her head as she took a long pull on Jesspersson's ale. "Fum never speaks, but you always seem to know what he is thinking."

Jesspersson drained his cup and waved for Gudrun to go fill it again.

She stood. "Actually, Fum always seems to know what *you* are thinking."

"That's scary." Gath gulped hard. "Is he a wizard?"

"No," said Jesspersson. "But in the summer he is as one with the forest. He goes out all day and comes back with huge honeycombs and not a bee sting on him."

"Does he always look at strangers that way?"

"No," said Jesspersson carefully. "But when he does you feel 'im inside your head. He is so…pure…it is hard t' even be angry when he's aroun'." Gudrun came back with three filled cups.

She squeezed close to Jesspersson. "We were surprised. He seldom stares at people like he did to you."

"Well, he startled me. It's like when you are hunting and suddenly get a feeling you'd better turn around and you find a wolf creeping up on you. It shakes you."

She laughed. "I wouldn't know. The only wolf I find hunting me is Jess here, and his mouth doesn't bite."

"Seriously? No wolves here?" Gath sucked in a deep breath and sipped his ale. "We have had a great black wolf haunting the forest around Drakestad for a month or more."

"Ha' you seen 'im lately?" Jesspersson squinted through bleary eyes. "We had one here 'bout two weeks ago. There have been other sightings too."

"Ah! I thought I saw wolf sign as we came in."

"They've kep' their distance 'cept t' frighten some of the goat herds. Howling and all."

"They don't scare me." Gudrun snickered. "But Jess here does."

"How can you be scared with s' much food and ale t' eat?" said Jesspersson, reaching for more ham.

They laughed, and the conversation turned to people, sleds, and the quality of the ale.

Firth and Gath stayed about an hour before Gath caught Firth's eye. Firth nodded and they took their leave. Brun saw them out the gate and gave them torches against the growing darkness.

They thanked him and started up the path. Just over the hill Gath stopped behind a tree and worked hard to clear his throat. He hacked and spit heavily. Even in the twilight, it showed bright red against the white snow.

Firth pulled up, looked around, and threw snow on the stain. Gath took several deep breaths. "Sorry. We had to leave. I couldn't have held it much longer." Firth shrugged.

They stopped a little further on and Gath picked up a hidden deer-skin bag. Firth scoffed. "I said you wouldn't need your gear."

Gath shouldered the bag. "It was wrong to offer me as our trade. The temptation would have swayed lesser men."

Firth shrugged.

Gath pressed him. "What if they had found I had the breathing sickness before they left? We would have been exposed as liars, cheats."

"Our sled would have been gone already and the whole thing would fall into confusion. They could never win the race then."

"That's not the point." Gath spit again. "We tried to deceive them. We did deceive them."

"When did you get so particular? Yesterday you were bargaining for more silver for your part in this."

"I need silver for my parents. I hated doing this."

"Be happy. Your family will eat. I wanted an edge. You won. Let's get moving. I want some rest before the sled leaves tomorrow."

Gath closed his hand around the wooden cross on his chest. He looked back at the lights from the distant palisade and thought he heard a wolf howl, and then a thin bone whistle.

As the feast wore down, Stjärna and Keri slipped out of the hall toward the woods. Moonlight sparkled off the snow outside the yellow circle of their torchlight.

Annika stood alone by the path. "Have you seen Pekka? He asked me to meet him. He promised he would take me down to see the mill in the moonlight."

Keri and Stjärna exchanged winks. "Nope, his father was looking for him earlier." Annika slumped and walked back toward the village.

Stjärna and Keri scampered up the trail, laughing. "Look," said Keri. "The evening star. I think of it as your star."

She nuzzled into him. "Can I be your morning star too?"

"When I see it on the trek to Hilhelm, I will know you are here, calling me home."

She kissed his cheek and pulled him up the trail. Rounding a corner, they found Jesspersson hugging Gudrun against a tree. He threw his hands in the air as Gudrun giggled, then burped. He gestured higher up the path. "You won't fin' a quiet place up 'ere either. Eli an' Laurel are not far off."

The girls began to talk excitedly as the boys exchanged wry looks.

"I thought I heard an elk herd," Eli said, following Laurel down the path.

Laurel elbowed him as she took Stjärna's hands. Her smile included Gudrun. "This may be the last time until after harvest we are all together. That is a long time and we need to plan some way to keep busy lest we succumb to Sami and his dreadful brothers."

The girls laughed but the boys glanced at each other with eyes wide open.

"No, really, we should pray or something. It could be a long time before we are together again."

"Bro'er Hamar prays plenty f' me." Jesspersson grabbed Gudrun's hand. "Come on, this could be our las' chance."

Gudrun giggled. "I have a couple prayers to get answered before Father knows I am gone." She curtseyed to the group, almost fell, and they started off.

"Do you need a torch?" Keri called.

Jesspersson waved. "Nope, I got m' own fire." They both giggled.

Laurel looked concerned but Eli hugged her. "Come on! Worry about us for a minute. I'm leaving too."

She smiled. "Six is a safer number than just two. You realize they are heading towards Cnute's old cabin…where Liisa died."

Eli frowned. "Not my problem, except that now we have to find a place to go."

Keri pointed. "I left some tree trunks up here to dry. They would be easy to clear, and we could get a fire up."

Laurel grabbed his arm. "Where?"

Keri led them to the spot and they stayed talking and whispering quiet promises until Brun blew his horn at the closing gate. Far away they heard the horn echoed by the call of a wolf. They lit a torch and ran laughing to the village.

They were not the last ones in, which caused much shouting at Gudrun's house later that night.

BATHED IN PRAYER

Families sat to awkward dinners the night before the sled left. No less so at Ellishouse. The blacksmith sighed as he watched Keri's mother, with a tearstained face, hold Keri's hand and just look at him. She occasionally touched his cheek or brushed aside his hair. His older sister and brother-in-law smiled, trying to know what to say now that they had all wished him luck and prayed. They hushed Soren when he tried to talk about Keri's axe or the war. Baby Galina sprawled sound asleep.

They had already said how much they would miss each other and would pray for each other and be good several times, but that was understood at this point and had lost any impact.

Ellis swished a last gulp of ale in his cup. "We must to bed now. We all need sleep to face tomorrow." He finished his ale and cleared his throat. He fixed his eyes on Keri and they gazed at each other for a moment. "Keri, tonight you will sleep one last time under my protection and our love." He paused to collect himself and choked back a sob. "Tomorrow you will leave here feeling like a son…but I see a man. Come back feeling like a man who is my son."

Well after most were asleep, Ellis heard Pekka's father, Rainar, calling at the gate for Brother Hamar. "Please. Come quickly to the mill. Pekka has fallen and won't wake up. Help. Please hurry." Ellis fell asleep praying.

Fum listened while Brother Hamar prayed with Rentvatten's people huddled around the great hall in the pre-dawn. A cold mist turned the ground and sky white, so only the trees loomed black. The buildings and sleds added their own shapes to the strange gray morning.

"Amen." Hamar sagged. It had been a long night.

"Amen," said the crowd. Then they broke away to the sleds.

"Sweet words." Tharn patted the monk's arm.

Hamar shook his hanging head. "Ah, ye know, the bards love t' sing o' great deeds and o' gods movin' among mankind. Their songs are full of brave words, they are, and longin' looks, and even wisdom, but by the Saints, no woman has heard a ballad that described the agony she felt at seein' her man depart, especially to go to war. God bless 'em."

Tharn nodded. "Seneca said, 'There is no easy way from the earth to the stars.'"

Hamar sighed. "May my prayers reach the stars. Amen."

Fum smiled.

Tharn sighed. "You speak good words. You have a good heart. Watch over our village. And Pekka. Can you say what happened?"

"Unconscious, he is. Lost a powerful lot o' blood from his scalp. Broken arm, twisted knee. God help 'im. Rainar said he must ha' fallen through the trapdoor at the mill. His mother is nearly hysterical. God bless her. Annika's a' stayin' with her."

"Will he be all right?"

"By God's grace. Hard t' say. A limp at best. Addled in the head or even death at worst, don't ye know. Rainar...Rainar seems relieved, he does, t' be goin' in Pekka's place."

Fum put his hand to his eyes.

"Maybe we should have let Rainar replace him when this all first came up. At least we would have had time to build up his birdie legs," said Tharn.

"What?"

"Birdie legs. That's what his father calls him."

Hamar crossed himself, shaking his head. "God's will it is, either way. Ye be keepin' an eye on Rainar. I don't think he knows what he's into. God be with you all."

"Amen. And with you."

"Amen."

Tharn moved to the smaller sled. Fum followed, touching an anxious child here and there as he went. Fum stood behind Timonen's family a few moments, and then Bue's. Then he climbed to the highest spot on the bigger sled, shifting his gaze from one man to another.

Hamar followed behind as the villagers pushed the sleds out the gate and down the hill. The pink and orange line on the far horizon broke into a golden eye as the sun rose, melting the morning fog. Here the pull was easy. Children and young boys stumbled underfoot helping.

After two hours the sun went behind a cloud as they came to a white meadow. A frozen streambed cut a sizable gash through the snow and earth. Everyone piled snow into the gap to build a snow bridge. The men pushed the sleds across. Without signal or fanfare, they went back for a final word or touch.

Mantas and some others waved to their wives who stood higher up the hill chanting by a tree where three goats hung by the neck. Mantas touched the horns of Odin he wore at his throat.

Below, the trees thinned out among the rocks and the horizon fell a thousand feet through ridges, drifts, and sharp fingers of stone. Fum climbed down from his perch and waited by the bridge. As the men crossed again, he touched each of them. Some smiled, some shivered. Mantas jumped. Cnute said, "Thank you."

Brun called the crew to their posts. He briefly bowed his head and then looked up with his fierce twin-bearded grin. "Rentvatten, take up the slack! Steady! Pull!" He put his shoulder to the big sled and pushed. "SSSuuuut –tah!" and they lurched off.

People lined the streambed to watch them go. Brother Hamar stepped onto the snow bridge and bowed his head. The villagers stood until nearly noon watching the men move down the hill.

Fum climbed high in a tree, overseeing them all, including the several wolves who loped along the ridges above the sleds. Then the skies darkened, and a snow squall devoured both sleds and watchers. The mournful wails of the littlest ones covered the sniffling of the adults as they trudged up the mountainside to their village.

Almost a day's walk north, Fum could see Drakestad had no less sorrow, but those left behind stayed late in their beds and wondered about their men who left the day before.

PART 2

WHEN MEN LEAVE HOME THEY'RE NOT ALONE
THEIR FAMILIES' PRAYERS WOULD BIND THEM.
BUT DEMONS PRAY THEY'LL GET THEIR PREY
SOME PLACE WHERE GOD CAN'T FIND THEM.

BUT, LO, THE WOLVES HAD THREATENED LONGER
AND DROOLED AS FIEND FROM CLOSE TO YONDER
AND GAVE THE WISE MEN PAUSE TO PONDER
"WHICH IS WORSE AND WHICH IS STRONGER?"

From *The Ballad of the Blacksmith's Son*

FIRST DAY

K eri's harness leader, Sturl, sired seven sons and wore a squirrel cap with seven tails to remember them. By accident of height his crew included most of the younger men in the group, which made Brun glad. He figured Sturl knew how to handle young men. Except for his hat, Sturl's approach was always practical, from his short brown beard to his short, clipped sentences.

His young men pulled the small sled late that first afternoon with clouds of frosty breath enveloping them. The sun dropped below the cloud cover and cast long blue shadows from the peaks pointing their way east. Keri and Sturl pulled the two longest harnesses out front. Gantson and Jesspersson wore the shorter harnesses while Gaar and Alex Broke Tooth pushed on the flanks to keep the sled steady.

The larger sled, about thirty paces in front, used three crews under Tharn, Gotthard, and Eldman. Brun put two of his men on the flanks and the rest in front, picking, clearing, and marking the path. They carried wooden shovels to smooth the way. Brun carried a thin pole the width of the big sled to measure the space between boulders and the scrub trees that scrabbled for footing in the snow-covered rocks. Brun had initially

assigned Pekka the measuring duty, but Brun did it now. Rainar, who replaced his son, proved to be inept on skis and could not keep up.

Several men knew this ground, but they still referred to the map. It
was detailed close to Rentvatten but vague where they must cross the
river and then the Tunturri. The route through the snow desert showed
few well-defined landmarks.

For now, the last low eastern hills that marked the beginning of the
Tunturri stood at least twelve days ahead, while behind them the white
peaks of home ripped the sky like canine teeth. A series of ridges and
passes guarded broad snowfields whose gradual slopes rose and fell like
wrinkles on a mussed blanket. Every two hundred paces forward and
down included a push up a dozen steps followed by a short slide down
the other side. Rock outcroppings and brittle mounds of frozen talus
forced them this way and that.

The packed snow supported the men's weight well, but the sleds
needed every bit of their wide runners to keep from sinking too deep.
Keri's shoulders ached and his breath came out in huge clouds. Though
they completed harder pulls in practice, few were as long as this first
day and the men were tired. Their initial enthusiasm died several hills
behind them where Rainar stumbled to catch up.

Cnute, with Brun's men, relayed back the order to halt. Keri stood
panting. Sturl looked back at his crew. "All right, Gaar and Alex, come
take the front harness. Keri, you and I will push until the next stop."

"How about a drink?" asked Jesspersson.

Sturl checked on Brun's activity and nodded. Jesspersson quickly
grabbed the two cups riding on a tether above the ready keg. He turned
the tap for him and Gantson. They gulped down the thick drink and
helped Keri and Sturl repeat the process.

Keri glanced back for Rainar. "Any idea what happened to Pekka?"

Sturl followed Keri's gaze. "Rainar said he fell and broke his arm at
the mill last night."

"How'd he do that?"

"I haven't heard. All I know is Rainar showed up this morning with his own box and told Brun he was Pekka's replacement. Brun was furious."

Gantson shrugged. "Do you suppose Pekka got scared?"

Keri shook his head. "Doubt it. He's really taken to Brun and would follow him anywhere."

Jesspersson contemplated the last inch of ale in his second cup. "Did you know that too much ale can…" He stopped and looked up. Keri was listening and raised an eyebrow. "Uh, well, Gudrun felt sick that last night at the party and, ah…things didn't go so well."

Keri poured himself some more. "What are you talking about?"

Gaar walked up, gulping air like a grounded fish. "When will we stop today?"

Sturl handed him a cup. "Either when Brun finds a problem too big to solve quickly or when he can't see fifty paces to the front."

"He could go quite a while tonight," said Gantson. "That full moon rises early. He might try to go by moonlight and give us some extra time to beat Drakestad."

Eli skied up with a swoosh. Laurel had given him a deep green wool cap with long earflaps that flew two feet in the wind behind him. He learned to make it flip and fly as he moved. Keri wore a long blue scarf from Stjärna.

Eli smiled. "Brun's sent me to find Rainar and bring him in. He said to get some ale for him." He waved a tankard with a hinged top.

Jesspersson reached for the cup. "Nice. Is that silver? Where'd you get it?"

"Rainar's box. Did you see? His box is bigger than the food boxes. There's a bunch of stuff in there besides clothes, even a candle holder."

"Why didn't Birdie Legs just use Pekka's box? He doesn't need all that junk."

Eli shrugged. "Maybe he is used to living like a rich jarl. I don't know."

Jesspersson scoffed.

"Did you hear any more about Pekka?" Gantson tucked his hands into his sleeves for warmth.

"All I heard was he was knocked senseless and Rainar took his place."

Keri nudged Eli. "So, you're his babysitter and servant?"

"No, I'm your rear guard because you are always in the rear." He flipped Keri's blue scarf into his face. Keri snatched at it and remembered the warmth of its giver. He sighed.

Gaar snickered. "Leave Birdie Legs and bring back Pekka."

"Take a torch too," said Sturl over the banter. "You may not get back before dark."

Eli grabbed a pre-made torch from the sled and checked for his tinder box. Then he tromped up the hill looking for Rainar.

"Find out what happened to Pekka!" called Keri.

Gantson sighed. "By dark I'm usually in a cozy barn sitting on a stool with a half-dozen cows. I don't know if my legs will work after dark."

"Moo," said Keri. "Feel at home?"

Sturl drained his cup. "You just keep moving your feet and you'll be fine. All right, back to your places."

Jesspersson knocked snow off his boots. "First I have to feel my feet." He looked back the way they came. "I wonder what they are doing in Rentvatten now."

Keri laughed. "Maybe Gudrun is praying for your feet."

"Well, it's not her feet I am missing." Jesspersson spit into the snow.

Keri cocked his head. "Huh?"

"Let's go," hollered Brun from up front. He bowed his head for a moment as the men took their places. Grinning he put his shoulder to the corner. "SSSuuuut –tah!" and Rentvatten lunged off again.

The moon lit the sparkling blue snow and cast vague shadows off the struggling men. They moved at half speed because of the weak light. Men on the flanks and front carried torch and spear.

Keri heaved at the back of the smaller sled, shivering as his sweat-soaked tunic turned icy. He released one hand to try to flip his scarf around his neck but slipped and fell instead.

"New scarf's gonna kill you," mumbled Jesspersson, pushing on his right.

"Shut up. I'll be fine."

"Right." Jesspersson's Adam's apple bobbed in his long throat. "Just ask that wolf to help you."

Keri, sitting in the snow, laughed, then looked over his shoulder into the grotesque shadows behind him. He jumped up and ran the half-dozen steps to catch up. It wasn't any lighter but at least he was with a fellow human.

Jesspersson laughed.

They heard Brun up front calling his men and both smiled to hear "Halt!" Brun placed the sleds to form two walls against the wind with a large rock outcropping at their other flank. It formed an enclosure big enough for a fire and the men to sleep.

Brun assigned teams to tasks. Sturl's group took charge of unloading the food and kegs. Tharn's team built a fire and unloaded the men's boxes, while Eldman's stretched several large skins for overhead cover.

"Two cups of ale per man tonight," said Tharn. "We need to conserve. If you're still thirsty, we'll put a kettle by the fire to melt snow. Drink all the water you want." Men reached for their cups.

Brun slapped a hand on one man's back. "Goran Flat Nose, your chubby belly elected you cook; besides, you can count higher than your fingers and toes. You also make good ale. Stir up some food. Gotthard! Tharn's plan says your crew does kitchen chores tonight. Ask Goran what he needs. We're famished. Feed us! And remember the pre-dawn guard wakes Goran up so he can get breakfast ready."

The men all chimed in with advice and admonishments to hurry but Goran just laughed and set about his job as he planned it. "Cold grub tonight so you can eat quick and sleep, but something hot at dawn. Enjoy the bread because there won't be much left in a week or so."

Keri grabbed a big hunk of bread from Goran's basket while they formed a line. He threw Jesspersson a piece. The men groaned but laughed as Goran passed out hefty pre-apportioned packets of dried fish, dried beets, and hard cheese.

Tharn glanced at the forty-two separate boxes of food for the forty days of the crossing. "Looks like enough."

Goran shook his head. "I thought so until I saw Keri and Jesspersson eat at the feast. There are a couple other big eaters here too. Mantas for one. They are going to gripe."

Brun walked away from the fire, looking back up the hills. Keri and Tharn followed.

Keri pointed. "Over on the right. A spark against the black." The spark grew as Eli and Rainar crested a small hill. Their torch sputtered as they started down the last slopes.

"Praise God," said Tharn.

Brun grunted, "Amen," and turned back to camp. "I think we did an extra morning's walk after sunset."

Timonen beat the snow off his boots by the sled wall. "If we can do that every day we should cut at least a full day off our arrival in Hilhelm."

Brun kicked the snow. "We can't count on that. We lose a lot of speed at night and the full moon won't be there in a few days. Tonight we were lucky…clear horizon. Picking the trail out is tough. Every shadow looks like a ravine and every ravine looks like a shadow. Clouds would make it impossible."

Timonen pulled on a dry sock. "True, but if we can get just a half-day lead on Drakestad we can win this race…maybe get home sooner. I already miss my wife, and my little Ragnar is ready for his first hunt."

Tharn sat on a rock. "Aye, but we still have weather and wolves and the river and God knows what other surprises in front of us."

Brun grimaced. "And Rainar is no decent replacement for Pekka."

"It proves the proverb," said Tharn, "'Tomorrow is a stranger.'"

FATHER'S WINGS

Stjärna finished arranging Laurel's long braid into a bun. Gudrun sat fiddling with a copper ring she wore on a thong. Laurel said, "Brother Hamar said he would teach me how to read. Want to join me?"

Gudrun made a face. "No, thank you. I'd rather learn something useful."

"Mother says we make cheese today," said Stjärna.

"Cheese and spinning. Every day! There must be more to waiting." Gudrun slumped.

Laurel tilted her head. "It's a start, but we are not the only three left behind. There are about eighteen wives who might enjoy a friendly face."

"It's not like they are all alone." Gudrun furrowed her pale orange eyebrows. "Most have children or parents. Besides, like you say there are eighteen of them."

"True, but they might like some company or help with water or the kids."

Stjärna nodded. "This village gossips so quickly. They might

180

appreciate just having someone around. Mikal brags he's going to have first choice of the ladies at the well. I was worried for Annika, but she is busy now nursing Pekka."

"How's he doing?" asked Gudrun.

"I don't see Annika anymore, so I haven't heard. Did he wake up?"

"Humph!" Laurel made a face. "Whether he's awake or not the village wags already talk of Annika. The lone wives will be next. We can hide under our fathers' wings, but someone needs to protect the sled crew's wives. At least two fell to other men during Sigvard's trek."

Stjärna pushed a hair in place. "I'll ask Oldefar to keep Sami and Mikal at bay. He's looking for God's next mission."

"Brother Hamar will help too, but they can't be everywhere."

Stjärna shrugged. "Only God can be everywhere."

"Oh, I hope not." Gudrun giggled.

Laurel raised an eyebrow.

"Well, there are some times I don't need Him to be looking at me." Gudrun giggled again.

"Those are probably times when He needs to look at you the most."

"Oh, don't be such a stuffy goose, Mother Laurel." Gudrun put out her chin. "I'm sure you remember a few moments you and Eli did not want God looking over your shoulder."

Laurel glared but her neck turned red.

Stjärna stepped between them to get a bone comb. "That's kind of scary. I mean, I think about that night in Cnute's cabin with Keri and wonder what God thought about all that."

"Exactly!" Gudrun put her hands on her hips. "You may never tell us what really happened but if God stood there watching, He knows the truth and you wish He did not!"

Stjärna stamped her foot. "Nothing happened!" Her frame sagged. "It's just that sometimes I feel like I need to go to confession or something."

Gudrun sighed. "I know what you mean. And that's why I don't need God looking at me all the time. Fum showing up is bad enough."

"Fum?"

"Yeah. He was everywhere we went last month. It was like he followed us. After the race we had to hide."

Laurel sighed, "Really? I thought he was just stalking me. But don't we want God to be everywhere all the time protecting us?"

Gudrun thought. "Well, yes, but not Fum."

Stjärna tucked the blue stone necklace into her collar.

Laurel spread her hands. "Then God is our answer. He allowed us into this mess for who knows what reason, so let's ask Him to get us through it."

Stjärna touched her father's shield on the wall. "Oldefar says his grandfathers prayed while they rowed the dragon ships. They may have prayed to the wrong gods, but the point is that you need to do something while you wait for God to act."

"Well," said Gudrun, "with Jesspersson gone, God can go wherever He wants. Fum, too. I'll pray. I've got nothing to hide."

"Really? Nothing?" Laurel laughed. "Then pray for someone else. I know a sled crew who may need prayer when it comes to temptations in Hilhelm."

The three girls exchanged glances. Gudrun started to speak, but Laurel put a finger to her lips. "No protests. Jesspersson, Keri, and even Eli are no better than any other living human. And don't forget my father. They all need to be prayed for and watched over by God."

"All right, I said I'd pray." Gudrun raised her brows. "By the way, has anybody actually seen Fum recently?"

MORNINGS

Long before dawn Keri heard Brun waking first Goran, then the harness leaders. Most of the men slept in pairs under pelts designed for one man to wrap up in. Two or three men together on top of one pelt and under another made everyone warmer. The men favored bearskins. Brun grabbed the skin under Keri and Jesspersson and rolled them out into the snow. "Up, lads, up. I need your long legs today."

As they blinked in the early twilight Brun walked toward the sunrise. The wind blew directly in his face from the east. It lifted dry snow off the hills and swirled it down among the men as they awoke. Brun bowed his head and was still.

Jesspersson clutched his bearskin. "Is he praying?"

"I think so."

"Women's work."

"Don't let Brother Hamar hear you say that."

"Well, yeah, but every day?"

Keri stretched. "It seems to make him feel good."

"I'd rather sleep."

"Didn't Eli's mother used to say, 'Prayer is better than sleep'?"

"No that was his oldemar, the Bedouin slave."

Brun burst upon the crew, bellowing, "Everyone changes boots to-day! And socks. Make sure you have dry feet when you put them on."

People shuffled this way and that with leaders prodding the sleepy ones to get the gear packed. Goran's pot steamed over the flames. A general groaning and joking acted as a background to the murmuring of the fire.

The sky began to lighten and the last stars faded away. "Stjärna," whispered Keri when he found the morning star.

Goran swirled his massive iron ladle and smiled. "Bring your cups!" He filled each cup with hot barley porridge.

Lars, Laurel's father, grabbed a hunk of bread from the pile and sniffed his cup. "Just like Mother's."

Mantas poked Goran in the belly. "Only if your mother was ugly and shaved under her nose."

"Then this ought to suit you fine," said Goran, smiling.

Keri laughed. Eli came over while he tied his boots.

"I didn't see you much yesterday, Keri."

"You were looking the wrong direction. I saw plenty of your be-hind. Every time we changed positions, you were on sled or scout in front of me."

"Maybe, but at least Rainar didn't make you late for dinner."

"Did he say anything about what happened to Pekka?"

"He chattered at first. Probably nervous from being alone. Then he couldn't talk for all the panting."

"Yeah, but what happened?"

Eli brushed his faint mustache. "He said Pekka fell from the grind-ing floor to the storeroom through the trapdoor."

"What was Pekka doing on the grinding floor? There's no grinding this time of year. Why would he go up there? They sleep in the house beside the mill when they're not in town."

"I don't know. Rainar said grandfather Leksa found him in the storeroom."

"I wonder how he missed seeing an open trapdoor."

"Well, it was night."

Keri wrapped his blue scarf to have a tail to flap behind him. "Yeah…but it's his house. He would know where everything is."

Jesspersson came by. "Sturl says we are on scout first today, Keri. Get your skis."

"Great," said Keri. "Funny about Pekka, though." Keri grabbed his skis off the rack.

Sturl came by, checked his men's boots and socks. "If you're done with the porridge, Goran's putting the ale out now. Two drafts this morning and we're off."

Keri used his knife to flip the last morsels of barley into his mouth. Jesspersson went to the keg, drew off a full draft, and drank it straight down.

Goran watched. "Nice going, king of the keg. Give your stomach a chance. Drink the next one more slowly or you'll be sick."

"Ale doesn't bother me," said Jesspersson.

"Jesspersson, older men than you have said that and then fallen off the bench."

"Clean up. Reload!" Brun was in full throat. "Let's go, crew leaders! We should be moving already. Push these men. I want these sleds moving from the moment I can see a hundred paces until the moment I can't! What are you doing? Waiting for the daffodils to pop through the snow?"

Cnute approached Brun. "'Can't ge' Rainar movin'. He's all cramped up an' cryin'."

Keri and Jesspersson glanced at each other.

Brun went over to the pile of fur with Rainar inside. There was an exchange of words which started softly and then turned impatient. Brun looked around. "Keri, Jesspersson, come here. Help me grab this fur ball and throw it on the sled."

They grinned. With Brun and Jesspersson on one end and Keri at the other, they made two tentative swings and threw a scrambling pile of furs, including an ermine pillow and Rainar, on the top of the big sled. He protested but everyone just laughed and moved to their assigned places. When Rainar's head appeared, Goran threw him a hunk of bread and closed the food box.

Brun readjusted his men around the small sled to work without Rainar. He glanced at the sun. "Scouts, find us a path. Get going."

Keri finished his ale, tucked his cup in his tunic, and stamped his skis. He and Jesspersson started after Sturl.

Brun bowed his head briefly, put his shoulder against the bigger sled, and flexed his legs. "All right, Rentvatten. Let's go. Take up the slack. Pull, push. SSSSuut – tah!" He heaved and the sled lurched forward.

In all the chatter only Rainar saw the silver-gray wolf among some rocks. Wide-eyed, he pointed, but nobody noticed.

TANGLED

Down and down they went, sometimes through blinding sunshine and sometimes through blinding snowfall. After two days, cloudy weather forced them to travel only by daylight through sharp passes into wide white meadows. Snowdrifts squatted deep on one side of the valleys like huge white bubbles ready to burst. The windblown opposite side scraped rocky and hard on the sleds' runners. Keri and Eli gaped at the muscular formations, blue glaciers, and sudden deep crevices. Spirits soared at the sights, but the work crushed the bodies. Gudrun's uncle Gotthard spat into the morning fire and called the terrain "a beautiful hell."

The same wind that formed the drifts found its way into their clothes and turned their uncovered ears bright red. Keri and Eli, with no beards, wound their faces in their long-tailed wraps. On bad mornings the bitter breeze moaned like an anguished witch. The pitch changed as the wind intensified and found new raw peaks to scratch.

The low sun cast long shadows that looked like obstacles from afar. The scouts traveled twice the distance of the sleds, going further out to see whether an apparent rock ridge or ravine was really just a shadow.

Eli proved particularly adept at finding routes, and Brun often turned to him.

They occasionally saw rabbit or other rodent sign, but the scrub brush or sprigs of dead grass offered them little fodder. Traps set at night caught skinny prey. Even the cheerful grosbeak and waxwing birds disappeared. The wind found only rocks, snow, and men to bristle against.

Eli, out of sight of the sleds and his partner, scouted for a way around a stream cut. He hesitated at the top of a slope that looked useful. The talus at the edge of the crumbled streambank might offer a crossing. The powdered snow came up to Eli's calves and the gentlest of winds brushed it across his path. He poked his ski pole into the powder. Shuffling his skis down the slope to test it, he fell sideways, head below his feet on a sharp incline. He disappeared in a fluff of snow that rose and settled again like flies disturbed on a carcass.

"Crap!"

His skis twisted on the uneven bank and wedged into the snow-covered rocks. Grunting, he struggled to get free but instead found his feet strapped and pinned by the skis above him. Any movement dropped his upper body deeper into the frozen streambed. His bow pushed up into his face and only his left arm remained out of the snow. He dragged the bow out of his way and shoved the green cap off his eyebrows. Sweeping the snow away from his leg, he could see his left boot. He fumbled with the boot strap, but his gloved hand could not grip it. Biting his glove, he pulled it off, but he still could not untie the knot. The rocks and snow beneath him pushed pain and cold into his right side. As he tried to pull himself up, the edge of a rock dug into his ribs, taking his breath away. He eased down and steeled himself for another try.

Wiggling, he forced his right arm under him. It hurt but he had purchase and it took some weight off his side. Picturing the knot, he thought about how to approach it. He took a deep breath and pushed up. His left hand found the knot and he tried to get a grip on one cord to loosen it. His right hand ached, crushed by his weight, and his left hand turned icy numb in a fruitless effort. His thumbnail snapped back.

"'s wounds!"

Thumb went to mouth and tasted of blood. A glance showed the damage. He cursed slowly, "By...God's...wounds!" He stuck it back in his mouth as much for the warmth as the pain relief. His fingers tingled, so he grabbed his glove. He could not get it on straight without crushing his right side.

"Arrgghh!" He slumped into the drift, arching his back to free his right hand.

An eddy of wind swept through, making the air as white as the ground and leaving him momentarily disoriented. The wind died and the disturbed flakes settled like a light blanket.

"Jaako!" The snow muffled his voice. His scouting partner searched in the other direction when they found the streambed. "Jaako!" He listened. Nothing. The snow buried all noise in an awful weight. He heard no sound; not the wind, not the men on the sleds, not even his own breathing disturbed the stillness. He remembered a Brother Hamar sermon: "Hell is eternal, absolute nothingness." He leaned back and looked over his forehead. The world was upside down. The slope fell away forever and blended into the like-colored sky with nary a soul between him and the end of the world.

"Oh, God," he sighed, then smiled. "Sorry about the ''s wounds.'"

He heard a crunch. His eyes turned to the sound. Up the slope a diminutive gray she-wolf with a twig of pine needles tangled behind her ear stood examining him.

"Jesus."

The wolf tilted her head as if to listen.

Eli reached for the knife in his belt. His half-on glove wouldn't grip it.

The wolf watched…interested…took a step.

"Oh, Jesus." Eli bit off his glove. His freezing bare hand fumbled but pulled the knife and pointed it at the wolf.

The wolf lowered her head and her green eyes flared. One foot rose, hesitated, stepped. She cocked her head and then rolled her eyes as if looking behind him.

Eli glanced back, saw nothing but snow. He turned back and the wolf stood at his boot. He raised the knife, but paused: a scent…evergreen…pine…but not a tree within three day's march.

The large pink tongue licked out as she sniffed his snagged ski.

"Jesus, help me." Eli braced to lunge, hoping the knife would at least cut the black nose nuzzling his foot. He tensed, gathering strength.

The wolf suddenly bit the knot at his ski. A tooth found leather and she pulled.

Eli could feel an individual lace slipping out of the knot.

She looked him in the eye, and winked.

He could feel the knot release his foot. The wolf stepped back and settled in the snow, watching.

Jerking his foot free, he slid partway down the slope in a tumble of snow, arrows, and skis. He waved his knife and struggled to one knee with other ski splayed behind him. His hands so numb he could barely keep the knife straight.

The wolf's ears laid back and she began to growl.

Mesmerized by her green eyes, Eli just stared.

The wolf tensed, its ears perked. Eli lowered the knife. Ears suddenly turned back, the wolf leapt clear over him and bounded away down the slope.

"Eli!" Jaako, Brun, and Tharn ran down to him. Brun glared down the slope, spear at the ready. The wolf vanished.

With four extra hands, they pulled Eli free. Jaako grabbed him.

"We couldn't find you. The snow filled your tracks. Why didn't you call out?"

"I did."

"We didn't hear you."

"I didn't call you."

"Huh?"

Tharn smiled. "They say that everyone who fears calls on God."

"That seems to be true." Eli flapped his arms for warmth. "And He sent help. But I wasn't sorry He brought you along too."

Eli kept the rest of the story to himself.

PROVERBS

Over the days Rainar's muscles worked into passable shape. As he was still clumsy, no one welcomed him as a pushing partner, but even his body was needed as others fell temporarily injured or developed coughs. After the first week, it seemed someone new rode the sleds every day to recover from something. Nighttime, the camp settled into a routine of repair, quiet conversation, and loud snores. Goran handed out salve and willow tea for the aches.

In the eternal twilight of the valleys, nighttime came slowly, turning the thin white clouds in the thin white sky to a deep blue black. Creeping down the mountainsides, huge dark clouds loomed like ominous cobalt trolls oozing over the peaks. Late returning scouts said the golden campfire flickered like a tiny sun against the tormented rocks.

After twilight the sky frequently hung clear and black above them. Gauzy clouds hedged in the horizon, forming an illusion they camped in a deep bowl with the fire at its bottom. When the stars glowed a holy white in the midnight velvet, the earth held none of its heat and the temperatures dropped. Beards frosted over. Food was never hot. The men huddled under their furs like children.

Having only the general direction of the sun on the southern horizon and the vague map to guide them, the sleds traveled on instinct and faith. Only Eldman, Tharn, and Rainar read well and they struggled with Brun to clarify and interpret their predecessors' map. They estimated another week to get to the Tunturri, where the slippery slope became an endless plain of rolling snow and ice.

Only a week out, Brun sounded hoarse from shouting all day. Goran made him some warm water with salt. Brun gargled and spit into the snow outside the circle of light. He stood staring at the night sky.

Tharn joined him. "You should pace yourself better. The old wives say that 'a dry cough is death's trumpet.' Let the harness leaders do more individual leading."

"True, they know their men better than I."

Tharn crossed his arms. "Anybody new look lame or sick to you?"

"Viktor is better and won't need to ride tomorrow. Keep an eye on Eldman. He's the oldest and is pushing himself to keep up. He may pull something in his pride. Timonen may be pressing too hard as well."

"Eldman looked exhausted when we stopped. I think he fell asleep during the blessing at dinner. He's lost a lot of weight."

"Make sure he is eating and drinking his ration." Brun sniffled.

Tharn leaned in toward him. "I think the youngsters are holding up physically. Are you seeing any homesickness?"

"Jesspersson seems a little moody, but Eli and Keri are all right. Godwin too. Still goofing around. Kids. Maybe a little too much ale. I'll try to spend some time with them."

"How's Cnute look to you?"

"I haven't seen him this well since he married Liisa. New man. Losing his gut. Put his old red cap back on. His beard's trimmed. It's white. Wasn't it brown before?"

"Maybe. But I'm sure it wasn't white."

"I think he's growing his hair back too under that red cap. As his hair grows out his stomach grows in and he seems to be stronger. He even seems to have rid himself of lice."

Tharn rocked back and forth. "Perhaps, but that empty eye hole is vulnerable to the cold. I think it hurts his head. He tries to cover it when he skis."

"Hmm…" Brun pursed his lips. "I'll keep an eye on him."

They looked at each other, then laughed.

Brun glanced at the sleeping men. "Remind me to ask Mantas and Gotthard to keep down the swearing. We don't need the boys learning that. May be too late with Eli."

"Not Gotthard's fault. Eli's been toying with it since last fall. He's still a little embarrassed when he cusses. He said he apologized to God after the wolf incident and is trying to stop. Vow or something."

"Well, I don't want to get a reputation in Hilhelm of being crude. They already think we're high country oafs."

"I can't recall Cnute cussing lately. Another nice change."

Brun turned to Thran. "Have you gotten any more out of Rainar about Pekka?"

"Nope. Same story. He fell through the trapdoor. Grandfather Leksa found him."

"Was he drunk?"

"Pekka? Maybe. Rainar didn't say. Maybe he was drinking for courage."

Brun shook his head. "That doesn't sound like him. Rainar swore he would come on this trip and here he is."

"Maybe Pekka couldn't sleep. The proverb says, 'Grief will sleep but anxiety will not.'"

"Prayer helps me sleep." Brun moved to the fire. "You don't suppose he had a girl there and Rainar caught him?"

"Rainar said Pekka didn't like girls."

"Ach," scoffed Brun. "Annika was after him at the race, and by the feast Pekka was chasing Annika. Gayle pointed it out. Didn't you see?"

"Maybe she is trying to fulfill the old saying that 'the first to the mill is the first to grind.'"

Brun chuckled. "Saints! Where do you get those sayings? But you could be right. There's a lot of wealth in Pekka's marriage."

"Well, whatever happened quenched Rainar's idea that this trek would be a fun adventure."

"Maybe, and it proves that silver can't buy muscles." Brun shook his head. "There are ten other men in the village I would rather have here to take Pekka's place."

Tharn yawned. "Well, Rainar doesn't ride much now and we are making pretty good time."

"Yeah." Brun pulled his sleeping fur from his box. "Most of our men look good and the slope helps move the sleds."

"Hmmm, but that ice… The Psalmist says, 'Surely you place them on slippery ground; you cast them down to destruction.'"

"Isn't that saying about sliding into sin?"

Tharn smiled. "Well, yes, but isn't the earth just proof of God's sayings? Just as people slip easily from thinking carelessly about sin to actually doing it, so do we think carelessly about ice and then fall down its slippery slope."

"Always the philosopher. Right now I think we have more chance to fall to ice than to sin."

"Perhaps. But the wise man says, 'Only he who sleeps doesn't sin.'"

Brun laughed. "No more sayings! I'm going to sleep." They went to their furs.

A few steps away Jesspersson pulled his arms in tighter and shuddered under the furs back to back with Keri.

"You all right?" murmured Keri.

"Yeah, but after what I dreamed about Gudrun last night, I'm not so sure you can't sin in your sleep."

"Stop thinking about it."

"How? From what you and Stjärna did you should know about as much as...never mind."

"Shut up or you'll be sleeping by yourself." Keri lay with his eyes wide open and staring into the fire.

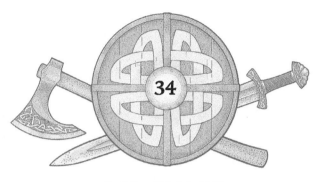

ON GUARD

Keri and Jesspersson stumbled to their feet in the midnight cold. They exchanged warm sleeping furs for spears and guard duty.

Sturl grabbed each lad by a shoulder. "We've put the next allotment of logs by the fire. Just keep it going, and bright. You know the instructions. Watch the food cache for varmints; don't look at the fire. Don't lose your night vision. Great northern lights tonight."

Keri nodded, still stupid with sleep. Sturl disappeared.

Jesspersson nudged him. "Just like before?"

"Yep, you walk around one way, I'll go the other. Keep moving, stay warm."

"With no clouds, nothing is warm. It's so cold my spit turns to ice before it hits the ground."

"Be happy. It makes the sleds go easier."

"Yeah, but it also turns the morning porridge to ice."

Keri put a hand to the fire. "Take bigger bites."

"I need your bigger mouth."

Jesspersson hunched into his cloak and plodded around the big sled. Keri listened a moment to the variety of snores and trudged off in the other direction.

When they met, Keri stopped. "Did you hear a whistle earlier tonight?"

"A whistle?"

"Yeah, like Fum plays."

"Nope. But I was so tired I might have slept through a dog fight."

"Maybe it was a dream. But I thought I heard it the other night too."

"Maybe you're homesick, Keri. Maybe your ears are too big."

They resumed their rounds.

The waning moon riding the horizon cast a dim blue light on the snow, forming fuzzy, fantastic shadows on the rocks and drifts. Hummocks of snow looked like tiny huts snug and inviting. Keri gazed into the sky, fascinated by the northern lights blurring the heavens with their random pastel patterns. Sometimes sharp with spirals, other times like smeared green blood on a cloth, the mysterious cloud-like formations floated across the sky.

Keri watched one stem rise from a distant peak before spreading across the northern horizon as if windblown. Keri stood remembering when he first saw the lights with his father from the watchtowers.

Twenty leagues west Laurel stood with Stjärna at Rentvatten's watchtower, gazing at the northern sky seemingly filled with colored pollen swirling in a lazy stream. Somewhere in the dark village Fum played his tune.

Stjärna leaned into Laurel. "What's your favorite story about the lights? Souls of dead maidens? The tail of the giant fox brushing up the snow?"

Laurel shrugged. "I don't hold to those so much as the idea that the God who created heaven and earth decided that the colors of the trees and sky were wonderful for the day. Sunsets and sunrises were fine for marking dawn and dusk, but He needed something to decorate the night."

"Weren't the moon and stars enough?"

"Sure, for people who sleep in warm lands where the moon and stars are cool at best and cold at worst. For those of us up here in the snow country, God commanded the lights in the night to let us know He is there even when pagans think He is sleeping. He fills the northern sky to sing us to sleep in His arms. It is better than a Brother Hamar homily any time to make me a believer in God's power...and to help me sleep."

"Well, I hope that power is flowing down on Eli and Keri about now." Stjärna sighed. "Can you see their fire tonight?"

"No, they are too far away for us to see anything, even on a clear night like this. We were lucky to see their glow that second night."

"They could be down in a ravine where their firelight would be blocked."

Laurel shook her head. "I hope they are just too far away. They need to make good time."

"Sami says they have already been eaten by wolves and that's why no one has seen any sign of them for nine days."

"Sami is trying to scare someone into his bed. I hope they like fleas."

Both girls shivered.

Stjärna laughed. "Which reminds me, have you seen Gudrun or Annika recently? My sister says they must be hiding with Fum."

"I spoke with Annika by the gate. She's still staying at the mill, nursing Pekka. He's awake now but his mother won't let him out of the house. Annika is concerned. Says his arm hurts badly and he is still addled from that lump on the back of his head."

"How did I not notice when Annika and Pekka got together?"

Laurel turned to Stjärna. "She's been stalking him since he started working with the sled. Couldn't you see? He's filled out a little and when you get him into working clothes, he doesn't seem so soft."

"No. I'm afraid Keri blinded me for a while. What about Gudrun? She was here every night at first, and at the well, you know, showing off the copper ring Jesspersson gave her. But suddenly she's gone. Could she be looking around?"

Laurel snorted. "I doubt she's with Sami. Though I think he offered her fleas a while back."

"Yeah, but they don't seem to be friends, especially after his fight with Grandfather. Besides, Jesspersson may be poor but he isn't so bad." Stjärna shrugged. "Maybe too many days of no sightings made her decide to stay in bed."

Laurel yawned. "Bed sounds good to me. Mother is tired of me coming back late and waking them up. She sleeps lightly with Father gone. I guess I should go home and let God watch over Eli and Father."

"And Keri…"

"And all of them, and all of us," said Sigvard, who had climbed up quietly behind them.

"Oldefar!" Stjärna hugged him. "You are up late."

"I seldom sleep through the night at my age. Besides, with so many men gone, I find I am called by the Spirit to the watchtowers just to keep an eye on things. Twice I've found Sami or Mikal lurking in the shadows."

"What did you do?"

"Ha! I spanked them and sent them to bed."

"Oh, Oldefar." Stjärna laughed.

Laurel clutched her cloak tighter. "Have you seen Fum? We hear him, but no one has seen him since the sled left."

Sigvard shrugged. "Nope, Brother Hamar hasn't either. I don't know where he is, but I do hear him on nights like this. When I follow the tune, it just moves to another spot."

"It's not like him to disappear like that."

"Has he really disappeared?" Sigvard shrugged. "We know he's here somewhere from his music."

"Yeah. Maybe he's acting as a watchman with you, Oldefar."

"Maybe. There are outsiders who might seek to do some mischief to our weakened village."

"Why us?" Laurel stifled a yawn. "We are not a rich town."

"You are riches enough for some people, young lady. You two would bring much gold in the markets of Byzantium. Eli's oldemar did."

The girls exchanged glances. "Well, then, we need to add extra prayers for us as well as the sled crew."

"The sled should be well enough for now." Sigvard rubbed his beard. He gazed to the east. "The first two weeks are mostly down-hill and the load gets lighter. Once they cross the sawtooth passes and reach the Tunturri there's a whole new set of problems. They need good weather and good luck. Barring some accident or a storm, their weariness doesn't really begin until they cross the Usko River."

"What happens after that?"

"It is hard to say. There's a long, barren stretch towards Hilhelm. It's when the wolves really make themselves felt. Everyone's exhausted and the enthusiasm's worn off. Tempers flare and the selfish personalities of the weaker men come out. That's why Ole walked guard duty alone that night the wolves took him: his partner went back to bed. It is a time of trial for the group and individuals. And the river crossing? Like a bear, not easy. The ice might not bear the weight. We disassembled the sled and carried it over pieces at a time."

Stjärna gazed east. "When will we know if they crossed safely?"

"Sometime late next fall after the season for wars ends and the men come home. Not before."

A large cloud drifted over the mountain and obscured the baleful northern lights. Fum's whistle stopped.

THE WHITE STONE

The sleds waited in the morning light by the edge of a short, steep ridge. Brun took Eli and Sturl to find a shallower slope. The crew rested around and on top of the sleds. Keri and Cnute sat on a wind-cleared rock.

Cnute squinted his one eye and pointed east. "How far's it t' that peak? I can't judge distance no more."

"I'd give it about a league." Keri looked at the dark eyehole in Cnute's otherwise pink and white bearded face.

Cnute growled and covered the space with his red knit cap.

Keri looked away. "Sorry."

"Same's anybody. Ever'body's curious." His voice sounded like a wooden shovel scraping gravel.

"Well, it seems like it would make you cold or something."

"Who cares?" Cnute slapped the eye socket through the cap then hung his head. His voice softened. "Sometimes I packs a little wool in't."

"Hope that helps." Keri gazed down the ridge. "Why did you do it?"

Cnute kept his head down. The breeze flipped the tail of his cap. He caught it and caressed the fabric. "The eye?"

"Yeah, I mean, what's more precious than your eyes?"

He sighed and looked up. "'Guess that's the point: delib'rate important sacrifice t' clear m' guilt an' cleanse m' heart. I figured m' eye was important an' it had helped me t' sin so..." He fiddled with his gloves.

"It must have hurt."

"Yeah...I's pretty numb t' everything what with m' Liisa dead an' weeks in a' snow."

"Did it help?"

"Plucking m' eye? Not hardly. When I woke tied t' Brother Hamar's cot I still felt th' anger an' rage...like God didn' approve. An' t' eye hurt like hell. Sorry. Brun said not t' cuss. Looks ign'rant."

Keri shrugged. "Brother Hamar said you were lucky to live through it."

"He's right. Packed in a bunch o' herbs an' stuff. Prayin' every time I woke up. Lotta hot water too." Cnute kicked ice off his boot.

"But something changed recently." Keri paused. "You're not the same as when I first delivered wood to you."

Cnute shrugged. "Nothin's changed 'cept me. Wife still gone. Wolf still lives. Voice gone. Tongue bit, won't obey. All I got's charcoal." He looked up at Keri. "But then I pulled th' white stone. Before...m' life was a trek t' get revenge. All I saw's failure an' that devil wolf. I's trying t' show God I could do it...prove I was a man. That white stone... slapped me. I looked t' God, an' said 'What do you want o' me?'"

Keri studied Cnute as he kept talking. "I tried t' repent a couple times after th' eye by trying t' stop m' drinking, m' anger. I failed. I's still too angry at the wolf...an' God. Now I'm changed. Askin' God what He's laid out fer me 'stead of telling Him what I wants laid out. I'm letting God do the thinkin' an' take th' responsibility. Funny. I haven't felt this alive, this free, since m' Liisa died."

Keri nodded. "I'm sorry. It must be hard."

Cnute let out a breath and looked at Keri. "No, I'm sorry. I been rude t' ye in a past. Ye been patient an' steady wi' me 'bove all men save yer father an' Brother Hamar. I hopes ye can forgive me. Call m' frien', or at least companion." He stripped off a glove and reached his hand out to Keri.

Keri turned to him surprised and took his hand. "I am your friend, Cnute. As Brun said, this sled has made us all brothers."

"Thanks anyways."

They sat silent, staring out.

"So you don't care about the black wolf anymore?"

"Oh, no! I want 'at firstborn devil t' eat m' spear point much as ever. But God called t' me...wants me fer somethin', some task. Can't see it yet. But I think God wants t' do it *with* me 'stead of me trying t' do it by m'self."

"Do you think the wolf will be out here?" Keri gestured down the hill.

"Not sure." Cnute absently fingered a crudely carved wooden cross hanging about his neck. "But God has a better chance t' put him before me than I do of a catching 'im."

"I haven't seen many wolves yet," said Keri. "I haven't even heard one."

"That's when they's most dangerous...when ye don't see 'em or hear 'em."

Keri laughed. "I think I keep hearing Fum's whistle at night. Have you?"

Cnute smiled and his hand went to his wool vest but stopped. "Nope. Not Fum's." Then he frowned. "But I didn't hear no wolves f' years, neither. Then I opened that door t' our cabin. There he was: crouchin'."

Down the ridge Brun started waving. Tharn called the leaders to harness their crews. "Keri, organize Sturl's men until we get down there."

"Yes, sir."

Cnute stood up. "Yer a powerful man, Keri, but don't ever un-ner-estimate the 'bility of a wolf t' sneak up on ye. Even one ye think ye tamed."

SHADOWS

Down, down, up and down the terrain fought the men and the sleds. The ground refused to cooperate. Joints wiggled loose, the runners took a beating, and harnesses snapped in the cold. Eldman the carpenter fussed with constant repairs. Even skis found ways to crack or split and put their owners afoot.

Stress plagued their clothing. Seams in boots and pants leaked and ripped. The men spent hours at night reapplying wax and pine tar to patches and stiches. They hotly contested places close to the fire's heat and light for mending. No one ever felt completely dry.

Shoulders and necks ached. Men woke in the night to paralyzing cramps in their calves that left a shadow of pain long after the muscled knot released. Most of the men fought sniffles that froze yellow in their beards and raked their throats in the cold air. Viksten was fighting a debilitating cough.

Brun approached Rainar at dinner. "Hey, Rainar, you're Viksten's fur mate. He pulled a lot of extra sled for you when we started. Can you pull guard duty tonight without him? Let him get some extra sleep, maybe cure that cough?"

Rainar shrugged. "Why not? Same order as usual?"

"Yep."

Brun and Cnute woke Rainar that night, set him up, and went to their furs.

Rainar hoisted his spear and pulled his bearskin cloak around his shoulders. He paused and stared at the furs where Viksten snored. Sniffling, he walked to the gap between the two sleds and the rock where Brun left an entrance to their protected area. Rainar scratched his ribs, yawned, and wrapped a lamb's wool scarf around his once groomed face.

With the fire behind him, his shadow wobbled in the snowdrifts. Rainar glowered at the darkness. He cursed his sniffles. He cursed the cold. He cursed his nickname. He cursed the journey. He decided he was sick, weak, alone, and surrounded by men he hated. He cursed their jokes. He cursed his father's stinginess. "A plague on him!" he said aloud. It didn't make him feel better and created a measure of superstitious religious guilt to add to his misery. He hung his head.

The fire flared and his shadow rose tall in the snowbanks. Rainar made what he imagined was a gruff face and exaggerated the shadow by raising his spear and cloak. His image in the snow became a mighty warrior slaying first a great wolf, then the yellow horsemen. The shadow grew and he pantomimed saving the sled from annihilation at the cliffs. Arrogantly he tossed curt comments to his cowed sled companions who begged him to lead them. Finally, his dark specter became the sole healthy survivor dragging the pitiful men of Rentvatten into the cheering crowds at Hilhelm, where his father emerged to beg for forgiveness.

He was engulfed by a very fluid sneeze, which tinseled his beard, the fantasy shattered. Rainar's eyes teared up as he gasped for air and pulled the cloak close to him. He remembered his father's last words. "Don't disgrace us and die ugly, Birdie Legs." He cursed again. His shadow shrank back to nearly normal size and a wolf howl filled the empty night.

He wiped his eyes and tried to focus as he backed up with his spear pointing into the dark. A large silver wolf examined him from the edge of the light and then loped away.

Several men mumbled from the sleeping area. "Shut up for God's sake."

Heavier, deeper, the howl came across the night again.

"Jeez," said Mantas, "that's a blasted wolf."

Several men leapt up and grabbed for their weapons. "Where's the guard?"

"I'm here." Mesmerized, Rainar stood firm by the food boxes. "I'm right here. It's out there somewhere. Not here."

Timonen threw more wood on the fire.

Brun was up. "Timonen, stop! Don't waste tonight's allotment. Haven't you ever heard a wolf before? Back to sleep. Tomorrow comes soon enough and Rainar has us covered. Sleep, you mighty men. You'll need your energy when the wolves finally do show up."

Brun went quietly to Rainar. "Did you see anything?"

"Maybe a shadow."

"Have you heard anything?"

"No, just that wolf."

Brun looked closely at him in the firelight. "I knew you would do all right. I remember you on the boar hunts when we were kids." Rainar smiled. "You can handle this, but no one should be on guard duty alone. I shouldn't have asked you to do it. I'll finish the watch with you."

"I'm all right. I was startled by the sudden noise, but it didn't scare me much."

Brun noticed their shadows bouncing on the drifts. "Good. How are your legs doing? You've been pushing the sleds better lately. Come on, I'll walk with you a bit."

They walked the perimeter talking of hunting and old friends.

The wolves didn't howl again.

They just watched.

Brun and Rainar were relieved by Eli and Viktor, who walked in opposite directions around the camp. "The wind shifted," said Viktor as Eli passed him the tenth time. "If it comes from the west for long it usually brings snow."

Eli looked up in the sky and saw nothing. The stars had disappeared into the high, thin clouds. "Did you hear a whistle last night?" he asked on the fifteenth pass.

"Nope. I dreamed of home but no whistles."

"I thought I heard Fum."

"Probably a wishful, homesick dream. I dream of my family."

"I wish I dreamed of Laurel."

"No, you don't. It makes the absence hurt more."

"It might be a nice hurt."

"Bittersweet is more like it." Viktor glanced at the sky. "I think it's time to wake up Goran."

Eli grunted with his face hunched deep in the exaggerated earflaps of Laurel's green cap. His watery eyes peered out at the pre-dawn's light blue snowfields, but his mind was as far west as the wind that blew on Rentvatten.

FLAKES

Laurel came out of the shadows and caught up to Gudrun, who walked to the well in the pre-dawn snowfall.

Laurel smiled. "You're up early."

"No more than you." Gudrun kept her back to Laurel.

"Trouble sleeping?" Laurel jogged a couple steps to get closer.

"No." Her face changed from frown to polite smile. She turned. "With my sister married there is more work to do for those of us left behind."

"She's been married a year or more."

Gudrun turned away. Silence except for the dry snow squeaking under their footsteps and the whispers of the wind in the trees.

Laurel ducked her head to try to look into Gudrun's eyes. "We've missed you, Stjärna and I, around the well and such."

"I've been busy."

"It's been sad and quiet with the boys gone. Are you missing Jesspersson?"

"No! Yes…of course." She took a breath. Her hand went to the copper ring hanging from her neck. "It's been no fun."

"Stjärna and I find being with friends helps."

"Well, it can't help me." Gudrun twisted away and walked off with her bucket still empty.

Laurel watched her leave as the snow fell harder. She looked up, calculating the sky and air as people who live close to the land do. She blinked some flakes out of her eyes and shook her head. "Big snow coming."

Far to the east the snow didn't begin to fall until late morning. Thick and clumpy splats fell fast among lighter flakes winging and dancing to the ground. After a half hour, all the flakes were smaller and more determined in their dive to the earth.

Jesspersson caught some snow in his mouth. "At least the wind is behind us now." He stumbled as they pushed up yet one more slope.

Keri caught the extra weight and grunted. "Yeah, but remember small flakes mean a big snow."

"Well, if it keeps snowing, it may be a little warmer tonight. You know, cloud cover holds the heat."

"It's hard to breathe with snow on your nose." They cleared the small rise, and the sled shuddered down the other side.

Jesspersson raised his arms and stretched to his full height. "I bet you had plenty of heat when Stjärna thawed out in your arms."

"Hey, why do you always come back to that? Nothing happened! I was more scared than anything." Keri kicked at the sled.

"Well, I've been there too, only my girl wasn't so icy and I tell you there's nothing to be scared of." Jesspersson chuckled.

Keri stopped pushing. "What?!"

The sled veered. Gaar and Alex pushing at the other side cried out. "Hey, what are you guys doing over there!" said Gaar.

"Sorry." Keri caught up and put his weight to the sled. "What do you mean, 'nothing to be scared of'?"

"Well, since you and Stjärna did it, I convinced Gudrun that we could do it. Nobody except Sami stayed mad at you, so I figured...you know."

"We didn't do anything!"

"What?" It was Gaar again.

"Nothing!"

Jesspersson leaned closer to Keri. "Half the village thinks you did, and the other half is pretty sure Eli and Laurel have been doing it too. They're laughing behind their hands. And if you really didn't, you are really missing out."

"I can't talk about this right now," gasped Keri as they joggled the sled over a rock. "You're making me angry."

"We'll have to ration the ale even more," said Goran, skiing alongside Brun and Tharn. "They drink so much during the day that I can't make enough to keep up. Plus, we are running through our supplies of malt and barley faster than we planned."

Brun smiled. "I like fresh ale."

"So does everyone else, but it still takes two days to make it. Three is better. Besides, we use more wood to make more ale and I don't know how long we can do that."

"What do we do?" asked Tharn.

"Let them have ale while they pull, but let's go with hot water at night. The water tends to freeze during the day anyway. I'll set aside a water-only kettle by the fire."

Brun shook his head. "Melted snow tastes funny. Ale is better."

Goran raised his hands. "Ach, true, but warm water heals the chilly body as well as the tingle of ale. And the men don't need any alcohol encouragement to sleep."

"Fine with me." Tharn shrugged. "Somebody said pure water is the world's first medicine."

Brun sighed. "Yeah, but I'm not sick. So, whenever you can, slip us a mug of ale."

The cook glanced at his food boxes. "Maybe I can find an herb to help the snow water taste better."

"Just don't make it turn yellow."

Tharn frowned. "How's the food holding out?"

"We are eating a box a day as we planned, but neither the traps nor our bow-carrying scouts have brought in what we'd hoped."

"Yeah, and everybody is losing weight."

Brun waved at the men. "Everyone is burning food like a hearth burns wood."

"Well, I packed each box to feed forty and it is disappearing like we were feeding fifty. Some of the kids are still growing. I think Keri could eat two rations every meal."

"Do we have any dried apples or anything that could supplement the meals?"

"Yep, each box carries extra crackers, cheese, or dried fruit. And they finish it every night. So, that's what we have. Plus, of course, two days' emergency boxes."

"Well, it's too early to think about using that. Maybe when we sight the Hilhelm mountains."

Tharn raised his index finger. "The Good Book says, 'The plans of the diligent surely lead to abundance.'"

The cook laughed. "Maybe, but I think Keri, and Jesspersson for that matter, would eat both the plans and the diligent right now if I boiled them."

BEING FIRST

The wind and snow grew worse as they broke for midday rest. The scouts disappeared in and out of squalls all morning and the sun wasn't even a bright spot in the haze. Brun reckoned they cleared another pass and were down a turn in a wide valley. While they rested, the air thickened until they couldn't see both ends of the sled at the same time. Brun called it quits. He positioned the sleds below a rise that provided relief from the wind and formed a protective half circle. He found Goran choosing a ration box. "Good day to make ale. You should have some extra time," he shouted over the wind.

"Maybe so, but I think you may be glad for that extra fire pretty soon anyway. It's going to get cold and wet early tonight."

Sturl and the other leaders gathered around. "Looks like a bad one, Brun."

Tharn leaned in. "They say there is no bad weather, only bad clothing."

Brun ignored Tharn. "What do you suggest?"

Sturl shouted above the hissing snow. "Prepare now for the night.

Get the fire in a protected place, stretch the overhead cover, make the shovels handy, eat while we can."

Eldman agreed. "Then bundle up and stay close together. If anyone walks off they could disappear forever."

Brun swatted snow out of his forked beard. "Sturl, have somebody stretch a line from the front of the sled. We'll follow it out and back to relieve ourselves. We may be here a while and I don't want to roll our furs into a smelly barn floor."

Sturl grunted and walked off.

"Eldman, get Lars and Timonen to help Goran unload what he needs for tomorrow morning as well as tonight. He's going to get some double duty out of the fire by brewing ale." Brun coughed and scratched his forehead. "Tharn, have your guys find the shovels and let's get ahead in clearing a space to work and sleep. This kind of snow usually turns sticky. Maybe we can make a snow wall for shelter. My folks will unload the sleeping gear." He spit into the snow, shivered, and trudged off.

Goran turned out some thick soup. Keri sucked his down and didn't feel so chilled with a warm belly. The snow popped in the fire and melted against the sides of the copper pots. At first Goran found plenty of company from the harness crews crammed around his fire, but exhaustion took over and the men fell dozing against the sleds.

Keri found Eli and they huddled on the snow-packed ground under a sleeping fur while quizzing Jesspersson.

"What do you mean you 'did it first'? We didn't do anything," said Eli, scratching his scruffy face.

"Really? After the race, Laurel didn't...you know...reward you or something? Gudrun and I were laughing about it and then..."

Eli shook his head "no."

Jesspersson smirked. "Well, maybe we did do it first."

Keri pushed at him. "You are the only ones who've done it!"

"Well, that's what Gudrun thought, but then she said Stjärna acted so contented and happy that she was sure you had done it, you know, at Cnute's cabin."

Keri raised his voice. "But I told you."

"Doesn't matter. Sami and everyone else said it was clear you did. And the older folks laughed about how kids from their days snuck around, and… Did you ever hear about how Bue the Elder had to hide in the grain shed for a week?" Jesspersson laughed.

Eli frowned. "Why didn't you and Gudrun go ahead and at least announce your banns? I mean if you're in love and all…do it right."

"We didn't much talk about that. We just sort of got hungry, you know? Thinking about what you did…we decided to have a go."

"We didn't do anything!" said Keri and Eli together.

"Well, maybe not, but we didn't know that. And we had both been thinking about how Eli and Laurel kept disappearing and sort of talked about it. Next thing you know we decided we'd waited long enough. The only hard part was getting away from Fum."

Eli put his hands to his face. "Well, I hope you both went to confession before we left."

"When did you get so religious?"

"I'm not so religious but this isn't just swiping apples or pulling your sister's hair. This is a big sin. That's probably why Fum was dogging you."

"Ha." Jesspersson smirked. "God doesn't care about this. He's busy with the weather and kings and crops and stuff, not us little folks. Besides, God honors love."

Eli put a finger in his face. "You're nuts. You said you guys never talked about love. And if God doesn't care about ordinary people, why do the Ten Commandments focus on ordinary people?"

"We didn't break the Ten Commandments. That's adultery." Jesspersson raised a palm. "She's not married, so I didn't take her away from anyone."

Keri listened with clouded eyes. "Well, until you get her father to give her to you, she is someone else's property. You stole her from her father. That's a commandment."

Eli nudged Keri. "Now you're nuts. She's not property to be bought and sold."

"Really? What's a dowry then?"

"She pays that to me," said Jesspersson.

Eli shook his head. "No, her father pays it to her."

Keri spread his hands. "In any case, it shows what she is worth. The fathers determine her value by agreeing on a dowry."

Now Jesspersson was shaking his head. "Hardly, Gudrun has no value to him. Since her little brother turned eleven, her father spends all his time with Yaro, teaching him woodcraft."

"He'd thrash you if he knew you were teaching Gudrun bed craft," said Eli.

Jesspersson sneered. "Well, he's not here."

"Then I'll do it for him!" roared Gotthard, Gudrun's uncle, ripping the fur off the three young men.

Half the crew was listening around where the boys were huddled. Their expressions ranged from humor to anger. Gotthard grabbed Jesspersson by the cloak and jerked him to his feet. A swift uppercut put him right back on the ground, where Gotthard began to curse and kick him.

"Stop!" Tharn and Brun ran over.

Gotthard stomped down hard on Jesspersson's chest. Keri jumped in and pushed Gotthard back a few steps. Mantas pushed Gotthard forward again as Jesspersson scrambled to his feet, but Keri pushed the older man and knocked him on his seat.

"Hey! You spilled my broth," wailed Mantas.

The snow flew thick, steaming on the fire and clinging to their clothes. Nobody heard the wolf howl over all the shouting.

Brun yelled, "Everyone back to your furs. We settle this with words first."

"By the old gods, I will thrash this pup into the next mountain." Gotthard jumped up, fists clenched.

Tharn put a hand to his arm. "We need him to pull his weight on the sled."

Gotthard jerked away. "Gudrun's back there carrying his weight all by herself."

"Carry what? Nothing happened." Jesspersson shivered.

"What if she's pregnant?"

Jesspersson dabbed blood from his lip. "We only did it four times."

"Four times!" Gotthard charged again.

The teen held up his fists, but Keri kept them apart. Cnute helped.

Jesspersson stuck out his chin. "Everybody knows it takes at least four months of marriage for a wife to get pregnant. Look at Jodis Jurgensdottir or Marti Sigvardsdottir. It took them years. They have to get used to it or something."

Most of the men laughed out loud. Mantas nearly choked.

Brun glared at Jesspersson. "Now I may thrash you for your ignorance. One of God's greatest gifts is children, and some women get them after years while others get them with barely a wink at their husband. You could be a father before we get back."

Tharn rolled his eyes. "Gallant fools say courting is all flowers and fun until someone gets pregnant."

Gotthard and Jesspersson yelled at each other over Keri and Cnute.

"Why would God punish Gudrun? She's just lonely, looking for a little attention. Besides, it's her body."

"Then what were you doing there?"

"She invited me."

"You invited yourself and talked her into it!"

"Well, she seemed curious too."

Brun pulled Jesspersson aside. "This is serious business. That's why we have rules."

"Our grandfathers' rules were better."

"Our grandfathers didn't know God's rules," said Tharn.

Jesspersson waved at everyone. "And you've never broken those rules?"

"Other rules, yes. But I married my woman before…and am still glad it went that way," said Brun.

Several men nodded. Others looked down. Tharn spoke up. "The good book says, 'Let he who is without sin cast the first stone.' It also says, 'all have sinned.' So, maybe we should stop throwing stones, thank God He hasn't crushed us, and maybe get some sleep. Let's take some time to think about what to do."

Brun turned to Gudrun's uncle. "Your anger is just, Gotthard. You will serve us all better, however, if you can stand in for your brother-in-law after we reach Hilhelm. We need all hands until then, even foolish ones like his…and ones like yours and mine that are not exactly clean."

Tharn slipped between Gotthard and Brun. "The Romans said that anger is the one thing made better by delay."

Gotthard spit. "Then I will delay for the sake of the sled. Ha! And the ale. But you owe me a setting for a proper thrashing, Brun. I will hold you to it." He turned to Jesspersson. "You ignorant pup. I will make you whine like the cur you are. You'll tuck your hungry tail between your legs when I kick you down the castle steps. By the old gods, I will!" He turned, grabbed his furs, and threw himself into a snowy seat against the sled.

Jesspersson stood quivering, working his lips, but nothing came out.

Brun turned his back to Gotthard. "All right, let's get this snow cleared away so we aren't buried by morning. Who's putting snow in the kettle for Goran's ale? Where's my snow wall? Let's go, let's go!" The harness leaders chased everyone off to their designated tasks.

Laurel's father found Eli with Keri working behind the sled. "I am glad to hear you tell your friends my daughter is still…uh, pure."

"It is true, sir, we are of one mind. We like the idea that when we wed, we will have one secret about each other that no one else can share."

Lars looked keenly at him, his lips pursed, nodding. "Aye. It is a comfortable bond between husband and wife. It helps you through difficult times and hard arguments. And to hear our grandfathers talk, it binds a couple well against the day when the thrill is…let's say, less urgent."

"Yes, sir."

Keri blushed and turned away from their conversation.

"But did I hear you say 'marry'? I don't recall hearing that from you, or her, so far."

"I know it is in my heart, sir, but I dare not ask until I get back from this war."

"Hmmm… Well, let's see that you do…get back from the war, that is. War changes people." Lars slapped Eli on the shoulder and went to his own duties.

Jesspersson stood alone in the blowing cold. He hung his head and a tear froze on his nose. He tried to picture Gudrun as his wife. He shook his head to clear the idea but the image of her body remained. He lingered there a moment and then caught Gotthard glaring at him across the fire. He sneered, turned away, and pulled his cloak over his head. Hiding under his hood he tried to keep from sniffling.

FISSURE

K eri followed the line to the latrine area. After twenty steps he sensed movement. Drawing his knife, he moved cautiously until he found snow swirling against a rising cliff face with an overhanging ledge. Thinking it might provide overhead cover, he brought Sturl and Brun back with a shovel. They poked it along the overhang when the shovel nearly disappeared into the snow. Digging deeper they found a fissure in the rock that continued into the cliff. Brun sent for more shovels. They widened the gap and discovered a narrow cave opening before them.

Brun turned to Sturl, his best hunter. "Bears, maybe?" His voice sounded muffled by the snow.

Sturl shrugged. "Bears don't hibernate this far down the mountains. No trees or leaves to pad the den."

"I don't smell any, but you've hunted more bears than I."

"Hard to catch a scent in this wind." Sturl hefted his spear. "Why don't we look?"

"Eli, Jaako, get your bows. Keri, a torch. Everyone get a spear."

With spears and torches Sturl and Brun crept into the cave. They

221

came right back, calling for the harness leaders. "It's pretty dry, tall enough and deep enough to hold us. There's a wider cavern of sorts in the back. It's worth the effort to move the sleds closer to make a wind-break at the opening. Since it will hold the heat better, we can use less wood. And we can cut the guard to one. It will be tight, but it's worth it."

Timonen eyed the dark opening. "How will we see?"

"We will have the fire at the far end and our eyes will adjust," said Brun. "Let's get Goran in there first with the fire, the ale, and dinner."

Timonen bit his lip. "Looks like a tomb."

Eldman stepped in out of the weather. "It's better than wind and snow."

Rainar joined Timonen looking out toward the invisible sky. "We could be here for days."

Timonen stayed outside looking in. "We could be here forever." Lars patted him on the back as he went in.

A black wolf lay still on a ledge looking down on them. The snow swirled around him like sand in a wave. His red tongue licked his lips.

The valley acted as a natural conduit for the storm that roared outside. While Goran brewed ale, guards cleared away drifts threatening the opening. They worked around Timonen, who could not abide caves and was sleeping on boxes in the lee of the big sled. The snow on the windward side drifted to the height of the sleds by midnight.

Somewhere in the darkest of the night they heard a low rumble up the pass they crossed that morning. The ground shook and woke most of them.

Rainar jumped up. "What was that?"

"Avalanche behind us," said Timonen, standing at the entrance.

"But that means we can't go back," said Rainer, his voice rising. "We're trapped. We're going to die." Other voices joined his.

"Hold on!" said Brun, calm but firm above the chatter. He looked out the opening. "We're safe here. This hill with the cave isn't steep or big enough to slide much snow. When we have this much snow back home, we dig out. Same tomorrow. Now sleep."

Rainar groaned. "Why does God hate me?"

Viksten, his bedroll mate, pulled up the furs. "Shut up. God doesn't hate you any more than He hates me. He just challenges us to remember He's out there. Sleep. Let God take care of the snow."

"By the Holy Saint Eulalia!" Brun mumbled as he peered into the thick gray night. "Do you hate us, Lord?" Brun caught movement in the corner of his eye and glanced up. Pure black against the whirling snow, a wolf crouched by the boxes. It turned its head as if to hear Brun better.

Brun grabbed a shovel and hurled it at the wolf. As quickly as Brun moved, the wolf disappeared into the all-devouring snow.

"Watch out!" barked Timonen, adjusting his furs.

Brun said, "Sorry. Sleep deep, Timonen, it is not your time yet." He looked at the empty hole in the night and shuddered. "All right, God. You don't hate us but sometimes you scare us." He doubled the guard to two, gave them a torch, and posted them where they could see Timonen on the boxes.

"We should pray," said Tharn as Brun rolled into their furs.

"Sleep," said Brun.

"We should eat," said Keri next to them.

"Sleep."

"Was that Fum I heard?" said Timonen outside, but no one answered.

The falling snow held back the morning. Watches changed, the ale bubbled. The guards cleared the snow again and again. Men snored while the snow piled against the sleds.

By the time Keri and Jesspersson took guard duty it seemed like the world lay under a thick blanket of dark wool lit only by their yellow spitting torch. Theirs was supposed to be the last watch before dawn but they could see no dawn. They stared hard into the gray. The snow deadened every sound, every snore, every footstep, every crackle in the flames. The fuzzy air was like being under water. The eddies of wind lifted and dropped snowflakes randomly, giving no visual clue as to which way was up. Only gravity gave a sense of which way was down.

Unheard by human ears, a black she-wolf with a tinge of orange around her ears padded up one of the drifts above the sleds and looked down at the cave mouth. Even the slightest light reflected off her snow-jeweled coat. She lay down and watched Jesspersson as the snow piled deeper. Her ears perked up. She looked into the still dense sky and turned her head to listen more carefully. Then without a backward glance, she slipped into the darkness.

From far away Jesspersson and Keri heard a deep-throated rumble like distant thunder. It didn't crack like summer lightning and there was no flash, but the air was filled with the sound, and the ground, for the second time that night, began to shake.

Jesspersson steadied himself with a hand on the cave entrance. "Mother of God, what was that?"

Keri peered into the snow. "Avalanche. A big one north and east of us. Probably in the next valley. Relax, Jess, it's over."

Viksten elbowed Rainar. "See, Rainar, God doesn't hate you. He hates the next valley over."

Rainar and ten other men rolled out of their furs and reached for their things as if they should do something. Their faces reflected fear and consternation. Brun walked among them. "Calm down. Listen to Keri. It's over. We're safe. Listen. Quiet snowfall."

Then, like a sailor rolling his shoulders before he hauls an anchor, the mountain shrugged, flexing its peaks and valleys. Snow slipped from the cliff sides and washed down the valley as if a huge hand swept it from a tabletop. Drifts packed one upon another until the avalanche took on the strength of a tidal wave. It gushed down the valley toward the curve where the sleds sheltered the cave.

The stampede of snow came with a roar in the air and a groan in the earth. Momentum thrust it straight past the valley's curve and into the cliff three hundred paces opposite the cave. The snow mounded there and then veered down the valley, venting its fury on the slopes below. As the main force plunged down the hill, the edges flipped the big sled like a child's toy into the cave mouth, burying it against the entrance.

Snow plowed up by the sled entombed Keri and Jesspersson at the cave entrance. In the cave, pandemonium: dancing shadows, falling rock, noise, and yells. Those who rushed to the entrance found only a pile of tightly packed snow.

Suddenly it ended. Nature fell quiet but the cave rocked with panic, men shouting, praying, cursing, weeping as each tried to get his bearings.

Keri clawed his way out of the snow pile. He gasped for air and then turned back, digging until he felt an arm. He dropped to his knees and pulled until Jesspersson erupted from the pile, coughing and wheezing.

"Timonen!" Keri attacked the snow followed by Brun. They used a shield as a scoop, pulling back bushels of snow.

"Torch!"

Sticking from the snow was Timonen's outstretched arm. They pulled. It came out, leaving a blood trail in the snow. Timonen didn't come with it. Keri lurched back, sucking in his breath. Using both hands Brun dug along the red trail about an arrow's length until he hit a sled runner. Blood flowed there, freezing and congealing as it came. Then it stopped. Keri turned and retched. Brun just stared at the tell-tale pool. He coughed. The men behind them murmured.

Gotthard grunted. "Well, sleeping outside the cave was smart. I think I would have been happier getting dead quick instead of suffocating slowly in here with you smelly goats." He pushed his way to the back. Mantas followed.

Rainar stared at the blood, panting. "Why, God, why? I'm so close." He dropped his head. "I'm so close."

But for a few sniffles and coughs, the cave fell almost silent. Tharn picked up a log and shoved the embers back together. He blew until the fire grew again and placed the log on the growing flames. The crackles of fire brought the men back to life.

Brun placed Timonen's arm to one side and packed it reverently in snow. He bowed his head a moment, took a breath, and turned to the men. "Do you wish to sit and die? Let's get busy digging ourselves out."

Several men slumped to the ground, but others stepped forward. Gotthard snorted and sat down, poking at the fire with his toe. "When you dig, Brun, where will you put the snow you dig out? In here? Will you bury some of us like Timonen's arm so you can burrow your way to freedom? This cave can't hold all the snow between us and freedom."

"And how do you know?"

"Did you hear that avalanche? That was Thor's own foot stomping a mountain down on our little hole."

Two more men hung their heads and sat. One began to weep.

Cnute spoke from the shadows. "This 'ere hole be a blessing o' God. If we'd a been out there, we'd be dead." He stepped into the light. "God saved us fer somethin'. Let's dig an' see wha' 'tis."

Gotthard laughed. "You think you can dig through all that?"

Tharn chimed in. "The good book says, 'I can do all things through Christ, who strengthens me.'"

Gotthard clapped his hands to his head. "By Odin's eye! Must I die with a goat-faced saint telling me of the blood of Christ and my unrepented sins?"

"You may die if you wish," said Keri, "but Cnute is right. I dig."

Rainar quivered as he spoke. "Son of God, son of Odin, son of Cnute, I care not, but I will not stand here doing nothing." He tried to control his voice but it rose in tenor. "I hate caves and this one is closing in."

He turned to the entrance, found a shovel, and began working.

"Wait," said Tharn. "We should pray. Asking for help after we are worn shows no faith."

"You pray," snapped Rainar over his shoulder. "I think we are caught here because of God's help. Somebody give me a hand."

Antanas and a few more stepped up but the entrance only allowed one or two to work at the front. Paddling like dogs they shoveled snow onto a shield and hauled it to the back.

Tharn, Lars, Cnute, and a half-dozen others gathered to one side. Eli grabbed Keri, still groaning with nausea, and brought him to the group. Tharn glanced around and then back to Cnute. "You've prayed in the wilderness before and you seem to know what God wants of you. I see no man here more qualified than you to lead us now."

Lars glanced at Tharn with his eyes and mouth wide open.

Cnute shook his head. "I'm n' monk. I ne'er prayed 'loud afore."

Tharn smiled. "If your prayers are good enough for God in private, they are good enough for God in open village. Pray from your heart and we'll come along."

Brun winked at Cnute. "Jesus answered the lepers' prayers, why not yours?"

Cnute saw everyone looking at him. He nodded and bowed his head. "Lord...I been here afore, desp'rate, afraid, haunted...ye saw fit t' save me. Ye got som'thin' for me t'do... som'thin' f' all of us. Git us outta here, an' we'll try t'do it... An' take care o' Timon'n...thank ye. In Jesus' name. 'men." He crossed himself as did most of those listening.

Tharn smiled and said, "A-MEN! They say even short prayers penetrate the heavens."

Brun sniffed. "Now let's get to work." He slapped Keri on the back.

Gotthard scoffed from his shadow on the floor. "Shall we look for a lightning bolt to melt the snow?"

Tharn nudged Cnute. "If 'a kind word turns away wrath,' I wonder what works on fools."

Gotthard kicked at Tharn, but Tharn just walked away.

Brun and Eldman stared at the snow-packed entrance with a torch. Rainar and the others had cleared the snow up to where the sled blocked their exit. "What do you think?"

Eldman skewed his mouth. "The problem is the sled." He scratched his beard. "This is the bottom. It's been thrown on its side somehow. See here? Those two logs crossing? That's like the keel and the main crossbeam. They hold everything in place."

Tharn squeezed beside them. "We are down to about an hour's wood. And Goran says breakfast is out there in today's food box."

"Wood we can get." Brun gestured at the sled.

Eldman shook his head. "Not if we want to live. If we cut the sled here to get wood we disrupt the sled's strength. I'm not sure it will carry half what it does now if we cut the bottom here. It may not work at all. Besides, we would still have to dig a path through the wood piled in the sled to get out. The wood would have to go in here. I doubt there is room for us, the snow, and the wood."

"Do you have a suggestion?"

"Let me think." Eldman tugged different places on the sled. He wiggled his fingers through the gaps in the sled's deck and felt around. "Maybe we don't cut…maybe we tap out the wooden pegs with a punch and untie the ropes…" He was thinking out loud. Brun waited. Suddenly he turned. "Don't let them burn all the wood. I need to make a punch from some oak. And we need a hammer. And someone with small hands…"

Brun nodded. "Right."

LOOK UP

Cnute sat against the cave wall with the others waiting for orders. He fingered the white stone he kept in his glove, the one he drew from the kettle months ago. *Ye testin' me agin, God?* He closed his eyes. *All I see's a white robe an' a bearded man talkin' t' folks by the sea.* "Keri," said Cnute out loud, "tell m' somethin' ye remember o' Brother Hamar's churchin'."

Keri thought a moment. "Jesus said, 'The water I give shall give everlasting life.'"

Mantas snorted. "Don't need no water, need light, and a way out."

"Jesus is supposed to be the light too," said Keri.

Cnute shrugged. *That didn't help.* He stared into the cave's darkness until he fell asleep.

Brun nudged Cnute awake. "Need you, Cnute. Help Eldman tap his punch under the sled." The fire flared and Cnute saw Goran binding Eli's hands. Brun followed Cnute's gaze. "Eli squeezed his arm and a knife into the sled to cut strips of wood for the fire. His hands are bleeding, but we have some wood."

Cnute shivered and rubbed his eyes. "Why's my hand wet, my jacket?"

"Huh?" said Brun.

"It's drippin' on me," said Cnute, looking up. A drop hit him in the eye. Cnute jostled Brun as he jumped up. "We's doin' it wrong." He punched Keri in the shoulder. "God ain't down, He's up!"

"Easy," said Keri. "We'll be all right."

"No, God's up. Jesus, th' water o' life…it's coming from up. Th' light's up too. I's dripped on from up! Cain't ye see?"

Mantas flopped over in his sleep. "By the gods, shut him up."

"Listen t' me! Jesus's tryin' t' tell me. If we digs in t' th' sled, we're diggin' unner how much snow? But if we digs up, we find an openin' t' th' sky, t' th' heavens. Cliff's 'tween us an' th' avalanche. Can't be too far up."

Cnute quivered as he spoke. Suddenly he dropped his head and said, "Thank ye, Jesus. Thank ye, Jesus."

Brun stared.

Tharn looked up. "He's right. The first part of the cave is a fissure, not a cave. It has no top. That's just snow up there. The smoke from the fire has been going up all night. I'm guessing the heat melted a smoke hole. So…since the sled is at the exit, we are actually out of the cave and in the crevice, which is covered with snow we can dig up through."

"'s wounds," said Gotthard, rubbing his eyes. He looked up and then at Cnute, who was still mumbling thanks to Jesus.

"Yes, but how do we climb out?" said Rainar. "It's the height of our mill and nearly straight up. The top will be just snow with no handholds."

Keri flicked a thumb at Eli. "He's a good climber. And skinny. Not too much weight."

Goran spoke up. "Not now. His hands are covered in salve. They're all cut up." Eli shrugged.

Keri grabbed Bue. "You're not too big. Give it a try. We'll help you start."

Keri and Jesspersson lifted Bue up the face of the sled. He dug his boots into the upturned deck, securing a foothold. He found a hand grip on the rock wall and tried his weight. Brun handed him a spear and he poked at the smoke hole now visible in the white ceiling. Snow fell all around them. A big chunk came loose. So did Bue.

He slammed into the sled before Keri and Jesspersson caught him. Bue cried out and reached for his left shoulder, sucking air through clenched teeth. They laid him on his back and Brun felt under his tunic. "You can feel the joint pushing out," said Brun.

Tharn nodded. "Pull or rotate?"

"Pull. Quickly!" snapped Bue.

Brun looked at Keri. "Me or you?"

Keri's eyes went wide. "I've never..."

"Me." Goran came up. "My father's shoulder came out all the time. I've done this a lot." He looked at Bue. "Too bad you're not drunk like he was. The pain is nasty but quick. Watch now, Keri."

Goran placed his fur hat under Bue's armpit and sat on the ground next to him. He put his foot on the hat in the armpit, took Bue's hand, and began to pull. "Hang on."

Bue gasped, gritted his teeth and curled his legs as Goran hauled on his arm. Suddenly his eyes went wide and he cried out.

"Done." Goran stood up. "Next time you, Keri."

Keri retched.

Brun laughed. He looked around. "Who wants a try climbing out of our snow cave?"

Silence.

"Come on now, who will go for us?"

"I'm goin'." Cnute fiddled with his bootstraps.

Keri and Eli exchanged glances.

"If I takes off m' boots I can get a better toehold. I be takin' off m' coat too, so's I can hug the wall better. And tie a rope aroun' m' ankle so's I can tie it t' somethin' up there and ye can climb up after me. Somebody get t' throwin' that spear up now 'til we makes an opening t' th' sky. Then I can keep both han's free t' hold on."

Brun caressed his fraying beards. "Right...Sturl, you and Jesspersson see if you can't spear open a hole. Do we have any rope?"

"No," said Tharn. "All outside."

Cnute shrugged. He wiggled his toes and looked up. "Well, then, when God gets m' up 'ere, He'll just hafta fin' me a rope."

Brun smiled. "Rope's in the front of the small sled. Or get some harnesses."

The men cheered. Jesspersson's last spear throw found daylight. From the small opening a golden shaft of light pierced the smoke from the fire.

Tharn raised his hands. "Thank God."

"Hey, thank me," said Jesspersson.

Cnute smiled at the sparkling light. "God's sayin', 'Yer welcome.'"

Gotthard stared open-mouthed at Cnute.

Mantas elbowed Gotthard. "He'll never make it."

"I dunno. I think he's got powers. His god seems to favor him. He chased wolves in the dark, you know."

"Bet a copper he falls?"

Cnute laughed. "I'll take yer bet an' I'm gonna win 'cause I's not th' one responsible fer gettin' me t' th' top."

"Huh?"

Gotthard pushed at Mantas. "Just watch."

Cnute stripped to his tunic. Everyone's eyes questioned him. "Hey, I've been naked in the snow before." Keri and Jesspersson lifted him, and Cnute's feet searched for footholds. "Ouch! Splinter 'r somethin'..." He shook out one foot. Gingerly he lifted it and tried a stick jutting out of the snow. It gave under his weight. He kicked it and out fell a serviceable torch. "Look out." He stuck his foot in the hole. It took his weight. His ungloved hands explored the rock wall for grips. He looked up. "Lord."

The uneven rock face bulged in places. He hugged it as he crept a hand's breadth at a time higher and higher. When it narrowed he pressed his back against the wall behind him while he found hand-holds. His tunic, caught on a jagged stone, slowly ripped as he inched up the rock.

Keri and Brun waited with arms outstretched to break a fall. Keri pulled back his hand and showed it to Brun. Blood. Brun nodded. "His back's bleeding, I think."

Only pausing for breath or to shake out a muscle, Cnute reached the top of the crevice. "I'm at t' top o' the rock; it's level here, but there's still a man's height o' snow t' th' surface." He pulled his shoulders into the snow and began pushing it over the ledge to clear a place to stand. Some of it fell spotted red.

"His hands and feet too," whispered Keri.

Cnute cleared a small pocket in the packed snow and pulled himself up. He turned around and sat gasping in the fading sunshine with his feet hanging over the edge. They dripped bloody ice. "I's cold."

Brun cupped his hands but when he took a breath to call out, he began coughing.

Keri called out, "Rest a minute, Cnute. Try to swing your arms and warm up your hands. Goran, heat his boots and stuff his socks in them. We have to warm him up. Get his gloves in there too."

Goran looked at Brun, who nodded.

In a few moments, they tossed up Cnute's boots one after the other, but his hands were too numb to grab them. Cnute shrugged and waved them off. "Later." He shuddered a deep breath and reached overhead to make his pocket cave taller. As the snow fell it broke into a thousand flakes reflecting the fading sunshine. Gotthard elbowed Mantas, who stood staring.

The higher he dug, the more the avalanche-packed snow fought

Cnute's bare hands. Using his hands like trowels, he scraped ever upward, shivering and leaving blood trails in the snow. When he cleared enough room to stand he was still half his own height short of the top.

"Look at his back," said Keri. "It's torn all to pieces from the rock."

"The man has strength," said Brun.

Cnute's face hung down over the edge. "Haff t' make a tunnel t' get ow'."

Brun handed Keri a shovel. "We'll throw you the shovel."

Keri threw the shovel ten times but Cnute's numb, bleeding hands could not catch it.

Sturl stepped up. "Stand back, Cnute. I'm going to throw a spear to stick in the snow above in your clearing. Dig with it."

Keri held out a hand. "Wait. Tie his boots and gloves to it. He needs them."

With no room or angle to throw normally, Sturl squatted with one hand under the spear butt and the other to guide it. The spear flew straight, but the boots hit the wall and it ricocheted into Cnute's cave.

The spear grazed Cnute. "Arrgh!" He grasped it with one hand clapped to his side. He hissed and pulled his bloody hand away from the wound. "Not yer fault."

Keri called up. "Put on your boots and gloves. Warm up."

Cnute struggled into his socks. With one boot on he collapsed against the snow. His eyes rolled up at the opening above and he rolled forward, almost falling out. Prone now he rested his head on a gloved hand. "Light fadin'. Cold…must sleep. Dig later…Lord, he'p m'."

Brun sucked air between his teeth. "He's in trouble."

Tharn rubbed his hands together. "Freezing."

Brun eyed the climb up and shook his head.

Goran walked up. "We are almost out of firewood."

Brun stomped his foot. "God! Can it get any harder!"

Blue in the fading light, a clump of snow fell on the men below.

Suddenly it went dark. A shadow filled the spear hole. Fangs bared, the black wolf glared down, blocking the last of the dying twilight. He sniffed, moved to where he could see Cnute, then growled and disappeared. The men could hear it digging.

LIFE OF GATH

Sigvard, who carried his spear of late, and Valdemar prepared to close the village gate. Valdemar blew his horn to tell any strays that Rentvatten was shutting down for the night. He knew parents around the village heard and did a mental head count of their family in case someone might need to be worried about. Late returners could use the pedestrian gate after hours if one banged loud enough and Jodis Jurgensdottir knew them. But still, mothers worry, and goats are sometimes slow in the lengthening days.

Soren appeared at the ridge pulling a sled with baskets of charcoal. Valdemar and Sigvard waited. Soren stopped, waved, and pointed north. A tall man appeared on skis, his glide irregular, as if winded or drunk. He stopped by Soren, spoke, and started erratically down to the gate.

Valdemar squinted at him. "I think that's the large fellow Firth brought from Drakestad."

"Gath? The one they wanted to give us for the sled?"

"Yes. He should be three weeks gone by now with their sled."

"You don't suppose they turned back, do you?"

236

"Maybe. They could have broken their sled, or all come down with the grippe."

About forty paces from the gate Gath staggered forward, slipped, fell sideways, and belched bright red blood in snow.

"Plague!" cried Sigvard. "Stay back! Soren, get away from him!" They all stepped back.

Gath lay in the snow shivering, shaking his head, and mumbling.

Soren dropped his sled harness and ran over to Gath. "No, he said it's the coughing disease. Come help him."

Valdemar made a sharp gesture. "Stay away from him, Soren! He can still give you the sickness." Valdemar and Sigvard approached cautiously. Gath coughed and spit blood, thrashing like a grounded fish.

Sigvard stepped up and handed Gath his ski pole. "Can you get inside?" Between gasps and coughs, Gath shook his head.

Sigvard looked at Valdemar, pursing his lips. "Maybe Widow Jonsdottir will take him in."

Valdemar pointed at Soren. "Fetch Brother Hamar and then Widow Jonsdottir. Tell her the council will pay to put him up." They propped Gath against Soren's sled.

Suddenly there was Fum looking down at them.

"Fum!"

"Fum?"

"Oh, Fum," said a half-dozen voices as people came to the scene.

Gath wheezed and reached out. Fum kneeled and laid his hand on Gath's shoulder. Gath fumbled in his shirt and brought out the cross Fum had given him. He was gasping. "What…did you want…when you gave…me this?"

Fum said nothing but looked into Gath's eyes.

Gath could barely whisper. "What…am I supposed…to do?"

Fum put a second hand on the young giant's shoulders.

Hamar arrived and crouched next to them both. He smiled at Fum and turned to Gath. "Is it that ye been sick very long? Saints, you've lost weight."

Gath gagged back another round of coughs. "Several months."

"An' is it that Firth knew?"

Gath hesitated. Fum squeezed his shoulder. Gath nodded. "I needed...the money...for my family." Tears formed in his eyes and froze as they dribbled down his cheeks. "Forgive me."

"I'll be takin' that as a confession, don't ye know," said Hamar. "God forgives ye, lad." He made the sign of the cross over Gath's forehead.

Valdemar and Sigvard exchanged raised eyebrows and frowns. Others arriving heard and began talking.

Hamar shushed them with a hand but never took his eyes off Gath. "I donna ken why yer here."

"Confess...beg...forgiveness...to know..." He coughed long and hard. When the fit ended he lay still, exhausted.

Hamar gestured for some nearby men to undo Gath's skis. "Saints allow, an' we will have time for that later. Let's be gettin' him some rest and milk. My Brigid, God rest her, was always sayin' goat milk for consumption."

Gath grabbed Fum's arm. "And to see...him." Fum smiled. "What do you want? Why...me...this?" Gath clutched the cross.

Fum just smiled.

"Why won't...he speak?" Gath looked at Hamar.

"That's that way o' him. He says nothin', yet he says everythin'. Like the blessed Jesus on the cross, he doesn't speak, but ye know when he's a thinkin' o' you, or watchin'."

"Woman at Drakes'd...says he heals." Gath's eyes were bloodshot.

"Saints be praised, I've never seen 'im heal, but I seen him love the unlovable an' bring them life. He knows where to be, he does, an' when to play his whistle, an' when t' just touch someone."

"Will he...save my life?"

"Now, that's not his job, don't ye know? It's really between you and Jesus."

"Jesus…died for…sins, but…" Gath gasped. "Will He…save my life?"

Hamar nodded and smiled. "If ye believe what ye just said, He already has."

"But…the cough?"

"The cough ain't yer life, my son."

Another bout of wheezing and blood wracked his body. Soren brought the widow Jonsdottir. She took one look at the blood and shook her head. "He'll have to sleep in the stable side of the house." The men laid him on Soren's sled. They pulled him down the street, leaving Soren's coal baskets behind. Fum walked beside the sled with one hand resting on Gath.

Valdemar looked at Sigvard. "They were going to cheat."

"Do you suppose they planned more than just Gath?"

"We should ask him."

"We'd better hurry." Sigvard watched them turn the corner. "I saw folks die overnight of that in Hilhelm and they were in better shape than him."

Brother Hamar came out the next morning and found Sigvard and Valdemar waiting. "What did he say about the Drakestad sled?"

"Now ye know I can't be revealin' a confession."

Sigvard laughed. "I doubt that lad was the center of any scheming. What he may have told you was not his to confess."

Hamar slumped a little and spread his hands. "Yer right. The devil's in it. Firth set up waystations along the first part of the route, ye know. Stocked they were with food an' wood an' a shelter. An', God smite 'em, they left a day early."

Valdemar nodded slowly. "I warned Brun."

Hamar smiled. "For Brun, all life's a game, you know."

Sigvard stamped his foot. "Well, the bet is off!"

"They won't know that in Hilhelm," said Valdemar.

"How is the boy?" asked Sigvard.

"Saints be praised an' he's gone o' this world. Died late last night, Fum at his side. Away for a moment, I was; come back an' he was gone forever." Hamar looked up. "Fum. Fum? Was it this way he came? Have you seen him this morning?"

"Nope."

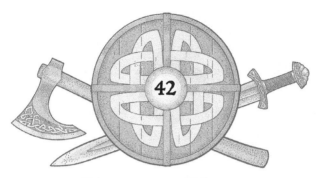

FIRE OR FOOD

Keri looked up where the wolf had been. "Eli, you can hit a squirrel shooting up. Can you hit a wolf?"

"I'll get my bow. You decide which eye to hit." Eli went to his pack.

Brun turned to Eldman. "We have to cut the sled. Now."

"But…"

"Show me where we'll do the least damage. Keri, get an axe. Chop where he tells you."

"Right."

"Eldman, I need a long pole and cross pieces to make a ladder. Pick a place to cut. Build us a ladder. We will solve the sled problem outside with a full stomach and warm hands."

Eli strung his bow, but the wolf was gone. Eli grabbed the torch Cnute found and, using a piece of broken bowstring, tied some of the sticky torch head to his arrow. "The wolf's not there now, but maybe I can put some fire in Cnute's cave. It might warm or wake him."

Brun nodded. Eli drew his bow. Goran lit the torch residue and it flared into flame. The angle was bad and the fire kept swinging down on Eli's arm. Keri rested the flame on his axe.

"Thanks."

"Shoot soft."

"Yep."

The shot was true, sticking a hand's breadth inside the snow over Cnute's head. The fire dangled down on the string. Cnute stirred.

Eli prepared a second arrow, which hit just outside the cave, adding more light. The day was fading to black and the ball of torch material hung like a sun against the darkening sky.

The wolf's face appeared in the hole again, his muzzle wreathed in snow. He growled at the arrow and swiped at the burning light well below him. Eli whipped out another arrow but the wolf disappeared. They heard it digging.

Tharn sucked in a breath. "The prophet says, 'Those who do evil hate the light, it exposes their deeds.'"

"That may not help Cnute if he freezes to death," said Brun.

The string on the first arrow burned through and dropped its fading fireball on Cnute's outstretched arm. He shook and then yelped, shaking it off. Through sleepy eyes he saw the flame and then the second one hanging outside his snow cave. He staggered to his knees and palmed both arrows awkwardly. He put the fires together on the rock ledge and snapped the arrows to form a pyramid over the small flame. The tiny fire caught and he warmed his hands.

"There's a wolf digging down to you!" shouted Keri.

"Uh…" Cnute waved his hand.

Eli shot two more arrows to feed the flames. Cnute reached them and huddled over his fire. After a while he leaned out the opening and waved a gloved hand. "Try t' shovel. I t'ink I c'n catch it."

"Do you hear the wolf?" said Keri.

"Yep. He's 'n ol' frien'. But he hates fire. Any torch lef'?"

They threw up the shovel and the remains of the torch. It took a few tries but he caught them both. They tried to throw his coat but it kept catching on the walls and he gave up. "'Stay warm diggin'.'"

Keri folded his arms. "He probably will. He's the best digger in the village."

"Look out!" Snow began to fall from the cave above. "He's digging along the rocky top of the crevice like a mole until he finds an opening," said Tharn.

After a few minutes Cnute appeared at the top of Jesspersson's spear hole. He had the torch in one hand and the spear in the other. "I'm out. N' wolf yet. 'Goin' fer rope."

"Bring wood too!" said Brun. He began coughing.

"And food!" shouted Keri.

Everyone strained to hear what was going on above: crunches in the snow...Cnute shouted...snarling...yips...silence. And more silence. The fire in the cave crackled. A dollop of wet snow fell with a dismal splat. Keri's stomach grumbled. A few stars peeked through the smoke hole, but Keri couldn't see Stjärna's star. A whisper of wind brushed some snow off the edge of the hole above them. Someone shifted and his knife scraped the stone floor. "Hush!" said a half-dozen voices. Another drop of water. Brun coughed.

Then a grunting sound above, a swish in the snow. Fire. There was Cnute with a new torch wearing a smile and a heavy coat. "Are ye hungry? Would ye rather ha' wood?"

Everyone answered something different. Cnute laughed. "Stan' back. Wood first." He dropped down a half-dozen split logs. "Here's sausage an' cheese!" He dropped the food down padded in some clothes. "Save me a bite. Wolves dug int'a couple o' food boxes."

Brun wheezed. He nudged Keri. "My voice is gone. Ask him what happened."

"What happened up there?"

"Later. D' ye wan' t' get out t'night or stay sheltered till mornin'?"

Brun waved at Keri, who called up, "What do you think is best?"

"Stay outta th' wind. N' place t' camp up here. But I needs help to' guard th' food."

Rainar stepped up. "I'll go. I can't take it in here anymore."

Brun stood under the hole. "How do we get out?" He broke into a coughing fit.

"I ties harnesses t'gether an' lead 'em down th' tunnel."

"Do it." Brun turned to the group. He gasped. "Who wants to go? Wait. Cnute and Rainar are on my crew. Let's keep together. My men will go. Tharn, Sturl, you harness leaders…are you all right with that?"

Tharn looked at Brun. "You are obviously getting sick. Remember, 'Sleep restores the body as faith restores the soul.' You need to stay and sleep."

Brun shook his head. "Who said that?"

"I did. Brun, let me or Sturl go up. Or Keri. He knows Cnute."

Antanas spoke up. "I'd like to go too. Timonen was my friend. I don't want him with the wolves."

Brun waved off Tharn. "All right. Antanas and my men go. I'll be fine. Just a cold. Besides, Keri is not paying attention."

They looked at Keri, who was looking at Goran. "Do I smell sausage?"

"Still pretty cold."

"Don't care," said Keri.

The men ate and hot water helped Brun's throat. Soon Cnute dropped down the harnesses and the evacuation began. Brun insisted on leading, pointing out footholds. At the top he leaned on the up-turned sled wheezing while Cnute helped the others up.

The small sled stood upright but hard against the cliff wall. Broken boxes and food jars littered the area. Cnute waved a torch. "Th' wolves did most o' th' diggin' work fer me. Jus' as wel, m'back's wrecked. I opened a couple more boxes fer some warm clothes. I dug 'nother tunnel t' th' top o' th' big sled t' git wood. T'night? Maybe a snow cave here 'gainst th' sled. Dig out t'morrow."

Brun coughed. "All right, we'll start here."

Antanas took Cnute's arm. "Wait. Did you find Timonen?"

Cnute shook his head and pointed at the big sled. "No, n' yet. Guessin' he's there."

Antanas stared at the immense pile of snow in the eerie yellow light. He sighed. "I'll stand guard there."

Brun nodded and gave him a torch. "Let's the rest of us dig a shelter against the sled, get some fire, post guards."

After things settled, Brun found Cnute by the fire. "So how did you handle the wolf?"

"When I heerd 'im diggin', I think he's comin' after me. So I waits with torch an' spear, but he never come. So I starts diggin' from my end. Found he'd been tryin' t' bury me so's I couldn't get out. Snow piled ever'where.

"When I shows th' light he stalks off. I sees th' top o' the small sled sticking out th' snow. Torches on th' corners're snuffed out by the avalanche but I got 'em goin' ag'in. I used 'em t' chase th' wolves offa th' food boxes an' get back t' ye."

Rainar asked, "Are they gone?" He squinted into the night.

"Naw, they just out o' th' light."

Brun stared at the dark, working to stay awake. "Well, they have certainly found us now and had a taste of our famous smoked salmon. They'll be back."

"Yep. Fire's a bes' answer."

"And no one walks alone."

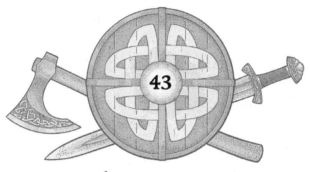

WET CHEESE

At dawn they brought up the rest of the men. Keri stared at the destruction around the sleds. About a third of the spears lay broken or missing as well as eight pairs of skis and half the shields.

Eldman lifted a broken shield. "The spears can be kindling now, maybe torches, maybe short thrusting spears, but I don't have the wood for long shafts. Same for the skis. These broken shields? Firewood."

"We make new ones in Hilhelm," said Keri.

"Yep."

Brun set Goran to re-pack the small sled and assess the remaining food. "And get some salve on Cnute's back."

Keri groaned when he saw the scattered and open food boxes as Sturl's men were sent to the big sled. Much of the firewood scattered when the sled capsized. The men needed to take the rest out to right the sled. They worked quietly knowing Timonen lay buried under the wreck. When they found him, work slowed while they determined how to empty that part of the sled without disturbing his body. Keri and a couple of men were sick at the sight and it wasn't any better when they dragged the sled away from the cliff so they could lift it off him. They wrapped Timonen in his sleeping fur. Keri couldn't watch.

Tharn looked at Brun. "What next?"

"We can't afford the wood for a proper pyre."

Eli stood at the cave. "We could put him in here and seal it like Jesus."

Antanas shook his head. "No. Timonen hated closed spaces. He would want to be out here."

Eldman kicked at the broken cave entrance. "Rocks. We build a cairn against the cliff wall. Keeps the wolves off. Mark it with his shield."

"Is his still in one piece?" asked Tharn.

"Nope," said Antanas.

Brun was coughing. He waved assent.

Rainar offered a fancy tunic to dress Timonen in exchange for a more useful wool sweater from Timonen's box. Antanas took Timonen's sword for his family and Tharn said the words. With gentle frankness and a somber prayer, the burial was done before noon.

As they walked away, Eli said to Keri, "Not quite the scarlet uniform and glorious adventure we sought."

Keri fought back against his stomach. "How can you stand the blood? The stench?"

"It's not like killing a deer, is it?"

The falling snowflakes turned to clumps and the sun broke through the clouds all at once, bringing the camp into painful brightness. The wind shifted southerly and the air turned warmer, making everything slushy and wet. The scene around them chilled Keri's heart. He nudged Jesspersson and nodded to the cliffs heaped with the packed snow.

Jesspersson shivered and then pointed east. Below them was a sea of chest-high lumps like waves of broken snow heading down the valley: the flotsam of the avalanche. "That's gonna be hard to push through."

Keri leaned on his shovel. "Yep. I'll bet the sleds just sink in and stop."

Grasping the sled and coughing, Brun sent Eli and Jaako to scout. The snow stuck to their skis as they struggled out. They fought for every foot of forward motion. Eli called back as they cleared the first rise. "It is like we are skiing on wet cheese."

Brun turned to the men. "Let's go! Harness leaders, keep your men moving. We need to load this sled, clear a path, and see if we can get the sleds to slide on this...cheese."

Shadows added to the cold. When the scouts came back the sleds weren't ready. As the sun dropped, so did the temperature. Slush turned to ice under the runners.

Keri's group pushed at the food sled. "One more time," Brun said huskily. "One, two, three!"

The men heaved in straining, grunting agony.

Brun found a place for his shoulder and pushed. "One, two, three... SSSSSuut-TAAhhh!" The sled broke free. Then he sneezed, coughed, staggered, and fell down.

Half the crew lay in the icy muck after the sled lurched out from under them. Keri stood soaked and shivering. Jesspersson squeezed water from his cloak. Brun stood sodden, hacking, and looking at the sky, his beard glistening with snow. Sturl turned to the cook. "Goran, keep a little of that fire going. We will need to dry some clothes and feet by the time we get the big sled free."

Brun rasped, "Kill the fire and save the wood, Goran. We'll have to warm up from within. This avalanche cost us at least a day's travel and half a day's wood. We don't have enough to waste a stick."

Sturl banged his soaked boot against the sled. "It's hardly waste when it keeps us from frostbite or the shriveled foot mold."

Brun tossed his hand, dismissing him. "We'll survive. We can do this." He turned to the men. "Eldman, Gotthard, have your men change into dry gear in the cave. Everyone else, let's break the big sled free. Then you can change."

"Wait, Brun." Sturl grabbed Gotthard, who had started to the cave. "We can't put our stuff away wet. It will be useless tonight when the temperatures drop again. Look at that sky. Not a cloud. You know that means an extra nasty cold and with all our furs and clothes wet, we will freeze. We must dry it before we pack it, or we will have no protection at all."

"We don't have time!"

"We should make time," said Eldman, joining in. "Let half the men dry their clothes now while the rest load the wood. Then we switch."

Brun spit. "By God's wounds, we don't have enough wood." He wiped at his nose.

"We don't know that," said Eldman.

"We *do* know the men are freezing now." Sturl gestured at the crew.

"Hellfire cold," said Gotthard, shivering.

Brun looked around. Eli, Jesspersson, and others nodded in agreement. Only Cnute and Keri stood by the sled ready to push.

Keri shrugged. "They're right."

"You too?" Brun lifted his hands to the scene. "I can't be responsible for everything if you won't listen to me. We are in trouble. We must go now."

Tharn clumped up, wiping wet snow from his coat. "We don't want you to be responsible for everything. We want God to be responsible for everything."

"Is that where you are going with this? You think I... All right..." Brun took a wheezing breath. "All right... How about this? God made us stewards of so much wood and so much food and gave us a huge task. He does not want us wasting it."

"But He does want us relying on Him, not you."

Brun clenched his fists and was about to shout when suddenly his eyes opened wide and he pointed to a cleft in the rocks fifty paces away.

Everyone turned. Someone whispered, "Wolf."

It was black but the snow on its coat made it flash silver-white against the dull rocks. Its shoulders were waist high to most men and its head hung down like a snake from a tree limb. It turned as if to listen.

Brun grabbed the nearest man and shoved him toward the sled. "Come on! We need to move."

But no one moved. The men stood mesmerized. Then there was a "whup" as Eli, still armed from the reconnaissance, loosed an arrow. The shaft disappeared into the snow at the foot of the rocks. The wolf turned its back, slouched into the shadows, and disappeared.

Keri's mouth hung open. "That's the worst arrow you've ever shot."

Eli gaped at his bow. He tested the string with a twang and shrugged.

Cnute spit into the snow. "Naw, yer bow can't kill tha' wolf. He's mine. There's another one or more out there fer each o' ye. Tha's who our struggle's 'gainst. Not our frozen flesh and icy blood, but the powers o' this shiftin' world o' snow an' wolves. But tha' wolf? He's mine an' *you* can't kill 'im."

Brun stomped his foot, sending slush all around. "Well, he doesn't seem to want to fight today. So, we must get moving. God has promised us neither manna nor wood."

"We can't move in this condition." Eldman shivered.

Sturl put his soaked seven-tail hat in front of Brun's face. "How about one crew dries out everyone's furs while the other four work the sled?"

The men looked at Brun. He wrung out his own soaking glove and found he could not force his red chapped hands back into it. He gulped. His body sagged. "I give up. It's in God's hands. Eldman, take your men to the fire first." Then he broke into a coughing fit.

BLACK TO SILVER

Pekka marched into the village with a slight limp and his right arm wrapped snugly against his body. His mother talked at him, but he said nothing. Annika trailed behind them. Pekka went straight to Valdemar, who sent for Sigvard and the members of the council. They met in the great hall.

Pekka looked pale, thin, and grim. As people filed in, he squinted at them.

Valdemar silenced the room and invited Pekka to speak.

Pekka remained seated. "I must sit, sir, if you don't mind. I am still regaining strength."

Valdemar gestured, "As you wish."

Pekka took a slow breath. "I think Rainar, my father, attacked me, pushed me down the trapdoor of the mill, and has run away. I don't think he intends to come back."

Council and audience members alike leaned back on their benches as if pushed by an invisible hand. Murmurs washed the room. Pekka's mother bleated into her apron.

"It has taken me weeks to remember it all." He leaned forward

251

and gripped the council table. "But I know the night of the feast I went back to the mill. I was surprised to see a candle lit up on the grinding floor. I went up to see who was there. That is the last thing I remember."

Arn pointed a finger at him. "Why did you go to the mill?"

"I had a farewell present for Annika under my bed and I wanted a fur to wrap her in while we…talked. My pallet is on the ground floor."

The room murmured.

Valdemar poured himself some ale and glanced at the crowd. "Quiet, please. Now what makes you think your father did this?"

"His best clothes are missing, also his favorite flagon, much of the silver, and Grandfather cannot find the coin bag with the family's money. I think Father took it and intends to start a new life in Hilhelm."

His mother sobbed.

"And," Pekka swept his arm at the crowd, "I hear everyone thinks I fell the night before they left. I remember nothing of that day. I was attacked and unconscious from the night of the feast. And my mother knows it."

Face in her apron, she nodded affirmation.

Pekka exhaled as if exhausted. Annika placed her hand on his shoulder. He took the hand. Suddenly he was crying and she held him. Everyone found something else to look at.

After a few moments, Valdemar cleared his throat. "These are serious charges, young Rainarsson."

Pekka nodded.

Valdemar spread his hands. "If Rainar comes back he will have his say in this matter and we can determine what to do, but I am at a loss as to what to do now."

Pekka looked up. "We expect nothing, but with the money gone, we must close the village house until harvest and move everything into the mill compound. We cannot afford wood for two houses and my injury prevents me from working. Besides, Oldefar refuses to leave the mill. We must also dismiss our two servants, Widow Berdine and her daughter, which may bring a burden on their families. But we have no coin to pay them. I fear we will also have to call in some of the loans we have made."

Several couples looked anxiously at one another.

Valdemar nodded. "These sound like issues your grandfather Leksa should direct."

"Perhaps." Pekka stood rubbing his temple. "But Grandfather is not… himself. He has not been for a while. Mother and I have taken a stronger business role, though he resents it mightily."

"Hmmm…" Valdemar stared into his ale cup. He grimaced, then looked up. "Anything else? No? Well then, on behalf of the council, we wish you good healing. We express our regret at your accident and at the distress of your family. We hold in reserve any judgment on Rainar until he returns. We add you and yours to our prayers. God speed."

Pekka took Annika by one hand and motioned his mother out the door. Valdemar gestured for the council to stay behind. Brother Hamar stood and poured the last of the ale for the council while the room cleared.

Arn tapped his lips. "It seems doing a good thing for the kingdom has turned into bad luck for the village. Is God mad at us? We need Leksa to run his mill."

Valdemar waved a hand. "God doesn't work that way."

Hamar studied the group. "No, but Satan does. He always attacks when we step up for the Kingdom or are most vulnerable. We are both right now."

"Well, we are all tired from the extra work. Even the families that sent no one are feeling the strain of helping their neighbors." Valdemar rubbed his neck.

"Not all of them," said Arn. "I know several who have raised the price of their goods, taking advantage of no competitors. With Timonen on the sled, our other barrel maker, Normund, raised his prices. He drew black at the lottery and is trying to turn it into silver."

Sigvard snorted. "Wait until Timonen gets back. Normund's neighbors will shun him."

Arn shrugged. "Or Timonen will raise his prices too."

Valdemar sighed. "I will speak to Normund."

"As will I," said Brother Hamar. "But remember what I said first. Rainar, if he is indeed guilty, plus Normund, and even Sami, all were inclined by their own desires to do some wrong. Satan caught them at a moment of stress or pressure and helped them turn a weak thought into a sinful action. We have to pray not to have that first desire."

Arn scoffed. "That's easy for you to say. Most of us still have wives and kids at home. They hunger, and the harvest is far away. My desire to see my family healthy is not a sin. I focus on the good steward commands and keep a sharp eye on my larder. If I must raise the price of curds to buy Normund's firkins for my cheese, I will."

Hamar raised a finger to Arn. "Elijah and the widow were satisfied on the strength of their faith. Their larder was never full, but their stomachs were never empty."

Arn pressed his temples. "Maybe, but Elijah never tried to feed four children, a wife, a mother-in-law, and twelve milk goats through a northern winter. Which reminds me, I have work to do." He finished Hamar's ale and left.

POWER

All but one harness crew took their turn at the drying fire before the big sled stood ready to move. Keri's waited still wet. His eyes darted between the setting sun and Goran's fire. He didn't know what hurt worse: his frozen feet or his empty stomach.

Brun feared a hard freeze and made them move the small sled back and forth during the afternoon to keep it loose. Now he wanted to try the big one. They gathered. They pushed. "SSSSSuut-TAAhhh!" It didn't budge. They waited while Brun coughed.

Eldman pointed at the skids. "It's actually down to the mud." The trampled snow around the sled was a frosty brown slush up to their ankles.

"We must get it on snow or it will freeze to the ground." Brun took a breath. "Everyone on the sled…ready? One, two, SSSSSuut…" Brun fell coughing. The sled stood firm.

Tharn ran over. "That's it. The sun is almost down. We will take tonight to recover and dry out. Goran, can you make something warm to eat?"

Brun pointed toward the fading sky. "We are losing an entire day. I have to get the sled on the snow before it freezes. The men need a little success today."

Keri spoke from among the men. "Getting the sleds dug out is a success. So is getting out of the cave. Rest would reward our effort."

Tharn nodded. "He's right. Between the physical misery, the body's exhaustion, and frankly the boredom of the work, we are in no mood to push. Let's take an early night and then an early start."

"But the wolf…" Brun's voice faded.

"Double the guard and give us a chance to dry out more clothes. We don't need to wake up wet and miserable tomorrow."

Goran called over. He was putting salve on Cnute's back. "And I have a second batch of ale finished. We can give every man a second cup and another at dawn. Stew will be ready shortly."

Keri's stomach leapt for joy.

Tharn smiled. "They say, 'The night heals what the day has damaged.' And you especially need healing."

"Ale? Two cups?" Brun sighed. "But we start early."

They ate and drank. Dozing by the fire, Brun opened one eye and wheezed at Cnute. "Get your whistle. Play for us."

"What?" said a dozen voices. "Who?"

"Cnute?" said Mantas.

Keri nudged Jesspersson. "I knew I heard a whistle."

Eli sat up. "Me too."

Cnute scowled at Brun. "Goat's breath! Ye know 'ow bad I play."

"You're all the music we have. Play."

Cnute sighed and reached into his tunic. He pulled out a white bone whistle.

"Where'd you get that?" asked Keri.

Cnute shrugged. "I foun' it in m' spare socks 'bout th' third day out. Dunno who put it there."

Keri reached for the whistle. "It looks like Fum's. Was Fum playing when we left?" He looked around. Men shrugged. "It could be his."

Eli scratched his head. "I really don't remember, but I think so."

Keri handed it back. "When did you learn to play?"

Brun laughed, then coughed. "He's been learning on guard duty."

"Oh…" said a half-dozen voices at once. "Well, play then."

Halting and awkwardly Cnute played Fum's tune. No one laughed. No one griped. And everyone thought of home as the snow drifted down from the black sky into the yellow glow of the fire. Keri searched for the evening star.

Almost dry, somewhat rested, but grumpy and underfed, the men assembled ready to go before dawn, except for Brun, who they wrapped in furs on the small sled. He said it was merely a cold, but Goran saw the mass of shakes, fever, and stuffed head. "No ale for you, Brun. Here, hot willow tea."

Brun protested, but Tharn held him in place. "Almost everyone else has spent a couple days riding."

Brun griped but delegated his duties to Tharn, Cnute, and Sturl. Then he asked for Keri. Brun looked up through bleary eyes. "You've seen me get this sled going for almost three weeks. Can you do what I did and get it going today?"

Keri looked back and forth from Brun to the sled. "I don't know."

Brun scowled. "Do you really think I am stronger than you are? Look at yourself. You're bigger than I am in every direction. When are you going to use that God-gifted power?" Brun breathed in the steam off his wooden mug.

Tharn smiled. "The Holy Book says, 'I can do all things through Christ, who strengthens me.'"

Brun laughed. "You already used that one."

"All right. How about the great Alexander? 'There is nothing impossible to him who will try.'"

"He sounds like Jesus," said Keri.

"Maybe, but I hear Alexander is dead and Jesus is not," said Tharn.

"Let's go with Jesus, and get moving," said Brun. "Keri?"

"I'll try."

"Just like I do it." Brun propped up on an elbow. "Small sled first."

Sturl placed double crews on the small sled and Keri took Brun's back corner. "Ready?" he said. "One, two, push!" Keri strained and the sled popped free of the frozen mud, almost skipping up onto the crusty snow.

"You did it!" Tharn slapped him on the back.

Sturl moved over to the larger sled. "Now the big one. Just like Brun." He positioned the men.

Keri took Brun's corner. "One, two, push!"

Muscles flexed and pressed against the wood. Men slipped. The air filled with groans, but the sled did not budge. "Push!" called Brun from his nest in the other sled. "Find that power!" Then he went into a coughing spasm.

"Stop," said Sturl. The crew stood panting. He changed out a few men while everyone caught their breath. "You heard Brun. Find your strength. Ready?"

"Wait." Keri stood up. "Just like Brun...wait." He stepped away from the sled a moment. He bowed his head. Then he took his place again and nodded to Sturl.

Brun winked at Tharn and smiled.

Keri took a breath. "One, two, push!"

Again, they strained. Again, they groaned. Again, nothing budged until Keri's voice hissed out, "SSSSuuut! Tah!" The sled broke free. Men fell as it jerked forward, but Keri pushed on with a dozen others, gathering momentum until they were out of the mud and on the snow.

Sturl ran alongside. "Stop! Let's regroup."

Jesspersson looked up from where he had fallen. "'s wounds, Keri, who are you?"

Eli jumped on his back. Others cheered. Keri glanced at Brun, who grinned.

"Always remember where your power comes from," said Brun.

Keri smiled and turned to the crew, "Let's go!"

They went, but the crusty snow disputed them every step. The scouts on skis flew over the now icy top layer but the big sled kept fouling the undercarriage when it broke through the surface to deep snow. Dropping down the undulating valley took twice the normal time even when Sturl called in the scouts to help clear the sleds instead of finding a route.

Keri served as Sturl's emergency muscle whenever a sled tilted or began to stick. Never on scout, he pushed all day and could barely move his legs when Brun drove them an hour into the night. He ached so much that he forgot to look for the evening star.

Brun rose partway out of his furs, looking back up the dim slopes. "God's blood! We've hardly gone half a day's journey. Tharn! Get these sleds into a windbreak." He broke into a cough. "Goran, cold ration now, cold breakfast tomorrow. We must sleep now, move sooner in the morning. And we need to conserve wood!"

Several men groaned. "Not fair, you've been warm all day."

"Shut up," Brun wheezed. "We've lost a day and a half. By Sigvard's reckoning we should be at the Tunturri already. Do you want to die up here?" He gasped between sentences.

Tharn spoke softly. "Easy, Brun. There is no remedy for a thunder-bolt. Surely, we need to be aggressive, but let us do it so that none are singed by the fire in the eyes of another. As the Romans said, 'Victory comes from harmony.'"

Brun's shoulders slumped. "I feel like all nature is against me: this cough, the snow, wet, wind, cold, fleas, hills, moon, Timonen! Our boots and clothes are starting to wear. Our guts are always hungry. Our sleep is interrupted. The first wolves dog us and they savaged our food. And, oh, Lord, I ache!"

Keri brought Brun his cup full of ale. "You have brought us far. Your training is paying off."

Tharn nodded vigorously in the light of Goran's growing fire. "We persevere! We are doing well against that power that wants us to fail. God is good!"

Brun lowered his cup. "Really? He allows all this, and you still say, 'God is good'?"

Tharn said, "You have never had a challenge like this. For thirty years God shaped you for this day. He prepares all of us for our roles. He will only push you as far as He has given you strength to endure."

"I feel like I have no strength left."

Keri shivered. "Many of us feel we have no strength left."

Tharn smiled. "That's exactly when you get closer to God."

"You have an answer for everything." Brun shivered.

"No, I really don't. But God does."

"Well, I hope His answer includes sleep and enough food and wood until we get there." Brun coughed until his eyes watered. The tears froze on his cheek.

Tharn took the empty cup. "The Psalmist says, 'In God we trust. I am not afraid. What can man do to me?'"

"It's not man I am worried about." Brun sank into his furs with a groan.

Keri turned toward the sound of food.

In his furs Keri listened as Sturl posted guards. A few men talked and mended by the fire while others went to sleep. The moon dropped below the mountains and the sky became a crystal black bottomless sea studded by bits of frozen starlight. The fire crackled in the still air.

Then there came a sound: soft at first, but soon the icy night filled with a deep, clear tone. Beautiful it was, like a pure golden song singing from the heart of a lovely girl. It didn't frighten; it called. Sleepers awoke. Talkers paused mid-sentence. Guards lowered weapons, slowed their breathing, and listened. Keri shivered, the hair rising on his neck. "Stjärna?"

"Laurel?" whispered Eli.

Antanas, on watch, moved his head to find the source. "That's Timonen." He walked out of the firelight. Bue, on guard with him, followed.

"Wait!" shouted Tharn. He grabbed Bue by the arm. "It's not Timonen; it's a spirit calling you from the light."

Bue stopped but Antanas continued as if sleepwalking. Gotthard brushed past Tharn and ran up behind Antanas. He hit him in the head with his closed fist and Antanas fell unconscious in the snow. Mantas laughed. "It's Loki, you fool. Antanas is spooked; addled since we rocked in Timonen. Keri, give us a hand gettin' him to his furs."

Keri shook himself into the present. They wrapped up Antanas and placed him near Brun.

The sound, the tone changed from beauty to the soulless wail of a wolf, lost in the blackest of pits. Eli whispered, "Sounds like a man who's lost his father."

Jesspersson choked back a sob.

Other wolves answered the first, and soon desperate howls filled the skies like arrows arcing over a castle wall.

Cnute stood by Brun. "Tha's th' true voice o' Satan. Heard it afore out here."

Keri glanced at Cnute and into the dark.

Brun closed his eyes, falling back in the furs. "Don't go spooking the men with religious talk of devil-wolves. More than a few here don't believe as you do. Their ignorance will turn to fear."

Tharn said, "Isaiah wrote, 'Those who hope in the Lord will renew their strength.' These men need some hope."

Brun took Tharn's arm. "Those wolves don't sound like God or hope to them. For them hope and safety and God are in the solid walls of Hilhelm. In the meantime, it is muscle, smoked salmon, and steel to get us through. Don't distract the men from that."

"Humph." Cnute walked to the fire. He pulled out Fum's whistle and found the first notes of "O Gladsome Light," a hymn they'd learned from Hamar. He struggled but on his third try, he noticed the wolves stopped their wailing. The men settled down. He spit at the darkness.

Keri recognized the hymn and tried to remember the words: something about praising the Father at evening. Curled in his furs the thought lulled him to sleep.

OH MY, GOD

Since Brun still lay ill, Keri started the sleds the next morning and then joined Sturl's crew to scout. Keri squinted into the fog. Tharn speculated they awoke in a wide valley, but the gray air hid the side walls.

"Keep the sun on your right and plant an upright log every forty paces or so," Sturl said. "As each pair of you runs out of logs, stand fast and wait for the sleds to catch up. Don't let any mark behind you or the scouts ahead of you get out of sight. Remember, we have seen wolf sign already. Nobody walks alone. Keri, you and Jess lead. Go."

Keri and Jesspersson could hear muffled men and sleds well behind them but could not see more than fifty paces in any direction. Only the glow in the sky belied the approximate direction of the sun. Keri paused, shading his eyes.

Jesspersson fussed with his boots. "I must have a leak in my box. All my socks were wet this morning."

Keri touched his chest while staring into the white. "Next time we get a break, I'll lend you some of mine. I carry a dry pair in my tunic."

"Thanks."

Jesspersson peered behind them, looking for the following scouts. His shadow grew sharp and long as the sun broke through to the southeast and the fog evaporated like a dream.

"Oh, my God," whispered Keri. "Look what the Lord has done. It's beautiful and pure like a crystal." Jesspersson turned. Down a steep slope a thousand sparkles gleamed from the infinite plain below them. Little hummocks like white haystacks dotted the flat terrain to the southeast. A perfectly flat frozen blue lake stretched north and east. Keri fell to his knees with his skis splayed out behind him.

Jesspersson slid up next to him and stared. "Look what God has done."

"Oh, my gods," said Mantas, exasperated, when the big sled caught up. The frozen lake gleamed like a blue jewel. "That's a frozen hellhole. What have the gods done?"

"Oh, my God," said Brun enthusiastically from his fur nest. "I've heard it was spectacular, but…it's…magnificent. More than I imagined. Flat and frozen, it will be easy to cross. Look what God has done for us!"

Tharn dropped his harness and stepped forward. "It is like that new heaven and earth with the crystal sea Brother Hamar talks about."

"Oh, my God," whimpered Rainar, limping up from behind the last sled. "It never ends. We'll never make it across there. It's too big." He gasped, "What has God done to me?"

"Oh, my God," said Brother Hamar, praying with his congregation in Rentvatten. "We thank you for what you have done. We know you designed the future and the past. Be with our men and those of Drakestad and the other villages crossing your creation. Watch over them as you watched over your chosen Israel in the desert and your son, Jesus, in the wilderness. Grant us grace and protection in your creation."

"Amen," prayed the families on their knees.

On a high rock overlooking all God has done, Fum smiled and played his whistle.

The men struggled down a cut in the ridge and paused on the last small rise before the terrain flattened out to endless plains of snow and ice. A few blue shadows of frozen streambeds cut the pure white in the distance. Occasionally tufts of yellow grass or reeds poked through the windswept snow and the frozen lake. The men stared.

Brun, wrapped in fur, stepped to the front. "The Tunturri," his voice almost a prayer. "Frozen in winter, marsh in summer, but only on top. The ground below never thaws. Beautiful fields of low flowers in spring, but spring only lasts a couple weeks before the snows finish melting. It floods into marsh and travel is impossible for men. The streams fill with fish, but the skies fill with hawks and eagles, so life for fur and fin is dangerous. The rabbits and voles come out of their winter sleep to be chased by the lynx and wolves. If you come here to hunt and manage to escape the wolves, you will likely be eaten by mosquitoes beyond number. They hang like a mist in the air. Woe to a hairless man's face who falls asleep within ten leagues of this place."

Sturl cleared his throat. "Down south they call this tundra." Cold mist rolled from his mouth. "It stretches to the taiga forests of the southern low hills. You'll see naught but wolf sign here until spring.

The windblown snow hides the sleeping critters' holes and flattens out the terrain. Be careful where you step; a snowdrift may cover the ledge of a streambed."

Tharn studied the map. "You can't see it yet but out there winding like a snake is the Usko River. Fed by a hundred streams of melting mountain snow and the occasional artesian hot spring. It's slow, cold, and not very deep. It changes course each summer. Pray it is frozen enough to carry our sled. With a goat's height of ice on top, it may not have enough water to drown you, but you will probably freeze before you find out."

Brun nodded. "Aye, and we need the river and the Tunturri to stay frozen or we die. If spring comes too soon it will get soggy. No sled can slide on that surface."

Tharn handed the map to Brun. "So, pray for clear, cold skies for another month. The next time we see hills we will be within a day or two of Hilhelm."

Eli pointed to a pile of rocks several hundred paces to the south. "What is that?"

Tharn laughed. "That must be the Ebenezer Sigvard's sled built all those years ago. It's here on the map. It means we are on the right path!"

"Ebenezer?" Keri struggled with the word.

Tharn shaded his eyes looking. "In the Bible Israel set up a stone to thank God for His help against the Philistines. We are in God's hands. Who shall we fear?"

Mantas wiped his nose with his sleeve. "Pretty brave talk, Tharn, when you know there is no one here to face us."

Cnute spoke toward the snow plains. "I's not been 'ere, lad, but I been out like this 'lone, far from any human, in a snow, in a weather... there's plenty out here t' cause us fear. An' I've seen eyes in a night that had a name, I jus' didn't know it. Be 'fraid, boy, be 'fraid. There be more behind t' wild an' t' weather than jus' nature."

Mantas spit. "I'll respect what you've seen, old man, but your god never stilled a storm for me. I don't think any power big enough to create this wilderness would give an owl hoot in the dark about me. I believe there's a creator, but he's moved on. Left us here with nature and some drunken gods. We are on our own. Even Odin is said to just wander the earth."

Tharn shook his head. "That must make you feel very lonely and fearful."

"No time for proverbs," said Brun, wheezing. "We are only a third the way there and we've already used over half our wood and eaten or lost more than three-quarters of our food. We need to get off this rise and debate God at dinner."

The murmurs of the men as they manned the sleds partially drowned out the wolf howl that drifted plaintively down the mountains behind them. It hung in the air for a moment before being blown by a wind gust into the vast Tunturri. Only a few heard it. They looked puzzled into the sky. Keri missed it as did Eli, but Jesspersson and Gotthard heard it and exchanged sharp glances.

Once on the flat, the sleds moved briskly. The great crystal lake disappeared behind them, its silver-blue ice reflecting the sky like a perfect mirror. In the half day since they left the Ebenezer, Keri estimated they went as far as their best time for a full day in the frowning mountains. The pace raised spirits. Men called out in boyish jest and challenge. They called on Cnute to play Fum's tune at every stop.

On the second afternoon Keri gave the commands to start. He placed his shoulder to the big sled and twenty-nine voices cried "SSSuuuut –tah!" together as they lurched toward the eastern horizon. Keri's laugh rose above the sleds' noises. "Step...step...step..." he called. The men found a rhythm with their feet that mimicked the harvest dances of home. The sled itself seemed merry.

267

Tharn's crew tried chanting a rowing cadence of their grandfathers. The sound carried back two hundred years to the trade routes from the Varangian Sea to Kiev. The first Viking earls and Slavic princes met and their combined heritage began. Viktor and Rainer provided a deep monotone bass beneath the feisty lyrics of the others. The men pulled like their heroes. Soon all the harness crews chanted.

"SSSuuuut –tah!" called Keri and they pushed off at another dawn, sailing through the snow. Pride in their strength and power lifted their heads. A fresh batch of ale didn't hurt spirits either.

Eldman smiled to see the sleds getting lighter each day with a lower center of gravity. The same sight worried Brun.

ICE

The Usko River appeared as a shiny ribbon stretching to the distant Arctic Sea. When Keri first saw it, a light mist ghosted along its frozen surface. They stopped at the riverbank and stared at this last landmark before the hills of Hilhelm. Eldman cleared away some snow on the frozen river and examined the ice. He took a short log from the sled and flipped it as a man might play with a sheath knife. He pondered its weight, then threw it in a high arc on to the river. The solid ice clanged like a hammer on a cracked anvil and echoed with every bounce of the log.

"Like summer lightning," said Keri.

Everyone felt compelled to throw a log and hear the strange noise. The ice didn't break. It only cracked with fine lines running from the point of impact like a spider web in a nightmare.

Brun called his leaders. He sent Eli and Viktor south and two others north to scout for a narrower spot to cross. Fuming at his own weakness, Brun sent Cnute and Sturl east across the ice to see if the river doubled back. They didn't want to have to cross twice.

While they waited for the scouts' return the wind turned south. Keri noticed his footsteps getting mushy. "South wind, warm wind."

"Yep." Eldman nodded. "Makes the sleds stick to the snow like sap to your finger."

Brun said, "Where are those scouts?"

Keri went to him. "The snow is getting soft. Probably slows their skis. Give them time."

Goran came over scratching. "We've got bad weather."

Tharn shook his head. "There is no bad weather, only bad clothes."

Brun snapped, "You said that already…ten times!"

"Well, it's at least partly true," said Keri.

"It better not be." Brun wheezed inside his fur cocoon. "I checked everyone's clothes."

Tharn sighed. "Yeah, four weeks ago."

"And we're already running low on pine tar," said Goran.

Brun waved at the clouds. "Then add clear skies to your prayers. Never saw a snowpack that didn't freeze under a clear night sky."

"We're moving by day," said Eldman.

"Then we'll get up earlier, move sooner, and catch more freeze before it goes sloppy on us. Where are those scouts?" Brun started to get up.

Tharn put out his hand. "You stay put. We need you healthy."

"I'm feeling better."

"You still sound like a goat in heat."

"More ale would help." Brun strained to see north and south.

Goran shrugged. "Maybe two weeks of ingredients left. Shall we drink it all now and save the weight?"

"Well, I'm tired of your sotted teas."

Keri climbed up on the big sled. "Here come Eli and Viktor."

Brun flopped back to his furs. "Thank God!"

Eli reported lumpy ice upstream. "The ice here seems smoother, shiny even."

The other scouts dribbled in. Cnute and Sturl found a big loop in the river just to the northeast, so they decided to cross here and then head southeast.

Eldman said the river would only support the sleds if they were empty. They discussed dismantling the smaller sled and using it for firewood.

Keri was listening. "It looks like we have room in the bigger sled for everything, but both sleds move easily now with lighter loads. It's nice to have the smaller sled for an additional windbreak."

Brun studied Keri. "Good idea. Keep both."

Eldman spoke up. "Let's take apart the upper half of the big sled and carry it over in pieces. No sense taking chances."

Brun nodded, drooping, dopey for more sleep. "Good. Move the small sled first. Morning's almost gone. Move soon or lose the day."

The south wind made the day warmer and snow thickened with moisture. They emptied the small sled and carried the food and clothes boxes across the river. Eldman supervised unloading and dismantling the big sled while Sturl gathered his men and Eldman's to move the small sled to the other side.

Halfway across, Gantson slipped and landed on his rump.

Jesspersson laughed. "Why do you sit while we work?" Jesspersson lost his footing but grabbed the sled and hung on.

"You look like a haunch of deer hanging in the smokehouse," said Gantson, wobbling to his feet.

"Save your jibes for tonight," said Keri. "Push steady now."

"Who made you boss?" said Jesspersson.

"Easy, guys. I just don't trust this ice."

"But Keri, I thought broken ice was your favorite way to meet girls," said Jesspersson.

Gantson giggled. Keri blushed. Sturl spoke. "More to the left. Keri, grab the shovel and see if you can level the slope on that riverbank."

Keri attacked the frozen earth and managed to break down its sharp edge. The ice groaned as the sled crunched into the bank. Keri shoveled snow in front of both the runners. He gripped one front corner and gestured Antanas to the other. The remaining men grabbed the sides with Sturl and Jesspersson in back. "Ready? One, two, three, go!"

They strained. The sled started up the angled bank then stalled. There was a loud crack. The back runners broke through the ice by Jesspersson and Sturl.

Keri heaved. "SSSSSuut-TAAhhh!" The sled jerked forward and on to level snow. Keri fell gasping.

Jesspersson slid into a crack along the shore and into water up to his calves. Antanas pulled him up the bank, where he cussed and swatted at his wet legs.

The crack widened, chasing Sturl away from the sled and into the middle of the river. Bue, halfway across with a load of wood, didn't see the fissure coming. He disappeared into the ice like a hand into a glove, leaving only the wood scattered behind.

Sturl fled toward the western side. He almost made it to the bank but ice cracks spread out around him like a fishing net. He tried to go faster and fell.

"Don't move, lie down, and spread your weight," yelled Tharn. He threw a harness end to Sturl but it fell short.

Sturl wiggled forward. "Quickly! Water is seeping into my clothes."

Cnute edged out on some ice-coated rocks and threw another line. Sturl caught it and they pulled him to shore. He scrambled to his feet, brushing at the wet and frosted spots on his coat.

Brun staggered over in his furs. "Are you all right?" Tharn wrapped Sturl in his coat.

"Bue? Bue!" Eli ran along the bank.

Eldman pointed at a darker patch flowing under the ice. "There!"

Eli stepped onto the river but the ice snapped. Viktor jerked him back. Eli broke free but the dark patch was gone. They stood and stared at the ice. Eli sobbed and fell to his knees. Viktor swore. Most of the others came to the spot. Brun shouldered his way forward. "Anything?"

Eli sobbed harder. Eldman coughed. Brun put an arm on Eli.

Sturl squinted at the men across the river. "It looks like they are all right over there. I think a couple of them may have wet feet, but the sled is up. I see them changing their boots and wrapping feet. Is he building a fire? It's lucky the clothes boxes made it over the ice before the sled."

"Lucky for who?" said Tharn absently. "If the ice is so soft we can't cross, they have the food and the furs and we have the firewood."

Brun stared at the river, working his jaws. Sturl glanced at him and then turned to Tharn. "The men who went in the water need fire quickly. We have no food. We need some decisions."

Eldman rubbed his beard, looking at the re-freezing crack that took Bue. "There's more to this soft ice than just the south wind." He gestured behind him. "Look, the snow on the sled runners is not melting. The air is cold enough. What's wrong with the river?"

"I don't know," said Tharn, "but the more immediate problem is Bue."

Brun turned. His eyes were blank; he had no expression. His voice was flat. "No. The more immediate problem is making it through the night. Bue is gone. The best we can do is leave him an Ebenezer."

"Doesn't an Ebenezer thank God?" said Tharn.

"A cairn then. Build it now with river rocks. We won't have time later. Do it now." Brun wheezed and collapsed on the sled.

The men worked silently, wrapped in their own thoughts.

STEPPING UP

On the far side, Keri gave orders. "We all have flint; who has tinder?" He had his own harness mates plus most of Eldman's men. With three wet people, he wanted a fire now. No one answered. "Does anyone have some in their gear box?"

Jorvik stared at the river. Antanas shrugged. "I think Goran had some."

"Check it. Did any firewood come across yet?"

Lars looked at the river. "Bue was bringing the first load."

"Where is he?"

Jorvik stirred. "Gone."

Keri stopped. "Gone?"

Jorvik shook as he spoke, still facing the ice. "It was like a pike hits a baby duck. The river just swallowed him." He pointed. "See? There's the wood he was carrying."

Keri saw the scattered wood. The crack was sealing up. Across the river, the men ran down to the edge and stopped near Eli on his knees.

"Gone? Under the ice?" said Keri. His voice cracked.

Jorvik nodded slowly and turned to Lars. "He was my nephew, you know. Asbjorn's son. I should have kept a better watch on him."

Lars put his hands on Jorvik's shoulders. "He was a man, Jorvik. He died doing a man's work. He will be remembered as well as missed."

"I don't think he was ever baptized."

"He attended church, so we will pray anyway. God is merciful."

The others stood by dumbfounded. Keri felt a little lightheaded.

Jesspersson stamped his wet boots. "I can't feel my feet." No one responded.

Keri took off his blue scarf and ran a hand through his hair. "I'm sorry, Jorvik. It doesn't seem right or make sense. Bue was so…happy. He made us happy. We'll see how Brun wants to handle it, but right now we have to handle us."

Keri took a shuddering breath. "Antanas, you and Gantson check the food boxes. See if any of them are almost empty. Consolidate a couple, start a fire with the empty. You three, get your boots off before they freeze to your feet. Do we have a broken shield we could burn? Lars, get Jorvik into a fur too."

The older men looked up at Keri. Lars tightened his face in anger, then sighed and relaxed. His lips worked. "Ummm…" He glanced at the others. They all shrugged. "Well, that's what we'll do…son."

Keri blushed. "Oh, I'm sorry. It's not my place… It's just… I was… but we kind of need a plan. No offense meant. Can you think of anything else we should do?"

Lars smiled. "Nope. And no offense taken. We probably expected it eventually. Just kind of strange to see it happen all of a sudden." They all moved off as ordered.

Keri's shoulders slumped. He bit his lip. "Who do you think you are?" he murmured to himself.

Antanas improvised some tinder from fuzz in his hood while Gantson broke up a box with a hand axe. "Looks like we were supposed to have the king's smoked salmon for dinner."

Antanas spoke over his shoulder. "We may be the only ones. We have all the food."

275

"And the furs," said Lars. "But no spare wood. At least not enough to get through the night."

Keri toyed with a mallet, waiting for someone to volunteer an idea. "What if we take apart some of the sled?" They looked at him. "Gantson, see if we can get any wood off the sled."

Jorvik came over. "Burn this shield. It was Bue's."

Keri took it gently. "Thank you." Jorvik walked away and sat by the river.

Jesspersson opened his box. "Raging goat farts! Everything under the sleeping fur is wet: clothes, socks, everything."

"Don't you dry your stuff?" asked Gaar.

"Every night." Jesspersson sighed. "How's it wet? There wasn't any snow since yesterday. And they stink like mildew or something. The outside of the box isn't wet, and the box below isn't wet. Nothing is melting anywhere else."

Keri looked. "Well, the boxes shuffled around in the move. Must have dropped some snow inside. Take a pair of my socks while you dry those out. This is what, third time?"

"Yeah, but how?"

Keri shrugged. He glanced at the river, the fading daylight, and the empty small sled. "We'll sleep inside the sled. That will offer us some protection since we won't have much fire. Pile the boxes like a wall at the front so we can open the gate and extend the space a bit."

Antanas studied the space. "It will be cozy, just like home. Eight to a bed. Very warm if you're in the middle."

When they settled it was three men on each of the two shelves in the sled with two very nervous guards, Keri and Jesspersson, staring into the dark. They could hear snuffles and padded paw steps, and occasionally saw a wolf silhouette in the pus-white moonlight.

Keri pointed to the clear sky northeast. He whispered, "Smoke?"

Jesspersson saw a tiny vertical streak on the horizon. "Could be. Drakestad?"

"Probably. Eli said he saw smoke last night. Who else could it be?"

The wisp disappeared in the wind. They squinted at movement by the fire across the river, but everything else lower than the horizon stayed black.

Keri shivered. "It's like being in the cave again."

"The cave didn't have eyes." Jesspersson turned Keri away from the river. "Look."

To the east, they peered over their box wall into a dozen eyes reflecting the flames across the river, some red, some green, some yellow. The eyes moved and bobbed and disappeared to reappear like pairs of bubbles in a simmering pot of black night. When the wolves didn't move, the reflecting fire writhed in each eye like a maiden burning at a stake.

They finished their shift back to back in complete silence. Their hands clenched their spears so hard it hurt.

AMEN

After midnight Alex Broke Tooth woke them shouting, "It's a dragon!"

Everyone awoke in a tumble of furs and confusion with Jesspersson's voice loudest of all. "What? Where?" He grabbed for his spear and fell over Keri. The sled rocked.

"There! At the river! It's coming this way!"

Confusion turned into panic as each man grabbed something to fight with. Two dancing flaming orange eyes came from the riverbank. They gripped the sides of the sled as the eyes grew bigger. They laughed in relief as the two orange eyes evolved into two torches in the hands of Cnute and Tharn. Eli followed with an armful of firewood. Every other eye around the sled disappeared.

While Eli laughed Tharn explained. "Eldman thought the night-time temperature drop would re-freeze the ice. We should be able to get the sled across before the dawn brings another thaw. Get your boots on! We have work to do."

"Wait." Jesspersson's voice was higher. "Is this safe? We've been see-ing wolves all night. Even with torches we cannot see more than a dozen paces. We will work nearly blind and if anyone goes through the ice or slips, we may never find him."

"Ye 'fraid?" said Cnute.

"No!" He paused. "Just practical. Bue's gone and I've been in the river once today already." He looked around. "Who stands with me to not move the sled until dawn? Give the river all night to freeze."

Two men with their heads down peeked up. They nodded and Jorvik stepped up next to Jesspersson. "We should wait until dawn. Remember Bue. He never saw it coming."

Tharn pondered the group. "Keri," he said, "what are you thinking?"

Keri scratched. "Well, Jesspersson's right, the river will be frozen at dawn, but then it will start to melt again. I think we need to bring the wood now while we know it is solid. We'll bring the sled itself just as the sun rises."

"You don't know..." started Jesspersson. Eli and Cnute interrupted. An argument began, somebody shoved somebody, and a wolf howled from the darkness. Everybody stopped.

Tharn cleared his throat. "The ancients threw dice to make decisions. Hamar says prayer is better."

"It can't hurt," said Lars. "Then maybe we can talk."

Tharn prayed aloud, giving praise, thanks, and then his petition for their safety. "And give us the courage you gave Peter to step out of the boat. Let us step out on this ice with our trust in you to keep us safe. In Jesus' name, amen."

Several men echoed his "amen." Cnute's voice rose high above the rest. "Amen!" he shouted. "Amen an' amen an' amen! Lord, F'rgive us our fear. Ye can handle ice. Ye can handle wolves. Fill m' wi' confidence that ye have somethin' f' me! Gi' m' strength t' walk where's ye wants me. Amen! Amen! Amen!"

Tharn started to speak, but Cnute kept going. "Keri, Eli, ye been mute. D' ye think God's a magic trick? A show? If yer convinced yer gonna die anyways, whyna die in a hands o' th' God who offers ye 'nother life?" He grabbed both by the arms.

Keri stood fast. "I believe everything ever said by Tharn, Brother Hamar, and sometimes even you, but…"

"Great," said Cnute, "then say 'amen' wi' all yer heart an' prove it by followin' m' 'cross th' ice. Show these men an' God yer faith!"

Caught in the moment, and Cnute's push, Keri and Eli stepped out. Keri gulped. "Amen," he said quietly. "Amen," he said louder. "Amen!" he shouted with Eli as they jumped with Cnute off the bank and onto the ice. The surface disintegrated in a flurry of crackles and icy splinters, dropping them into the water. Keri's feet hit bottom. His mind screamed "death by freezing" but his skin said "warmth." He pushed up and next to Eli in waist-high water, ready to panic. But it was warm. *Am I dreaming? Is it an illusion? Am I in heaven?*

Shouts, arms, and spear butts reached out to them. Cnute splashed alongside holding his red cap. "It's a miracle, b' God's grace we're saved!" He laughed as he pushed them toward land. They climbed on shore but began to chill in the frozen night air.

Tharn called for a fire but Cnute just broke loose from the helping hands and jumped back in, pulling Keri and Eli with him. "It's warm! Get our dry clothes an' a cloth 'r two an' we'll come out an' dry off when th' fire's up."

Antanas shook his head. "He's gone mad, shaken by the sudden cold."

Tharn bent his knee to touch the water. "No, it's a miracle."

Several men followed him. "It is warm."

"There must be a hot spring nearby," said Keri, shaking his head. "This part of the river will never have totally stable ice."

Lars started a fire. Jesspersson dug for clothes in Cnute, Keri, and Eli's boxes. Sitting in the water Keri looked up. "If there is a hot spring, then if we can get upstream of it, we can find strong ice. The hot water will flow downstream."

"Yes!" said Tharn. "We can cross safely in daylight. Well, thank you, Jesus."

Keri and Eli sat in the water with steam rising out of their hair. Eli pumped his head under and spit water as he came up. "Hey, the water is washing away the fleas. *There's* a miracle."

They got the fire going and Cnute danced around it wearing only his steaming hat and playing his whistle. The men stared at the scabs on his back. Tharn made him stop and dress. He soon went back to the whistle, occasionally stopping to laugh and say, "Thank you, Jesus!"

Jesspersson frowned. "Is he drunk?"

Keri, still dressing, laughed. "No. He's just filled with a happy spirit."

"He sounds drunk."

"Nope. He's actually been giving Gotthard and Brun his ale."

"Really?"

"Yep. I think it's helped keep Gotthard off your back." Keri wrung out Stjärna's blue scarf.

"What has? The music or the ale?"

"He gives Gotthard ale and talks about God."

Jesspersson eyed Cnute. "I don't care if he talks about goats; if he keeps Gotthard off my back, he's my friend."

"All right," said Tharn. "Like Keri said, we'll wait until dawn to move the sled. Tonight we move the wood and get Goran to cooking."

Everyone jumped to it…upstream.

WATCHING

Keri stirred when Eli woke Tharn and Goran at dawn.

"I think we found your hot spring," said Eli. He pointed to a thick mist rising from the ground a hundred paces away. Grabbing spears, they went around a curve in the river and found a foggy flowing streambed. Upstream fifty paces sat a dozen large rocks around a large pool of lightly steaming water. Green grass grew at the edges of the rocks and they could feel warmth as they approached.

Keri and Brun came up with Brun still in his furs. "This is not on the map."

"Neither was that cave," said Tharn. "But here is an answer to prayer. A place to rest, get warm, and recover. You're not the only one who is cold, you know."

Keri touched the water. "It's as warm as Stjärna." The men laughed, and he blushed. "Hot almost. Far more than the river."

Goran fingered his tunic. "We could even wash."

"Oh, yes," said Eldman, walking up. "Oh, to be warm."

Tharn smiled. "The proverb says, 'If pine tar and a sauna cannot heal you, you will die.'"

"Why didn't we see this before." Brun looked around. "Here's rabbit tracks but no wolf tracks. Where are the wolves?"

"Who cares? Perhaps the wind blew the mist or whatever away, so we didn't notice it." Sturl laughed. "Perhaps we are north or south of the route, so it has never been noticed. Perhaps it's new since Sigvard's time."

Tharn pointed. "Sturl, get the others. We'll cross the big sled and put it here by the spring. Then we'll move the small sled here and reload."

"No." Brun coughed and grabbed his chest. He was gasping. "We've no time to waste."

Tharn half helped and half forced Brun to sit near the warm water. "Exactly. Let's get cleaned up and warmed up for tomorrow."

Brun struggled to speak. "No, don't you see? Now that we've found the spring we know where we can safely cross. We can cover a half a day's march before sunset."

More men arrived. They called back to the others until nearly the whole crew was there. Everyone touched the water. Eldman sat on a rock and started to take off his boots. Four others started to do the same.

"Stop!" shouted Keri as he saw the rush to the water. "We need to get the big sled over now while the ice is most solid. Once we are packed and reorganized for tomorrow, then everyone can enjoy the water. And a warm night's sleep. Isn't that right, Brun?"

Brun was shaking his head "no" but Keri had a firm grip on his shoulder. Keri looked him in the eye. "Can't be helped. We need the fixing; both the sleds and us."

Brun broke into a coughing fit. "Follow Keri," he said, gasping.

Eldman put on his boots.

Seeing their reward close at hand, the men worked hard, and by midafternoon the sleds sat ready. Keri and Tharn dismissed two crews at a time to bathe in the hot spring while the others washed clothes downstream. They put Brun in a warm spot between two rocks and he slept, breathing the steamy air.

After dinner, Eli climbed on Keri's shoulders to look for Drakestad's fire. They found the smoke to the north as the evening star rose. Keri smiled. He hadn't seen Stjärna's sign for several days.

Eli studied the smoke. "Considering the avalanche and the river, they're not much farther ahead of us than yesterday. And we don't know if they've crossed the river yet. We can still beat them."

Brun woke to eat and order double guards but there was not a wolf in sight. Tharn reduced the order after Brun fell asleep and soon almost the whole crew snored on the warm ground.

Keri woke up to a distant wolf howl and realized the fire was almost out. He woke Jesspersson. "Where's the guard?"

"Is it our turn?"

"I don't know. Where is the guard?"

"Whose turn is it?"

"I don't know! Get up. There is no guard."

"Just a minute more."

Keri rolled him out of the furs. "Get up. We're on guard duty."

"All right. All right."

Keri stoked the fire and poked his finger toward each pile of sleeping furs. His lips moved as he did it. "Count the men. I see twenty-seven."

Jesspersson counted. "You're right. Twenty-seven. Who's missing?"

"Twen'y-eight, lads. Go back t'yer furs. Sleep," said Cnute. He sat rock-still atop the big sled. "I's guardin' from up here."

"Who is your partner?"

"Brun, but let 'im sleep."

"Who's your relief?"

"Me. Can't sleep no ways, so's I'll jus' take it."

Jesspersson sighed. "Great." He headed for the furs.

Keri walked over to Cnute. "Why'd you let the fire go down?"

"Wanted t' see if th' wolves'd come in."

Keri's eyes darted into the shadows. "Did they?"

"Only th' one. An' he jus' wants t' look. Over there 'bout fifty paces."

Keri looked but saw nothing. He climbed up on the sled. Cnute pointed. "Black on white snow, he is, an' looks like a shadow. M' ol' frien', maybe."

"*That* wolf?"

"Yep. He's a comin' for m'. He's proud. Jes' like I was." Cnute stared stock-still into the black and white shadows.

"Where's your spear?"

"N' worry. Won't come near th' fire, n' matter how small. G' back t' yer furs. I'll wake Goran when it's time."

"You need to sleep."

"Don't want t'. Nightmares, ye know."

"Oh... About the wolf?"

Cnute sighed, glanced at Keri, and then stared back into the night. "No. Wolf don't scare m' n' more. Can't hurt m' neither. Well, 'cept for th' dreams an' th' memories of Liisa. When I 'pologized t' God fer th' ale, an' th' cussin' at folks, those dreams faded 'way. But I can't shake the dreams o' Liisa: cussin', laughin' at her. I think I hit 'er when I'se drunk... 'Specially bad dreams t'night." He hung his head.

"I thought sins washed away when you love Jesus."

"Guess tha's so but Hamar says ye gots to 'pologize. Liisa's dead. Can't tell 'er." He took a long breath.

Keri, embarrassed, sat staring at the dark. He thought he saw movement as if a head was raised. Cnute wiped his nose as Keri spoke. "Do you think Liisa's in heaven?"

Cnute's head snapped up. His eye flared, reflecting the fire. "Y' think she's not?"

"No, no. I'm just thinking that if she is, you can apologize to her through Jesus, can't you?"

Cnute looked into the night again. His head began to nod. "Ma'be so...could try... Good idea."

"Cnute, let me get someone to take guard duty."

"I'll take it for 'em. Love m' 'r not, they's family now. Mine." He pointed. "See? He's a movin' off."

Keri tried to follow where the arm pointed but saw nothing.

"Go back t' sleep, young un. I gots t' think. Leave m' be." He fished out Fum's whistle and began to play.

Keri laid some wood on the fire and then slept. Cnute had the watch.

IDLE HANDS

The sun bathed Brun's face as he awoke from a dream of home. He heard Tharn talking and deep, relaxed snores. Eldman walked into view from outside the perimeter, adjusting his pants.

Brun flung back his furs and winced from the ache in his chest. Tharn saw him and came over with some ale. "Relax," he said, handing Brun the cup. "Harness leaders decided another day of rest would not hurt us at all. Goran will make more ale, men can repair their gear, and we can all catch up on sleep."

"Are you possessed?" Brun took careful deep breaths between sentences. "We have to get going! Drakestad has been on the road for probably three hours!"

"That's what Keri said." Tharn smiled. "The wise men say, 'A step over the threshold is half the journey.' We crossed the mountains and the river, so we crossed *two* thresholds! Let the men rest a day. Goran says we will be on short rations but Jorvik and Antanas hooked four good fish already and traps added two rabbits, so there's fresh food. We're not using much wood because the ground is warm. We need the rest and so does Drakestad. They'll never match our pace once we restart. Rest now."

Brun looked at all the men still sleeping or lolling in their furs. "Surely you, Tharn, know a dozen sayings against procrastination."

"True, but 'a job started is two parts done' and we are half done and our biggest obstacles lie behind us. Take a day off! Besides, your snores turned almost civil last night. I think you're starting to get better. The sauna cures."

"Ohhhh," moaned Eldman a few feet away as he eased his wrinkled, naked body into the hot spring. "So nice…"

Brun glanced again at the stirring camp. He had not been in the water yet. He scratched a flea and felt the dried sweat on his clothes and furs. He looked at Eldman luxuriating. "Is there any breakfast left?"

Tharn laughed. "Yep. And even some more ale. I'll get you something."

Brun sat up. Eli and Sturl fletched arrows while Keri practiced swinging his battle-axe. Viktor applied pine tar to his boots. Jesspersson pulled wet gear from his box. Cnute played his whistle. Goran measured malt. Tharn came back with a cup and a sausage.

Brun sipped. He sighed and lay back. "All right, but I want a meeting of all the harness leaders at midday." He motioned at the sleds. "This afternoon we will consolidate the two sleds into one and reorganize the loads. We cannot waste a day doing nothing."

"Fine but remember what the Romans said: 'When fools try to avoid one vice, they sometimes rush to another.'"

"Maybe," said Brun, "but here's a Proverb I know: 'Whoever strays from the path of prudence comes to rest in the company of the dead.'"

Tharn laughed. Brun did not.

Keri burped. Supper had been a happy, if short rationed, affair with fresh ale, fresh clothes, fresh bodies, and fresh spirits. And two bites of fresh fish. Brun, feeling better, asked, and Goran reluctantly agreed, to double the ration of ale. Men sang or slept or sat drowsy in the hot water. Some roared over raucous stories as the unaccustomed alcohol took them. The ale made others morose for loved ones left behind. Cnute lay dozing atop the sled.

Gotthard walked stiff-legged over to where Keri and most of Sturl's young crew sat. Mantas came with him, the firelight flickering as they walked. Standing behind Jesspersson, Gotthard deliberately dropped his pants and prepared to urinate.

Gantson and Keri jumped up shouting, "Hey!" but the performance started and Jesspersson took a full blast of hot urine. He rolled out of the way as Gantson knocked Gotthard off target. Mantas laughed until he caught the errant stream across his ale mug. He shoved Gotthard, causing him to fall on his back, cursing and messing his own clothes in the cool grass. By now everyone stood laughing, yelling, or asking what happened.

Too late Keri saw the knife. Jesspersson threw it into Gotthard's shoulder.

Carnival turned to riot. Other knives flashed. Keri and Gantson held back Jesspersson from another attack, and Cnute plus four men held back Gotthard's mates. Tharn and Goran kept Gotthard on the ground. He raged and gasped as they tried to stop his bleeding. Brun ran up but after a couple of shouts and shoves he fell coughing to one side. Keri and Sturl managed to separate everyone and shout them to silence.

"Who started this?" Brun wheezed at Jesspersson.

"He pissed on me. And I think he's been pissing on my clothes box for nigh on two weeks."

Keri nodded. "So that's what it was."

Brun's eyes opened wide. He turned to Goran, who was examining Gotthard's wound. "How bad?"

Goran shrugged. "Cut's not too deep. Shouldn't use his shoulder for a spell. It'll heal nicely with pine tar."

Brun leaned closer to Gotthard. He paused for a deep breath. "Did you piss on Jesspersson?"

Before he could answer, several members of his crew spoke at once. "Sure did…had a bet with Mantas…I saw him…only a little, the rest missed…"

Brun waved a hand to hush the group. He cleared his throat and focused on Gotthard. "Have you been pissing on Jesspersson's clothes box?"

Gotthard clenched his jaw and turned away.

Brun snapped around and looked at Mantas. "You two stand guard together. Has he been pissing on Jesspersson's box?"

Mantas hesitated, studied his ale cup. Took a sip, grimaced, spit, and poured the rest out. He looked up. "Son of a bitch deserved it. Revenge for Gudrun. Besides, it gives us something to do on guard duty."

Some men laughed, some groaned. Keri shook his head.

Brun glared at Gotthard but spoke to the whole group. "Goran! The ale keg is closed. Who has Jesspersson's knife? Give it to me. Sturl, get me Gotthard's knife. Everyone to your furs. Keri, get your crew on the far side of the fire from Gotthard's. We leave before dawn. Move! Harness leaders to me behind the sled. We need to talk." He paused to cough. "Keri, join us. Everyone move now!" They moved. Brun snatched his furs from the ground and walked wheezing behind the sled.

ATTITUDE

Well before dawn Rentvatten formed up on the Tunturri. The gray snow looked like an ocean on a calm day with gentle rollers frozen in mid-motion. The distant northern horizon glowed like a cobalt-blue glass while the southern horizon traced a thin line of gold to mark the edge of the earth. Sparks from Goran's dying cook fire drifted lazily into the clear, frozen air.

Keri gazed north. "Seen Drakestad's smoke?"

"Nope," said Jesspersson.

Keri shaded his eyes. "Wonder where they are."

"Didn't look. Don't care."

"Come on, Jess. We may still have a chance."

Jesspersson kicked snow at the sled. "A pox on Drakestad. And Gotthard. And Brun. And Gudrun. Half the camp hates me now, so a pox on the whole God-cursed trip."

"Yeah," said Gantson, passing by with Alex. "And a pox on you, Jesspersson. Brun is so angry he cut the food ration again and won't let us get a last dip in the hot spring. We may as well starve warm here than starve frozen out there."

"Yeah, a pox on you," said Alex. "The ale is cut for the day."

Keri patted them each on the back. "There will be saunas in Hilhelm and plenty of ale." They flinched away.

Jesspersson hung his head. "Yeah, and Gotthard to fight, too."

Gantson smirked. "You're dead."

Keri shrugged. "Brun will fix that."

"And a pox on Brun, except that he already has one. He's riding again."

Keri's face clouded and his voice turned stern. "Hey, I gave you guys stuff to do. Get ready, we're leaving."

"Yes, sir, Jarl Keri." Alex bowed. "I forgot you are the head man now."

"I didn't ask for this, Brun just did it. Sturl had to take Gotthard's group. Now get ready. We're all pulling today."

As they sauntered off Alex mumbled, "Must be nice to be huge."

Keri flexed his fists, "Lord…" but took a breath and went off looking for Eli. He passed men working listlessly in the gray light. The harness leaders snapped orders but elicited no spark in the men. He thought about the reorganized harness groups as they stumbled to their duties. Gotthard was now under Brun's direct supervision. Brun reformed a crew under Eldman with Cnute, Eli, and Jorvik as reserve pushers or scouts, and Goran still as the cook. Keri noted Jorvik pushed today in place of the wounded Gotthard. Would the new teams be surly with the new order? His mood brightened when he saw his friend.

"Hey, Eli."

"Not now," said Sturl, grabbing Eli and pushing him toward the sled. "Brun says you scout with me today, Eli. Grab your skis and catch up." Sturl skied off with his crew dragging behind.

"Take up the slack, you sluggards," shouted Brun from his furs in the big sled. Then he broke into a coughing fit. He wheezed at Keri, "Get the crew moving."

"Me? Where's Tharn? Eldman?"

"We don't need a proverb now; we need to move. Talk to the men. Get them going. Be my voice." He labored as he sucked in a breath. "They like you."

"Not now that I am in charge."

"Still…they will listen. Go. Try."

The smaller sled was gone: disassembled for burning and repacked as firewood in the big sled. The crew stood around sullen. The older men gazed at Keri with expressions showing boredom or bemusement. His peers sneered. Keri faced them. "So…we've got to catch up to Drakestad. They have at least a full day's march on us."

"Pox on Drakestad," said someone.

Keri flinched. "Yeah…all right… How about a pox on Rentvatten? If we don't push, your wives and kids will never see you again."

"Like Timonen? Bue?" another voice.

Keri grimaced. "No. We owe this to them. And to help their families."

"We're hungry."

"We just ate." Keri's stomach grumbled at the thought.

"That wasn't enough to fill my little Freya," said Mantas.

"We will eat later. Come on! We're killing time. We have to go or we die."

No one moved.

Eli had finished getting his skis on and slid up by Keri. He turned to the men. "A pox on Drakestad. Pox on no food and even on the king's war. But also a pox on virginity. I'm a virgin. So's he." He jerked a thumb at Keri. The men laughed. Eli stuck out his tongue. "And we're going to Hilhelm with or without you so we can get back home next fall and take care of that. Are you coming?" He skied away after Sturl and the others. Mantas dangled the harness in his hands. He snickered, shrugged, and put it over his shoulder to pull. Others began to move.

Keri squeezed his eyes, then laughed. "I hadn't thought of it that way." He blushed but walked among the men, smiling. With a gesture or pat on the back he moved them to the sled. Then he stepped away, bowed his head a moment, and took his corner. "Ready? Push! SSSuuuut –tah!" They were off.

The sled moved well even though heavy again and they soon found a rhythm on the even snow. Once they gathered momentum Keri stepped away and jogged alongside. "Rainar, you have a good bass. Give us a song."

Brun smiled and sank into his furs.

After a few hours, they halted to rotate the men. Keri called across to Goran. "No food, but a cup of ale for every man."

Goran looked at Brun, who flicked a hand out of his furs. Goran shrugged and went to the keg. The men cheered.

They didn't eat all day but made two more stops for ale before the sun set. They made excellent time and the mountains behind them sank under the western horizon. Keri pushed them for an hour after sunset, not seeing the evening star behind them that watched him go.

As the men made camp, he brought the harness leaders to Brun.

Tharn spoke to the group. Brun listened. "Goran says an almost full meal tonight because we didn't eat at midday. That ought to fill them up. Half rations from now on. We're that short. Ale on the trail but none at night."

Brun shook his head.

"Guards," said Eldman, still breathing hard. "...smallest of fires, short of wood."

"Yes." Tharn peeked at Brun. "I'll save my proverb on thrift, but we have no wood to spare especially if we run into another storm. Usual guard shifts. Any questions?"

Keri opened his mouth, but nothing came out.

"Go ahead, Keri," said Tharn.

Keri smiled, then furrowed his brow. "Well...what if we use the boxes like we did at the river to make a wall, a windbreak. It may take time to load them in the morning, but it will help us stay warm. Maybe use less wood?"

Eldman grunted approval. Tharn looked at the group. Brun nodded from his furs. Sturl smiled. "My bunch will do it."

They moved off to dinner.

After dinner Tharn met with Brun. "He's changed. Keri. He's even showing a little stubble on his face."

Brun accepted a cup of hot willow tea from Goran. His voice rattled as he talked. "Aren't you the one who says, 'Necessity teaches the naked woman how to spin'?"

"He's hardly naked and he's strong as a horse, maybe a bear."

"Always has been." Brun sipped. "You know why he never beat me in wrestling?"

"You were stronger?"

"Nope. He never believed he could do it. He didn't believe in himself."

"Well, I wouldn't wrestle him now."

"Not until I'm better, anyway." Brun sank into his furs.

PACKS

The next days passed as Keri once imagined all days should have passed. The men hauled with a will and the sled moved easily. Keri seldom needed to give directions. The snow stayed firm and the drifts manageable. People accepted the new roles and Jesspersson stayed away from Gotthard, so peace reigned at night too. Eli, standing on Keri's shoulders, estimated Drakestad's fire at a half-day's journey north and east. Each day it came closer as both sled crews navigated to converge at the ravine that led down to the bridge to Hilhelm.

On the fifth day from the Usko River they paused for a mid-morning water break. Tharn pointed. "Scouts are coming in. Fast."

Everyone craned to see what was happening. Sturl led his men in looking anxiously over his shoulder. Keri motioned to form a circle in front of Brun's nest.

"Wolves!" Sturl panted. He skied up to Brun. "Dozens, maybe three score! I've never seen so many at one time. Maybe four or five regular size packs together. Just over that little drift. Big yellow she-wolf in the middle of them."

Keri sniffed something in the air. *Bread?* He glanced around.

Brun sat up on an elbow. His eyes were clear now and his voice sounded better. "Did they attack you?"

"Not exactly. They just stood spread out all over the snow. One came close enough to Mantas that he could shove his spear at it. Then it moved."

"But they will move?"

"That one did."

"And they didn't attack?"

"Not as a group, but if you watched one wolf, another suddenly appeared from another direction."

"Like that!" shouted Mantas, lunging at a wolf slinking behind the sled. The creature loped away, the first one most men had seen in a week.

The men turned and stared. More wolves appeared in every direction, slipping in and out of sight behind hummocks and low spots in the ground. Some had mostly white coats that blended into the snow. Others were gray and dusty brown, featuring white underbellies. With heads hung low they slouched on hunched shoulders, gliding like a school of pike stalking bait fish. Two sat on nearby rises: the yellow she-wolf and a big silver. Keri studied them. The silver stared right at Rainar.

Cnute stepped toward a dirty brown wolf. It shied away. "If one gets close, watch t' ears. Their ears points t' what they's thinkin' 'bout."

Brun started to get up but Tharn pushed him back. "One more day, Brun. Goran says one more day."

Brun flopped back and grimaced. "Yes, Mother." The men chuckled, standing in a circle facing out. Tharn spoke from the middle. "This is strange, how the wolves act, but the tales warned us. It is said Tunturri wolves will only attack from behind or in the dark."

Eli flexed his bowstring and nocked an arrow. "At this range we could hit a few and drive them back."

Sturl stayed Eli's hand. "Sigvard warned us to save arrows until the end. If we have an attack, we will need them then. He said they try to get you to use up your weapons. One will offer himself as a target and another will try to grab your spear when you lunge. Be cautious."

Brun propped up on an elbow. "Eli, Jorvik, we need your bows riding on the back of the sled to protect the rear. Sturl, bring the scouts in closer. Keri, get us moving." He sniffled.

"Devilish strange," said Tharn. "But we finally have a proverb to keep us moving: 'The time for the mouse to yawn is when it's half inside the cat.'"

"Are we the cat or the mouse?" said Keri.

"We are a duck frozen in the ice." Jesspersson flinched as another she-wolf loomed around the sled, its muzzle trimmed in orange. He backed into the crowd. "How do we move?"

Cnute stomped at the beasts. They pulled back. "They fears th' strong man. Keep yer back covered an' push at 'em. An' remember, th' black wolf's mine." He scanned the pack.

Random and silent, the wolves sometimes moved together, and other times just drifted alone. One or two looked directly at specific men and then moved on. Keri caught the yellow she-wolf following his movements. The orange-tinged one followed Jesspersson.

"I can't count them," said Keri to Brun. "They keep disappearing and coming up somewhere else."

"Yep. This was always the unbelievable part of Sigvard's story: the wolves not attacking until dark."

"He said they don't like light. We should stop early and get a big fire going," said Keri.

"You think we have the wood?"

"According to Sigvard, we'll die if we don't," said Tharn.

Brun slowly shook his head.

Keri glanced at the sled and the wolves. "We will have to move slower now so guards can cover the pushers. You saw Cnute. They will back off when you face them, but we need more guards, which means fewer pushers and scouts."

Brun said, "What would you do?"

Keri took a deep breath. "Put Cnute, Sturl, and Gotthard at the front. On foot, not skis. They'll need their hands for weapons. Have them push on to some of the closer rises and figure where we need to go without having to go there themselves. It is not safe anymore for scouts to be out of sight."

Brun smiled. "Try it."

Gotthard glanced back at Brun. "Can I have my knife?"

"You can have a spear."

"Mine's broke. Besides, I need something to fight close with."

Brun hesitated.

"Hey, I didn't start the knife fight."

"All right. Take my spear, but be careful with your shoulder." Brun gave him the knife. "You're a tough man, Gotthard. Jesspersson's just a kid trying to figure out what kind of man he is. Let him mess up like your father let you mess up."

"My father beat the pine tar out of me."

"You'll get your chance at Hilhelm."

Gotthard nodded as he took the knife.

Brun turned to Keri, smiled again. "Hey, I didn't cough."

Keri smiled. "You can have your job back."

Tharn stepped up. "Not until tomorrow."

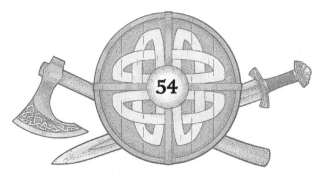

DELIBERATE

Out front Cnute indicated a shallow rise to Gotthard and Sturl. "Let's go." Several wolves came forward. Cnute snarled and walked straight at them. "God's wi' us, ye demons. Back off." The wolves peeled around them and continued their circuit.

Gotthard walked backward to face a wolf circling around them. "Jesus, Cnute, how can you just walk at 'em?"

"Jesus an' practice," said Cnute.

"How do you practice talking to wolves?"

"Ye don'. Ye practice trustin' Jesus."

"How do you practice trusting Jesus?" said Gotthard.

"Dunno. I jus' started. Stop worryin', I guess. Do th' bes' ye can wi' what ye 'ave."

Gotthard pointed his spear at an approaching wolf. The wolf kept coming. Gotthard stomped his foot and barked, "Jesus!"

The wolf backed off.

Gotthard glanced at Cnute and smiled.

Sturl pointed at a clear stretch that headed more south than east. "How about there?"

Cnute said, "We needs t' go more northeast."

"True, but the path is open and we could make good time. We'll probably find another stretch heading north before the day is out."

"Yeah," said Gotthard. "The sled is plodding. The wolves aren't moving away as quickly for Keri as they do for you. They would appreciate moving faster."

Cnute considered. "All right, no straight an' narrow f' us t'day." He called back and pointed to a gap in two drifts. Tharn waved and Keri turned the sled. The wolves parted as they entered the easier path. As the scouts moved, the wolves shied away. The sled picked up speed on the clear stretch for two hundred paces. Twice they repeated the pattern, making good time where they found a clear route.

By midday the wolves trotted alongside just out of danger and Cnute smiled as the sled recaptured its best speeds. "Like it's glidin' on a slope," he said. "You two keep goin' an' fin' a route to the northeast. I'se checkin' w' Brun and Tharn."

They went on and Cnute waited for the sled to catch up. He heard a yell, looked, and saw Gotthard but no Sturl. Wolves surrounded Gotthard. "Don' move," shouted Cnute, running toward him. He threw his spear through the belly of a wolf about to spring at Gotthard's back and drew his knife. Two wolves dragged off the spear. "Where's Sturl?"

"There." Gotthard gestured with his head while swinging his spear back and forth at approaching wolves.

Cnute saw a hole in the snow with Sturl squirming at the bottom about a man's height below him. Cnute waved at the sled. "Stop! Stop! Streambed! Stop!"

Keri, Tharn, Eldman all repeated the order. The men hauled backward but the sled carried momentum on the icy snow and barely slowed. Keri pulled his harness hard to the right. The sled veered a fraction. The crew hung on the sides and back, their feet plowing through the snow. Brun jerked awake in his furs and sat up just as Keri's full strength pulled and snapped the harness. When the sled lurched Brun tumbled off the top and under the careening sled.

Cnute saw forty wolves surge over the nearest rise like a wave on a beach. Eli and Jorvik fired arrows from their perch but the wild ride led to wild aim and only one scored a hit. Men shouted and snatched weapons from the staggering sled.

For Cnute time slowed to a crawl. The sled crept pace by pace toward him while Sturl sluggishly climbed up the streambed. As in a dream Eli fumbled for arrows, mouthing unintelligible words. Wolves hung like hummingbirds in the air as they leaped at the men. Gotthard's laugh was distorted when his lethargic knife sliced a wolf, its blood butterflying gracefully into the sky. Snow arched from Keri's feet while he dragged the front corner and pulled the sled gradually, ever so gradually, off course to break its speed. The craft tilted imperceptibly at first, then more and more, digging in its runners now sideways to its momentum. Languidly it came straight at Cnute, who stood fascinated as the structure, nearly as tall as his cabin, pushed by invisible hands, teetered above him. "Lord," he whispered. The sled's tall wall nudged him, and he fell into the streambed Sturl just escaped. The sled begrudgingly stopped at the ravine's edge.

When he hit the bottom, sound and speed came back to Cnute. Shouts, snarls, and cries filled his head. He scrambled to his feet in the ditch and jumped high enough to reach the runner above him. The runner moved and the earth gave way, dropping him and the sled a hand's breadth down the escarpment.

"Here!" It was Keri reaching down. Cnute jumped and Keri hauled him out.

Wolves pressed the men. Cnute pulled his long knife and flung Keri his battle-axe. Keri slipped the loop around his wrist, growled, and burst upon the wolves. He broke out of the circle of men and

302

swept around him with the axe. He hit one wolf on an upswing, severing its leg. He spun like a dancer and caught another behind him. He used the spear point on the shaft to stab deep in the throat of one on his back. With a roar he spun and spun into the pack. Cnute stared open-mouthed.

The wolves backed off, turned, and fled. Eli's arrows chased them as they disappeared. Keri stopped spinning and stood with his axe dripping. He gulped air and shook his head. The men stared at him in the center of a circle of blood and dismembered wolves. He saw the carnage, fell to his knees, and retched into the snow.

Cnute saw the wolves regrouping two hundred paces away. The great black wolf pushed up to the front, surveying the tilted sled and wounded men. He trotted closer, following the sled's tracks to a patch of red in the snow. He licked the blood and then stared directly at Cnute.

Cnute rolled his shoulders and wiped his knife in the snow. He snatched a hand axe from Tharn and walked toward the wolf. The beast lifted his leg at Cnute and then loped away to the north. His pack turned and followed. The silver wolf stared at Rainar before moving off.

Rainar shivered. "Where are they going?"

"I'se not sure," said Cnute. "But I'se sure glad I'm not on Drakestad's sled t'night."

Tharn's voice broke the sound of heavy breathing, groans, and retching. "Sturl! Keri! Help Brun!" Tharn stood at the back of the sled. Brun's arm stuck out from under the deck.

Keri wiped his mouth with some clean snow and ran over with Cnute and Goran. As in the cave, they dug into the snow under the arm. Cnute flopped down beside Keri and they scooped snow out on both sides, finding more and more of Brun. His fingers flexed. Sturl brought up the shovels and they loosened the body from the jaws of sled and snow that held it. They pulled him out. Wide-eyed, Brun gasped, then fainted.

"He's alive!" said Tharn. "Thank God he wasn't under the runners."

Brun's face bled from the nose, and his outer clothes were ripped. His breathing was ragged but the unnatural way his legs twisted caused Keri to break away and retch again.

Goran grabbed Brun's furs and wrapped him on the ground. "He isn't feeling anything right now. I have to try to set his legs straight while I can. Keri, Cnute, come hold him for me."

Keri gulped. "Can't."

Tharn put a hand on Keri. "If he wakes only you can hold him. He needs you."

Keri looked up into twenty faces. Eli nodded at him, winked. Keri swallowed, wiped his mouth with snow again, and went to Goran. As the men stepped aside, Keri said, "Sturl, would you post guards? Eldman, see about the sled." He turned to Cnute. "Where do you need me?"

Goran placed Keri's hands to hold Brun just so. "There. And there. Don't let him move."

Keri gagged. "Yep." Cnute gave him a grim smile. Keri stared into the wreck that had been Brun, choking back bile. While Goran worked, Keri saw Brun's rolled-back eyes, bloody face, and limp red beard. He felt the blood, sticky between his fingers, and the nasty smell of Brun's soiled clothes. *Lord, don't let me cry. Give me strength.* He thought he heard Fum's tune. He glanced at Cnute and saw the whistle hanging from his neck. Keri heard the tune again. No one else seemed to notice. *Lord...* He closed his eyes, shuddering, and felt at peace. He felt a compassion, a love for this broken man who so loved life. *Lord, have mercy on Brun. Have mercy on us all.* He opened his eyes. He could hear the men behind him panting, whispering, worrying. A memory of Hamar came to him. "Maybe God's plan for ye is out there on the sled, don't ye know?" Keri found he was breathing normally, his anxiety gone.

It took a while, but Goran finished an improvised splint from splintered skis and stood up. "Thank you, Cnute, Keri."

Keri rubbed his bloody hands in the snow and wiped them on his tunic. He rose, calling for harness leaders and the map. "Cnute, you have Brun's crew for now. Have your men set up for Goran while he finishes with our wounded. Then hot food. We camp here tonight. Sturl, design a wall using the boxes with our back to the ditch. Organize our guards. Eldman, tell me about the sled while Tharn figures out where we are."

After talking with Tharn and Eldman, Keri sent Eli with three men up the ravine while Cnute and three others went down to find a crossing point. Goran came wiping blood from his hands. "Brun will be in a lot of pain when he wakes up. If he was home he wouldn't walk again for at least a month or more. Out here...I won't have enough willow bark to ease that pain. Plus, I have at least three other men who will need some pain relief."

"How about ale?"

"It might take the edge off, but we're short of that too. The good thing is that Brun seemed to be almost over his chest sickness. At least he will be able to breathe while he heals."

Keri nodded, then led the men to unload the sled so they could lift it away from the ravine edge. When the scouts came back, Keri brought in the harness leaders and listened to their ideas. He folded his arms. "All right. Sturl built us a nice fort. That will allow us fewer guards and more sleep, but I also want to burn less wood. Tomorrow we backtrack a little and cross at that spot Eli found. We reload before dawn and leave when we can see fifty paces. Questions?"

"It's delib'rate, ye know," said Cnute.

Keri glanced over. "What?"

"Wolves knew. Plans it. Took us off track b' showin' us th' easy way."

"The wolves?"

"Yep. Give us th' easy path."

Tharn cleared his throat. "Like the Trojan said? 'Beware Greeks bearing gifts'?"

"Like that Loki," said Mantas, "always foolin' the gods."

Cnute rubbed his good eye and adjusted his red cap, covering more of his head and face. "More 'an that. I should a died a dozen times searchin' fer Liisa's revenge. Wolf was always jus' outta reach. Led m' on fer weeks. Never turned 'r killed me at night. Bastard knew God had somethin' I shoulda been doin'. Wolf kep' m' sidetracked. How much time'd I waste? Now he's here tryin' t' waste m' time ag'in."

Keri nodded.

"We gots t' focus on where we're goin', not what th' devil wolf wants."

BLESSED

Brother Hamar prayed alone in a corner as the proceedings began. Old Sigvard stood in his tattered trek gear in Rentvatten's great hall and addressed the council. "After we closed the gate last night I heard screams from Wiglif's house and ran in to find him beating his daughter, Gudrun, with a rope. She was nearly senseless." Sigvard gestured to Wiglif's wife, Ilmater. "She was beaten too." Wiglif, seated next to Ilmater on a bench opposite Sigvard, glared.

Valdemar and four councilmen nodded behind their table. That was not news.

Sigvard continued. "Wiglif said Gudrun was pregnant and he was going to demand satisfaction from Jesspersson's mother. Brother Hamar arrived and reminded Wiglif that Ilmater was pregnant when they married, and he had no room to be angry."

That raised an eyebrow on the council and a murmur from the spectators. Wiglif shouted, "But Jesspersson didn't marry Gudrun!"

"He didn't know he had to," snarled Sigvard.

"He should have anyway!" Wiglif jumped to his feet.

Sigvard pointed his age-knotted finger. "Would you have married Ilmater if her father hadn't made you?"

Wiglif's cheeks huffed above his fuzzy beard. Ilmater whimpered.

Gudrun, on a stool in a cleared space before the council, remained upright and stoic, her face bruised and cut. She stared at the cloth-covered altar in the back of the room.

Valdemar waved a hand to Sigvard. "Continue."

"Brother Hamar had me bring Wiglif here to the great hall to sleep off his anger. Hamar stayed with Ilmater and Gudrun."

"Anything else?"

"It took me awhile to get from the north tower to Wiglif's. You could hear the screams halfway across the village. Yet none of their so-called Christian neighbors went to help or even see what the problem was. I remember pagans who were better friends. And today there is gossip everywhere I go. Perhaps I should tell everything I see in the village at night."

The spectators murmured.

Valdemar thumped his ale cup. "Thank you, Sigvard. I meant was there anything else we need to know about Wiglif's actions with his family?"

"It was shameful, hypocritical, and cruel." Sigvard spat at Wiglif's feet and sat down on a side bench. Wiglif bristled but didn't move.

Valdemar rubbed his eyes and let out a deep sigh. "Brother Hamar, can you add anything?"

The monk stepped forward and pulled the dusty white cowl from his half-shaved head. He looked down and kept his hands inside his wool sleeves. "Now Gudrun had a knife, tryin' t' find strength t' stab herself, she was. But she was too woozy from the beating, I'm thinkin'. Saints be praised, but I led her to talkin' an' she gave up the knife." He gestured at Gudrun. "Bruised all over she was, especially her back, an' cut either from the punches or the rope…nasty gash on her neck, don't ye know, where Wiglif tore off the thong 'twas holdin' Jesspersson's copper ring. While I tends her wounds she was sobbin' she'd been… handled roughly by Sami last fall, sweet Mother of God. Jesspersson? He treated her nice, and she responded."

The crowd noise increased until Arn, now on the council, pointed to Gudrun. "So, the child is Jesspersson's." It was a statement. The fire crackled in the silence.

Hamar slowly shook his head. "'Twas not a formal confession, don't ye know, but me tellin' what I heard is close to violating my vows, God forgive me. But the child is *possibly* Jesspersson's, God willin'. Time may tell. In either case, Gudrun is a victim here, can't ye see? …of youth, loneliness, and the lust of two young men…maybe three, God help us. Somewhere in Gudrun's story Sami brought his brother…to help."

The crowd gasped and chattered. Hamar noted that Sami was not in the room. Ilmater went to her daughter and held her. They both sobbed.

"Quiet, please!" Valdemar paused.

Arn looked at Hamar. "Are you suggesting that Gudrun should not be punished?"

Sigvard jumped up. "For doing what her mother did? And others if you will give me leave to talk."

"But she is pregnant!" said Arn.

"God's will, it is," said Hamar. "Many ne'er have children."

"Are you saying this is a blessing? I say it is a punishment, a curse," said Arn.

"Is it that your children are a blessing or curse?"

"But my wife has a husband."

"Ah, that is the blessing, ye know: having someone t' share the joy o' children and t' help with the work. Gudrun now is at a disadvantage 'cause she has no one here now t' share this burden. But neither does Brun's wife, or Lars' wife. Their men are on the sleds, ye know."

"But they aren't pregnant!" stammered Arn.

"Are you sure?"

Valdemar rapped his wooden cup on the table. It splashed, and he shook the ale off his hands as he shouted, "Quiet! Quiet!" The noise subsided. "What are you saying, Brother Hamar?"

Hamar turned to face both the crowd and the council. "We canna have people beatin' their kin, don't ye know? We should be punishin' Wiglif for beating his wife and daughter. 'Twas sinful, unlawful rage, not discipline."

The women nodded. Most of the men grimaced. Terkel at the council table jumped to his feet. "It's Gudrun who violated the law! Wiglif has the right to discipline his household as he sees fit."

"Exactly," snorted Arn.

Brother Hamar cleared his throat and crossed himself. "An' now which law o' the village is broken? So few o' ye can read, ye made me writer o' your laws. I know no place that says a woman an' a man may not join before marriage. Yer mistakin' God's laws f' Man's laws."

"So?" said Arn. "She has broken God's laws and should be punished."

"Well now, Saints confess we have all broken God's laws," said Hamar. "Is it that the council should be punishin' the whole village?"

Terkel slapped the table. "But this is a big sin. Petty gossip and kids stealing apples are not the same."

Hamar waved a hand. "Ah…perhaps not in your mind, Terkel, but God says one sin 'tis bad as another. Not desirin' yer neighbor's donkey is but a few sentences from ye cannae murder. Scripture's put 'em in the same place, don't ye know?"

"Still," said Valdemar, interrupting, "we cannot allow this kind of blatant violation of public morals. Once one of the laws of the village is ignored, then all are open to ridicule and abuse. We must not allow this knothole in the wall to become a breach."

"Yes," shouted Arn. "Gudrun should be shunned until she gives birth, then exiled."

The room filled with loud voices. Ilmater dropped her head and cried.

"We have a proposal," shouted Valdemar, banging his cup. "It is worth considering. Our village is held together by moral ideas which depend on all of us adhering to the laws. We cannot have our moral and spiritual laws flouted any more than we can our council laws. It leads to internal destruction."

Sigvard moved to stand between Gudrun and the council. "What about wantonly beating another person?" he asked. "A person you swore before village and God to love?"

"That came after. Gudrun caused it all and she is the problem to solve," said Arn.

The room murmured and Sigvard rolled his eyes. "My old pagan neighbors had more sense than you new Christians."

Valdemar put his chin in his hand and pointed a bony finger at Hamar. "You would say mercy no doubt. But perhaps we should have you speak a sermon to her on sin and how the people cannot tolerate it."

Hamar crossed himself, took a deep breath, and covered his head with his cowl. The crowd stopped talking. "'Tis right ye are, we should be sayin' sin is wrong an' we donnae approve. Ye know without a standard for our behavior, we be collapsin' like a bad roof. But I cannae condemn poor Gudrun for joinin' before marriage, without makin' m'self a liar. An' I cannae keep from bein' a liar without breakin' a promise t' two young people in this village, which would be makin' me an oath breaker. God help me."

Gudrun jerked her eyes to Hamar. From under the cowl he raised his eyebrows at her. Her lips quivered and tears burst from her blackened eyes.

The room fell silent until Arn shook his head. "What? I don't know what you are saying."

Hamar shrugged and looked up. "It is Jesspersson's ring Gudrun was a wearin'..."

"So…you mean? By the beard of St. Peter," snorted Terkel. "They're married!"

Ilmater collapsed. The crowd erupted in laughter, shouts, and talking. Gudrun looked at the floor and wept.

"But there were no banns!" said Valdemar.

"And no legal ceremony!" said Arn.

Hamar held up his hands. "God willin', I willnae break a promise, an' I willnae speak a sermon ag'in poor Gudrun. By the saints, we are all sinners, an' while God wants obedience, He's preferin' mercy an' love over punishment. Do what ye think you must, but I be preachin' m' next sermon as the Holy Spirit tells me, praise God, not on what the village gossips think I ought."

The council erupted. Sigvard and Wiglif scowled at each other.

"Well, I wish you had told us this sooner," said Terkel. He stood up, finished his ale, and made to leave.

"Told ye what? Have I not week after week been a tellin' ye how t' live a life t' please God an' how t' find God's forgiveness when ye be sinnin'? By Saint Padarick himself, is that not the lesson we should be learnin' from poor Gudrun an' Jesspersson? An' Wiglif?"

"No, I mean told us about the wedding."

Hamar turned away. "If I said anything about a weddin', I would make m'self a liar, don't ye know?"

"Wait, wait." Valdemar leaned on the table. "Who else knows about this marriage?"

"If there's been a marriage, 'tis not mine t' talk of," said Hamar, stooping to lift Ilmater to a seat. "Nope, I've not spoken t' anyone about a marriage."

Benches scraped; people laughed or argued. The room descended into chaos.

Valdemar rubbed his temples under his wool cap. He rapped his cup on the table but still had to shout. "I think we can all go home and let Gudrun and Wiglif and Ilmater work this out. It is no longer village business."

People shuffled out still talking, laughing, and arguing like the end of a wrestling match. Ilmater fell on Gudrun again. Laurel came from the crowd and held them both. Ilmater's brother took Ilmater and Gudrun and led them out. Wiglif stormed past everyone.

Hamar thumped onto a bench and put his head in his hands. When the room emptied Valdemar came to him. He put a hand on the monk's shoulder and smiled a very old smile. "You are a blessing to this village."

"But, I…"

"No, listen, Brother Hamar. You are a clever peacemaker and a blessing to this village." He nodded as he walked away.

Hamar sat alone. A tear ran down into his beard. "Ah, Lord forgive me. Let the anger o' the people fall t' me an' be merciful t' poor Jesspersson and Gudrun. Forgive m' for 'tis against you an' you alone that I always seem to be sinnin'."

Fum's whistle played somewhere in the village.

GOOD FOR HEARTS

The morning after the ambush the wolves disappeared. Wary of another trap Keri led the crew out. Working their way around the deep streambed, they made good time though they slowed more than usual for drifts and turns. Every bump caused Brun to groan, a sound the men hated. Keri tried to get them to sing but their hearts remained chary and his attempts fell flat. He allowed ale at noon but one cup barely quenched thirst, much less diffused fear.

Keri and Sturl doubled the guard that night. The men went to their furs with spears or swords in reach. Keri groaned to find they only had ten spears and about eighty arrows between Sturl, Jorvik, and Eli. "The wolves snatched our arrows when we missed and took their dead when we hit. We lost every arrow we shot," said Sturl.

"No more arrows for hunting then," said Keri.

"Hunt what?" said Eli. "There hasn't been a bird, a rabbit, or anything since we hit the Tunturri."

The next dawn, Goran motioned to Keri and Tharn. "Someone's

been in the food," he said. He opened a box and showed them firewood where food should have been. "I'd guess they put the wood in so no one would notice it was lighter."

"But who?" said Keri.

"And when?" said Tharn. "We all see the boxes all the time."

"Not at night," said Goran.

"And not when we were in the cave," said Mantas, who heard them talking. "It could have been anyone, not just the guards. Maybe when we were separated at the river."

"We didn't have any wood to put in the boxes," said Keri.

Tharn shook his head. "How much do you think is gone, Goran?"

"I'd guess about a day's worth. That means it didn't happen all at once. No one could eat that much all at once."

Keri looked directly at Mantas. "OK, this could cause real problems among the men. Let's keep this quiet. If we get there with no more shortages, then there is no problem. But if word gets out…the men are edgy enough already without throwing a thief in the midst."

"Sure," said Mantas. "Not a word." He went off.

Keri pursed his lips and watched him go. "Goran, how many days' food do we have?"

"Maybe eight if we eat only half what we'd planned. Remember, the wolves destroyed most of two days' food at the cave, so there's no reserve anymore."

"Tharn, you said about ten more days to the bridge?"

"Yep, the same as Eldman said about wood."

"That counts cutting up the sled?"

"Yep."

He shook his head. "'s wounds…uh, I mean, raging weasels." He instinctively touched Stjärna's scarf and looked for her star.

Eli daydreamed of Laurel as Keri pushed the crew harder. It kept him from thinking of his aches and the cold. With still no sign of wolves Keri set the pace, pushing at the back and encouraging the men by name. Seeing Keri lead made Eli smile.

At noon they stopped. Eli started to help Goran unload his boxes, but Keri said, "We'll run while the wolves let us. Piece of cheese and a cracker is all we need. Is the water frozen? Yes? Ale then. One cup."

The men began to grumble as Keri walked away. They were hungry. Eli heard, paused, and joined in. "A cracker? You'd think a giant like that would want more to eat. How's he going to keep going on just a mouse portion?"

Rainar looked at his cheese. "And a skinny mouse at that. He's gonna kill us."

Eli snorted. "If I was in charge we'd eat like kings."

Antanas sniffed. "That's why you're not in charge, Eli. We'd have run out of food already and we still have a week to go. I'd rather eat a little every day than nothing for the last few days."

Mantas and most of Gotthard's old crew sat nearby. "Yeah, idiot. You'd have starved us all already."

Eli wanted to smile but stood and walked away. "Well, don't gripe to me when all you can produce tomorrow is a mouse-sized turd!"

Mantas threw snow at Eli's back. "Idiot. Keri knows what he's doing."

The others chimed in. "Yeah."

"Good sense."

"We can do this."

"Yeah."

Now Eli smiled.

They ate up the distance that day and the next, even when the wolves reappeared on their flanks. Brun regained his senses, but his stifled groans showed how he struggled with pain. He lived though, and it encouraged the men.

They tried to sing again. They knew it was almost over. When Keri beckoned them to the harness, the men hustled to regain the pace. At breaks they again talked and joked. Even with the wolves on their flanks and the growl in their stomachs.

Each man found a wolf he could identify and gave them names: Lop Ear, Serpent, Fat Tail, Lucy, Ale Eyes, Brown Bitch, Old Harry. Jesspersson picked the orange-eyed she-wolf and called it Goody. Mantas named one with a squinted eye Sausage Stealer. Eli spotted the green-eyed wolf with the pine twig and called it Laurel. The yellow wolf caught Keri's eye.

Brun summoned the leaders that evening and asked for suggestions. Eldman said they should dismantle more of the sled for firewood.

Keri demurred. "Its high walls are good protection at night. Let's burn all the wood and our boxes first." He looked at Brun.

"Agreed."

The group nodded.

For two days they moved cleanly through the wolves, most often led by Cnute and Gotthard. Others tried to lead but any hesitancy made the wolves bold. Rainar and Mantas faced outright hostility.

On their fourth night from the ambush Keri called the leaders to Brun. "How are we doing?"

Eldman grunted. "Gotta make more torches but we're running out of pitch."

"How about ski poles?" said Brun strapped in his pallet.

Eldman grunted. "Skis too. Only twelve pair left anyway, and skiers are having trouble keeping up with the sled."

Tharn gestured at the map. "Eldman's right. We are on that last rise heading towards the ravine where the Archangel River flows. The slope slows them down."

"Burn the skis," said Keri. He nodded at Goran. "Food?"

"We're stretching it already. How much longer?"

Brun wheezed, "Tomorrow is forty days. We've lost days to the cave and river, and we're guessing at our speed. It could be four more days or seven. And that assumes the storm we saw forming before sunset goes behind us."

"Seven is tough. We've run out of several things. Tomorrow we run out of ale."

Brun sighed. "Couldn't run out of cabbage instead?"

Goran shrugged. "A good wife never runs out of pickled cabbage. Isn't that in the Bible?"

Tharn laughed. "No, it was my grandmother: 'Cabbage is good for hearts and farts!'"

They laughed but Keri's stomach grumbled. "Harness leaders, are your men holding up? No one had to ride today."

Sturl shrugged. "They want to live."

Lars, Laurel's father, spoke. "Eli says Drakestad's fire is closer again tonight. The kid's got good eyes."

"He sure spotted your daughter." Sturl gave him a friendly thump.

"Ha! I'm glad he's here where I can watch him. Anyway, it's hard to say how far, but we are gaining ground if the boy is right."

"The finish line is the bridge over the Archangel," said Brun. "Out there." He pointed east. "At forty days we should have seen the hills already."

Tharn tapped the map. "Look for hills with a deep notch where the river passes Hilhelm. When we see that, we are still a couple days out and need to locate a knoll. It marks the drawdown off this plateau to the bridge. The knoll should be slightly north of the notch in the hills. If we've been drifting, it could be south. Who knows how far off track the wolves took us?"

"God knows," said Keri.

STORMS

The storm found them. Snow fell insistent, heavy, and wet. Buffeted by gusts, flakes became ice pellets stinging the eyes and exposed skin. They blasted horizontally across the camp and stuck on the sled like ice on a cliff face. Men walked hunched over. Snow buried their furs while they slept. At dawn Keri couldn't see far and the sled didn't budge. Ice froze everything almost as fast as they could chop it loose.

Frozen snot streaked the beards, and the clean-cheeked boys double-wrapped their faces. Eli wished Laurel made the earflaps on his cap longer. Goran struggled to keep the fire going as gusts blew shovels full of wet into the flames. The barley meal bubbled lukewarm when he served it and glazed over with slush before they could eat.

With visibility nil, Keri suggested they wait until the storm passed. Brun agreed, but they resented the enforced rest. The men grumbled under improvised overhead cover in their furs. At first the confident mood of the previous days buoyed them, but the cold and slim rations gnawed at their spirits. Food meant warmth and cheer, but there was little of either.

Keri sat at the edge of the dripping shelter watching the guards.

"They say, 'Let sleeping dogs lie.' Wolves are only a couple steps from dogs."

Eli tried to stretch his legs. "I wonder how many steps they are from Brother Hamar's lions?"

"I don't know. Do lions come in black and gray? There's even a silver wolf."

"Did you see that orange fur one? She looks right at me," said Jesspersson.

"The yellow one looks at me," said Keri. "She's the color of bread."

A guard pulled a brand from the fire and chased off a wolf. Tharn rubbed his eyes. "The Psalmist says, 'Fire goes before the Lord and consumes his foes. The earth trembles.'"

"The wolves tremble too," said Eli.

"Amen," said Keri. "But how much fire do we have left?"

Cnute, appearing to be asleep next to Eli, opened his eye. "In th' sled 'r in yer belly?" He snorted and rolled over.

Keri wondered.

The gray dawn emboldened the wolves. Keri started to give torches to the guards, but Eldman waved him off. The carpenter took several logs and sawed two perpendicular notches lengthwise partway down their lengths. He stood one log on its uncut end and put kindling into the notch. He lit it and the log burned slowly from the top down. He placed torch-logs at the corners and the wolves stayed away.

The small fires provided a meagre heat for Goran to make a little broth, which raised smiles until they realized that was all they'd get until dinner. Keri held off the last of the ale until they could move again. Small fires meant little chance to dry clothes or leaky boots. The only relief was sleep but there was no dry place to lie down.

At dawn the next day the storm raged on. Eldman made the last of the pre-cut wood into log torches. In the dim gray light he disassembled more of the sled. Frayed slats from the boxes would serve as makeshift torches. Eldman begged a pair of spare socks from each man to serve as wicks and confiscated Goran's remaining lard for fuel. He had little confidence they would burn very long. Jorvik and two others offered their shields to the fire. "Too heavy to carry anyway."

On guard duty the second night, Keri saw the storm fade back to a gentle snow. He woke Goran. "Something hot. The storm is passing. We leave before dawn."

Rolling their furs, the crew jumped when Goran called, "Food!" The men queued up with their cups and Goran ladled in some meal.

Gotthard looked in his cup. "Hey, where is the meat? We ain't sheep, you know."

Goran shrugged. "None left. Between what the wolves snatched and the extra days of the storm, we are out."

"We packed in extra food for extra days. I saw Brun and Tharn count it," said Gotthard, poking a finger at Goran. "The wolves didn't take that much. You've been stuffing yourself on the side, haven't you?"

"Look at my pants. Double cinched," said Goran. "I've lost so much weight my clothes look like a tent."

Gotthard squinted and frowned. "I know there was more. I helped pack it. Where's your hideout?" Gotthard turned to the pile of rolled furs and began tossing them about. Several men stepped up to protect their bundles, but Gotthard drew his knife and backed them off. "Which one is Goran's?"

Someone pointed and Gotthard cut the thong holding the bundle together. Out rolled socks, boots, clothes, and a hat, but no food. Goran came up and whacked Gotthard's hand with his iron ladle, spinning the knife into the furs. Gotthard reached for him, but Goran hit him in the jaw with the ladle and Gotthard went down.

Several men pulled their knives, but Goran swung around on them with the ladle in one hand and his cleaver in the other. "I warned Keri and Tharn two days ago that someone's been stealing food. Now we are almost out. I knew I would take the blame, but I didn't do it. One of you did."

Keri came beside him. "Back off. Let's open everyone's furs to see if someone has stolen food."

"We don't need to do that," said Mantas. "Gotthard's just hungry. We know the wolves stole it."

Gotthard glared at Goran. "The wolves stripped the sausage box, but they didn't get any cheese. My Siggy put in three cheese wheels marked with her rune. I've only seen two come out. I saw the other one untouched last week. Who's got it?"

Goran considered. "He's right. We should have had her other cheese this week."

Mantas snorted. "Whoever stole it probably ate it already."

"Or is saving it," said Eli. "It's too big to eat all at once."

Gotthard stood alternately rubbing his hand and his jaw.

Keri stepped to the middle. He pointed at the guards who had come to see the ruckus. "Guards, get back out. Be especially watchful; the wolves already surprised us once. Everyone else get your fur roll."

Almost eagerly the men kicked open their furs. Rainar was careful as he rolled out his, and Antanas stepped on his hand.

"What's that?" Antanas pointed while Rainar squealed. Two men pulled him away. Antanas flipped over a fold in the fur and there was a mug-sized piece of cheese.

"It's not mine," cried Rainar. His guards shook him. "It belongs to Mantas. He has the rest. He made me do it."

Mantas pulled his knife and lunged at Rainar. "You lying weasel." Goran hit Mantas' hand with the ladle and again knocked a knife into the furs. He smiled at the ladle.

Keri grabbed Mantas and looked him full in the eye. "You've been reluctant to investigate this since Goran reported it. Let's have a look at your furs." Mantas pulled away but Antanas grabbed him from behind.

"Fine," said Mantas. He shook off Antanas and walked to an un-rolled bundle.

"That one's mine," called Cnute from guard duty.

"Watch for wolves!" said Keri.

"Yes'r."

Godwin pointed. "This one."

Out rolled an apple and another hunk of cheese. Shouts, shoving, anger, threats. Keri raised his voice above the mob. "Quiet! We'll hear Mantas."

"Rainar put that there," said Mantas.

Rainar stiffened and faced Keri. "I did not. That first week when Brun left me behind Mantas said he would take care of me if I took care of him. He wanted silver at Hilhelm for the food he gave me on the Tunturri. I agreed."

Gotthard laughed. "So that's how you kept watch while I peed in Jesspersson's box."

"Liar," shouted Mantas. "Rainar's trying to get back at me for treating him like the goat barf he is. Snuck that food in there himself, he did."

"How?" asked Keri. "While you were asleep? Didn't you think it was strange to wake up with an apple in your shirt?"

Antanas grabbed Mantas from behind and Keri pulled an apple from his tunic. "We ran out of apples four days ago. Do you have a tree in there?" He tossed the apple to Goran. Everyone was yelling.

Tharn held up his hands. "There is no council out here to pronounce judgment on these two. But banishment, the usual punishment for theft, would be death on the Tunturri. I propose we allow Rainar and Mantas no food for the next two days. Then they share whatever is left for the last leg into Hilhelm. After that the king can decide what to do."

The men murmured. Rainar cried. Antanas and Mantas scowled at each other. The wolves howled in the pre-dawn.

Goran nudged Keri and gestured toward bubbling oats.

Keri spoke. "Hamar always counsels mercy, but he also says the Bible says earthly punishment should fit the crime. Rainar, Mantas, you have made others hungry. Now you will be hungry. You're on guard duty now. Everyone else to the oats."

The murmuring continued as the men went to eat. Keri took some oats to Brun. "You were not much help."

"You didn't need much help," said Brun.

"I've never done anything like that before. You should have stepped in."

Brun sucked his wooden spoon clean and pointed it at Keri. "I've never done anything like that before, either. And how do you propose I step into anything?" He waved at his pallet. "You did fine. Stepping up for right is half the fight. The hard part now is getting those two home alive."

"Those two or all of us? Hurry up and get well."

"From your lips to God's ears!"

58

ONE WAY

"The sled is so light now we don't need pushers," Keri said to Sturl. His cold lips slurred the words. "Put three more harnesses up front. We'll let the sled protect our rear as we pull."

Sturl's head, huddled into his chest, nodded assent.

They loaded and started out. Keri pushed the pace to a slow run, but the weakest had trouble keeping up. Boots gave out, gloves never dried, and the small night fires left their clothes clammy wet.

That evening Eli reported Drakestad's fire even with theirs. Keri smiled, then frowned. "They must be having problems too."

The second day after the storm, they burned the last food box, broke up the remaining shields, and drank warm water. Goran's larder was down to a bag of oats and some cold flatbread so hard the men let it sit in their mouths before they tried to chew it.

They lost count of the hours pulling, jogging, waving their few spears at the now brash wolves. Certain wolves continually dogged certain men. Keri's blonde she-wolf reminded him of bread and aggravated his hunger. More than one man felt sympathy for the caribou herds the wolves relentlessly pursued each summer.

The third dawn broke cold and clear. The men leaned against each other or sat on the remains of the sled. The sides were gone. Eldman's cache of torches, Brun's pallet plus the rolled and piled furs filled the reduced deck space and hung over the edges. When the sides came down, their improvised fort went with it. The wolves sensed weakness and the guards needed more torches to keep them away. No one slept well and they mourned the last of the oats. Ice-laden boots dragged in the dry snow as they prepared to move.

Goran laughed in the gloom. Condensed air puffed through the wool muffler over his mouth. "Now that's an Ebenezer!" His unneeded cooking gear stood in a small pyramid. "I've kept one pot for water and one tripod to hang it from. And I'm keeping my iron ladle. It's easier for my short arms than your long swords."

Gotthard snorted, but rubbed his jaw.

"Hey," said Goran, "show some respect. It whacked your knife. I'm going to give it a name, like Keri's 'Wild Boar.'"

The men stared at Goran's ladle tucked in his belt like a sword.

Jesspersson grunted. "How about you call it 'Empty Stomachs'?"

Goran shook his head.

Someone said, "Soup Smasher." There was a chuckle. Others jumped in.

"Turnip Tapper."

"The Cook's Killer."

"No, that's Goran!"

"Pig's Bane."

"Sausage Slammer!"

"No, that's Jesspersson!"

"Beef Basher!"

"How about 'Server of Death'?"

"Are you talking about its killing power or his cooking?"

The laughter felt good. Keri sighed stepping up. "Drop your ladles and let's get going before the wolves make us into a meal."

There was grumbling but it was punctuated with guffaws.

"Pork's Pride?"

"Keri's Dream Spoon!"

"Ready?" shouted Keri.

The dawn shadows stretched long but Eli noted a difference. He pointed east. "Look. The shadow is jagged. Those are hills."

The crew let out a collective sigh. Some laughed, others reached out to touch a friend. A few sobbed. They were too tired to cheer.

Keri turned away from them shaking. He grit his teeth and took deep breaths. Tears started that no one saw.

"Praise the Lord," said Tharn to the group. "Surely the righteous shall give thanks unto Thy name."

Gotthard mumbled, "By the lap of Freya…" He stopped and glanced at Cnute. "By the beard of St. Peter," he shouted. "We made it."

Brun propped up on an elbow, his beard a red tangle of snow and hair. "Antanas, stand aside!" He held out his hand. "I can cover them with my thumb. By Sigvard's reckoning that means about two more days."

Gotthard sneered at Mantas. "Without food."

"But I can't see the gap where the river cuts the hills," said Brun.

Eldman looked at the carcass of the sled. "Do we have the wood? What, maybe two runners, some shield bits, a few sock torches, and a piece of deck? I don't know if we can last one more night."

Keri turned back and clapped his gloves. They splatted. "We have to pick up the pace and try to make it in a day. Thank God, the days are longer now. Sturl, your crew on the sled. Everybody else, circle around them. Let's go."

"Wait!" said Keri. "Brun, start us."

"Huh?" said Brun from the pallet.

"You know, give us that big push." The men grunted.

Brun laughed. He bowed his head a moment and then dug one hand into the snow as if to paddle. "SSSSSSSSuh, Tah!" They were off.

The wolves stayed back but increased in number. The men murmured that only hell whelped packs so large. When the crew stopped for a drink of icy water the wolves surrounded them a spear's thrust away. The black wolf came and appraised them, but when Cnute stepped out to face him, he trotted north. "Coward!" Half the pack followed Cnute's wolf.

Goran sought Keri. "Gotthard's shoulder is bleeding again. And Eldman...can he run any farther?"

Keri glanced at the carpenter and the others huddling together for warmth, their eyes hollow and dark. He looked at the hills. They didn't seem any closer. "Tharn says, 'A lame man runs if he must.' We don't have a choice." He wrapped Stjärna's scarf tighter around his chin and tried to picture her. All he saw was snow and the yellow wolf.

They ran east.

Afternoon clouds obscured the hills and they couldn't see the landmark. They jogged until dark and then stumbled well into the night, clustered inside four sputtering torches. Everyone staggered. When Eldman put a hand on Tharn's shoulder they both fell to the ground. Keri called a halt. "Goran, fire here, then snow water."

The men dropped like wounded ducks. Keri pushed the guards to keep them waving their torches. He threw fur bundles at the men and shook them awake to wrap up.

"Why? There's no hope," cried Jesspersson.

"Sleep. Dream of Gudrun," said Keri. "Eli! You, me, and Cnute pull first guard."

Eldman limped up. "We have to disassemble the sled for wood tonight and...and...Brun can't walk." He shrugged.

Keri took a deep breath. "Keep the frame but take the slats from the pallet. Replace them with a fur slung from the frame. Put one runner under, like a wheeled barrel on a ski. He can hold whatever torches we don't use tonight."

"You've been thinking about this."

"It's better than thinking about walking."

The men fumbled into their furs. Keri stood tall in the center; firelight flicked across his face. "Tomorrow morning we make our own Ebenezer. Put on your best clothing, your weapons, and…well, I guess there is nothing else. If you have a good boot left, find somebody who does not and give it to him. Same with tunics, gloves, everything. We leave what we don't need. We run light tomorrow because tomorrow night there is no more wood. There is no choice but to keep going and we won't need our furs or have time to change socks. We'll run better without their bulk."

"Run where?" asked Jesspersson.

"Tharn?"

Tharn rose still panting. "The final instructions are 'Go two handbreadths to the north of the gap. Find the knoll and go half a league east to a draw. Then down to the river crossing."

"Handbreadths?" asked Jesspersson.

Brun spoke. "Put your arms out, palms up, hands side by side. Put the gap in the hills at your right little finger and the draw should be at your left little finger. The knoll is the last landmark."

Brun shuddered, pulling the furs tighter. "We haven't seen the knoll yet, so we continue east. If we see it to the south, we head towards it. If we see it to the north, the path down the ridge is about a league east of the knoll. If we get separated, you all need to remember that."

Eli gazed into the dark. "Is Hilhelm right there?"

"No," said Brun. "Hilhelm is a few leagues around the hills."

The men collapsed under the weight of the night. Keri grimaced as his feet tingled with frosty pain. Several men snored already.

Goran's fire fluttered. "Hey, dinner soon. Tonight we're having snow soup."

No one laughed.

"Keri, Tharn?" It was Brun. "I'm thinking that if we disassemble my pallet you'll have another hour's fire for tomorrow. And I don't mean to sound crazy or heroic, but if you bury me under the furs, I can distract the wolves and give you a head start."

Tharn spoke. "No, Brun, we'll get you there."

"No. You don't understand. I'll be the first in our family to draw blood with this sword in two generations." He cleared his throat, but his voice trembled. "I'm proud to do it."

Eldman spoke. "We have wood for tonight if we burn the pallet and save torches for tomorrow night. We can run with torches, but not with a campfire made of pallet. That means your idea for a barrel on skis won't work."

Cnute grunted, "An' we needs th' furs. They're better'n a shield on wolves. They can't fin' anything solid t' bite if ye drapes it loose aroun' ye."

Brun pursed his lips and fingered his sword. "Well, then. I won't hold them off so long, but I pray some bard will sing well of me."

Keri put a hand on his shoulder and turned to Cnute and Eldman. "All right, we will burn the pallet tonight, save the torches for tomorrow night, and carry our furs as shields against the wolves."

Sturl stood brushing off fresh snow. "I don't want to be dragged down like some deer by a pack of wolves. If I'm to die out here I want to face these demons."

Keri creased his eyebrows. "I agree. Then we run until we make it to the bridge or until we are down to the last torches. Then we make a stand."

Heads nodded.

Tharn sighed. "What about Brun?"

Heads hung. The fire fluttered. Goran started ladling out hot water.

"Antanas," said Keri, looking up. "Can you rig up a big harness like the ones I use at home to carry wood?"

"Yeah."

"Make one for me that can carry Brun. Chop up the rest of the harness for Goran to boil for breakfast."

Goran scratched his red nose. "Can't we carry him slung from a pole like a deer?"

"No wood long enough," said Eldman. "Spears aren't strong enough."

Brun began to protest, but Eli cut him short. "Relax, Keri will enjoy the warmth on his back. Stjärna did."

Keri swung a tired arm at Eli, who ducked.

Brun sobbed. "I can't let you do that. It will slow everyone down."

Keri said. "If you don't get in the sling tomorrow, I will drag you by your flaming beard. Rentvatten doesn't leave people to wolves."

In the pre-dawn the last of the pallet sputtered in the snow. The guards circled with hand torches, keeping the wolves back while the crew rolled their furs. Their numb fingers fumbled tying the straps. Wearing their weapons and a few helmets, they struggled to walk under the unaccustomed weight. Keri was glad he didn't have a helmet. Brun was heavy enough.

Tharn began to organize a prayer but Brun, hollering from Keri's back, cut it short. "Pray while you walk. We have to move."

Cnute pulled out Fum's whistle, weighed it in his hand, and started to put it in his tunic. A wolf crept toward him in a shadow, but he saw it and tooted the whistle. The wolf jumped back. "They don' like n' music."

Goran looked up from his pack. "Did you ever hear of a devil singing?"

"Nope, only angels."

"Well, there. Maybe you're a one-eyed angel in disguise," snorted Gotthard.

"If he's an angel, then I'm definitely not praying to go to your heaven," said Mantas.

Keri loomed over them. "Would your angelship explain to me why we aren't moving?"

"Rainar's not ready," said Gotthard. "His fur bundle won't close."

"Help him re-roll it."

"No." Rainar protected his furs. "It's mine. You can't."

"What do you mean, 'you can't'?" said Keri. "We're leaving now."

"He means you can't see what's in his furs," said Viksten, slapping his arms for warmth. "He has a couple bags of silver. They clink half the night when we sleep."

"What?" said Keri.

Rainar stood over his bundle. "We'll have expenses in Hilhelm. I'll need new clothes, food, lodging. That silver can't sell in Rentvatten. Candlesticks and the like. Nobody can afford it. I thought I'd sell them in Hilhelm. I can't just leave them behind."

Keri's voice went up an octave. "Do you expect the wolves will walk slower so you can have new clothes in Hilhelm?"

Rainar gulped. "Well, no. I'll carry them."

"You won't last two hours. Before noon we will have to carry you."

Rainar looked pleading to the group. "Will anyone help me? I can pay."

Several men opened their eyes, considering the prospect of money. "How much?" said Gotthard. His breath froze in the air.

"Two…no, six pieces of silver if you carry half. Six to someone else for the other half."

"Wait," snapped Keri. "No one is risking their lives to carry your silver."

"Listen," said Rainar. "What if every man carries just a little and I promise we split the money when we get there?"

Everyone paused. The silver wolf howled near the men, making them jump.

Gotthard eyed the wolf and turned back to Rainar. "How much is in there?"

"Probably three years' earnings," said Rainar. "Just think, when we divide it that's… two…three silvers for each."

"What's this thing weigh?" said Gotthard, picking up the bundle. Two leather bags fell out clanking.

Cnute stepped up, grabbed the nearest bag, and flung it toward the wolves. It opened, scattering silver plates, candlesticks, and cups that twinkled once or twice in the torchlight before disappearing into the glistening snow. Rainar started after it but Sturl grabbed him.

Keri laughed. "Roll that fur now or I'll have Cnute throw the other bag."

Mantas helped him, and Rainar packed through tears mixed with rage. Keri headed to the front where Cnute played Fum's tune.

"Good decision," said Brun through gritted teeth.

Keri looked over his shoulder. "He had a good idea, but I wager he throws the second bag by noon. What a waste."

The men started out with everybody close to the nearest torch praying for the sun. When it finally rose, haze obscured the horizon. They could not see the hills.

Keri plodded carrying Brun and their furs. Like everyone else he struggled to adjust from being a cart horse to being a pack mule. Brun's blood dripped down Keri's legs and he could sense Brun tensing to hold back the pain.

By the first rest stop, packs had settled, so Keri set a pace just below running. Grim, he chanted nonsense grunts as he led the way, shaming anyone with a lesser load to keep up. "Tah, uh, tah, uh…"

The wolves trotted away from Keri like a bow wave flees a boat. They parted when he closed on them and circled behind as more wolves formed a new sea that he would part again. The crew trudged behind him in an elongated diamond shape. "Tah, uh, tah, uh…"

As the sun melted the haze the snow sparkled pure and white, hurting their eyes. Keri squinted and remembered Stjärna waving from the hill the day they first kissed. Eli shouted and pointed east. Keri looked up. Tantalizingly close, the eastern hills beckoned like reflections of a distant lake on the horizon. "Keep moving. We can't stop. Tah, uh, tah, uh…"

Tharn's voice crackled like a crow. "There's the notch, the gap! North like we want it."

Brun held out his hands to measure for the draw. "Can anyone see the knoll?"

Eli ran to Jesspersson. "Give me a boost up!" Jesspersson made a step with his hands and Sturl helped keep Eli steady as he gazed northeast.

"Look to your wolves," shouted Keri. Everyone checked their back. Antanas turned, swinging his blade behind him. There was a yelp, and a gray wolf limped away, leaving a trail of blood.

"I see a black spot to the north that could be your knoll." Eli pointed.

Keri took a shuddering breath. "Good. Everyone get a mouthful of snow. Let's go. We're not there yet. Let's go! Tah, uh, tah, uh…"

Keri never allowed them to stop but they slowed to a walk several times. They scooped snow into their raw throats, making their teeth hurt. Men staggered. Friends adjusted one another's gear. Several boots split and their owners limped in ice-caked socks. Others wheezed and spit into the snow, red eyes staring out of their mufflers. "Tah, uh, tah, uh…"

The hills crept closer, but so did the wolves. They snapped at men's heels like sheep dogs. One or two ventured too close and limped off wounded. One or two men suffered nips. The cold multiplied their pain. "Tah, uh, tah, uh…"

Cnute had no air left for his whistle. Sturl and Tharn carried Eldman's pack for a while and Mantas took the silver pack from Rainar.

Brun passed out, limp in the sling. By noon their paces became the inconsistent tramping of an ox at a grind wheel. The last iron helmets dropped to the snow, left behind. "Tah, uh, tah, uh…"

As afternoon stretched on, overcast hid the notch. Tharn had the crew angle a little north, their steps heavy and sloppy. The wolves disappeared. No one spoke for an hour or more, each man's thought etched on his face: fear for some, regret for others, hope for few, all trying to push back the pain. Most could not feel their feet and each step was a jolt. His mind empty, Keri plodded on. "Tah, uh, tah, uh…"

Covering the rear with his bow, Eli gasped, "Sun's on the horizon. Shadow's creeping this way. Heaven help us, there's wolves in the shadow. Dozens of them."

"Shadow of death," mumbled Mantas.

Keri dropped his head and stopped. He laid down Brun, who groaned and woke up asking for water. They gave him snow. The shuffling men came up and fell to their knees in the gray twilight. The wolves circled like hungry crows around a dead squirrel. Looking out, each man spotted his named wolf.

Tharn had the map. "We've been drifting north all day like it says but with the cloud cover I can't tell how close we are. And I've yet to see a river valley or the knoll."

"Have we gone too far north?" Keri looked from his knees.

"I don't know, but we can only cross the river at the draw. Everywhere else the slope falls like a cliff."

"Maybe that won't matter since we don't have the sled," said Keri.

"Sigvard said there's only the one way to safety," Brun whispered.

Tharn panted on his knees. "How much longer can we go? The men are exhausted. Even Eli is dragging. And our few torches are mostly pig lard and socks."

"Do you want to die here or there?" said Keri, gesturing with his head.

"I want to die with a prayer on my lips and my family in my mind," said Tharn. "I'll follow until I can't, but I ask that we stop while we still have a little fire so the men can compose themselves."

The crew murmured.

Eldman looked forty years older. He spoke in gasps of fog. "This is futile... Look around... We have maybe...four hours of torches...if each one lasts a half hour... Let us find a place...make a stand...die facing these wolves...rather than running like blasted sheep."

"I promised you that, if the time comes," said Keri. "But I will not give up now. We have a little twilight now and a chance."

Tharn wheezed, "Cicero, I think, said, 'A man of courage is also full of faith.'"

"It's easier to have faith if you know God's plan. Ask Gideon," said Eli.

"Gideon who?" asked Keri. "Let's go. Pray as you walk. Didn't one of those guys say we should pray continuously?"

All walked and some prayed as darkness closed in on the feeble torches. High clouds parted infrequently to let a half-moon leer at them. Many limped and only swung half-heartedly when the wolves approached. They walked as to a funeral.

Approaching midnight, their lead man, Cnute, drooped. His torch fluttered low and he almost stumbled over a cliff edge. They stopped. They collapsed, too tired to cheer. Keri had to push the torch bearers to cover the rear.

"Left, or right?" Keri asked Tharn.

"Doesn't matter," said Eldman. "These three torches are the last... just burning socks... won't last half a league." He sat with a thump. Keri looked over the sharp cliff. Cnute's torch could not light the bottom. Eli dropped a snow crust. It fell for several heartbeats before they heard it hit. Then all they could hear was their own labored breathing.

Tharn broke the silence. "We could be standing on the edge of eternity." The men did not even look up. Leaning on their packs or their knees they just ached.

"Men of Rentvatten," Keri sighed. "Prepare to spend the night here."

CALLED

As the days grew longer the village worked longer. Stjärna's mother kept her busy all day but when night came Stjärna could not sleep. She heard Fum's whistle. Disentangling from her sleeping sisters, she slipped out of bed. A few minutes later, dressed and wrapped in her cloak, she stepped into the dark outside. The cold, dry air felt good and made the house seem stuffy. Fum's whistle played after dusk nearly every night, but tonight it called to her.

A half-moon watched her progress along the palisade wall toward the eastern watchtower. A crunch in the snow made her stop in a shadow.

Sigvard passed by, carrying shield and spear, as he did most nights. "Good evening, child," he said.

"Oldefar," she said, smiling. "Don't you ever sleep?"

"God's flipped me upside down these days. I sleep any time during the day, but nights? Never more than a wink. So I walk the old guard path and talk to old ghosts."

"Are there so many ghosts?"

"I hope not." He sighed. "I like to think they drink ale on some green hillside. Walk with me, girl, God still lets me get cold."

They crunched over the frozen snow. "Worried about Keri and the others?" he asked.

"Yes, when I think about it," she said. "They should be there by now, so I worry about things they might find in a big town."

"Ach! Men can find trouble anywhere. Look at Sami. Look at Jesspersson. Who ever heard of trouble in the wilderness?"

"I suppose, but Sami is quiet now that Gudrun has moved in with Jesspersson's family, and Wiglif is trying to catch him out."

Sigvard chuckled. "Calm before the storm, Stjärna, calm before the storm."

"Should I be worried?"

"Always…and yet Brother Hamar preaches, 'Fear not. Give it all to God,' he says."

"Yes, but Tharn says, 'Pray, but throw water on a burning house.'"

"Yep. Yep." Sigvard peered through a small gap between two palisade logs. Satisfied, he continued on. "Been hearing noises out there some nights. Never see anything."

Fum's tune seemed a little louder. Stjärna looked around. "Where is he?"

"Fum? Don't know. Always hear him, never see him. Tried to find him several times. Nothing." He shrugged.

"I'm going to look."

"You'd do better to sleep, child. Who knows what tomorrow brings?"

She hugged him. "Good night, Oldefar." Stjärna followed the tune down toward the Great Hall. She saw a flickering yellow light under the leather door. She peeked in the entrance, then laughed and entered.

"Stjärna!" said Laurel, sitting with five other women near the fire circle. "I stopped by your house and found your mother standing at the door. She said you had just left. How did you know?"

"Know what?"

"To come here, now? We are trying to figure out why we are here.

Do you know?" The women with Laurel all had their hair down as if for bed. One, Gotthard's wife, Siggy, had on only her sleeping tunic and a cloak. She poked another stick into the fire.

Brother Hamar adjusted his cowl as he came down from his pallet at one end of the hall. "Ladies, I am always glad for company, but it is late. Is there some problem? Is someone ill?"

Stjärna glanced at Hamar and then the ladies. "I came following Fum's music. I thought I might find him."

Hamar laughed. "Fum." He yawned. "I've had a half-dozen people show up since the crew left…following Fum's music. But they never see him. So we pray and they go home, usually hearing Fum's music just as when they came."

"Who else has come?" asked Laurel. Stjärna sat and touched Keri's necklace.

Hamar scratched his beard. "Well, I guess I'm not violating a confession or anything. It's not a sin for people to pray." He looked at the ceiling. "I guess Timonen's wife was first. She brought his father. Bue's parents came once. Siggy, this isn't your first time. Gudrun came. Brun's wife, Gayle, showed up a week ago."

The curtain door opened and Gayle walked in with Gudrun and Marta. "Oh, hello." She hesitated. "And there are four more sled wives right behind us."

"Welcome all." Hamar laughed. "I think Fum called a meeting."

Laurel stood. "Let's see, then." She looked around at the ladies. "Yes, everyone here is connected to the sled, somehow. Eli's has me and his mother. Gayle and Brun. Keri's got Stjärna and his mother." She nodded to two ladies. "Tharn's wife and sister, and you are Gantson's wife."

The door flap lifted again. Stjärna's mother came in with her sister-in-law, Jorvik's wife. Behind her was Rainar's wife with Pekka, their son. He shrugged. "She wouldn't come alone."

Stjärna felt a shiver. She closed her eyes and swallowed hard to keep her stomach from wrenching. Looking she saw almost twenty ladies biting their lips. Brother Hamar caught the sensation and reached for his rosary. His voice dropped to urgency. "Ladies, we should pray."

"Wait," said Pekka. "There is one more."

The flap opened and a short, stocky woman with an owl tattoo on her face came in, Mantas' wife. She looked around. "I usually only come here to feast. But tonight Fum woke me and came this way. I followed. What do you want?"

Several women wrinkled their noses. As if lifted by another hand, Stjärna rose and went to the woman. "Come. We are not judges. We are just people who believe in the power of prayer in the name of Christ. We have been called to pray. Will you join us?"

"No. Mantas hates your Christ."

"Mantas isn't here," said Stjärna, taking her hand. "And his opinion should not decide your god. Listen to our prayers, and if you wish, join us. If you have questions, you can talk to Hamar." Stjärna led her to a bench by Stjärna's mother. She hesitated and then sat.

Hamar stood. "Let us pray."

REMEMBER

Goran commandeered a torch and scooped gray snow into his pot to melt for drinking water. Keri started to organize the men. Tharn stopped him. "You promised us some time."

Keri nodded. "All right, but only a few minutes. Guards, keep your torches moving."

"Yep."

"I'll help," said Cnute. He played Fum's tune softly. The wolves backed further into the dark.

Everyone gathered around Brun's fur. Rainar dragged his bag through the snow. Tharn spoke. "This may be our last chance for a while to praise and thank God." Mantas snorted. "No, really," said Tharn. "We've come a long way and been blessed to do a lot of things in our lives. We should thank Him."

"We are not done yet," said Keri. "At dawn we are going to find the draw, leave the Tunturri, and sleep in Hilhelm."

"Or sleep in some wolf's belly," sneered Mantas. His hand clutched the horns of Odin around his neck. His voice broke. "Jes' lemme die with m' sword in m' hands."

Tharn bobbed his head. "Even if Mantas is right and we die to-night, we are blessed to know this could be our last moment on earth. Many are surprised by death. We will not be surprised. Use this time to talk, maybe mend arguments, say thanks. We have time to ask God for our forgiveness and to forgive others."

The men looked around.

"See who you should talk to. Talk to God. And make sure you have asked Jesus to be your savior on God's final judgment day. Nothing else you have done can erase your sins."

Mantas shivered. "M' father's gods will be glad to see m'. I'll be glad for the ale and a wench."

Tharn laid a hand on his shoulder. "Does your god really offer so little?"

Mantas turned roughly away. "Cnute, gimme yer torch. I'll guard."

Goran walked up with his pot full of warm water. It looked red in the torchlight. "It's not ale, but it's warm and it will give your body fresh life."

"Thank you," said Tharn. "And thank God for this moment to share it."

Everyone passed the pot around the circle, drinking deep. The warm metal radiated through Keri's tattered gloves and felt good. On his turn Gotthard laughed. "It's warm as blood." Still the water touched their thirst, and the warmth lifted their spirits.

Cnute drank and said, "I may remembers it as th' bes' drink I ever 'ad."

Goran smiled. "There's more. I packed two rye flat breads around my belly. They're almost warm. You will not die with an empty stom-ach." He passed around two plate-sized loaves and everyone broke off a piece. He caught the crumbs in one hand and ate them as his share.

"Thank you, God, and thank you, Goran!" said Tharn. "Now talk to your neighbors and talk to your God."

Keri looked for Eli, but Lars had taken him off. He found himself face-to-face with Jesspersson.

"I'm sorry I've been short with you," said Jesspersson. "I've been worried about Gudrun...oh, crap, Gotthard. Help me find him."

Gotthard was staring at the sky. The clouds' silver edges hid the half-moon. He turned at their approach. "You don't have to say anything."

"Yes, I do," said Jesspersson. "You are right to be angry about Gudrun."

"Maybe," said Gotthard. "But I knew you were sniffing around like I used to do. I just didn't care."

"Well, I'm still sorry I treated Gudrun like a bird I was hunting."

"I'm sorry you weren't a better aim with that knife." Gotthard sobbed.

"We'll be fine," said Keri. "Brother Hamar says God provides, you know."

Gotthard snarled. "Has Tharn so befuddled you with this Christian stuff that you think we are going to make it through the night? Who do you think is providing the wolves? I wish you'd killed me at the hot spring. I'm not sure I can face being torn apart by teeth."

Keri sighed. "The Jew told me I don't know enough about Christianity to defend it, but our experiences lately taught me something. Prayer helps. Whether you get what you ask for or something else, God responds and He's glad you asked. I will pray while we fight."

"Humph," snorted Gotthard. "Well, I'm glad you found something that works for you. I've had two parents and a child die while I prayed to your god and Mantas'. So, you can keep them all."

"I'm sorry that's so," said Keri. "But I can say that I would rather die with God's name on my lips than a curse."

Eli's voice rose above the men talking. "Drakestad's fire!" To the northeast a string of flickering light moved in the dark then sank and disappeared.

"How far?" Tharn asked.

Eli shook his head. "I couldn't tell. The darkness hides the distance. A league, maybe."

"Too far," said Eldman. "And too late. We're starting our last torches."

"Gather round," said Keri. "We have wolves to welcome."

The men moved in, leaving Goran and his torch on guard.

Keri handed Brun the last torch and drew in the snow. "We will form a half circle with our backs to the cliff so they can't get behind us. Make a snow wall, space the eight spears out. In front of each spear one or two men with a sword. Bows, together in the front, try to break their charge. Rainar, would you anchor the left side? Eldman, take the right. You two don't have to kill them, just slide them off the cliff. I'll be up front with the axe."

Cnute cleared his throat. "I got some sperience wi' wolves. That gi' me some ide's."

Keri nodded.

Cnute rubbed his eye. "First, don't stand s' tall. They likes t' grab legs. Think how they hunt deer: take th' legs firs'. So crouch. Second, slice a hole in yer sleepin' fur to put yer head through. When th' light goes out they can't see any better'n you can. They're devils, but they're not God. They'll scent ye an' hear ye, but th' folds of th' bearskin will hide yer shape. Third, they'll be too close t' fight good with yer swords. Some should be crouchin' b'tween the spears t' fight low an' close w' knives an' hatchets. An' last, when th' wolves jump at ye t' clear th' wall an' go for yer throats, ye spear holders use their speed t' fling 'em up an' over th' cliff. Jus' like we spears jumpin' salmon outta th' stream behind us onna ground. Oh…an' 'member: th' black wolf is mine. Ye all got plenty of yer own."

Keri scratched his stubbled face. "Good ideas. Let's try it. Brun, you command in the middle and get any that break through. Sturl, be his eyes after you empty your quiver. Questions?" The men turned to cutting their furs and building a snow wall. Rainar used his bag of silver to strengthen his wall by the cliff.

Keri propped Brun on his rolled fur. "Just throw any spares at me," said Brun. "I'll catch 'em right here on my knife." He grabbed Keri's arm. "Son, remember where your power comes from."

Keri nodded. "See you at dawn, Brun."

Cnute came over and grasped Brun's hand. "I'll throw ye a wolf, but don't ye go usin' it f' a blanket an' go t' sleep on us." They held the grip a moment. Tharn came by and pressed a hand to Brun's shoulder. "Do well, friend."

Keri moved to the top of the half circle behind a pile of snow, swinging his axe. The fur and the snow wall hindered his movement. He threw off the fur and stepped in front of the improvised fort, swinging the axe clear and free. He looked at the massing wolves to his front and whispered, "By God's...sorry, Lord...raging weasels." He smiled, remembering Stjärna. He touched her scarf.

The last two torches fluttered in the penetrating breeze. Goran held his torch high, casting weird shadows from the men to the wolves.

Brun gave Tharn his sock-fueled torch. "Pass this up to Keri."

Keri took the torch and glanced back at the men. He looked to the sky. "Lord, we don't know how fighting wolves is doing your will, but you brought us here, so we ask your blessing. By the wounds of Jesus Christ, we trust our souls to you."

The growls of the wolves intensified.

"Amen!" said Tharn.

HOLD

Sturl and Jorvik grabbed Eli and stepped to the front wall. Keri turned. "Hey, squirrel shooter, let's take this fight to them with what light we have."

"I would hit them better if they were in trees."

"Shoulders and throats," said Sturl, drawing his bow and flipping the seven squirrel tails of his cap back. Eli and Jorvik drew. "On three: one, two…" Sturl and Jorvik released in unison. The arrows thunked, two wolves yelped, and the pack charged. Keri threw the torch high in the air and lifted Wild Boar to the heavens.

Sturl sent a second arrow flying before the wolves hit the piled snow. Next to him Jesspersson staggered under the weight of the first wolf to hit his spear. He gasped like one who caught a fifty-weight bag of grain. Nearby Cnute slashed up with his knife at another. The front ranks of wolves peeled down the wall, disrupting spears and snapping at the flashing hatchets and knives. The men roared in defiance.

"Shoot, Eli, shoot!" yelled Sturl. In the sputtering flame of Goran's last torch Eli stood stock-still. Sturl shook him.

Eli gestured. "It's Laurel…" The green-eyed wolf was charging them. Sturl cuffed him. Eli shook, then nocked and shot. She fell at his feet whimpering, the scent of crushed pine in her fur. Cnute lifted the body and slashed its throat before he threw it over the wall. Tears streaming down his face, Eli fired until his arrows were gone and Sturl pulled him behind the spear line.

Keri's axe gleamed in a sliver of moonlight. Unable to see well he swung in a pattern that slashed up, across, and down from left to right and back again. The weight of the weapon and the keen edge of the blade cut or threw anything in its path. Sturl saw Cnute behind Keri taking on wolves who came for Keri's legs. One landed on Cnute's shoulders, pushing up his fur cover and ripping his already scarred back. Keri swept it off with a blow from his elbow.

Sturl checked Eldman on the right corner as he received direct charges from two wolves. The carpenter flung them sideways into the abyss with his spear. Swinging back, he found a third wolf on Antanas beside him. As the wolf bit down, it found only bear fur. Too close to spear, Eldman reached down and grabbed the beast behind the head. With Antanas' help they threw him wailing over the cliff.

Rainar at the other corner speared his first wolf and tumbled it into the darkness. He noticed the silver wolf in the faint light standing off watching. Two others hit Mantas to his side. Rainar bashed the spear down on the closest one several times and caused it to lose its footing. Mantas shoved his axe into the mouth of the other and pushed. Both animals suddenly slipped at the edge of the cliff and tried to climb over each other to solid ground. Another whack from Rainar and they were gone, replaced immediately by a third who threw himself at Mantas. Sturl nodded.

Jesspersson quivered as a wolf jumped and he caught it on his spear point. He used the animal's momentum to throw it in a flying arc beyond the men and over the cliff behind him. Then Goran's torch sputtered out and he could not see to skewer the next wolf. He cursed and fought blindly, jabbing the spear into the darkness over the heads of the men in front. His stomach a knot, he wanted to vomit.

Gotthard glared at a wolf hanging on his left arm. He hit it on the muzzle with the pommel of his sword until it fell off in a bloody thrashing pile. Another grabbed his leg and Gotthard nearly cut it in half. Gotthard staggered back from an attack on his blind side, falling as he tried to protect his throat. They wrestled for a moment and the wolf went limp. Gotthard heard Brun's voice from the ground beside him. "Thanks, at least I got one."

Sturl fell back with Eli. They dropped their bows and Sturl guided Eli forward again with his bearskin and a long knife. Sturl sensed Jesspersson next to him flailing with his spear. Grabbing him he yelled, "Take a knee. Point the spear up with the butt end against your back foot. Wait for the wolf to hit it, then throw him." It took a moment, but it worked. Jesspersson sent three wolves over the abyss before his spear broke under the large she-wolf Jesspersson called Goody. Her underbelly slammed into his face and her feet kicked his groin. Both tumbled to the edge of the ravine as if they would fall together but Brun rolled over to grab Jesspersson and stab the wolf. "Two," he said, gasping.

Grimacing, Goran used his iron ladle to crack wolf skulls as they appeared over the wall. He stunned three, but their bodies provided a ramp for the wolves behind. Goran had one by the throat but couldn't get a good shot at its head. A second wolf pushed them both to the ground. Suddenly a knife took the new wolf in the throat and Tharn pushed it back. "Ha," he snorted.

Goran whacked the ear of the one on top of him. He jumped up and waved the ladle at Tharn. "I'm going to call it the Iron Lady."

"Look," cried Eli above the din. "The fires of Drakestad are moving." Those who faced north glanced to see a flicker in the distance. "…away…"

Few of Rentvatten's spears remained. Most men fought from their knees, hacking and slashing with hand axes and knives. Several crawled to the rear with wounded forearms and bleeding faces. Brun called the line back to close the gaps but not everyone heard. A few fur bundles in the front lay ominously still. Surrounded on three sides Alex Broke Tooth went down in a furious battle with four wolves. Sturl pulled Eli back where he fell over Lars, who begged for water.

The circle slowly collapsed under Brun's orders and the fury of the attacks. Wolves savaged at least one body at the front and two others tried to drag Jorvik away.

Eldman crushed the windpipe of a wolf with his strong carpenter's hands but then fell exhausted to his knees beside Tharn, who struggled from under a wolf's body. Tharn jumped to his feet and pulled his sword. "Thou!" He swung. "Art!" He stabbed. "With!" He pushed an inert wolf back into the pack. "Me," he shouted. Then a wolf knocked him down.

The fight quickly taught Keri to crouch on his downswings to add his leg muscles to his upswings. Wolves flew first left then right, each spurting a mortal wound or broken bones. "Be with me, Lord," he said, gasping as he swooped the heavy weapon again and caught a wolf below the shoulder. Keri used the momentum of the swing and swept the axe over his head for a downward crash that split still another skull. Keri's huge shoulders and powerful legs seemed rooted to the earth and no wolf was able to move him. Round and round went the blade, slashing or crushing everything in reach.

Defending his corner Rainar lost his spear, axe, and finally knife. He drew his sword. Bleeding from a leg wound, he leaned on the snow wall. He'd lost sight of the silver wolf until it darted in and grabbed Rainar's bag. Rainar heard a clank and swept his sword at the sound. He missed. The wolf backed off, pulling the bag, and Rainar leapt over the crumbling wall. He slashed at the wolf and stepped on the silver. Two other wolves pulled at his fur, dragging him forward. Swinging weakly at the first wolf he grabbed the bag with his free hand. The wolf pulled. He pulled. The two others tugged his fur. He staggered but moved back step by step. Crouching, Rainar heaved on the bag of silver. All three wolves released their grips. He lurched backward, laughing, pulling the treasure to his heart. Top heavy, he stumbled back toward the crevice. The silver wolf jumped and hit him lightly in the chest. He began to fall. Mantas reached for Rainar but missed. The wolves tilted their heads, listening to Rainar's scream as he disappeared into the abyss. Then they turned on Mantas.

Sturl pushed Jesspersson into the gap left by Rainar. Three wolves attacked at once. He held off two, but one was at his leg. A lump of bear fur crawled over. Eli appeared and stabbed the wolf. Disappearing under the bearskin, he crawled off and surprised another wolf.

The pure golden howl the crew first heard in the mountains signaled the pack from the battle. The men sat stunned. Eli's voice rose above the panting and groaning. "Look. The morning star. Dawn comes within the hour. The night is passing."

Keri turned, but a cloud drifted over the star. "It's gone. She's gone. I can't…" His shoulders sagged.

Red weary eyes looked and hoped. Gasping they leaned on their weapons, some grabbing bloody snow and stuffing it in their mouths. They looked warily at the shadow of the pack licking its wounds only two dozen paces away. Eli pulled back Jorvik's still body. Tharn and Antanas hauled in another. The pack just watched.

Keri shook himself, saw the wolves, and pushed the men. "Get the wall back up." The half circle was smaller than it had been. Several men could not stand and leaned against each other. Others limped as they filled the gaps.

"Find your weapons. Feel around on the ground," said Keri. "Here is Jorvik's knife. Who needs it?"

The hidden sun reflected off the morning clouds and the men could almost distinguish each other's features. "The sun will scare them off," said Gantson.

"No," said Cnute. "Not t'day. Their blood's up. They prefer th' night but they's not limited. 'Sides, one's still got work t' do w'me." He picked up a hand axe, wiped the blood off his dagger, stepped outside the snow wall, and waited.

The pack parted and the great black wolf came to the front. While the others slouched, this wolf walked stiff and erect. It stood tall at the shoulder and easily weighed as much as Keri. Dawn reflected off the crystal snow on its coat. It stalked within ten paces of Cnute and stopped.

Keri stepped out between them. "Let him try my axe, Cnute."

The wolf moved to face Cnute.

Keri moved between them and the wolf moved again.

"Ye can't have this fight, Keri," said Cnute. "Yer axe ain't got th' p'wer."

Keri turned as if to face Cnute but swung the axe in a powerful roundabout that he aimed at the great wolf. The wolf leaped inside the swing, throwing his whole weight on Keri's shoulders. Keri fell back, slapping his head into the frozen snow. He lay stunned as the axe flew toward the pack and landed at the feet of the blonde wolf.

The black wolf stepped toward Cnute. Only the panting of men and wolves broke the silence.

"Hello, damned cub," said Cnute. "I took ye in an' treated ye well. But ye can't change what ye are: damned. Th' Lord God give ye a mission, He give me one too. I thought mine's t' save ye, but it was you He sent t' save me. Well, ye succeeded even though ye didn't mean t'. That's part o' yer curse. Yer best plans are all doomed t' fail. T'other curse is that I can't kill ye, but ye can't kill me neither." He wiped a bloody hand across his forehead. "Still, we mus' try."

The black wolf rose to its full height and growled.

"Ye don't scare m' now. I'se washed in a blood, fed on a bread, and drank from the cup. What can ye do?" He shrugged off his sleeping fur and stood nearly naked, dripping blood off his back and head into the snow. Cnute brought the whistle to his lips and played a bar of Fum's strange tune. The great wolf tilted its head.

The men heard the tune and stood a little taller.

"It's Fum," said Eli.

"It's Stjärna," said Keri, trying to rise.

"It's home," said Sturl.

"It's the spirit of all you hold dear," said Tharn.

The wolf quivered as Cnute played it again. The pack cringed and whined. Their chief gestured with its head and the wolves skulked around the men from both directions. It nodded. They rushed past Cnute and Keri and hit the reconstructed wall like an avalanche hits a village. The first row of wolves died at the wall, but the pack pushed their dead weight from behind. The wall crumbled under the sheer mass.

The black wolf leaped fantastically high at Cnute's head, snapping its jaws. The man ducked under the jump and slashed up with his dagger. The beast hit the ground, scattering snow, and turned its massive head and shoulders back to attack. It snapped toward Cnute's good eye, but the man waded into it, alternately hacking with the axe and feinting with the dagger. The wolf grabbed his axe and Cnute stabbed at its heart, but the dagger seemed to hit stone. He pulled it back and plunged it into the wolf's eye. The wolf pulled away with the dagger lodged in its face.

It attacked again, grabbing Cnute's left arm and shaking him. Cnute pressed into it and wrapped an arm under its front leg. He sunk his teeth into the wolf's neck but could not find flesh through all the fur. He could hardly breathe. Standing on its hind legs the wolf tried to force Cnute down, but the stocky man turned away from the weight and swung it around like a couple dancing. They spun toward the cliff's edge until Cnute's teeth finally found flesh under the neck. He bit and the beast panicked. It released Cnute's arm but Cnute's teeth gripped its throat. The blood tasted like ale. The wolf lurched but the man held and shoved it toward the cliff edge. With a great spasm, the wolf jerked away and planted four feet on the ground. Cnute grabbed a broken spear shaft, smashing it down on the wolf's head. Dazed, the fire went out of its eyes. Cnute pushed like a battering ram and forced the wolf toward the edge of the abyss. Cnute pushed again and the black wolf bit his hand as it slid over the precipice, pulling Cnute.

Keri wasn't watching. He stared at the blonde wolf. She sniffed at his axe and looked at him with eyes blue as the morning sky.

"Keri!" shouted Eli. He turned his head and saw Cnute slipping over the edge. Keri leaped over the snow, landing on his stomach and grabbing at Cnute's foot. Slippery with blood he could get no grip and Cnute disappeared over the cliff. Keri scrabbled to the edge.

The two bodies dropped like falling stars sparkling in the first rays of sunlight. They seemed to tumble forever but suddenly disappeared without a sound into the shadows below.

Keri's heart felt empty. He smelled fresh bread and his stomach knotted. She was there, beside him, licking his ear. He slumped in resignation, then suddenly rose in anger, flinging her by the neck into the pack. He screamed with a rage his men and the poets would try to describe for generations.

Charging barehanded into the melee he grabbed wolves and threw them. Some went over the cliff, some into the snow. He grabbed necks, legs, muzzles and threw them. "God curse you back to hell from which you came!" he cried, barreling into the piles of wolves and men. Yelps, cries, grunts filled the air. Wolves driven by the torment of the long chase, fury of the moment, and the downfall of their leader hurtled themselves over the bodies of the dead and dying to reach him.

Keri fought his way to his axe. The pack pushed him to the ground, grappling, a mass of fur and flesh. With a roar he rose, spinning the blade in a blur. Blood flew like wind-driven snow. The dead piled up. Still they attacked. Keri heard men chanting a rowing cadence.

At the wall, the pressure let up. Those wolves engaged fought on but the press at their backs slowed. The pack on Keri heard too. They jerked their ears, trying to decide whether to flee or face this new threat. They saw fire: torches in the hands of men running through the dim morning in a wedge. Their spears gleamed red. They swept around a small rise, driving through the wolves. They threw fire at the tight pack and burning arrows slapped into fur. There were at least fifty men and in their midst a horse-drawn sled half full of wood. The wolves backed away, hesitating.

The yellow wolf came to the front, watching Keri. Their eyes met and he glared. Framed by piles of dead and dying wolves, he absently brushed at something on his leg and realized it was a flap of his skin. He glanced down and back up. She was gone. The scent of bread lingered, then changed to offal and blood. Kicking his way through the bloody fur around him, he stepped between the new torches and the wavering pack. His eyes narrowed, his fists flexed, and he spit blood at the snow. He bellowed an inarticulate roar.

The surviving wolves ran.

Well done. My servant's wrath strikes terror like the roar of a lion. Keri turned to the voice but saw only the rising sun.

Tharn and Eldman sat stunned. Others cheered, laughed, fell, or cried holding each other. Some fainted. All blinked their eyes against the sudden heavenly brightness of the breaking dawn.

Their rescuers quickly built fires and formed a perimeter while others helped the wounded men. Their uniforms bore the insignia of the king. A white-bearded man astride a white horse waited in their midst, occasionally giving orders.

Among the sounds Brun's voice cracked. "Thank God, we thought we would die unknown."

The rider leaned down from his saddle. "Did ye not know I would be watching out for ye from the hillside above? Oh, my good and faithful subjects, hadst ye shown better light we would have been here sooner."

Brun collapsed onto a soldier.

"Fainted, sire."

The king surveyed the carnage. A horseman rode up. "Sire, the other group up north be safe now. We tended their wounded, and the wolves hath left them. One named Firth says they be from Drakestad."

"Drakestad? Hmmm…and who then be you?" he asked the men on the ground around him. No one responded, so he nudged the horse toward the only one standing: a large fellow with a naive square face, a stubble beard, and shaggy yellow hair, surrounded by dead wolves. "Who be ye, man?"

"Keri Ellisson," he said between shuddering breaths, staring where the wolves had fled.

"Indeed," said the king, crossing himself. "Kyrie Eleison, 'Lord have mercy' in our tongue. The battle cry of the Crusaders. An apt name."

The man rose to his full height and turned to the king. "No, my real name is Sakarias, Sakarias Ellison." He touched the bloody scarf and looked where the morning star might have been. He turned back, spit, and said, "Sir, my men need bread."

THE END

A COUPLE OF NOTES

The fact that Vikings helped found Russia was largely suppressed by the Soviets, but archeology has helped reveal the truth. They came to raid and trade and were apparently invited to stay. In 988 the Slavs and Scandinavian Rus became nominal Christians by command of Tsar Vladimir who sought treaty advantages with Christian Byzantium. Western culture has mostly ignored the Turk/Mongol/Muslim wars in that part of the world, but Eastern Europe remembers. Those wars still influence today's politics.

I adjusted the geography of northwest modern-day Russia for the book, but if one locates modern Veliky Novgorod and goes northeast to Kotlas (Hilhelm), most of the lakes and rivers are there.

Tunturri has various spellings and was originally defined in my research as Finnish treeless steppes. It is also used to describe the Scandinavian mountain range. I see it as a snow desert.

Though much of *Ballad* was inspired by the real main character, I owe many thanks to my patient wife, my honest beta-readers, and the Olympia Writers' Group who kicked an old English teacher into the 21st Century of publishing.

You may find me to complain or just chat at *rickistaylor.com*.

CPSIA information can be obtained
at www.ICGtesting.com
Printed in the USA
JSHW030520131222
34801JS00003B/6